CONDOR

A GABRIEL WOLFE THRILLER

ANDY MASLEN

TYTON PRESS

For Jane and Charles Kingsmill,
with love and affection.

1

GOD'S TEARS

THE NINETEEN-YEAR-OLD GIRL formerly known as Eloise Alice Virginia Payne, and now simply as Child Eloise, stood trembling in front of the older woman. She was naked but for a pair of white cotton briefs and a much-washed, plain white bra, the thin straps frayed at the points they crossed her bony shoulders. They'd given her an extra cup of the sacrament that morning, and now she was blinking rapidly and couldn't stop clenching her jaw. She was thin, and her skin was so pale the blue of her veins showed clearly down her neck onto her breastbone, and on the insides of her thighs.

The insides of her forearms were laddered with fine white scars.

The room in which she was standing was on the top floor of a sand-coloured, terraced house on a crescent flanking London Zoo. It was flooded with pale September sunlight that caught the fine, blonde hairs on Child Eloise's arms and legs.

"Will it hurt, Aunt?" she asked.

The short, silver-haired woman pushed her glasses higher up on her beaky nose, and took the dressmaking pins from between her thin lips to answer.

"No, child. You will feel God's breath on you, that is all, just as Père Christophe taught you. Then you will be with the Creator, safe and sound. Now, hold still while I finish your raiment."

The young girl stood, trying to be still, but the muscles in her legs quivered in a relentless beat. She tried to imagine what it would be like. A flash of light and heat, and then some sort of awakening in Heaven. Would God actually be there to meet her? What if he was busy? But Père Christophe was clear on this point of doctrine. She was doing His will by serving Père Christophe, and of course He would be aware of that and would be there, ready to receive her.

As she shuddered and quivered, frowning with the effort of standing still, her aunt pulled the cotton garment over her head and down her narrow torso. It had no sleeves or collar. It did have a series of ten sagging pockets that circled her chest like something a hunter or a fisherman would have on his jacket, each three inches wide, three deep, and nine from top to bottom.

With a few deft stitches, her aunt sewed a narrow strip of cotton from front to back between the young woman's legs, forming a crude leotard.

"There!" Aunt said, standing back to admire her handiwork. "All finished. Now we just need to fill those pockets and you're ready for your glorification."

* * *

Three miles away, Harry Barnes was getting ready for another day's sightseeing. He was a trim sixty-three, and he liked to keep in shape playing golf and the odd game of tennis. He had a year-round tan, and he thought it set off his close-set, pale-blue eyes just fine. Since the divorce had come through, he'd been enjoying "every goddamned minute" of his life, as he'd put it to a fellow he'd met the previous night in a pub, over a couple of pints of that weird, flat, British beer. That included this no-expense-spared, two-week vacation to the UK.

The day looked like it was going to be fine. But Harry was from

Reno, Nevada, where he managed a casino, and counted anything below seventy as dangerously chilly. He shrugged on his fawn windbreaker over the sweater, and the tattersall shirt and undershirt he'd already tucked into his grey pants. What did the Brits call them? Trousers? Funny word.

He sauntered down the short path from his hotel to the street, pausing on the edge of the black-and-white-chequered tiles to admire the park and its trees opposite the hotel. Back where Harry came from, there wasn't a whole lot of greenery. Bayswater, in contrast, was verdant, and full of other tourists, folks heading to work, even a party of kids, all wearing plum-and-grey school uniforms with matching caps or floppy felt bonnets, like something out of Masterpiece Theatre. They were being led in a crocodile by a pretty young redhead in a lime-green dress with patent leather pumps. She reminded him of his daughter, who'd sided with his ex-wife and currently wasn't speaking to him.

No bus in sight, but Harry didn't mind. Linda had been the one who was always in such a hurry. Well, now she'd rushed off with half his money and her skiing instructor, so fuck her. Harry liked waiting. Gave a man time to think.

* * *

Gabriel Wolfe sat at a small, circular, brushed aluminium table outside an Italian café on the northern end of Regent Street. From his vantage point on Biaggi's pocket-handkerchief-sized terrace, he looked south to Oxford Circus, a throbbing crossroads where pedestrians swarmed around the junction, pushed and jostled their way down into the tube station beneath the pavement, or darted across the road in front of hooting taxis and buses groaning with passengers.

He sipped his flat white, savouring the smooth, strong coffee beneath the foamy milk, and took a mouthful of the delicately lemon-flavoured cake. It had been brought to him a few minutes earlier by the owner, a scrawny old guy who still spoke in a strong

Italian accent despite having lived in London, as he told Gabriel, "since the sixties. Swingin' London an' all that, innit?"

The day was bright, and the bite in the air was counterbalanced by the warmth of the sunshine on his face. It was "a real Indian summer," as his father would have declared it before finishing his tea and toast, folding his newspaper under his arm, ruffling his son's straight black hair and heading off to his job as a diplomat in Hong Kong.

Gabriel's three-piece Glen plaid suit in a lightweight grey wool was perfectly suited to the temperature. Today, he'd paired it with a pale lavender shirt, a knitted black silk tie, and a pair of highly polished black brogues. He was on his way to meet a prospective client: the CEO of a firm that offered close protection to foreign celebrities and VIPs visiting London. She wanted help training her operatives, as she called them. Firearms, unarmed combat, defensive driving—bread and butter for Gabriel, and very well-paid bread and butter at that. Early for the meeting, he'd stopped for breakfast on this wide boulevard, only a hundred yards or so from the streaming crowds of London's main east-west thoroughfare, but as quiet as a village high street in comparison.

With a clatter from its diesel engine, a very high-mileage example to judge from the grey smoke rolling out from its exhaust pipe, a car drew up at the kerb, blocking his view across the street. Nothing fancy. A silver Ford Mondeo, one of millions like it on Britain's roads, with the rear windows blacked out with plastic film. A common-enough modification these days, when every suburban middle-manager wanted to look like a drug dealer. From the rear seat, a young woman got out. Her hair was blonde and cut short, but nothing stylish. In fact, it looked like someone had done it for her at home using kitchen scissors. Her shoulders were hunched inside a black, padded jacket, and the muscles around her pale blue eyes were tight. She kept grimacing as if she had just tasted something unpleasant. Her mouth would stretch wide, then release again. He caught a glimpse of a middle-aged woman ushering her from her seat, gold-framed glasses glinting as a shaft of sunlight penetrated the gloomy interior of the car.

4

Without looking back, the young woman shuffled down the street towards Oxford Circus.

* * *

Harry was enjoying himself. He'd caught the 94 bus after ten minutes' wait and was sitting on the top deck chatting with a new friend. Her name was Vivienne Frost. She was a little younger than Harry, fifty-eight or nine, maybe. No wedding ring. She was a looker all right, and Harry told her so after a little idle conversation about the weather.

"My ex-wife would kill for hair like yours," he said. "Real natural blonde, none of that peroxide stuff. It kills the shine, and probably the planet too, for all I know."

"Quite the Sir Galahad, aren't you?" Vivienne replied, patting her hair and smiling. Her lips were a pale pink and seemed to shimmer in the light coming through the grimy windows of the bus. Harry was close enough to see the way traces of lipstick had worked their way into thin creases that ran over the edge of her upper lip.

"Hey, at my age, we call it like we see it. Am I right? Plus, we got taught good manners, which in my book includes complimenting a beautiful woman on her looks."

He really hoped he hadn't just overdone it, but Vivienne seemed happy enough with this gentle flirting. Her figure was just what Harry liked, too—round in all the right places, and none of that bony, sucked-in look so many of his ex-wife's friends paid so much to achieve. "Why wouldn't a woman want to look like a woman?" Harry had asked Linda one day when they were still talking.

"Jesus, Harry, you're such a fucking dinosaur," had been her baffling reply, leaving Harry none the wiser but one tick closer to hiring a divorce lawyer.

As the bus lumbered along the start of Oxford Street, they stared down at the tacky tourist shops. Displays of T-shirts emblazoned with union jacks jostled for pavement space with circular racks of sunglasses and displays of miniature red telephone boxes, bearskinned soldiers in sentry boxes, and teddy bears dressed like Yeomen of the Guard. Just in front of them, a bright-yellow metal fitting was vibrating in time with the big diesel engine some ten feet below them. The buzz was loud enough to make Harry have to raise his voice.

"This could be a bit forward of me," Harry said, after clearing his throat, "but would you have some time this morning to see a couple of sights with an American on his first trip to the United Kingdom of Great Britain?"

He held his breath as he waited for Vivienne to answer. She checked her watch. Rolex Oyster Lady-Datejust, a nice model, Harry noted with a professional's glance. You could tell a lot about a person by their choice of watch. Then she looked at him. And smiled.

"You know what, Harry? I think I might."

Harry smiled right back.

* * *

Something about the young woman had troubled Gabriel. Now, his antennae were flickering and twitching, and a thin blade of fear was lying on its edge inside his stomach. She'd looked anxious, but so did lots of people. She was so tense she couldn't walk easily. Her coltish legs looked uncoordinated, as if she had only learned how to use them a few hours earlier. A job interview? The clothes didn't look right. Black jeans, black quilted jacket. And no makeup, which would have been a good idea, as her eyes were red from crying. She'd looked skinny. The jeans were narrow cut, but her thighs didn't even fill them. Her wrists looked bony, too. Yet her body appeared bulbous, bulky somehow, even allowing for the stuffing of the jacket.

No, it wasn't the woman herself. It was her ride. After she'd left the car, the driver had executed a rapid U-turn in the street, tyres screeching on full lock as their treads scraped across the tarmac, forcing a taxi to slam its brakes on and the cabbie to curse, loudly and fluently, from his open window. Acrid, blue rubber-smoke had drifted towards Gabriel's table.

* * *

Child Eloise waited at the bus stop on Oxford Street. She looked behind her at the shop window. It was filled with a display of what she had initially taken to be fruit or perhaps cakes, but which, on closer inspection, turned out to be handmade soaps, things called 'roulades' and 'bath bombs'. Funny name. Her neighbours in the queue were all busy with their phones, swiping, scrolling and tapping. The women wore bright clothes and high-heeled shoes, and they were slathered in makeup. Painted like whores. *Sinful.* The men ogled the women, peering at their breasts or eyeing their stockinged legs. *Lascivious.* All seemed more interested in the little slivers of plastic and glass in their hands than in God's creation around them, even if it was mostly concrete and steel here. *Decadent.*

Despite her quilted nylon jacket, she couldn't stop shivering. She grunted involuntarily from time to time and her tongue kept poking out between her lips, causing one or two people around her to smirk before looking away. Aunt had told her not to be afraid and had given her a sweetie, "to bring you a little calmness as you do God's work, child", but she felt frightened all the same.

Under her jacket, the cotton leotard was packed with seven pounds of homemade explosive—a mixture of diesel oil, bleach, wax and potassium chloride from a health foods website. Each of the ten pockets was packed with a sausage of it. She had helped Uncle and Aunt mould them herself, rolling the sticky, greyish stuff between her palms and inserting a blasting cap and a length of detonator wire into the tops. Around the sausages lay the shiny steel spheres Uncle called, "God's tears".

The ball bearings were twenty-one millimetres across. Uncle had been most specific on that point when ordering them from the factory. He said the number was significant because it was the product of the seven deadly sins and the Holy Trinity. Together they'd dropped twenty-five into each of the ten pockets, where they nestled against the yielding surface of the explosives.

The girl looked around again. Her phone wasn't as shiny as these others. It didn't even have a camera. Not that she could have reached it to take a picture, in any case. It, too, was sewn into her vest, in a channel sitting right over her heart. The wires from the explosives ended in a control box soldered onto the phone's battery charger socket.

* * *

Harry and Vivienne's bus pulled up outside a shop selling soaps and bath products. Through the narrow windows on the top deck, wafts of scent—tropical, spicy, lemony—insinuated themselves, causing Harry to smile without realising why. He was happy. Happy Harry.

Vivienne's thigh was pressed against his, and even though he knew it was just an accident caused by the stingy seating arrangements, he felt a prickle of desire. And it had been a long time since that had happened. Linda had stopped putting out for him years ago, and he'd never been a guy to go off looking for pleasure in a cathouse or a strip club. Not that he'd have had time, the hours he put in.

"Look at her," Vivienne said, prodding the glass on her left and gazing downwards. "Poor thing looks so miserable. And on a beautiful day like today. You'd think she'd manage a smile."

Harry leaned across, taking the opportunity to glance down the front of Vivienne's blouse. *Great rack!*

"Who? Her? The skinny one in the puffy jacket? Yeah, she does look kind of sad."

* * *

Gabriel finished his coffee, dabbed a wet fingertip into the yellow crumbs dusting his plate, sucked them into his mouth, and then stood. His meeting was in an office on a side street leading east from Regent Street. He took one final glance towards Oxford Circus, then picked up his battered Hartmann briefcase and strode off towards Great Portland Street.

His phone rang. He saw the small circle enclosing a face he

knew and smiled. He swiped his thumb to the right to answer the call.

"Hi, Britta, how are you? *Where* are you?"

"Hey, Gabriel. I'm good. I'm at my place in Chiswick, actually, painting my nails. My boss pretty well ordered me to take some leave. Been burning the midnight oil at both ends."

Gabriel laughed. However good her English was, Britta Falskog hadn't quite mastered all the subtleties of idiom. On the other hand, he liked her very much; always had. They'd run joint ops for a while, back in the day, she in Swedish Special Forces, he in the SAS. And there had been the odd overnight stay. Now, since she'd been seconded to MI5, working out of Thames House on Millbank, maybe there was something in the air between them.

"So, do you want to meet up?" he said. "I'm in town too. Going to see a new client."

"I would like that. Do you want to get dinner?"

"Sure. Then I'm heading back to Salisbury."

"Oh, OK. Well, you know, I do have a few days to kill, so maybe …"

"A trip to the countryside? Sounds like a lovely idea."

While they bantered, Gabriel made his way along the uncrowded roads to the north of Oxford Street, heading for the offices of Faulds & Vambrace (VIP Protection) Ltd.

* * *

Eloise Payne slid her Oyster card over the scuffed magnetic reader and made her way to the stairs of the bus, which she climbed, gripping the handrail tightly. There was one free seat, about halfway back, behind a couple who were chatting away about museums and art galleries. The man reminded her of Uncle. He had the same short, white hair. Only this man spoke with an American accent.

She took the seat next to a black woman in her thirties who was chatting into her phone and admiring her fingernails, which she extended in front of her in a fan. There seemed to be yellow flecks, like gold, floating in the orange varnish, and the tips were white.

* * *

Standing by the drawing room window, in the elegant terraced house where Eloise Payne had so recently been stitched into the garment that was to become her shroud, was a grey-haired man named Robert Slater, known to the Children as "Uncle Robert". He looked out at the oaks, beeches and hornbeams dotting Regent's Park. He was six foot, slim, and wearing a white shirt and white trousers. He wore wire-rimmed glasses that magnified his eyes. They were the blue of a sunny day in February, promising warmth, but delivering none. In the distance, he could make out the long, dappled necks of a pair of giraffes grazing in their enclosure in the zoo. Through the open window, he could smell burning leaves from a bonfire somewhere in the park.

In his hand, he held a smartphone, a number keyed in and ready to be called. Beside him, Irene Stevens, Eloise Payne's Aunt and a former manager of a dressmaking business, spoke.

"Père Christophe will be pleased."

"Yes. We have proved our worthiness."

Then he tapped the green phone icon.

* * *

Inside the neat, stitched channel covering Eloise Payne's heart, the phone's circuitry woke up as the incoming call was beamed in from a cell tower on top of an office block two hundred yards to the north.

The electric current it generated was tiny. Just enough to cause a glimmer from a Christmas tree light. Or to impel a child's toy robot to take a buzzing half-step across a polished tabletop. But also enough to excite the atoms in ten, foot-long pieces of copper wire. The wave of energy travelled along the wires at the speed of light until it reached the fat cylinders of explosive corseting their wearer.

There, something curious happened. The energy of that tiny electrical charge multiplied itself billions of times as the chemical reaction it initiated gathered pace and violence.

Exactly seventy-three milliseconds later, the atoms comprising the charges became unstable and, searching for equilibrium, set off a chain reaction that released all their pent-up energy into the surrounding space.

* * *

Gabriel had just turned into the side street where his client was based. He and Britta were fixing the details of a pre-dinner drink.

"So meet at six-thirty at the French House," Britta was saying. "Shall I book a restaurant?"

"Yes, please. Anywhere we can get a decent burgundy. And I hope you …"

Gabriel didn't finish his sentence. A roaring, shattering boom cut him off. He recognised the shape of it. It sounded like a truck bomb. There was a second or two of total silence, then distant screaming.

"Call you back!" he said. He stuffed the phone in his pocket, then spun round and ran back to the main road. He turned left at the junction and sprinted towards Oxford Circus. And hell.

* * *

Eloise Payne simply disappeared in a cloud of wet, pink specks that combusted into oxygen, carbon, and hydrogen atoms and a few trace elements. The explosion leapt outwards from her torso, popping her head from her neck like a cork from a shaken champagne bottle. The roof of the bus split apart into flying shards of red metal, allowing the roughly spherical object, trailing bright arterial blood and gin-clear cerebrospinal fluid, to travel diagonally upwards for one hundred and seventy-five feet, and roughly south.

The force of the explosion blasted Harry Barnes and his new friend Vivienne Frost into a fine mist of flesh and blood. They had been discussing which museum they should visit first and had just settled on the Victoria and Albert, Vivienne's choice.

The black woman with the orange nails was cut into rags. Later, a fireman would retrieve her feet from the wreckage where they had jammed against a twisted piece of steel tubing that had once been the frame of her seat.

Everybody else on the top deck of the bus was killed instantly, either by the compression wave of the blast itself or the ball bearings flying out in a sphere from their point of origin.

Downstairs, there were multiple fatalities from the blast itself and horrific injuries as limbs and bodies were torn and punctured by the God's Tears or the shrapnel created from the bodywork and fittings of the bus.

* * *

The shattered bus sat among piles of dead passengers and pedestrians. Body parts were scattered everywhere—lying on the ground, flung through shop windows that sliced them more cleanly than a butcher's knife, impaled on railings, and dangling from streetlamps. The street was inches deep in blood. People were screaming and moaning, clutching bloody stumps, bleeding heads, and each other. Many had horrific burns that had blackened and charred their exposed skin. Others stood around in a daze. On the periphery, the unharmed were already filming the carnage on their phones.

Gabriel barged past a young guy with a smartphone held above his head and knelt by a teenaged girl with both her legs blown off above the knee. She would bleed out within a minute. He undid his belt and yanked it out from the loops of his trousers before cinching it around her right thigh and pulling it tight to staunch the bleeding. She opened her mouth, but the scream was silent. Her face was pale and she was shaking violently.

"You!" he shouted at the young man with the phone. "Give me your belt. Now!" He held out his hand, and as soon as the man complied, dropping his belt onto Gabriel's palm with shaking fingers, Gabriel wrapped it around the girl's other leg, tightening it hard against her torn flesh until that leg stopped bleeding too. She whimpered in pain. He took off his suit jacket, removed his phone and wallet, then covered her chest with it. The young man had woken up to what was happening. He ripped off his bright red hoodie, folded it into a pad and eased it under her head.

"You're going to be fine," the young man said to her, looking down into her shock-widened eyes and reaching for her hand.

"Stay with her," Gabriel said, then stood and ran to the nearest victim, a middle-aged businessman, his head pouring with blood from a five-inch gash that had torn his scalp away from his skull.

Gabriel worked solidly for another hour, applying compression to bleeding wounds, fixing more makeshift tourniquets around limbs missing their extremities, and marshalling bystanders into trauma teams to do the same for as many people as they could manage. He implemented a basic triage system, telling people, "If they're screaming, they've got energy to survive. Treat them after the alive-but-silent. They need you first. The dead can wait."

As paramedics and firefighters arrived on the scene, he felt he had become more of a hindrance than a help. He staggered out of the devastated blast site, crunching over broken glass and mangled steel and plastic, before collapsing with his back against a wall. His shirt, waistcoat and trousers were soaked with blood. His face was spattered with it where the dying had coughed from ruined lungs. His hands were those of a slaughterman.

As he let the adrenaline metabolise out of his bloodstream, he felt a terrible fatigue settle over him. The scene reminded him of others he'd witnessed, as a soldier. One in particular.

He was thinking about Trooper Mickey "Smudge" Smith, the man he'd left, dead and mutilated in Mozambique after his final mission in the SAS had gone disastrously wrong. The man, though, wouldn't take death lying down; he continued to haunt Gabriel's sleeping—and waking—hours.

He looked down between his outstretched legs. Something shiny lay there. A silvery steel sphere, half-covered in blood. He picked it up and held it close to his eyes. He could see his own reflection. And someone else's. Someone with a black face and no lower jaw.

"*Hello, Boss,*" the face said.

"Hello, Smudge," Gabriel said out loud.

"Just like old times, eh?"

"Just like."

Then he put the ball bearing in his waistcoat pocket and began, very quietly, to cry.

2

PÈRE CHRISTOPHE

THE CHILDREN OF HEAVEN'S LEADER looked up at the young woman standing in front of him. She had been brought to his prayer room five minutes earlier by one of the Elect, a fifty-year-old former French insurance broker named Marianne Dix.

The young woman—little more than a girl, really—was nineteen years old, with fair, freckled skin, reddish hair cut short and razored in to the nape of her neck, and a slim build. Her eyes were set wide apart and coloured a startlingly bright shade of green, like the forest trees after rain.

She had forgotten her date of birth during her freeing, but Christophe Jardin knew her age for a fact. It was in the database of all his disciples—the ninety-seven Elect and the five hundred and sixty-eight Children—that he maintained on his MacBook. Her name used to be Frieda Brodbeck, back when she was a depressed undergraduate studying theology at the Humboldt University of Berlin.

There, she had met a young woman at a faculty party who told Frieda about her spiritual teacher and the group he had founded. A month later, Frieda quit her studies, left Berlin, and moved to a communal living space deep in the Bavarian forest.

After six months studying the leader's teachings, praying and handing out leaflets, and offering flowers to suspicious shoppers in the local town every Saturday and Sunday, she had been summoned to meet Père Christophe himself. In Brazil. The home compound. Eden, they called it. Deep in the rainforest thirty miles from a small town called Nova Cidade.

The room was furnished simply but, she thought, beautifully. The bed was antique, brass-framed, and dressed in white sheets with a scattering of pillows. The rugs were made from alpaca wool dyed in rich shades of earthy red, deep leaf-green and a blue that reminded her of the swimming hole at the foot of the compound's own waterfall. They were made nearby and traded at the gates of the compound by the local women who wove them on looms Père Christophe himself had provided.

She was in awe of the man sitting cross-legged on the floor, facing her. His white robe spoke of his rejection of Western materialism. His long grey-blond hair, moustache, and beard were unkempt. He refused to pander to the sinful preoccupation with appearance. She had never been alone in his presence, and she could feel her knees shaking inside her own simple, white cotton dress. She hoped Père Christophe hadn't noticed.

"Sit, Child," he said, extending his right arm and placing his palm on a folded blanket woven by the local Indians in a traditional Brazilian design of alligators and hibiscus flowers.

She obeyed, folding her legs beneath her and mirroring his pose as she sat beside him, just a foot from his right shoulder. He smelled of vanilla, rose, and a deeper, more masculine aroma beneath the floral perfume.

"Have I displeased you in some way, Père Christophe?" she asked, trying but failing to keep the tremor from her voice. "Aunt Marianne said you wanted to see me."

He smiled, stroking his beard, and stared at her hands, which were twisting around each other. Then he looked into her eyes and focused on her green irises, feeling her anxiety and stoking it with the intense gaze he practised in the mirror every morning before showering and washing his hair.

"Displeased me? Why would you think that, Child? You are blessed by the Creator. He sent you to serve me and you have only ever done your duty. You have always obeyed the First Order: Serve God through Père Christophe's will."

Her hands stopped their interlacing, her shoulders dropped, and a small smile broke out on her face.

"Then, forgive me for showing pride, but … have I been selected?"

He held her in the magnetic field of his purplish-blue eyes, willing his face to remain still, and the smile threatening to betray him to remain merely an impulse hovering behind the muscles of his cheeks. He nodded.

"Make yourself ready. Then we will pray together before your devotion."

She rose and began undressing.

Later, after he had dismissed the girl, Jardin lay on his back, sprawled across the king-size bed, the sheet kicked away, listening to the incessant song of the jungle insects and nocturnal creatures. He checked his vintage Cartier Tank watch, then placed it to his ear to listen to the wondrous whirrings and tickings of its intricate, handmade mechanism. A wide grin split his face in two; his teeth shone in the moonlight coming in through the open window. Child 105 had been obliterated, as per his orders, at the exact moment he'd been fucking the German bitch.

Too energised by the young girl to sleep, he lay there and recalled one of his father's many speeches.

"You are a waster, Christophe," the old man had said one evening, coming into his fifteen-year-old son's bedroom and interrupting his reading of an American crime novel. "You have no principles. Look at your mother and me. Every day we teach at the University in the hope we can bring about change in this decadent society of ours. Marxism-Leninism needs midwives. The French are too fond of their bourgeois comforts to see that their lives are enslaved to capitalism."

The boy had looked up at the bearded academic frowning down at him and imagined thrusting a dagger into his eye.

"But *Papa*," he said. "Between you and *Maman* there are so many fucking principles in this apartment. Any more would shatter the windows. You think you're going to change things by talking about them at your precious university? Get real! You need to take action, like they did in '68. When you were … oh, yes, on fucking holiday down south in your beach house. Tell me, how do you justify such bourgeois extravagance? Did comrade Trotsky ever own a second home? Did Lenin take a month off to stay in his ski chalet?"

Then he went back to his novel, leaving his father spluttering impotently in the doorway. He grinned to himself as he heard the old man stamping off to open another bottle of the foul, cheap red he tipped down his neck while marking his students' essays about *Maoism and the Rise of Chinese Self-determination*, or *Bourgeois Concepts of Independent Thought: A Marxist Critique*.

The year Jardin had been studying for his Baccalaureate, his parents had been killed by riot police attempting to dispel a student protest outside the American embassy in Paris. Finally, they had swapped their textbooks for placards and been killed for their troubles, a bullet each from a gendarme's assault rifle. Surprisingly, for a couple of Marxist academics, they had amassed a large and extremely valuable collection of twentieth-century French art. He'd always known that his mother had inherited money from her own mother, the heiress to a tobacco fortune. But the family discourse around capitalism's evils had led him to believe she had given it all away to good causes. Now, it appeared that at least one of the beneficiaries of her largesse was the Paris branch of a famous international auction house.

The paintings by Raoul Dufy, Berthe Morisot, Georges Braque, Marc Chagall, Chaïm Soutine, and others; the sculptures by Jean Arp, Max Ernst, and Alberto Giacometti. By the time he had disposed of the bulk of his parents' collection, he was a very rich young man.

Possessing none of his parents' scruples about capitalism, the young Christophe Jardin, independently wealthy already, had seen the opportunity in the nineties dotcom boom. He'd tripled his money with a series of stock market investments in companies started by pallid, bearded computer geeks who were now household names. Men so rich themselves that they could now afford to give away billions and still amass more wealth every year than the average man or woman could even dream about.

3

AFTERMATH

DETECTIVE CHIEF INSPECTOR SUSANNAH CHAMBERS liked to initiate all new members of her team with a mantra: "You can call me Boss, Guv, or DCI Chambers. If I invite you for dinner or a party at mine, you can call me Susannah. Call me Ma'am and I'll have your fucking arse in a sling." Most opted for Guv.

Today, the DCI felt as if it were *her* rear end that was swinging. The uniforms had secured the area of the blast and now Scene of Crime Officers were crawling, literally, all over it. The SOCOs' white, papery Tyvek romper suits were crimson with blood.

She ran a hand through her shaggy auburn hair, narrowing her eyes as she surveyed the ruined landscape in front of her. Then she turned to her detective sergeant, who had just returned from a circuit of the devastated junction that until an hour earlier had been simply a crossing of two of the world's most famous shopping streets.

"And?" Susannah said.

"Forty-nine dead at the scene. Thirty-seven from the bus, twelve on the street. Ninety-eight taken to hospitals, sixty-three in critical condition. Fucking hell, Guv, it's a mess. Looks like a war zone."

"Coming from you, Chels, that's not exactly encouraging."

The DS rubbed a hand across her face. She was new to the team, but not to scenes like this one. Chelsea Jones had served two tours in Iraq and one in Afghanistan before leaving the Army for a job in Civvy Street. Not too far from her old line of work, though. Still tracking down the bad guys and trying to maintain a semblance of law and order.

After the blast, it had taken just ten minutes before ambulances, fire engines, and police cars had converged, sirens wailing, on Oxford Circus. The police had set up road blocks at Tottenham Court Road to the east, Piccadilly Circus to the south, Hyde Park Corner to the west, and Euston Road to the north. They had, eventually, isolated the scene, with hundreds of uniformed police turning back motorists at side streets and junctions until the area was free from non-emergency vehicles for half a mile in all directions.

Susannah was the senior detective at the West End Central Police Station at 27 Savile Row. It had taken her ten minutes from the call coming in until she arrived, out of breath, at the top of Regent Street. She knew she had to lose some weight, and after her half-sprint-half-stagger up the broad curved half-mile of pavement, had resolved to go on a diet and join a gym at the very next opportunity. Chelsea had run ahead, the flaps of her black, chain-store suit jacket flying behind her, leaving her boss for dust, shouting over her shoulder that she'd meet her at the top.

Now they stood together, outside the blue-and-white police incident tape, shoes crunching on broken glass as they walked a little way further up Regent Street.

"What the fuck happened here, Chels?"

"It was a bomb, Guv."

Susannah turned to her DS, eyebrows raised.

"You think?"

"Sorry." Chelsea blushed, caught out yet again by her own literal-mindedness when her Guvnor wanted insights, not statements of the bleeding obvious. "I mean, you've got blast trauma, tons of really bad injuries from shrapnel, civilians the target. Terrorists.

Obviously," she added hastily, to forestall another ironic gold star from Susannah. "Suicide bomber, I'd say. And I found this."

She held out her right hand, palm upwards, and unpeeled the corners of a paper tissue.

Sitting in the centre of its crumpled white wrapping was one of the God's Tears.

"That hanky better be a fresh one. If your snot or tears or lippy have contaminated that … thing … you're going to have some explaining to do."

Relieved that she could answer with a clear conscience, Chelsea nodded.

"Fresh from the packet. I found it outside Top Shop on the pavement. Don't worry," she said, as Susannah scowled, "it had rolled right against the wall. I didn't go inside the perimeter."

"Jesus!" Susannah wiped her eyes where smoke from a burning car was stinging them, then planted her hands on her hips. "What kind of sicko fucking evil bastard sends someone onto a crowded bus at Oxford fucking Circus on a Tuesday morning dressed in a fucking ball bearing waistcoat? And what kind of fucking idiot sicko freak goes, 'OK, yes, my glorious fucking overlord, I'll do that and blow myself up with a hundred innocent strangers.'?"

"We'll get them, Guv. We will."

"We'd better," Susannah said, pushing a hand into her jeans pocket and extracting her phone, which had started vibrating on her thigh. She peered at the screen. "Fuck! That's the Chief Super." She put the phone to her ear.

Chelsea watched, amazed, as her Guvnor dropped the Sweary Mary act and transformed into Super Cop, all clipped, efficient language, and professional calm.

"Yes, sir," Susannah was saying. "Crime scene secure, SOCOs evidence-gathering. Roadblocks instituted with a half-mile perimeter, uniforms talking to eyewitnesses plus getting contact details for in-person interviews at the station. My team, and DI Rixon's and DI Harper's are all here too, but as you know, there's not much we can do right now. We're just … yes, I know, sir, I already cancelled it. No leave until further notice and … well, sir, suicide bomber is our feeling. My DS is ex-Army. Iraq, Afghanistan. She called it and I agree." Susannah looked at Chelsea and nodded. *Little shout-out to the Chief Super for you, girl. Never does any harm.* Chelsea nodded back. *Thanks.* "Yes, sir. As soon as I'm back at the station. Absolutely, sir."

She ended the call and stuffed the phone back into her pocket. "Fucking wanker."

Chelsea laughed then stifled it with her hand, eyes wide. "Sorry, Guv. Not the time or the place." Tears started from the corners of her eyes and she wiped them away, frowning, angry with herself for this unprofessional show of emotion.

"It's OK, Chels," Susannah said. "Better to let it out in bits when you can. Either that or have a fucking great cry and drink a bottle of chardonnay tonight."

"What did the chief want then, Guv?"

"'My office, soon as you can. I want a full briefing'," Susannah said, slipping from her usual south London accent into a passable imitation of Chief Superintendent Graham Ford's flattened Manchester tones. "Which is going to be pretty fucking short unless a lead falls out of the sky."

Both women looked upwards, but the sky contained nothing but wispy clouds, their very insubstantiality an insult to the dead, dying, and maimed victims of Christophe Jardin's latest blow against sin.

* * *

On Great Marlborough Street, one block east of where Susannah and Chelsea were talking, stood the offices of a discreet stockbroking firm named Arbuthnot & Hammond. One hundred and eighty years earlier, the founding partners, Walter Arbuthnot and Frederick Hammond, had forgone the comforting embrace of the city's financial district for the anonymity and commercial hurly-burly of the West End. The shattering explosion had brought all the staff out onto the street at the assembly point opposite the Liberty department store. Now that it was clear they were not about to be annihilated themselves, the brokers, analysts, client advisers, IT staff, secretaries, and partners had trailed back inside, some grinding out cigarettes under their shoes, chattering nervously, and casting worried looks around them.

On the roof of the building, wedged between a defunct brick chimney stack and a sloping section of slate tiles in the centre, was Eloise Payne's battered and bloody head. Perching on the broken jawbone, its hooked beak jerking at a strip of muscle partially torn away from the left cheek by the impact, was a female peregrine falcon. Her eggs had hatched three weeks earlier and now she had two hungry chicks to feed. The piece of flesh snapped free of its sinews, causing the head to wobble, then tumble from its moorings. The falcon took off in alarm, wheeling away back to her nest on the neighbouring building. The head slithered and bounced down the sloping slates, gathering pace with each jarring collision. On its last bounce, it cleared a low parapet surrounding a six-foot square sheet of toughened glass that roofed the building's central atrium.

Toughened it may have been, but the glass was also old. And prolonged exposure to acid rain, ultraviolet light, and the relentless chemical attack of diesel particulates and petrol fumes had weakened it. The head hit the glass dead centre, with sufficient kinetic energy to burst through.

Annette de Freitas was the senior receptionist on duty at Arbuthnot & Hammond. The emergency evacuation had ruffled her composure. She could feel her heart racing beneath her immaculate cream silk blouse and twin strands of pearls. One didn't work in central London for thirty-five years without developing a certain *sangfroid* when it came to sirens, alarms, and screams. However, the fact that this was not a fire drill but a fully fledged bomb attack, not a hundred yards from the office, had frightened her. She was on the point of asking the elderly gentleman in front of her, a longstanding client of the firm's, to jot his details down in the visitors' book when the smash from the atrium's roof made them both look up. Two-and-a-half seconds later, the head and its corona of sparkling glass fragments crunched wetly onto the marble floor. It scored a direct hit on the four-foot diameter Arbuthnot & Hammond crest.

Annette screamed. The elderly gentleman whirled round, almost losing his balance as his cane clattered to the floor. And two other visitors, waiting on a burgundy leather sofa to be collected and taken to the offices proper, leapt to their feet.

On impact, the already damaged skull split apart along its sutures. Fragments of bone sprayed out in a rough circle, intermingling with the irregular chips of glass. But the remaining flesh held the major pieces of the skull together in a grey and scarlet mess of brain tissue and blood.

The two men who had been waiting for meetings turned away. One vomited noisily into a potted dracaena plant. While Annette stood, motionless, her eyes wide with terror, the elderly man barked an order.

"Call nine-nine-nine. Now!"

Annette roused herself and snatched the phone from its cradle to make the call.

"You there, sir," the elderly gentleman called over to the younger man rooted to the spot by the sofa. "Go and stand by the door. Nobody in, nobody out. Understand?"

The suited investor, who had only come to discuss his portfolio, now found himself cast in the role of sentry. He skirted the pool of blood and bone fragments, looking down, then looking away, and stationed himself at the mahogany door, his right hand resting on the brass push-bar, looking out onto the street.

Behind him, the elderly gentleman approached the other visitor, now wiping his mouth on a white pocket square he'd pulled from his jacket.

"If you're feeling all right now, I need you to go and comfort that lady behind the reception desk. Her name is Annette."

The man did as he was asked, so shocked by the violence of the previous twenty seconds that he would have danced naked on the table had he been bid.

With the two men occupied, Major-General Angus "Jock"

Stuart, (Retd.), reached into the inside breast pocket of his tweed jacket for his phone, and called his wife.

"It's me, darling. Going to be late home, I'm afraid … You did? Bloody media. Vultures, the lot of them. Well, anyway, I'm fine. Heard the bloody thing though. I'm at A&H. Damnedest thing just happened … What? Oh, it doesn't matter. But I'm going to be here for a while … Yes. I love you too. Bye for now. Bye."

* * *

"Guv?" It was Chelsea. She'd just taken a call.

"What is it? Please don't tell me there's been another one."

"No, thank God. Only, Control have just taken a triple-nine. From just over there. Thought you'd want to take it personally."

"Why?" Susannah said, turning now to face her DS.

"Because a head just came through a skylight in an office building on Great Marlborough Street."

Without answering, Susannah strode towards the side road opening onto Regent Street, Chelsea at her heels. Then she stopped, causing her DS to stumble in her efforts not to crash into her. She pointed to a man sitting with his legs splayed in front of him against a shop doorway, a tan leather briefcase at his side. His head was down and he had lost his suit jacket somewhere: his shirtsleeves, waistcoat, and trousers were drenched in blood.

"Go and see if that bloke's OK. Paramedics must have missed him. Fuck, he's bled buckets."

4

A WOUNDED MAN

CHELSEA LEANED DOWN AND TOUCHED Gabriel on the left shoulder. His head jerked up and his blank expression whisked her back to Afghanistan. She knew that look. Slack muscle tone, eyes unfocused but red-rimmed. Like a "Closed for lunch" sign hung on a soldier's soul.

"Sir? Are you hurt? There's a lot of blood."

Gabriel looked down. "It's OK," he said. "It isn't mine. I was just helping."

"Can I ask your name?"

"It's Gabriel." He frowned. "Gabriel Wolfe."

She smiled and squatted beside him.

"Gabriel, did you see what happened?"

He wiped a hand over his face, smearing the blood.

"Not the explosion, no. I heard it, though. I was on Regent Street, up there," he said, pointing north. "I was early for a meeting so I was having a coffee. There was a girl. She lost her legs. And a man. His head was a mess. Lots of people wounded. A little Arab girl with her parents. She … I did what I could."

"I'm sure you did." Chelsea looked around and spotted a paramedic leaning against a shop window, smoking. She beckoned him over. He levered himself away from the glass, dropped the cigarette and ground it out, then jogged over. "I have to catch up with my Guvnor, but I would like to speak to you again. Later on, when you're sorted out. I want you to let my colleague here take a look at you. This is me." She proffered her business card. "Can you call me? As soon as you can?"

Gabriel took the card, examined both sides, then tucked it into his waistcoat pocket.

"Call you? Yes. I can call you."

Chelsea stood and ran to catch up with Susannah, leaving the paramedic to begin checking Gabriel for physical injuries and the shock from which she was sure he was suffering.

Inside the office building, Chelsea took in the scene with a glance. On the rare days when she had some time off for lunch, she enjoyed spending time in the National Gallery, on the north side of Trafalgar Square. This reception area looked like a tableau imagined by one of the old-school religious painters—one with a particularly gory turn of mind.

The centre of the composition was a misshapen human head, flattened and distorted, but still recognisable. She couldn't tell the gender from what was left of the face, and the blonde hair was cut short, so no clues there.

The head was surrounded by a halo of blood and brain matter, in which fragments of glass winked like jewels in the dust-edged shaft of sunlight spearing down from the smashed window overhead. Surrounding it were four people: a middle-aged woman and three men, one elderly, two in their thirties. The woman was being comforted by one of the younger men. She was sitting in a chair by the reception desk, and he was positioned to her side, kneeling and patting her hand, head bent towards her as he whispered words of comfort. The other younger man stood to the side of the door through which Chelsea had just entered. He was holding himself stiff and straight like a guardsman.

Standing with his back to the gruesome mess in the centre of the floor was an elderly man. White hair cut very short, watery, pale-blue eyes, neatly clipped white moustache, and the bearing of someone used to being in command. Ex-Army. Probably senior. She looked again at the tweed coat with its plum-coloured velvet collar. Was that a row of medal ribbons on his suit jacket, peeping out from the left-hand lapel? Probably very senior.

He approached her.

"Name's Stuart. Major-General Angus Stuart. But you," he winked, "can call me Jock."

"Thank you, sir," Chelsea said, almost saluting, so authoritative was his tone. "I'm Detective Sergeant Chelsea Jones. They used to call me 'Bun' in the Army. Not very imaginative, but, you know …"

"Army, eh? Regiment?"

"Royal Artillery, sir."

"A gunner, eh? Very good. Letting girls in, though. Bit of a change from my day."

Chelsea smiled. The old guy wasn't being snide, just flirting, she supposed, in a retired-general kind of way.

"Oh, we took a bit of flak from the guys, but once you've shot the balls off an insurgent with an SA80, they give you a bit more respect."

The general harrumphed, taken aback at this sudden coarseness, his cheeks flushing an even deeper shade of pink.

"Yes, well. I expect you want to interview everyone here. I told them all to keep away from," he turned and pointed, "that."

"Thank you, sir. And, yes, we will want to speak to you all individually. There's my Guvnor, excuse me."

Susannah was coming down a flight of stairs in the far corner of the reception area. She was accompanied by a fortyish man in a charcoal-grey suit and navy bow tie, his paunch straining the material of his waistcoat so that ellipses of white shirt showed between the buttons. He was polishing a pair of tortoiseshell spectacles on a white-spotted navy handkerchief. She looked over and caught Chelsea's eye.

"Over here, Sergeant, please."

Keeping to the edge of the room, Chelsea made her way round to her boss.

"This is Simon Hammond. He's the managing partner here."

The man held out his hand and Chelsea shook it briefly. It was soft, and damp. He spoke.

"I was just explaining to the Detective Chief Inspector here, if there's anything at all I can do, please let me know. This is just a terrible thing to have happened."

"Could we have a room to interview these witnesses in, please, sir?" Chelsea said. "We might need it for an hour or so."

"Yes, of course. Come this way."

Susannah paused and turned to Chelsea.

"Get a couple of uniforms in here. Keep the witnesses from leaving."

Chelsea nodded and pulled out her phone.

Hammond led the detectives through a door and into a corridor lined with old and expensive-looking oil paintings. Scenes of London in the nineteenth century, sailing ships on the Thames, portraits of whiskery men sporting gold watch-chains across their stomachs. He stopped outside a door.

"This used to be our boardroom, but we meet on the top floor now. Better Wi-Fi reception up there for transatlantic Skype calls and …" Susannah coughed quietly by his side. "Yes. Well, it's yours for as long as you need it," he finished.

The room was furnished with a long mahogany table, nine matching chairs to a side, upholstered in green and white striped fabric, and a carver chair at one end. The table was positioned beneath a pair of portraits of elegantly dressed middle-aged men with stern expressions, even bigger paunches than the current boss, and plentiful facial hair. The founders, Chelsea assumed.

"If there's nothing else?" Hammond said. "I do have some pressing matters to attend to."

"You've been very helpful, Mr Hammond," Susannah said.

He nodded, then excused himself, leaving a faint aroma of spicy, woody aftershave in his wake.

The two female detectives settled themselves across the table.

"Get the pathologist over here, pronto," Susannah said. "I want that head back at Savile Row and on his table as soon as possible. Could be another victim …"

"Or could be the bomber, Guv?"

Chelsea watched as her boss stared down at the polished surface of the table, following Susannah's gaze and seeing her frowning reflection.

"Yes. It could be the cunt who did it. And I want to know."

* * *

While Susannah and Chelsea spoke to the witnesses from Arbuthnot & Hammond, gathering a lot of consistent, but not very useful information—basically, smash, splat, scream, sick—Gabriel was recovering, sitting on the boot lip of the paramedic's yellow-and-green-chequered estate car. He was drinking a mug of tea that had arrived courtesy of a coffee shop that had turned itself into a combination dressing station and canteen.

He'd seen the effects of roadside bombs and suicide bombers before. But never in London. Never somewhere he thought of as civilised. Worst of all, he knew that within a couple of days, everything would be back to normal. Sure, there'd be damage to put right, but apart from the victims and their friends and families, people would slowly, and surely, forget.

Except for the odd snippets of video that found their way onto the Internet, the whole miserable scene would fade from view. Well, not for him. The face of the young girl he'd saved in the first moments after the blast—skin white with shock, eyes wide, mouth frozen open emitting frantic, shallow gasps—wouldn't let him. *Well, are you going to sit here all day, Wolfe, or are you going to do something about it?*

He pulled out his phone. Why wait to see if Don wanted him? He wanted Don. He called the man who'd commanded him in 22 SAS Regiment: Colonel Don Webster. Now retired from the Army, Webster ran a discreet organisation from a base in Essex—MoD Rothford.

Called simply The Department, it existed to bring the most evil men and women to justice. Not, as Don was fond of saying, into custody. There were plenty of terrorists out there who viewed a stint in prison as a chance to regroup and inculcate impressionable young men, and occasionally women, into their twisted philosophies. Plenty who used prison, assuming the Crown Prosecution Service's barristers were smart enough to secure a conviction, as another operating division. They ran their organisations from cells as comfortable as many people's living rooms. In short, plenty of very evil people who deserved more than a slap on the wrist. More like a very powerful slap to the body or head, in sizes ranging from 5.56mm to 9mm, with the odd .338 or .50-inch caning when getting up close and personal wasn't an option.

Gabriel had already completed a successful mission for The Department, rescuing the kidnapped wife and daughter of a British pharmaceuticals CEO and disrupting a plan to disable Britain's best fast-jet pilots. On that occasion, Don had come to him. This time, Gabriel wanted in on the ground floor.

Don answered on the first ring.

5

THE SECOND ORDER

MILLIONS OF PEOPLE TAKE PSYCHOACTIVE drugs perfectly legally. Leaving aside products whose mind-altering properties are a secondary feature of their production (at least if you believe the advertising of their manufacturers) such as alcohol and tobacco, there are mountains of others. Billions of antidepressants, sedatives, sleeping pills, anxiolytics, stimulants, and antipsychotics, every single year.

The daily dose of tranquillisers swallowed gratefully, or at least obediently, by the Children of Heaven would hardly count as a pebble kicked off the path to the foothills of those mountains. Nevertheless, they did a magnificent job of maintaining a pliable docility in the young people of both sexes recruited into the cult by its Elect of "Aunts," "Uncles," and more experienced acolytes.

Initially, Jardin had not found the tranquillisers necessary to instil discipline in his followers. His charisma, their readiness to believe, and a healthy dose of psychologically disorientating induction techniques had served to bind them tightly to him.

But as his following had grown in the late nineties, and with it, satellite communities in Berlin, Manhattan, and England's Berkshire countryside, he had hit on the idea of using drugs to simplify—or eliminate altogether—the problem of discipline.

The choice was fairly clear cut: uppers or downers. He believed his daily sermons would provide such uplift as was needed. So he opted for downers. Specifically, the class of antidepressants known as benzodiazepines, their most common manufactured form being diazepam, the active ingredient in Valium.

He took pains to cultivate relationships with criminal gangs in Albania, Turkey, London, and New York. In this way, he secured supplies of the drug in sufficient quantities to put his followers under the chemical cosh. After experimenting with the drug in tablet form, he and his main supplier, a then up-and-coming Colombian drug lord named Diego Toron, hit upon the idea of using a liquid formulation. This had the advantage of being impossible to hide under the tongue and also deliverable in soft drinks. He'd borrowed from that other leader of the lost, Jim Jones, and his Kool-Aid capers in the jungles of Guyana.

Now it was time to dose the flock. He left his house on the southwest fringe of the village square, robe flowing, hair blowing in the breeze that soughed across the grassland he had had chopped out of the forest, and made his way to the meeting space in front of the Temple.

Approaching the large wooden building, resplendent with an immense wooden cross outside and stained glass windows to each side of the double-doored entrance, he composed his features into something he felt was suitably messianic. Drop the grin. Crinkle the brow. And, for added saintliness, fix the gaze on a point thirty degrees above the horizontal, while trying to remember the names of all the women he'd fucked since setting up home in the jungles of Brazil.

One of the Uncles hurried over.

"Père Christophe! We were worried. It's later than normal, and when you didn't appear, we thought something must have happened. Your being so punctual, I mean."

Jardin returned his gaze to Earth and fixed his purplish-blue eyes on the man. "I was meditating. Forgive me for communing with God when there was admin to take care of."

"Oh no, I mean, of course, your spiritual practice must come first." The younger man was blushing now, aware he'd displeased his master. "The Children are gathered for the obeisance."

"Good. Come on, then. Let's dose them up and get it over with."

"Père Christophe?"

Jardin shook his head. He felt like saying, *did I say that out loud?*, but contented himself with a saintly smile.

"I said, let's perform the obeisance ceremony. Did you not hear me?"

Panicked now, the Uncle nodded several times, keeping his eyes to the ground.

The Children were assembled in rows, dozens upon dozens of them, all dressed in white. Walking amongst them, the Uncles and Aunts placed hands on heads, murmured blessings, and patted hands. They carried brushed aluminium flasks that sloshed as they bumped on their thighs.

Jardin arrived in front of the crowd and mounted a dais constructed from planks of hardwood harvested from the trees growing all over the compound. Silence fell.

The Uncles and Aunts set up the flasks on collapsible camp tables placed at the end of each row of Children. Each table was equipped with a hosepipe connected to a pump in a corner of the compound. Beside them were stacked clear plastic cups of the type used at outdoor parties and barbecues, and bottles of fruit cordials in deep, jewel colours of maroon, lime-green and bright, acid orange.

Beneath the rough-plank platform, yellow cables as thick as a man's finger snaked away to a plain, white, clapboard hut on the edge of the assembly area. There, a thousand-watt PA system stood ready to transmit his words to every corner of the compound, both here and way over in the vegetable-growing area, the water treatment plant, the workshops, the printing shed where the cult would create its leaflets to be distributed in towns and cities throughout Amazonas State, and the generator room. He slid the transparent cheek mic over his right ear and plugged its jack into the transmitter box under his robe. Then, assuming his slow, smooth, deep "Père Christophe" voice, Jardin began speaking.

"My Children. Blessings be upon you for following the First Order."

They chanted back at him in a low murmur that, owing to the sheer weight of numbers, reverberated around the compound's central village. "Serve God through Père Christophe's will."

"And you do it with grace and peace in your hearts. Today, we celebrate one of our family who yesterday carried out the Second Order."

Again, the chant. "Give your life to cleanse the world of sin."

"Child Eloise carried out a cleansing in London, that city of sin. She resides in the house of the Lord, now. She sits by his side, anointed by fire, handmaiden to the Creator."

The rows of Children smiled at this news, turning their tanned, unlined faces to each other and nodding, each daring to hope that one day Père Christophe would give them the Second Order.

"There is much wickedness in the World," Jardin continued. "Much sin. Greed, corruption, covetousness, lust, atheism. The great cities of the world have transformed themselves into modern-day Babylons, peopled by whores, fornicators and idolaters. Our God is not their God. For they HAVE no God. They pursue pleasure at all COSTS. They hanker for the empty acquisition of material goods and IGNORE the spiritual wealth God has already made theirs if they would only ASK."

Jardin could feel his pulse ticking over quietly in the background as he adopted the rhythmic cadences and pauses of the seasoned preacher. He'd found the speeches of Martin Luther King, Jr. online and practised until he could emulate the civil rights leader's every vocal leap and bound.

"We are the righteous ones who will CLEANSE this planet … we are the righteous. Who will UPROOT wickedness and consign it to the FLAMES of redemption … we are the righteous. Who will burn out SIN wherever it FESTERS … we are the righteous. Who will return this world to God's grace. WE ARE THE RIGHTEOUS," he thundered. His last shout flushed a flock of emerald-green parrots from a stand of banana palms at the edge of the gathering. They erupted from the foliage with a clatter of wings and a squawk of alarm.

He could feel an erection growing steadily larger beneath his robe and decided to cut this particular sermon short. There was a slim-figured blonde girl in the front row who had caught his eye and was even now gazing rapturously up at him.

"It is time for your obeisance, Children. Drink our sacrament. May the blessing of the Lord be upon your heads."

"And upon yours," the Children murmured in response.

With that, he dismounted the dais. He stood, watching, as the horde of Children queued like sheep to take their blackcurrant, lime or orange-flavoured tranquilliser. They were formerly the disillusioned, disturbed, disgruntled or just plain disaffected. The offspring of wealthy professional people with more time for their careers than their children's well-being. Now they were now *his* Children. His to control. To play with. And, when he felt like it, to destroy.

The blonde had selected lime. He watched as she knocked back the sweet liquid in one. Then, when her eyes came to rest on him, as he knew they would, he smiled and beckoned. She blushed. Then she looked down at her feet, which moved towards Jardin.

6

_____

INVITATION TO COBRA

"HELLO, OLD SPORT. I WONDERED how long it would take you to call. Heard about the bombing in London, then?"

"I didn't hear *about* it, Don. I actually heard it. I was on Regent Street when the thing went off. I spent the last hour patching up victims. It's like bloody Kabul down here." Gabriel looked at his bloodstained hand, turning it this way and that. It was trembling. He shoved it between his thighs and clamped them around it.

"Jesus! How are you doing?"

"I'm fine. Bit tired, and I think my suit's had it, but I'm good. Basically. Yes, good."

Apart from the reappearance of a certain SAS trooper we both knew back in the day.

"And you're calling me because …?"

"You know why I'm calling you."

"Well, there's nothing much to do at the moment. We need something to go on before The Department can be of much use. Hopefully the police will come up with some forensic evidence to give us a direction to start poking around in. Or MI5 will supply some credible intel. But at the moment, I'm on what the media would call high readiness, and you and I would call sitting on our hands doing sweet Fanny Adams. Once we know more, I'll be putting a team together. And you'd like to be on it, I assume?"

"Yes. Very much so. I'm …"

"Hold on, got a call coming in from the PM."

Gabriel heard a click as Don switched to the other call. He finished his tea and put the cup down on the pavement beside him. One of the young staff from the coffee shop rushed over, plucked it up, and dropped it into her black bin bag. She was very young, still a teenager, with pale skin, dark eye makeup, and a piercing in her left eyebrow, a little steel cone. Her T-shirt was black. It said Barista in Training across the chest. She smiled nervously at him and he realised he was staring. He looked away. As he waited for Don, a squad of infantrymen disgorged from the back of an army truck that had lumbered up Regent Street. They grabbed shovels and were marched off by a sergeant towards Oxford Circus.

He looked at the screen of his phone. Nine missed calls. All from Britta. Don came back on the line.

"Sorry about that, but when the PM beckons, one must come running."

"So what did she want?"

"Meeting at two-thirty this afternoon at the Cabinet Office Briefing Rooms, which the media, and our own dear leader, love to call COBRA. You want to come? I told the PM one of my team was directly involved. She'd like to meet you."

"I'm not exactly dressed for it. I look like I've taken a few rounds from a Kalashnikov."

"I can fix that for you. We've a couple of safe houses in town. One is unoccupied. You can get cleaned up and then meet me in Whitehall. I'll text you both addresses and call ahead to have someone there to let you in. Got to go."

The line went dead. Gabriel stared off into the middle distance. There was something he'd been meaning to do but now couldn't remember.

Britta!

Gabriel tapped out a text to her.

 · · ·

Am fine. Don't worry. Will call. G

A few moments later, Gabriel's phone beeped as the text arrived from Don with the locations of the safe house in Victoria and the Cabinet Office building in Whitehall. He was just wondering how best to reach the safe house when the two detectives came out from Great Marlborough Street and hurried across the road towards him. There was no traffic but they reflexively checked in both directions.

The one who'd given her his card, Chelsea, spoke first.

"Gabriel? This is Detective Chief Inspector Chambers. She's my Guvnor. Can we speak to you, please? Now?"

Gabriel checked his watch.

"You can, but I've just been told I'm meeting the prime minister this afternoon and …"

Susannah spoke.

"You need new clothes, right? And a shower? We can make that work, can't we Chels? Do you live in London?"

Gabriel had to think for a moment, He ran his hand over his hair and scratched the back of his head.

"No. I live in Salisbury." And because, often, people didn't know where that was, he added, "It's near Stonehenge."

Chelsea smiled at him and he noticed she had a mole on the right of her top lip, halfway between the outer edge of her nostril and the corner of her mouth. Her deep brown eyes were round, fringed with long dark lashes, and her lips were wide and full.

"I know Salisbury," she said. "I had a mate stationed just outside in a town called Tidworth. Do you know it?"

"Of course! I drive through it on my way to meet a friend in Hungerford."

"All of which is lovely," Susannah interrupted. "Forgive me if I try and hurry this along, both of you, but where can we take you, Gabriel? We can talk on the way."

Chelsea blushed, her pale skin tinting pink as the blood vessels dilated from her throat all the way up to her cheek bones.

"Sorry, Guv. So, Gabriel, do you have a friend or someone you can visit to get cleaned up?"

Gabriel showed her the screen of his phone.

"Can you take me there, please?"

She glanced down. "Sure. Come with us."

Together they made their way back down Regent Street, through the roadblock, towards Savile Row. Pedestrians ambled between the stranded vehicles or stood around by the statue of Eros at Piccadilly Circus, taking selfies or videos of the huge neon advertising signs. The traffic was gridlocked, and the noise from horns and engines was deafening.

"Fucking idiots," Susannah said. "Like hooting's going to make things any better."

She marched into the road and used one knuckle to knock on the window of a big black Audi saloon, whose driver was leaning repeatedly on the centre of the steering wheel, adding his air horns to the racket.

He buzzed the window down and she squatted beside him, holding her warrant card up where he could get a good look at it. Gabriel noticed a thin strip of red lace above the waistband of her jeans.

"Sorry to bother you, sir," she said in a sweet and reasonable tone, brushing her hair back from her eyes. "Do you happen to know exactly why the traffic's so bad this morning?"

"No, officer, not really," he said, looking down at his hands and then over at her again.

"Well, allow me to enlighten you, sir. About an hour ago, some antisocial nutcase blew themselves up on the top deck of a bus up there," she said, pointing back towards Oxford Circus. Her voice took on a singsong rhythm. "And now, there are firefighters … paramedics … police … and soldiers trying to clean up all the blood and mess and so on. So, I wonder, as a personal favour to me, if you wouldn't mind, awfully, not blowing your little horn, all, fucking, morning. Would that be OK? Sir?"

The man nodded, looking at Susannah then out of the

windscreen again, unable to hold her gaze. "Sorry, officer, of course. It's just, you know, frustrating."

"Of course it is, sir," Susannah said, all smiles and sweet reason again. "For all of us."

She pushed herself to her feet, grunting with the effort, hitched up her jeans and strode back to the pavement and the wide-eyed stares of a knot of pedestrians.

"Come on," she said to Gabriel and Chelsea. "Let's get a car, stick on the blues and twos and get somewhere quieter."

Susannah drove the unmarked silver BMW 5 Series fast down The Mall, heading for the safe house. The combination of the siren and the concealed, grille-mounted blue lights helped her carve a path through the traffic. Even so, she was sometimes forced to a standstill as the drivers of the cars and trucks in front of and beside her got tangled up with each other in their efforts to clear out of her way. While she concentrated on the route, Chelsea questioned Gabriel.

"So, where were you before the bomb went off, Gabriel?"

"At a café on Regent Street, north of Oxford Circus. It's called Biaggi's."

"I know it," Chelsea said, making a note. "Then what happened?"

"I left, and was walking to meet a new client. Then the bomb detonated."

"What did you do next?"

"I ran down towards Oxford Circus. When I got there, I just started helping people. Basic battlefield first aid: tourniquets, compression. There wasn't much I could do for a lot of them, but I got a few people to put their phones away and help out instead. Then I just, you know, I had to get somewhere to sit down for a minute. Then you came over to talk to me. Oh, and I found this."

He reached into his waistcoat pocket and took out the ball bearing. He handed it to Chelsea, without looking at its shiny, distorting surface, smeared scarlet with a stranger's blood.

"Yeah," she said with a frown. "You shouldn't really have taken that. It's evidence. But," she hurried on, as a sigh of exasperation from her boss hissed between the front and rear seats, "We'll have quite a collection of these evil little things by the end of the day, so one stuffed into your pocket probably isn't critical. We'll check them all for fingerprints but I'm not too hopeful. The blast will probably have destroyed them all." She draped a clean paper handkerchief over it and folded it into her jacket pocket. "So, apart from hearing the explosion and doing your bit with the wounded, is there anything else you can remember that we could use? Don't prejudge it; just let me hear it. Anything at all?"

Gabriel closed his eyes. "Let me be still a moment," he said. He willed his breathing to slow, and his heartbeat too. He tuned out the car's siren and quieted his mind, just as his childhood tutor in Hong Kong, Master Zhao, had taught him. Nothing. Just the sweet, lemon-scented cake and the strong coffee, then the call with Britta, then the huge bang as the bomb shattered so many bodies, and lives, in one terrible instant. No. Not nothing. The girl. Yes! The anxious-looking girl with the bulky jacket.

He opened his eyes.

"I think I saw the bomber."

7

REMEMBERING ELOISE PAYNE

SUSANNAH JERKED HER HEAD ROUND at Gabriel's words, then faced forward again after a white van with three men squashed together in the front blasted its horn as she veered towards its driver's door.

"You saw him?" she asked, giving the aggrieved builders the benefit of a full-on death stare.

Chelsea turned sideways to look at Gabriel directly. "How can you be sure?" she said.

"First of all, it wasn't a him. It was a her."

"Christ!" Susannah said.

"Second, I can't be sure. Not exactly. It was when I was having my coffee. A car pulled up and this skinny girl climbed out. She looked really nervous—terrified, really. And she had a bulky, padded jacket on. Then the car pulled a U-turn, a real tyre-squealer, and headed back up Regent Street towards the Euston Road.

"Could have been anyone," Susannah said. "Any number of reasons for a young girl to look nervous. Could have been a tart being taken to her first-ever client. Could've been anything."

But Chelsea wasn't prepared to write the lead off so quickly.

"The Guvnor's right, Gabriel. So how come you think she was the bomber?"

Gabriel wiped his hand over his face. The dried blood specks on his skin were itching and the smell from his clothes in the cloying, heated air of the car was making him nauseous. He felt his gut roll over.

"Can you pull over, please? I'm going to be sick."

"Shit! OK, hold on," Susannah said. Timing her braking to slide between a couple of black cabs, she brought the car to a screeching halt by a black and gold rubbish bin.

Gabriel wrenched the door open, leapt out and vomited painfully into the bin, his stomach cramping as it ejected a thin stream of yellow bile. Wiping his mouth on a handkerchief he pulled from his trouser pocket, he climbed back in to the car.

"Sorry," he said.

"No need to apologise," Susannah said. "I'm surprised you didn't chuck up sooner after what you saw this morning. So, look. Let's take this seriously for a minute." Then she slammed the palm of her hand onto the steering wheel, sounding the horn and forcing a motorcyclist into the bus lane as she powered through on her way round the road junction curving north in front of Buckingham Palace. "What's the matter, arsehole?" she yelled at the closed window. "You colour-blind or something? Thought these were flashing fucking fairy lights, did you?"

Gabriel spoke, his voice level.

"She was thin. I remember, she had bony wrists and her legs were like sticks. But inside the jacket, she looked, I don't know, wrong somehow. I know it was a Puffa, but you can still tell when they're mostly padding, can't you? This one looked like she was filling it. I think she had a suicide vest on underneath it. There were two people in the car with her. A man driving and a middle-aged woman in the back with her."

This time it was Chelsea who played the sceptic.

"Could be anorexic. Mum and Dad taking her to some clinic. Big jumper under the Puffa jacket. They get cold. No fat."

"Yeah, not like some of us, worse luck," Susannah chipped in from the front seat. "I could do with a few of those two-grape dinners myself." Gabriel said nothing. "Sorry. Bad taste? It's copper humour. You might have to get used to it while you're riding with Chels and me. We see so much horrible stuff, the jokes are how we cope."

"Don't worry about it," he said, "we used to do the same in the Army. Look, maybe she wasn't the bomber. But there'll be CCTV footage of her, won't there? Heading down Regent Street to Oxford Circus, she'd have passed, what, five cameras? Ten?"

"We'll be reviewing CCTV, so yes, OK, we'll keep an eye out. Might need you to lend us your eyes though. You saw her, after all. Now, we're here."

Susannah pulled up outside a row of plain, cream-painted, Regency houses in a side street, a couple of blocks back from Victoria Street. As Gabriel got out, she leaned over and spoke through the open passenger-side window.

"You have DS Jones's card, right?"

He nodded.

"OK, so get cleaned up, go and meet the prime minister, and then call. I want you at our nick tomorrow, first thing, if possible. OK?"

"Yes, fine. Thanks for the lift. I'll see you tomorrow."

"Bye, Gabriel. Thanks," Chelsea said.

He closed the door and watched as Susannah accelerated then executed a perfect sliding turn in the road, causing an oncoming taxi to screech to a halt, its horn blaring. From Victoria Station, a few hundred yards away, came the sounds of train brakes squealing and station announcements drifting on the wind. Gabriel screwed his face up against the noise. *Too much. Too much blood. Too much death.* His stomach churned and cramped again and he looked around for a bush or another bin. Then the spasm passed and he straightened up and turned to the front door of the house.

Unusual for a safe house to have a doorman, he thought. Especially a dead one.

"All right, Smudge?"

"Good, thanks, Boss. Never better. Apart from the face, obviously." The

dark-skinned soldier pointed at the place where his lower jaw should have been and made a tutting sound with his lolling red tongue against the roof of his mouth. *"Just wait there. They'll open the door for you."* He pointed up at a tiny video camera tucked away between the wall and a cream-painted drainpipe. *"Smile. You're on Candid Camera."*

Sure enough, the door opened silently. A man in his late twenties stood there, smiling. He wore a dove grey suit, a plain royal blue silk tie, and shiny black brogues. He beckoned Gabriel inside. Gabriel turned back to the street, but Smudge, as he'd expected, had vanished.

Once the door was closed behind him, Gabriel began to shake, uncontrollably. He felt the sweat break out all over his body in a sickly wave of clammy cold.

"I'm sorry," he said, leaning against the wall. "I'm feeling really not good. Is there somewhere I can lie down for a bit, or preferably have a bath?"

"Of course, sir. Follow me," the young man said, his face creased with concern, his eyes flicking up and down over Gabriel's bloody clothes. "I'm James, by the way."

"Gabriel."

Trailing his left hand along the wall as he climbed the stairs to the first floor, Gabriel could feel tears starting from his eyes and he let them come, tracking down over his cheeks and dropping off his chin to mingle with the blood on the front of his waistcoat.

James stopped outside a white-painted, panelled door with a brass handle.

"You'll find everything you need in there, sir. If you'd like to leave your clothes outside the door, I can have them cleaned for you. We have some spare stuff kept for visitors. I'll pull out some togs for you. You're about the same size as the last chap we had staying with us, and they fitted him fine."

With that, he turned and walked down the hallway towards the stairs.

Gabriel pushed the door in front of him. It opened onto a bathroom, complete with claw-footed bath fed from polished copper pipes emerging from well-worn, honey-coloured floorboards. He turned on the taps and looked around the cavernous room. It was easily fifteen feet square and housed a leather sofa as well as a sink and a large wooden cupboard that turned out to contain a hot water tank and, more importantly, a tall pile of fluffy white towels that smelled faintly of lavender. On the back of the door hung a white towelling robe. Best of all, on a wooden chest set against the wall between a pair of white-painted sash windows was an ice bucket. It contained a bottle of Chablis, already uncorked. A single glass stood next to it.

While the bath was filling, steam rising from the churning surface of the water, he poured wine into the glass, drained it, then poured again. With the alcohol soothing his tattered nerves and quietening the fluttering creatures fighting for room in his stomach, he retrieved his phone, wallet, and house keys from various pockets then stripped off the ruined clothes, folded them as best he could, and left them together with his socks and shoes outside the door.

He climbed into the bath then climbed out again to retrieve the glass and the ice bucket. After taking a long pull on the wine—not what its makers would have wanted, he was sure—he placed the glass on the floor beside the bath, feeling the cold beads of condensation under his fingertips. Then he lowered himself once again into the scalding hot water and closed his eyes. He let himself slide down until the water closed over his head. For a brief moment, he considered simply taking a deep breath. It would be a certain end to the hallucinations, the panic attacks, and the nightmares. It was also a coward's way out. And there was help available in the shape of his psychiatrist, Professor Fariyah Crace. He'd begun seeing her once a month on Don's recommendation.

She had confirmed what Don knew and Gabriel himself had already suspected. He was suffering—and that was definitely the right word—from Post-Traumatic Stress Disorder. He'd only met her for an initial consultation, but she'd told him he could be treated. He meant to sort it out, too. The problem was fitting in appointments around his increasingly hectic, and dangerous, work.

He surfaced with a gasp, splashing water over the sides of the tub and looking down at the pinkish water. *No. Not today. If death wants me, he's going to have to chase me down.* There was soap and shampoo on a shelf by the sink. He fetched it and began, methodically, to clean every square inch of his body, bloodied or not.

The spooks, or whoever they were, had thought of everything. The mirror-fronted cabinet above the sink held disposable razors, toothbrushes, shaving foam and all the other things you'd need to get the stink and the grime of a bomb blast off you. He finished off the second glass of wine as he shaved and was sitting on the wooden chest with a refill when there was a quiet double-knock at the door.

"Sir? It's James. I've left you some clothes outside the door. There's a bedroom next to the bathroom. I've been instructed by Mr Webster to let you sleep until one forty-five. He's sending a car to collect you at two."

Gabriel called his thanks through the door, took a sip of the wine, and fetched the clothes. Jeans, white cotton button-down shirt, and a navy V-neck sweater. Socks and underwear, and his own shoes, freshly polished and gleaming in the light from the shaded lamp overhead. The clothes were a good fit, though the combination of denim and polished black brogues gave him the look of a not-very-astute drugs squad officer trying to blend in at a festival. Still, probably good enough for the prime minister.

The ice bucket dangling from a finger by its handle, he headed next door, where he found a double bed. He finished the wine in his glass and lay down. Sat up again. Reached for his phone. Called Britta.

She answered without the phone even ringing.

"Oh, shit, Gabriel. Are you fine? Really? Swear to me or I will come and get you and …" then she stopped and he could hear her gulping for air.

"I am. I swear. It detonated a few streets away, and I went to help. I'm in one of Don's safe houses now. I'm going after the people who did it."

"Oh, thank God. It's all over the news. People are tweeting these horrific pictures. It's worse than Bosnia when we found that village. Do you remember?"

Gabriel did remember. As part of a joint Swedish-British Special Forces operation, Captains Wolfe and Falskog had been among the first soldiers to fight their way through heavily-armed Serbian resistance and retake a village largely inhabited by Bosnian Muslims. The Serbs had left nobody alive. Or intact. The smell of blood hung in the air like a dark, meaty fog and there had been nothing to do but place bodies, and body parts, of men, women and children into heavy-duty, black zip-up bags and wait for ambulances to take them away for burial.

"Listen," he said, shaking his head to dispel the images of bayoneted children, and men with their hands cut off and their eyes removed, "we may have to cancel dinner. I'm sorry."

"Don't be stupid. I'm not cancelling anything. Just a rain check. That's all. You call me when you know what your schedule is, and we are having dinner together. And you can come and stay here, too. Promise me."

"Britta, I ..."

"Promise me!"

"OK, I promise. I have to go. I need to sleep. Don's got me an appointment with the prime minister."

"OK. Sleep tight, you. I ..."

"Bye, Britta."

Gabriel ended the call. Whether it was the shock, the Chablis, the bath, the call with Britta, or a combination of all four, he was asleep twenty seconds later.

* * *

At one forty p.m., Gabriel awoke to the sound of surf and seagulls. For a moment, he thought he was at the seaside. Then he reached over and silenced his phone. He felt refreshed and calm, despite the nightmare of the preceding few hours. He dressed quickly and was downstairs five minutes later.

"Ah, there you are, sir," James said, emerging from the kitchen as Gabriel's feet landed on the carpeted floor of the hallway. "There's a car waiting for you outside, ready to take you to Whitehall. Shall I hold onto your clothes for now? We can courier them to your home address whenever you're ready."

"Thanks," Gabriel said, then they shook hands, and he was through the front door and climbing into the back seat of a gleaming, black Jaguar XJR with blacked-out windows and a set of gunmetal alloy wheels. The car smelled as if it hadn't been long out of the showroom—a mixture of expensive leather, beeswax polish, and a whiff of something that might have been vanilla in the air-conditioned atmosphere cocooning him and the chauffeur from the warmth of the September sunshine.

"Afternoon, sir," the driver said in a brisk, efficient voice Gabriel had always associated with company sergeant majors and other long-serving NCOs. "Whitehall, is it?"

Suspecting the man already had his orders, Gabriel simply agreed without furnishing the full address.

"Yes, please."

"Very good, sir. Shan't take us long; traffic's eased up since lunchtime. In that business in the West End, were you, sir?" he asked.

8

INVESTOR MEETING

"HOLD ON TIGHT, PÈRE CHRISTOPHE," the pilot said. Thirty minutes into the flight from Eden's airfield to El Dorado Airport in Bogotá, the Cessna 206 bounced and hopped through the sky, dropping alarmingly once for a couple of seconds as clear-air turbulence sucked the lift from under its wings. Sitting next to the pilot, one of the Elect, Jardin swore. The man grappling with the stick glanced to his right at the profanity.

"Relax, Robert," Jardin said. "I'm sure God would forgive me an oath under these conditions."

The pilot inclined his head and returned his gaze to the front. The plane steadied and they flew on.

Ninety minutes later, at 12.30 local time, the little aircraft was scudding along the tarmac in a landing slot allocated by the Colombian control tower between jets arriving from Medellín and Houston, Texas. The pilot feathered the throttle, then taxied along the runway and an access road. He brought the plane to a stop half a mile from the passenger terminal, on a pale concrete apron fronting part of a cargo building. He killed the engine. It spun down to a stop with a whine from the propeller shafts.

Jardin unsnapped his harness and stepped down from the plane.

He was stiff from the flight, and his arms and hands were tense from gripping the sides of his seat during the choppy ride. The only bad point to a compound sited in a location inaccessible except by air was the air itself. He hated flying.

Bogotá was enjoying warm weather and he began to relax, unhitching the muscles of his shoulders and rolling his head from side to side, eyes closed in what he hoped Robert would see as a sign of spiritual realignment. *Fucking idiot.*

Overhead, a jet screamed towards the runway, its landing gear down—the Houston flight. Full of fat Texan oilmen, no doubt. Maybe one of these days I'll put one of my Children on a flight with you.

As he reflected on the logistical difficulties of getting a teenaged acolyte wrapped in dynamite and ball bearings onto a commercial flight to the USA, a white car approached from the passenger terminal. An SUV of some kind. Cars didn't interest Jardin; it was the people inside them who piqued his curiosity. And this vehicle contained someone very interesting indeed: his business partner. He stroked his beard and pushed his long, thin fingers through his hair, raking it back behind his ears then pulling it forward again. *Every inch the prophet, Christophe.*

The car pulled up ten yards from the plane's starboard wingtip. The driver was a thickset man with a dark complexion and greased-back hair tied in a ponytail. Well over six feet, Jardin estimated, and with all his muscle concentrated in his upper body. He had thick gold hoops threaded through both earlobes giving him the look of a pirate, albeit one dressed like an FBI agent in a black suit, white shirt and black tie. He jumped down and scurried around to the rear to hold open the door for his passenger.

Jardin waited. The wind, which had sprung up as the car arrived, whipped his robe about his legs so that the coarse cotton stung his calves. He was calm. But then, he was always calm. Apart from those fucking flights.

The man who stepped down from the car was Diego Toron, the head of the Muerte Eterna drug cartel. His operation wasn't as big as its more famous Cali and Medellín cousins had been in their heyday, before greed and government determination destroyed them, but it was equally ready to get rid of its enemies with extreme violence. He was taller than Jardin, five-eleven to the older man's five-eight, and he was muscular, though good living had produced a rounded belly, made visible when his white silk shirt was blown against it. His top lip and his jawline, softened by the same luxury that had rounded his gut, were shaded with dark stubble. A thin white scar ran from his right ear under his cheekbone and down past the corner of his mouth. His nose was stubby, with wide, flaring nostrils. His lips were soft and full, almost like a woman's.

He strolled over to the plane while buttoning his jacket, removed his sunglasses and looked Jardin in the eye, scowling. Then a wide smile split his face revealing dazzling white teeth. He leaned forward to embrace Jardin, kissing him on both cheeks, before stepping back and poking him in the chest.

"Buenos días, Christophe. You still look like you're auditioning for *Joseph and His Technicolor Dreamcoat*! When are you going to get yourself a nice suit like this one?"

He unbuttoned his jacket again and let the navy linen fly back from his torso as the wind caught it. The lining was electric blue silk. Jardin caught the Italian brand name sewn in capitals onto a black label on the left-hand pocket. He smiled at Toron.

"When I turn into a fashion model, which," he lifted the side of his robe away from his body and let it fall, "as you can see, is no time soon."

The pleasantries out of the way, the two men climbed into the SUV, sitting side by side on the back seat. Jardin sniffed.

"Smells like a whorehouse in here."

"That's because we were taking some girls over to Medellín in it yesterday. It practically *was* a whorehouse."

The two men laughed and, as the driver pulled away, began discussing business.

"So, you're not happy with our current arrangement," Toron said, frowning. "I thought running coke up to Texas was a nice little income stream for you. Keeps you in prayer books and incense, doesn't it?"

Jardin smiled, laying a reassuring hand on the other man's knee for a couple of seconds, enjoying his discomfort at the overly friendly physical contact.

"More than happy, Diego. America is a sick society. Their idiot presidents bleat on about the war on drugs when it's their own citizens who suck half the cocaine in Colombia up their stupid, fat noses. You know what they ought to start, if they were serious about saving the lives of their people?"

"What?" Toron said, biting at a loose piece of skin at the side of his thumb.

"The war on guns. But somehow, I can't see that happening, can you? So if we can profit from their hypocrisy, so much the better."

"Well, what is this all about then?" Toron said.

"I have a business proposal for you. You see, I think what we need is a little vertical integration at Eden. A manufacturing and processing plant. Maybe even a plantation. We have the land, and a more-than-willing workforce, believe me."

Toron scratched the bristles stippling his chin.

"Vertical integration, eh? You know a lot of business talk for a man of God."

"Listen, my friend. I keep the Children of Heaven in line using God and the Valium you so kindly supply as part of our arrangement. For myself, I'd cheerfully blow up every church, mosque, synagogue and temple from here to Jerusalem. Take every priest, imam, and rabbi and shoot them in the face. In fact, one day I might just do that. Now, as I was saying …"

By the time they arrived at the restaurant in the centre of Bogotá, the outline of the plan was in place. Toron would supply raw product, machinery, and expert staff to set up a cocaine production facility inside the Eden compound. Stretching, as it did, over two thousand acres of rainforest, with a supply of water from a tributary of the Rio Negro, there was plenty of space where no prying eyes from the Brazilian authorities would ever alight. Instructed that their new work was covered by the First Order, the Children of Heaven would willingly, or at least passively, go to work. They'd turn bales of coca leaves into blocks of pure-grade cocaine to be flown north and into the USA for final cutting and distribution. The executives, rock musicians, students, and soccer moms would get their fix. The US customs officials, DEA agents, and police who required them would get their bribes and their kickbacks. And Jardin and Toron would get rich. Correction: richer.

The maître d' at Copa d'Oro was familiar with Diego Toron, and he never allowed the Colombian's lack of a tie to cause him any problems. Not that it would be wise to raise any objections anyway. A year earlier, one of Toron's bodyguards had spent a couple of days in Bogotá spreading a tale about his master's nocturnal activities that would secure him the best table in any restaurant in the city, even if he turned up stark naked.

The duty manager at a French restaurant across town from Copa D'Oro had once refused Toron entry for not wearing a tie. Toron had returned with a couple of heavies at two in the morning as the restaurant was closing, bundled the unfortunate restaurant manager into the boot of a Cadillac, and taken him to "the baptistry"—a warehouse owned by the Muerte Eterna, whose central space was empty except for a gleaming porcelain bathtub in purest white.

They had dragged the man over to the tub, handed him a hose connected to a distant tap, and instructed him to fill it.

As the water splashed into the tub, Toron spoke to the man, who was white with fear and shaking so hard he could barely keep the hose pointed in the right direction.

"My name is Diego Toron. But everyone—everyone, it would seem, apart from you, my friend—knows me by another name. El Bautista. You know? Like John the Baptist?"

The man nodded, bobbing his head up and down in rapid jerks as if he could forestall whatever was coming by the fervency of his agreement.

"Well, now it is your turn to be redeemed."

Then, he seized the man by the scruff of his neck and thrust him face down into the water. It was still only a few inches deep, but, as swimming teachers and anxious parents tell their children, that is still enough to drown in.

Knowing of Toron's reputation, Rafael De Angelis, Copa D'Oro's duty manager on this particular sitting, smiled a welcome to his powerful guest. However, he couldn't help wrinkling his bulbous nose as he took in the man Toron had brought as his guest.

Noticing the fleeting expression of disgust, Toron leaned towards De Angelis and beckoned with a crooked finger. De Angelis leaned forward, ear towards Toron's mouth.

"He is a very holy man," Toron mumbled, forcing De Angelis to lean closer still, until his ear was almost touching Toron's lips. "A spiritual leader. A guide for fallen souls over there," he jerked his thumb over his right shoulder, "in Brazil. Amazonas. I would consider it a personal favour if you would waive Copa's dress code for him."

De Angelis straightened, flashed his best VIP smile at Jardin, and picked up two menus from the brushed steel stand next to him. He motioned the men forward towards a pair of deep green velvet curtains.

"Gentlemen?" he said. "Welcome to Copa D'Oro. I have a very good table for you. Please. Follow me."

They started with ceviche, the thin slices of raw black clam perfectly cured by lime juice and chilli and garnished with fragrant chopped coriander. As they ate, Toron and Jardin discussed contractual details and the logistics of building, equipping and staffing the production facility, and how they would integrate it into the Muerte Eterna supply chain.

Jardin took a sip of his wine. "This Chilean sauvignon blanc is good, Diego. Almost as good as a Sancerre." Then he winked. "Just kidding. I wouldn't use that French piss to put out a fire. So, tell me, how is your family?"

Toron's face broke into a smile. His eyes widened and he took a sip from his own glass.

"Isabella has just been picked for the volleyball team. She's only nine, but already she is so talented. A natural athlete. And my baby, Serafina. Two years behind her sister and she wants to overtake her. Her gift is painting. Dolores and I have hopes she will go to art school."

"And the beautiful Dolores Maria Cristabel. How is she?" Jardin popped another slice of clam into his mouth as he watched the man talk about his wife and kids. The combination of heat, smoky clam, salt and citrus from the ceviche was almost too good to bear. He groaned quietly to himself, masking the sound by lifting his wineglass to his lips.

"She is well, thank you. Still perhaps a little too in love with the church, you know? She finds my line of work hard to square with her conscience. But she is a loyal wife."

"And you, my friend," Jardin asked, dabbing a trickle of lime juice from the corner of his mouth with his napkin. "How are you?"

"Me?" Toron appeared to find this question strange. He furrowed his brow and pulled his chin down, producing a wrinkled collar of flesh. "You know, I run my businesses. I have my health, thank God. I enjoy myself when I can. The opera, time permitting."

"And your line of work. Can you square it with your conscience?" How I love to mess with people's minds, you dumb Latino drug dealer.

Toron frowned, producing deep grooves in his high forehead.

"I provide for my family. I give to orphanages and charities. I go to confession."

"And your priest. He must need a stiff drink after a visit from El Bautista, no?"

A flash of anger crossed Toron's face. His brow lowered and his lips tightened over his teeth, compressing into a thin line.

"Watch your step, holy man. Make sure you don't end up at the baptistry yourself."

Normally, a threat such as this would have men pissing

themselves in fear. Jardin merely laughed before draining his glass and signalling a passing water for a wine list.

"Calm yourself, Diego. My apologies. I was simply enquiring after your spiritual well-being. Confession is one of the Catholic Church's best innovations. You can pull a man's tongue out through a slit in his throat, but as long as you wag your own to a priest in a little latticed cubicle the next day, you're back in God's favour. Now, where are our steaks?"

The meal, and the deal, completed, the two men left. Outside the restaurant, the temperature had dropped from twenty-one to nine degrees Celsius. Bogotá was experiencing its famous *sol de lluvia* —"rain's sun". The earlier blue sky had been occluded by a thick blanket of grey clouds, and now fat drops of freezing rain were pelting pedestrians like machine gun bullets, driving them inside shops and office blocks for cover. Toron's car was waiting at the kerb, engine idling to maintain the SUV's internal temperature. Spying his master, the driver exited the car and stood holding the rear door open, the rain drenching him as he maintained his pose like a statue. Toron and Jardin dashed the few yards from the end of the restaurant's dark green and gold marquee and into the open door at the rear of the car.

Back inside Eden's verdant embrace, Jardin relaxed again. The flight home had been even worse than the one out to meet Toron, and his robe was flecked with vomit. He stripped it off and stood under the shower, reflecting once again on his wisdom in recruiting engineers to the Elect. Though the Children endured primitive cold-water plumbing, he and his lieutenants enjoyed hot and cold running water and electrical power, courtesy of a sophisticated arrangement of hydroelectric and diesel generators.

Dressed in another robe he lifted from the pile in his wardrobe, he checked his satellite phone. There was a message from Slater in London.

. . .

Fewer sinners in London than yesterday. Insurance shares plummeted on news. Our short positions hit jackpot.

Jardin smiled. Time to select a new target. He unlocked the door to his office and ran his finger along the row of travel guides. Picked one out.

"Beverly Hills," he said. "False idols as far as the eye can see."

9

A MEETING WITH BARBARA SUTHERLAND

"NASTY BUSINESS WAS IT, SIR?" Gabriel's driver asked. Gabriel stared out of the darkened window, which made the people, buildings and cars he was looking at somehow distant, at one remove from reality.

"I'm afraid it was. It was bad. Really, very bad."

"Ought to shoot the bloody bastards what done it, 'scuse my French, sir."

Yes. You've definitely seen a parade ground from the front.

"But that's the trouble, isn't it? We don't know who did it, do we?"

"No, we don't. But I reckon you and Colonel Webster are going to sort it out, sir."

Gabriel wondered how much his driver knew about Don and The Department.

"So, do you work directly for Colonel Webster, then?" he said. "Sorry, I don't know your name. And you can drop the 'sir' bit, by the way. Gabriel's fine by me."

"Very good, sir. Gabriel, I mean. Since you ask, it's Tony, and yes I do know Colonel Webster quite well. Been driving him for the last two years, and I was fortunate enough to serve under him before he transferred into The Regiment. As I believe you did? Once he took over 22 SAS, I mean?"

"That's right. But you're OK being a driver after all that action?"

"Oh, not really. I'd much rather be out there taking it to the enemy, if you know what I mean. But the wife, she's much happier now I've got what you might call a steady job. Regular hours, most of the time. Home for tea, game of golf at the weekend, that sort of thing."

Gabriel thought of his cottage in a village just outside Salisbury. He hadn't been home for tea in a while. A lot of travel. A lot of hotels. A recent trip to Estonia on what he had been asked to call "government business". He found he didn't mind.

As the car moved slowly through the traffic towards Parliament Square before turning left into Whitehall, he watched a group of protesters, waving placards and yelling about human rights and how the police, the Army, the government, and essentially everybody in Britain not actively marching should be ashamed. And he wondered idly how they'd be treated in some of the countries where he'd run covert operations. Funny how the people who criticised the UK from the heart of its democracy could only do so in safety because of the very political system they seemed to hate.

As a soldier, he'd ignored politics almost as a duty. You served your country through its elected politicians and if they said, "Come on, chaps, we're at war again, go over to Country X and shoot the shit out of them," well, that's what you did. But now he was a civilian, even if his particular brand of Civvy Street still seemed to involve a great deal of automatic weapons and sneaking around after dark in camouflage. And he had begun to question things. After the morning's outrage, one of the things he was beginning to question was the right of anyone to stay free and alive while planning and executing—apposite word—horrific crimes of mass murder against innocent civilians.

His train of thought was derailed by the driver's turning left into a short road that ended in a pair of wrought-iron gates. There were a couple of guardsmen on duty beside the gates, resplendent in black trousers with razor-sharp creases, round-toed boots so shiny you could shave in them, scarlet dress jackets bedecked with gold buttons, and, of course, those ridiculous bearskins—almost two feet of glossy fur hat that took the average wearer to almost eight feet in height. They carried SA80 assault rifles with short, sharp-pointed bayonets fixed below the muzzles. But it was the unobtrusive brick office to the side and rear of the gates that held the real power to defend the building beyond.

Inside sat two men manning remote-controlled cameras with infrared capability. Each was dressed in dark clothes, nothing that would make them stand out on any London street. Each carried an array of weapons that would make short work of anyone foolish enough to try to gain entry without an extremely good reason and some very good credentials. Slung across their chests, each carried a Heckler & Koch MP5K submachine gun, their box magazines loaded with thirty 9 x 19mm Parabellum rounds. They wore shoulder holsters housing Glock 17 semi-automatic pistols, also chambered with the 9mm Parabellum rounds. They carried Special Forces ceramic knives in ankle sheaths. And each had his own SA80 assault rifle clipped into a steel rack on the back wall of the building, ready to rock with a magazine containing thirty 5.56 x 45mm NATO rounds.

If pressed, a large red button on the security console on the desk in front of them would trigger a range of countermeasures designed to thwart any attempt at forced entry.

Within fractions of a second, three circular steel columns, each measuring two feet from base to top and one foot in diameter, would spring from their flush-mounted silos in the road surface behind the wrought-iron gates, propelled by air rams each capable of exerting enough force to lift a three-tonne truck right off the ground.

Two miniguns, more often deployed on Apache gunship helicopters, were mounted in stainless steel housings high on the walls looking down onto the short length of road that led from the gates to the front door of the building. They were mounted with infrared and heat-seeking targeting software and loaded with High Explosive Incendiary Armour Piercing rounds—HEIAP in the jargon. If somehow a terrorist vehicle managed to defeat the steel barrier posts, the miniguns would whirr and swivel into action. They'd track the heat signature of the engine and unleash a hail of 7.62mm calibre bullets that would literally shred a car—even one with armoured bodywork—into fragments of torn and ruptured metal and plastic. As for the occupants, the six-thousand-rounds-per-minute rate of fire would reduce them to little more than mince.

Assuming that even this barrage was insufficient to defeat the insurgents, the men in the office were authorised to use deadly force. Shoot to kill, in other words. And they would. Efficiently. Unemotionally. And with ruthless determination.

Why all this security for a bunch of civil servants?

Because this particular complex of buildings housed the meeting rooms where the prime minister of the day convened the country's most senior law enforcement, military, and counterintelligence officers in the event of a crisis deemed to be a clear and present danger to the security of the United Kingdom.

Gabriel reached to his throat to straighten his tie, realised he was still wearing the borrowed clothes from the safe house, and let his hand fall to his lap again.

"Well, sir. Sorry, Gabriel. Here we are. If you'd just wait in the car, I'll sort out our clearance to proceed."

The driver strolled past the left-hand guardsman and knocked on the street-side door of the brick office. Gabriel watched as the green-painted door opened just enough to admit him before closing again.

Thirty seconds passed. Then another thirty. His pulse ratcheted up, and he closed his eyes and breathed slowly to lower it again.

Just as he was wondering whether there'd been a mix-up and the meeting with the prime minister was on a different day, or in a different part of the country, the door opened and the driver walked back to the car. His face was expressionless as he opened the door and climbed in. He turned round in his seat.

"All done. Just a little hiccup with the computer. Apparently the Colonel or his secretary had you down as Wolf without the 'e'. You'd think that wouldn't matter, but you know what computers are.

Now, we'll drive in, then you have to present yourself back at the office there to have your mugshot done and your security pass issued. I've to wait in the courtyard, which is fine by me. I've got a book to finish. *The Thirty-Nine Steps*. Very good boys' own adventure, if you need a recommendation."

The wrought-iron gates swung inwards and Tony eased the Jaguar into the courtyard, stopping just a few feet beyond the gates, which clanged shut behind them.

Five minutes later, Gabriel was walking towards the double doors of the building at the rear of the courtyard, a laminated ID bearing his pixelated face swinging from a pea-green lanyard round his neck. The day was still warm and he could feel the sweat under his arms beginning to roll down the inside of his shirt. London Planetrees fringed the courtyard, their mottled bark reminiscent of World War I camouflage patterns: tessellated irregular ovals in shades of sage green, dove grey, and beige.

At the black-painted door, he stopped, glancing around for a bell push or intercom. There was neither. He looked up. A white camera aimed at his face winked its red operating light as if to say hello.

Just as he was wondering how he was to gain entry, the door opened. A young woman appeared, mid-twenties he judged from the clarity and smoothness of her complexion. She, too, bore one of the laminated IDs around her long neck, which emerged from a scarlet polo-neck jumper made of some fine wool or perhaps silk. Expensive, anyway. Her tortoiseshell glasses magnified her brown eyes and gave her an owlish look.

"You must be Gabriel," she said with a smile. "Please follow me. The prime minister is expecting you."

Gabriel realised he had only ever seen the prime minister on TV or from a great distance on various military parades. As Secretary of State for Defence, she had once flown to Iraq when he had been stationed there. At the time, he was on a close target reconnaissance of a tribal warlord's compound many miles from the camp, so he had missed her visit altogether. Apparently she'd been a great hit with the lads, sharing some decidedly un-ministerial humour in her flat Yorkshire accent and also some beer she'd brought with her in specially cooled packaging.

A while back, he had helped to save her life from domestic terrorists, but the whole affair had been hushed up, and as soon as the dust had settled, he had disappeared back into the anonymity that Don Webster insisted on as a condition of his employing Gabriel on continuing covert missions for The Department.

He stopped for a moment to look at a portrait of Winston Churchill hanging on the wall between two closed doors. Then he hurried to catch up with his guide, though not so quickly he didn't have time to take in the shapely curves of her bottom in her tight-fitting tweed skirt.

Ahead, a door opened and the buzz of conversation drifted towards him. A loud and unmistakable laugh erupted from the room inside, and then out stepped the most powerful woman in the UK: Barbara Sutherland.

10

THE COBRA WAKES

BLACK STILETTO HEELS CLICKING, BARBARA Sutherland emerged from the meeting room, turned left, and strode towards Gabriel. Somehow, he had imagined she'd look grim-faced. Instead, her wide mouth, highlighted with her trademark slash of deep-red lipstick, was smiling. She stuck out her hand as she reached him. He shook it, reflexively.

"Well, well, here's my knight in shining armour," she said, her flat Yorkshire vowels sounding a challenge to the centuries of deference and privilege woven into the very fabric of the building they stood in. "Gabriel Wolfe, I think I owe you a bloody big hug and a couple of bottles of something expensive from the cellar in Number Ten."

The second surprise: after waving his owl-eyed escort away, causing the chunky gold bracelets on her right wrist to clank together, she grabbed hold of him and pulled him into an embrace, patting him on the back, and kissing him on the cheek for good measure.

When she let him go, his cheeks were flaring with a rush of blood. Being cuddled by prime ministers was not an activity his years in the SAS had prepared him for. In her heels, she was an inch or so taller than Gabriel and, he realised, very attractive. Slate-blue eyes, long dark lashes, and a strong straight nose.

"Oh, look, I've disconcerted you. Sorry. Come on," she said, all business, now, "there are a couple of people I'd like you to meet."

"If you don't mind my asking, Prime Minister, why were you laughing in there? When I arrived, I mean?"

"Thought I should have been crying, did you? Rending my garments, tearing my hair?"

Wrong-footed again, and starting to understand how this formidable woman from Yorkshire farming stock had risen to the top, Gabriel tried to explain.

"It's not that. I mean you just seemed, I don't know, happy. I can't see much to laugh about."

She paused, her hand on the doorknob, and turned to him, face stern now, dark eyes boring into his.

"Since I took office, Gabriel, we've lost a couple of dozen troops in various operations around the world. Our embassy in Tehran was firebombed. That maniac in Glasgow took out nineteen people with his articulated lorry on a crowded shopping street. I had to visit the scene of the Birmingham school fire, the Felixstowe chemical plant explosion, and, oh yes, I attended the funerals of those little Asian girls taken by that paedophile ring. If I didn't find a little shred of humour amidst the dark, you know what? I think yours truly would go completely, fucking mad with grief."

She shook her head as if trying to dislodge those bleak memories, then tucked her hair behind her ears.

"I'm sorry, Prime Minister. I didn't mean to say that you weren't, you know, your empathy—everyone says that about you. But ..."

She put a steadying hand on his shoulder.

"It's OK. We're going to nail the bastard or bastards who did this to us. And you're going to help. Now," she changed her tone to one of brisk efficiency, "let's introduce you to the others, shall we?"

The room looked like a corporate boardroom, complete with a bank of screens mounted on the far wall. This was one of the Cabinet

Office Briefing Rooms, referred to by the media, and apparently the PM herself, as COBRA. Seated around the table in the windowless room were four people, two of whom he recognised, two of whom he did not.

Barbara Sutherland took the seat at the head of the table and motioned for Gabriel to sit to her left.

"Well, lady and gentlemen, let's begin. We've got a few things to get through this afternoon, and I don't know about you, but I could really use a drink. So, to business. Let's start with introductions."

She turned to her right.

"Justine, for the record, would you mind giving us your full name and job title?"

The woman, one of the two people Gabriel recognised, had the bright, professional smile of the seasoned politician. The corners of her eyes were fanned with crow's feet, the lines between the wings of her nose and the outer corners of her mouth deeply grooved. A helmet of brassy blonde hair framed her face.

"Hello, Gabriel. I'm Justine Creech, Home Secretary."

"Hi. I did, you know, recognise you anyway." Trying to break the ice here. Feeling a little out of my comfort zone.

"Well, that's a relief," she said. "No need to fire my press secretary, then?"

That did the trick. Everyone laughed and from then on the atmosphere changed to a more collegial feeling. The man to Creech's right, an ugly brute with thick, coarse features and the florid complexion of a heavy drinker, turned to Gabriel. He was squat, a waistcoat adorned with a gold watch-chain stretched tight across his belly.

"Gregor Standing. Head of the Metropolitan Police Anti-Terrorism Division. Used to call me 'Last Man' in the Guards."

Across the table from Standing were two more men. Don spoke next.

"Don Webster, as I think you know, Old Sport. Head of The Department." Gabriel took in his former commander's appearance, once again. Greying hair cut short, grey chain-store suit, no scars, tattoos or other identifying marks, and an avuncular bearing more like that of the headmaster of a provincial prep school than a deadly security organisation buried deep within the British defence apparatus.

Last to speak was a man of such bland appearance, he could have run up to you in the street brandishing a machine gun and five minutes later, you'd have had no idea what he looked like. Mousy hair with a side-parting, mid-brown eyes, a pleasant smile. Identikit spook was Gabriel's initial assessment. Not far off as it turned out.

"Andrew Jeavons. Director, MI5."

OK, so you run the counter-spooks, but close enough.

Gabriel felt the eyes of the room on him. He swallowed.

"Gabriel Wolfe. I, that is, my firm is Wolfe and Cunningham. We're independent security consultants, but I seem to be working for Don, I mean Colonel Webster, a lot these days."

"Blimey, Gabriel," the prime minister said, "If that's your elevator pitch, love, it's a miracle you're making enough to live on."

More laughter. Gabriel felt able to join in, just. He noticed the others kept looking at him—not quite in the eye, off to one side a little. It made him uncomfortable, and he looked down at the polished table top, running a hand through his short black hair as he did so.

"One other thing, if I may, Prime Minister," Don said. She nodded. "Gabriel seems to have caught a bad habit from Tony, my driver. For the record, I'm no longer a colonel, as I think you all know. Wouldn't want anyone thinking I was trying to wheedle my way back into uniform."

"Thanks, Don. Noted," Sutherland said. "Perhaps we should all switch to first names to avoid any hemming and hawing over how to address each other. Agreed?"

There were mumbles of assent from the table.

Gabriel looked up again. Noticed there was a seventh person at the table. Nodded at Smudge, who nodded back.

"Good!" Barbara said, brightly. "So, we have a problem, which can be summed up as, some fucking psychopath terrorist set off a ball-bearing bomb on a packed London bus this morning, killed about fifty of our people and maimed dozens more. And I want him

—or her," she looked at Creech, "found. And stopped. Permanently."

She glared round the table, taking a moment to let her eyes rest on each person in turn. They all returned her stare with level gazes.

"Just to be clear, Barbara," the Home Secretary said, glancing at her then across at Gabriel again, with a slight smirk, "we're talking about an Executive Order here?"

"Yes, Justine, that is exactly what we're talking about." She turned to Gabriel and smiled. But it was the sort of smile a crocodile makes before eating something four-legged, up to its neck in a muddy brown river and whinnying in terror. "In the US, my counterpart has the power to authorise surgical strikes against enemies deemed so dangerous to the American people that no judicial oversight for the decision to terminate them is required." She paused. "Or to put that into words my dad would understand, he gets to take out the evil bastards on his own account. Judge, jury, and executioner. Nothing secret about it, either. He's done it one hundred and eighty-nine times since the start of last year. Freedom of Information. It's all there on the web."

"So we're going to track him down, then kill him. Or her."

"Smart boy. Don told me you were a quick study." She pushed a wayward strand of hair back behind her ear. "Now, what do we know? Gregor, why don't you start?"

Standing cleared his throat.

"We collected a couple of hundred steel ball bearings from the site. They're being processed for fingerprints at the moment. Top priority, obviously. The moment the lab techs discover anything, they're under instructions to call me. The explosives specialists are crawling over what's left of the bus, which was trailered to our ENCB facility in Vauxhall."

Barbara frowned. "Let's try to avoid the jargon, shall we?"

"Sorry. Explosives, Nuclear, Chemical, Biological. Bit of a mouthful, but there you are. May I?" She nodded. "Initial feeling, terrorist cell of some kind. Loners don't have the smarts or the resources for this type of thing. It's all machetes and samurai swords these days, since the handgun ban. We'll know more when we can pin down the composition of the charges."

Justine Creech spoke.

"Any idea on the nationality or race of the bomber, Gregor?"

"Not till we get some kind of DNA. On which subject, CID found a head. It made rather a mess of the reception area of a firm of stockbrokers behind Oxford Street. We'll know more once the pathologist has done his stuff. Other than that, at this point? Nothing."

"Thanks, Gregor," Barbara said. "For not dressing it up. I know we haven't got much to go on. Andrew, do you want to add anything?"

"I wish I could, Barbara. Once the Met can give us a steer, we can start cross-referencing to our surveillance feeds. But as of now, there's been no relevant chatter on any of the usual sites and chatrooms. I know it doesn't mean much, but at this point it doesn't feel like any of our friends in the Middle East. We're looking across the Irish Sea but, again, not really their MO."

There was a clearing of throats and a refilling of water glasses at this point. Maybe they'd been hoping for a simple conclusion. A ready-made enemy they could all rally against. Now Jeavons had plunged them back into uncertainty.

"Barbara, can I say something?"

"Go ahead, Justine."

"We need a story for the media. I know we have to get the people who did it. And I know," she said, looking around the table, "that we don't, at this point, have any idea who they are, but notwithstanding that, there's public confidence to be maintained. I was up there earlier today. Jesus Christ! Oxford Street was awash in blood." She swallowed and cleared her throat. "Can't we say something to reassure the public? I mean, we wouldn't be doing any damage to our position by hinting at an Islamic angle."

"If I may, Barbara?" It was Don who broke the uncomfortable silence.

The prime minister inclined her head, smiling briefly.

"Go on, Don."

"Whoever did this was evil. To their core. You don't need to label them at this point. Evil people did this, and good people lost their lives. But there are more good people working round the clock to find them. Don't point the finger. Not in a direction you may have cause to regret later on. Keep it metaphysical at this point."

"Goodness me, Don. I had no idea we had an amateur philosopher heading The Department. The last chap was more of a shoot-first-ask-questions-later type."

Don smiled. "Graham was an effective officer and a first-rate leader. I just happen to think we can manage public expectations without promising a crusade every second Tuesday."

Gabriel looked at the prime minister. She was staring down at her hands. They were clenched together on the tabletop, the knuckles bloodless and belying the relaxed banter she maintained with the quartet of powerful people ranged to her left and right. She turned to Gabriel.

"There's one person we haven't heard from so far. Someone who heard the bomb go off, and, by all accounts, saved not a few lives this morning. Gabriel. Why don't you give us your take on this?"

Gabriel sat up straight in his chair. He swept a hand over his hair and turned his deep brown eyes on the others in turn before speaking.

"I saw a young girl get out of a car on Regent Street. The bit to the north of Oxford Circus. She was behaving oddly. Frightened looking. Skinny, but wearing a bulky Puffa jacket. I told the detectives who brought me down to the safe house, I think she was the bomber."

They all leaned forward, alert now, hands steepling under chins, brows creasing.

"What makes you think that?" Standing said.

"White? Black? Muslim?" Creech added, showing a fine disregard for the difference between race and religion.

"Partly timing. She gets out of the car, five minutes later the bomb detonates. Partly she just looked wrong. I couldn't explain it to the detectives, and I can't really explain it to you, either. But my nerves were just, I don't know, jangling. There was a middle-aged woman inside the car ushering her out, you know. Like she didn't want to go. And the driver pulled a real stunt, U-turning in Regent Street at that time in the morning? Like he was in a real hurry to get out of there. I know it's all a bit vague and impressionistic, but that's how it took me." He looked at Creech. "She was white, by the way."

The corners of Creech's mouth turned down and she pursed her lips in disappointment.

"Barbara," Don said. "Don't discount this because Gabriel can't give you hard evidence. His instincts for threat are exceptional. I could reel off a list of instances where his gut kept his men, and non-combatants, safe, from Northern Ireland to the Balkans. It's why I asked you to have him here and why he's on my team to sort this mess out."

"Fine," she said. "But with the greatest respect, Don, and Gabriel," she looked to her left, "all this isn't worth bull-scutter unless we can pin down some basics. Motive. Type of explosive. Demands. Claims of responsibility. Unless anybody has anything else?"

Silence.

"Fine," she said, interlacing her carmine-tipped fingers and straightening in her chair. "I, Barbara Jane Sutherland, in my capacity as Prime Minister of the United Kingdom of Great Britain and Northern Ireland, First Lord of the Treasury, do hereby declare that an Executive Order is issued with immediate effect, targeted onto the person or persons unknown who perpetrated the atrocity in the West End this morning. In other words, find those fuckers and finish them. Any questions?" There were none. "In that case, thanks all. Now, I need a drink and something to eat. I'll be at Downing Street in five minutes, and you are all most welcome to join me." She turned to Gabriel. "You especially, sunshine. I hear you like a nice white Burgundy?"

"Yes, I do," Gabriel said.

"Right. I'll see you up the road shortly. Thanks all. Meeting adjourned."

With that, the group broke up.

Outside the meeting room, Gabriel drew Don to one side as the senior security officials and politicians left.

"What is it?" Don asked.

"Why did everyone keep looking at me? Have I got blood on my collar or something?"

The older man grinned and leaned towards him. "No, Old Sport. But you do have a rather fetching pair of lips printed on your cheek."

11

PLANNING ANOTHER CLEANSING

"SEND CLEANSING FIRE TO HOLLYWOOD," Jardin said, as he sat cross-legged on the floor in his house, facing the senior Uncle of the Children of Heaven. "Those idolaters foist their meaningless ideas on the world and persuade billions to abandon God for the transitory pleasures of their so-called 'silver screen'."

The Uncle sitting opposite Jardin had been the managing director of a regional French bakery chain in his former life. He creased his brow as he tried to anticipate his Master's wishes.

"We should reveal the shallowness of their dreams," he said. "Expose the spiritual rot at the heart of the big apple."

"That would be New York City, Uncle," Jardin said, not bothering to hide the contempt in his voice. "You did hear me say Hollywood?"

Caught out in an attempt to mimic Jardin's effortless flights of rhetoric, the man looked down at his clasped hands, now gripping each other so tightly the knuckles had turned ivory.

"Of course, Père Christophe," he said, trembling. "Hollywood. What did you have in mind?"

Jardin stroked his beard again, enjoying the silky texture of the fine hairs as they trailed through his long fingers.

"The Chinese want to get into film production. The Americans strive to keep them at bay. I will talk to some friends in Beijing. They can be ready to offer moral—and financial—support after the tragedy. Stand shoulder to shoulder with their American cousins. We might also drop a few well-chosen words into a few well-chosen ears in Los Angeles. Suggest that rebuffing such overtures of friendship might motivate whoever," he paused and smiled at the Uncle, "committed such an outrage to repeat the exercise."

"And us? How will we benefit?"

"We, as minority—*substantial* minority—investors in our Chinese friends' studios, will reap our share of the rewards accruing to them and their newfound success in America."

"So, another bomb, Père Christophe?" the Uncle asked, staring intently at his master's face, even though the eyes were closed.

"No. Not a bomb. I fancy a change. Tell me, Uncle Simeon," he said, stroking his beard, "how much do you suppose a petrol tanker costs?"

12

THE MEANING OF FREE SPEECH

GABRIEL WALKED UP WHITEHALL, DON at his side. A breeze had sprung up, and the temperature had dropped by a few degrees. Don touched him on the elbow.

"So what did you make of our glorious leader?"

Gabriel looked up, pursing his lips, then across at Don.

"A lot more likeable than I'd imagined. Everyone says she's this down-to-earth type, but you think, well, that's just PR spin for the media."

"Barbara's OK. I've met a few prime ministers over the years, ours and other people's, and she's been by far the easiest to deal with. And I'll tell you why. One," he started counting off points on his fingers, an old habit, "she never pretends to have all the answers. Two, she's decisive, as I think you saw inside the Cabinet Office. Three, as you're about to discover, she maintains a bloody excellent cellar."

Something ahead had caught Gabriel's eye. Instead of bantering with his boss, he nudged his right arm.

"Coming towards us, one o'clock."

Don looked where he'd been instructed. Four placard-bearing male protestors were swaggering along Whitehall's broad pavement.

The signs read STOP THE WAR, though it wasn't clear which war they might be referring to. One of the men, who were all wearing variations on a uniform of black jeans and T-shirts printed with anarchist slogans and symbols, leather biker jackets and black Dr. Martens boots, pointed straight at Gabriel and Don. He called out.

"Stop the war! Down with the class enemy!"

Perhaps it was Don's grey suit and tie that inflamed the bearded young man's sensibilities. Or simply that he and Gabriel had that unmistakable look, and bearing, that years of military service bestows on you, whether you like it or not. Either way, he'd elbowed his neighbour in the ribs and now the group had closed ranks and veered to their right, into the path of the oncoming "class enemies".

"I'll deal with this," Don said. "Can't have you getting mixed up in anything else today, now can we?"

As the four men approached, Don slowed, then stopped. He spread his hands out and smiled warmly at them. The bearded shouter stepped forward until he was within a foot of Don. Punching distance. His three scrawny lieutenants hung back.

"Why aren't you down there, with the people?" the man said, pointing past Don towards Parliament Square. "Don't you care what's being done in your name?"

"Oh, very much. In fact, it's because I care so much that I'm heading in this direction. So perhaps you and your friends would like to let us past and we'll leave you to join your colleagues."

"Colleagues? Did you hear that, boys? This wanker thinks we're going to some fucking board meeting."

The others snickered, shifting from foot to foot and catching each other's eyes.

Gabriel tensed, but Don laid a restraining hand on his wrist.

"I really don't think there's any need to call me a wanker," Don said mildly. "I'm actually happily married, so I'm probably getting it rather more regularly than you are."

"Fuck you, you Tory bastard!" the man shouted, then he dropped his placard and threw a punch.

The man's fist sailed into empty air past Don's left cheek, and he followed it in a graceless fall, as Don pulled hard and down on the wrist. Gabriel stepped in fast and placed a foot on the fallen man's neck.

"Stay down or I'll put you down," he said. The man complied, though he didn't stop struggling.

"You cunts!" he shouted. "You Tory cunts!"

Gabriel knelt by his head and hit him hard on the bridge of his nose. There was a loud crack and blood spurted out of his nostrils.

"What part of 'stay down' did you not understand?"

This time the man did comply, whining through his clogged nostrils about his human rights.

While Gabriel was dealing with the ringleader, Don had whirled round and elbowed one of the trio of lieutenants in the side of his head, dropping him where he stood. Then he stepped in quickly, pushing his face right up against that of the bigger protestor still upright, and grabbing a fistful of the last man's T-shirt.

"I'm not a Tory; I'm a socialist, as it happens. And I don't like little shits like you or your friend down there throwing their weight around. So either fuck off and do your protesting peacefully, or I'll have to exercise my rights to defend myself."

He pushed them both away and stood, feet apart, arms hanging loose at his sides.

"Fine. We're going," the bigger man muttered.

Leaving them to gather up their groggy friends, Don motioned for Gabriel to start walking. Then he beckoned a police officer coming towards them from the direction of Downing Street.

"See that foursome?" he said to the cop once he'd arrived. The policeman nodded.

"And I saw you getting into it with them. Everything OK, sir?"

"Right as rain, but I think a word of caution about assaulting innocent bystanders in the street mightn't go amiss."

"Couldn't agree more, sir. Look after yourself. Although it looks like you already have."

With a wink, the cop set off after the black-clad quartet, leaving Don to catch up with Gabriel.

"Well," he said, as he drew level, "always good to know one can still handle oneself. I've been pushing paper so long I thought maybe I was past it."

"You looked in pretty good shape to me," Gabriel said.

Tourists were busy taking photos of themselves posing by the Household Cavalry soldiers mounted on glossy black horses outside their barracks, some using selfie sticks almost as long as the men's ceremonial sabres. On a joint mission with the Irish Guards six years earlier, Gabriel had asked a captain how the men on duty outside government buildings and royal palaces managed not to laugh or twitch when the Americans, Italians, Japanese, Arabs, and Chinese were capering around them with cameras, trying to make them smile for the picture.

"Very simple," the Guards officer had said. "You imagine taking them to pieces with your bare hands. Does the trick wonderfully."

Now it was Don speaking. "Here we are, Old Sport. You can relax, now you've been," he tapped his own cheek and made a kissing sound, "blooded."

Gabriel smiled as they turned into Downing Street and stopped at another set of black, wrought-iron gates to have their security credentials verified by armed police. Once they were inside, Gabriel asked Don another question.

"How come down the road's guarded like a bloody fortress and here, she's only got a couple of cops with HKs on the gate?"

"Oh, don't worry, it's a lot more secure than it looks, but Downing Street's her home, and, well, the public face of the prime minister. When the serious shit hits the fan, there's a tunnel that connects Number Ten to COBRA. She and her family would be down there in seconds with an armed escort of useful chaps like you used to be. Not that you aren't useful now, of course …"

"It's OK, Don. I know what you mean."

Two more armed and uniformed police officers manned the front door of Number Ten. No more checks, and once they'd been admitted, Barbara Sutherland was there to greet them.

"Hello, boys," she said, suddenly looking tired. Her eyes were tight at the corners, her mouth downturned. "Ready for a drink? The others pleaded business. Good job, too, otherwise I'd have sacked them. So it's just us, I'm afraid. Come this way. I've got a nice bottle on ice in the sitting room."

The room she led them into was furnished comfortably, with two sofas covered in yellow, flowered chintz facing each other in front of an open fire. An aluminium ice bucket stood on a side table with a slender-necked bottle leaning against the rim. She offered the bottle to Gabriel as if she were a sommelier.

"What do you think?" she asked.

He read the label. A Puligny-Montrachet 2002 from a vineyard he'd read about in the Sunday papers.

"Wow, is what I think. Closely followed by, yes please!"

"Good lad." She poured three generous glasses and then took one end of the sofa furthest from the window and patted the cushion beside her. "Sit next to me, Gabriel. I've some questions I want to ask you. Oh, and I wondered whether you'd eaten today, so I've arranged to have some sandwiches sent in from the kitchen."

He did as she told him, while Don took a seat opposite them. He sipped the wine. It was chilled to the perfect temperature and tasted wonderful. He sighed as the cold liquid hit his stomach.

"So you've been helping Don out at The Department since saving me from those fucking neo-Nazis down your way?"

Gabriel nodded.

"And you're OK with his special remit? Sorry, bloody civil servant speak again. You know what I mean. Killing evil people to keep this country and its people safe."

"I did it once before."

"I know. I've read your service record."

Gabriel looked up suddenly. He'd remembered how MI5 had adjusted his Army personnel file to present him as a borderline fascist for the mission on which he'd saved the life of the woman in front of him.

She smiled at him now. "Relax. Everything back to normal. Good as gold. Loyal servant of the Crown, decorated for conspicuous gallantry. Worst thing anyone could say about you now is your infuriating habit of playing old jazz music too loudly on manoeuvres."

Gabriel returned the smile. He was liking Barbara Sutherland more and more. "You heard about that, then?"

Don spoke.

"Barbara wanted a detailed briefing on everyone I proposed bringing on board for this mission. Your exploit came up."

"It was a joke," Gabriel said. "The Yanks were playing bloody Wagner—"Ride of the Valkyries." Pretending they were in *Apocalypse Now*. I set up a sound system on our Bradley and put my Walkman through it. Bessie Smith singing "Nobody Knows You When You're Down and Out" at a hundred and ten decibels. They weren't happy because we had better speakers than them."

"I love Bessie Smith," Barbara said. "She, Billie Holiday, and Nina Simone are my three muses. However much shit I think I have to put up with, they keep it all in perspective. Oh yes," she continued, smiling as Gabriel's eyes widened, "we share a taste for old-time jazz as well as a decent drop of plonk. I was asking you about The Department's ethical framework. Because I wasn't joking down the road. I want this bastard found and brought to immediate and permanent justice."

"I'm fine with it, Barbara, really. But let me ask you something in return. If I may, I mean?"

"Of course. Go on then. Surprise me."

"Well, in the Army—the Paras and then the Regiment—we were one hundred percent sure who the enemy was. And that they *were* the enemy. Either they were in uniform or carrying weapons. How do you make sure you're targeting the right people?"

She took a sip of the Burgundy. Then she looked him directly in the eye. Hers seemed to glitter in the lamplight.

"I think we both know that even in wartime, the intelligence isn't always completely accurate. But even allowing for that, The Department is held to absolutely the highest standards of proof you can imagine. Way beyond reasonable doubt. Don can give you chapter and verse later if you really want it, but in terms of authorisation, I only give it if I'd be prepared to pull the trigger myself. No hearsay, blurry camera phone footage, or dodgy forensics. I'm talking about the kind of evidence that puts a noose around their neck and yanks the bloody knot tight."

Gabriel put his glass down. Looked first at Sutherland and then at Don.

"I like the work, don't get me wrong. So this is my last question. Why not use the forces you have that are under public scrutiny? Why have The Department at all?"

The Prime Minister of the United Kingdom and her loyal attack dog looked at each other. She spoke first.

"Shall you tell him, Don? A little history lesson?"

He nodded, took a sip from his glass, then cleared his throat and began.

13

DEPARTMENTAL PROTOCOL

"THAT BUSINESS DOWN IN YOUR neck of the woods, when you saved Barbara," Don said. "Do you remember I told you it had links back to the '74 plot for a coup against Harold Wilson?"

Gabriel nodded, sipping the delicious wine and enjoying the spreading warmth it brought.

"After that, Wilson created The Department. He never trusted MI5 or the Army again. Can't say I blame him after what they had planned for him. Its original brief was to work directly for the prime minister of the day, with oversight from the Privy Council. He handpicked the first five members himself, from outside the existing power structures. The story was he borrowed some Russian spooks to vet them, which was ironic given that's why the plotters wanted him out in the first place."

Don finished his wine and nodded his thanks as Barbara refilled his glass, and then moved to top up her own and Gabriel's.

"Anyway, initially their job was to provide intelligence to Wilson on who was talking to whom inside government and the intelligence agencies. They did rather feed his incipient paranoia, but he was happy. And then, like Topsy, it just grew and grew. Took on a more active role in preserving the security not just of the PM, but the country as a whole."

"So who funds it? I can't imagine you'd want it appearing in the budget."

"Do you know what a rounding error is?""

"Not exactly. Why?"

"There's a famous story, probably apocryphal, about a banking scam. The thieves supposedly reprogrammed a bank's computers so if any of their customers' accounts had a balance ending in a single penny, that penny was transferred to a dummy account set up by the criminals. Well, nobody missed those individual pennies because we don't look at our money down to that level of detail. Amounted to millions before it was discovered. Most people round up to the nearest pound, or even ten pounds, and simply don't focus on any amount smaller than that. The difference is called a rounding error. In terms of government funding, for departmental programmes and so on, that rounding error is usually at the level of a few tens of thousands of pounds. There's an algorithm buried deep in the Treasury's IT systems that sweeps all those spare thousands into The Department's coffers. Then there's match-funding from the Queen. A quid from Her Majesty for every quid we put in, no questions asked and thanks for the tax cut."

"You're joking," Gabriel said, scratching his head. "Aren't you?"

Barbara just smiled, and sipped from her glass. "Any other questions?"

"I do, actually. If that's OK with you, I mean?"

"I'm all ears."

"So, what about secrecy? Whitehall is notoriously leaky so how do you keep it all under wraps? The media would have a field day if this all came out."

"You're right, they would. Although the fact they haven't since '74 would suggest our protocols work."

"What are they?"

"Protocol One, plausible deniability. Nothing is ever written down, nothing is ever trackable. The entire operation is conducted by oral, face-to-face communication. In all the years it's been operating, there hasn't been a single memo, meeting minute, fax, or email. Protocol Two, anonymity. Everybody is selected personally and invited to join under the terms of Protocol One. No personnel records, no letters of appointment. Protocol Three, hygiene. The Department doesn't leave footprints. And if people feel they've contributed enough, they're free to leave, but their silence for life is required. We only select people who it's felt are completely trustworthy, but in any case, whistleblowing would be met with the same level of determination as main operations. No quarter, no sanctuary, anywhere. There's a code word that unlocks the door of any foreign embassy in London. That slimeball who recently leaked all those government emails would've been sitting in a windowless cell two hundred feet underground by now if we'd used it."

Don spoke. "Having an attack of the civil liberties, Old Sport?" He was smiling, but for the first time, Gabriel detected an edge behind the older man's genial manner.

"No. Not at all. Just getting it all straight in my head. Now I'm working for you. Just one other thing."

"Go on," Don said.

"Does it really make that much of a difference, not having the same levels of oversight as the Army and the security services?"

"It's not just about oversight, Gabriel," Barbara said. "It's about operational effectiveness. Sometimes we get intelligence that someone we want out of the way is in a particular place at a particular time. Well, you know how long it takes to get a military unit into place. And let me tell you, MI5 and MI6 aren't much better. The Department is fast. *Really* fast. And we can cherry-pick recruits from anywhere we like. Private-sector people like you. Men who maybe missed out on the SAS by a whisker and quit altogether rather than return to unit. All sorts. Now, I notice this bottle's empty. Shall we have another?"

Don and Gabriel looked at each other. Don spoke first.

"I have to get back to work, Barbara, but Gabriel, I think you should stay. Talk about jazz if all the spook stuff gets too boring."

He stood, and Barbara and Gabriel followed suit. He hugged Barbara briefly, then shook hands with Gabriel.

"I want to put Gabriel into the Met while they try to pin down their first lead. D'you think you could ask Justine Creech to square it with them?"

Barbara grinned, showing a single canine tooth.

"Oh, I'm sure my Right *Honourable* Friend would be more than happy to help," she said. "It'll give her an opportunity to build bridges with the police. She's not exactly flavour of the month since her speech at their conference."

"I'll be in touch," Don said to Gabriel, then he was gone.

Barbara pressed a button set into the wall, and within a couple of minutes, a young woman in white shirt, black trousers, and a black waistcoat appeared.

"Be a love and fetch us another bottle of this lovely wine, would you?" Barbara said with a warm smile.

After the young woman had left with the ice bucket, Barbara turned to Gabriel.

"I bet you're thinking, 'Champagne bloody socialist', aren't you?"

"Actually I wasn't. I was thinking about the girl I saw this morning. The one I thought was the bomber. Your hospitality staff, person, looked a bit like her."

"I want to hear more about that, but I have to tell you, being the prime minister's all very well, and I do still believe in all the principles my dad drilled into me, but there are times when, do you know what? Having a few people to carry your bags or fetch your wine is just bloody brilliant. I mean, you can see how the landed gentry got their taste for having servants, can't you?"

He nodded. "Though the only people I've met in the last few years with servants were, well, let's just say I'm glad the servants are looking for new jobs."

She laughed. "You mean that madman Toby Maitland, don't you?"

"He was top of my list, yes."

"Good riddance. Aha!" she said as the uniformed young woman returned with a refilled ice bucket and an uncorked bottle of the

Burgundy. "Here's our Cheryl back with the wine. Thanks, my love."

Glasses refilled, Barbara sat back and was just about to ask Gabriel about the bomber when the door banged open, and in charged a young boy wearing a maroon school blazer and tie. He was maybe five or six years old. He had the same shade of hair as Barbara, though his was messier than her professionally cut bob, and there was something about the set of his jawline that made their connection plain.

"Hello, Mummy," he said, running over and jumping onto her lap. "I got a sticker today for helping my friend Pradeep because he fell over and I got the first aid kit from Mrs Smith in the office and she said I was very responsible and I even put the plaster on and everything. And guess what …"

Gabriel smiled at the torrent of words and the unaffected enthusiasm Barbara's son showed as he related his day. When the boy he knew to be called Tom paused for breath, Barbara set him down on the floor and turned him gently but firmly by the shoulders to face Gabriel.

"Darling, this man is called Gabriel. He's helping me deal with some bad people. Say hello."

The boy stood straight, hands clamped to his sides like a new recruit on his first parade and looked Gabriel in the eye, squinting at him as if he would divine his true reason for being there by telepathy.

"Gabriel was an angel. He helped God. Is God going to punish the bad people? Are you an angel?"

Not used to talking to small children, Gabriel found his interrogator's direct question a little off-putting.

"I'm not an angel. I work for the, for your Mummy. But I'm sure that God …" he looked at Barbara, but if she had a view on whether he should discuss theology with her son or not, she wasn't revealing it through so much as a wink, "… if God knew about the bad people, he wouldn't be pleased."

"No, he wouldn't," Tom said, in his stride now. "What he'd do is, he'd put them on the really big naughty step. For probably ten hundred minutes. Or else he'd kill them."

"Darling!" Barbara said. "You know we don't talk about killing people just for being bad."

"But then they wouldn't be bad again, would they? Not if they were dead." He turned to Gabriel, who was marvelling, not for the first time, at how even the most sympathetic politicians could talk about the extra-judicial killing of terrorists one moment and then inveigh against the very same practice a moment later. "Have you ever killed anyone?"

Gabriel's mouth opened but then he realised he had no idea what to say next. Barbara seemed content to spectate on this interchange between the man and the man-in-waiting.

"Well, I was in the Army, so we did lots of fighting. But we were fighting to keep people safe. Children, like you, and their mummies and daddies." *Yes, this is going OK. Stick to this line, and pray she gets rid of him to his bedroom or nursery or whatever they have here.*

The boy rolled his eyes. "Yes, but did you actually fire a bullet into someone, and did they die?"

Gabriel slid off the sofa and knelt in front of the boy so they were on the same level. He spoke softly, seriously.

"Yes. I did."

"What was it like?"

"It made me feel bad inside. Because that person was dead and they might have had a family. But it was my duty. Do you know about duty?"

The boy puffed his chest out. "Of course I do. I'm on cloakroom duty this week. It's about being responsible. But do you know what I would do with bad people if I was God?"

"What?"

"If I was God, I'd parachute down to Earth, and I'd find the bad people with my X-ray vision, then I'd get them with my lightsaber, and then Mummy would probably give me a medal, and also a cake, which is what she does for brave people."

This was too much. Gabriel and Barbara both burst out laughing. She swept the boy up and carried him to the door. With a kiss and a tousle of his hair, she shooed him out with an instruction to "find Emma"—an au pair, Gabriel assumed.

"Sorry about that," she said when the room was quiet again. "He can be somewhat precocious, but it does him good to meet my guests from time to time. Since his dad left, he's been magnetically drawn to any bloke who visits. He's practically adopted Don."

"I read in the papers about the posting. Costa Rica, wasn't it?"

"That's right. John's advising them about pilot training. He'll be over there for six months. It's his last tour before he leaves the Air Force.

She stared out of the window, her face in repose drawn and sad. She looked tired, as if the effort of maintaining the bluff, no-nonsense persona had used up all her energy.

"I want whoever planned that bombing dead, Gabriel. I mean it. On God's fucking naughty step for all eternity." She stared at him, eyes blazing.

"That's what I'm here for, Barbara," he said quietly. "That's what I'm here for."

"People like that don't deserve to benefit from our legal system. Don't deserve human rights lawyers. They don't deserve it!" She shouted the last line then tipped her head back and swallowed the wine in her glass in a single gulp. "And I'll tell you why."

She leaned forward and he matched her body language, drawing on one of the techniques Master Zhao had instructed him in to get closer to someone's emotions.

"What happened?" he asked, struck by a sudden insight that her fervour was personal as well as political.

"Nine eleven is what happened. My sister was the fundraising director of a charity based in Manhattan. They were actually raising money for orphans in Iraq, if you can believe it. She was on American Airlines Flight 11. The North Tower. Now, I don't know who was behind this morning's atrocity. They could be extremist bloody Buddhists for all I care. But we're going to send them a message they won't forget, and I hope all the other twisted cranks sending other people to do their dirty work get the message too. If you fuck with us, you're going to regret it."

14

HOLLYWOOD AFLAME

THAT NIGHT, A FIREBALL BLOSSOMED above Grauman's Chinese Theatre on Hollywood Boulevard, destroying the sidewalk with its handprints, footprints, and autographs of movie stars, and turning the ornate Asian-style cinema into an inferno. The blast was contained, as it took place inside Christophe Jardin's head. But the devastation was comprehensive. He lay in his four-poster bed, and as the screams of the dying mingled with the sirens, he grinned.

"Oh, Papa, Maman," he said, staring up at the map of the world he'd had one of the Children paint as a fresco on his ceiling. "You always chided me for lying around doing nothing. But look at me now. You are dust; your flesh was eaten long ago by worms and beetles, while I am stamping my mark on the world."

He leaned over to his right, taking care not to wake the lithe, handsome girl sleeping soundly by his side, and slid open the drawer in the mahogany bedside cabinet. Slowly, and with exaggerated *shushing* noises from his thin lips, he extracted a Colt .45 semi-automatic pistol. He curled his fingers around the grip and inserted his index finger through the trigger guard.

He pointed the gun at the ceiling.

Reached up with his left hand and racked the slide.

Closed his left eye.

Moved the iron foresight until it lined up on the spot where he knew LA to be.

Then, smirking, he squeezed the trigger.

The bang was enormous and the room was instantly filled with the smell of burnt cordite, and threads of smoke.

The girl jolted awake with such suddenness that she fell out of bed, screaming as she regained consciousness, and landed in a tangle of slim, muscled limbs on the rug.

Flakes of paint and specks of plaster dust fluttered down onto them, covering Jardin and his naked companion in a fine rain of multi-coloured fragments of southwestern California.

Eyes wide, face drained of colour, the girl jumped back into the bed next to Jardin and curled herself around him like a frightened child, which, he supposed, she was, in a way.

"Père Christophe!" she gasped. "What was it? Are we called by Him? Is it the Second Order?"

He wrapped his arm around her, not bothering to hide the dark steel handgun that smoked in his other hand.

"No, Child. It was I, not Him. Back to sleep."

He looked down at the top of her head. She had inserted a thumb into her mouth and now shivered faintly against his ribcage.

He began an old French lullaby, crooning the words as he stroked her hair with the Colt's muzzle.

15

DEPUTISED

GABRIEL WOKE, REFRESHED AND READY to go to work. The bed in the safe house was soft and dressed in cool, white linens that had lulled him to sleep almost as soon as his head hit the pillow, despite the prime minister's vengeful words spinning around in his head. No doubt the wine and the inch of brandy he'd swallowed before retiring had helped. James, who had acquired the English butler's ability to disappear and appear just as he was needed without being either summoned or dismissed, certainly helped as well.

The two men sat at the kitchen table, munching bacon sandwiches and swigging from mugs of hot tea, chatting about places they'd been, things they'd done and seen.

"I was infantry before I landed this billet," James said, wiping the last of his bread around the edge of his plate to soak up the bacon grease and drips of brown sauce clinging to the rim. "Instructor on war courses, unarmed combat, that type of thing."

Gabriel grimaced, remembering some of the techniques he'd learned in his days serving in the Paras and then the Regiment. "You guys used to frighten the shit out of me," he said. "All that business with pencils and coins, and taking people out with broken bottles. Used to make my blood run cold."

"That was the general idea," James said, leaning back in his chair. "Useful stuff though, wasn't it?"

"Oh, without a doubt. More than once, I was glad of it. Listen, I have to be off and I need some new clothes. But thanks, you know, for looking after me yesterday. And this morning. Excellent breakfast."

He stood, and James followed suit. They shook hands, two fighting men walking different but parallel paths, both under the watchful eye of Don Webster and his minimally supervised Department.

A couple of hours later, Gabriel was back at the safe house, changing out of the mufti provided by James and back into his working gear, as he thought of it: a three-piece Prince of Wales suit in a light grey wool; a white cotton button-down shirt with French cuffs fixed with simple silver links; sea-green silk tie and matching pocket square, and his own polished black brogues. He'd bought some more underwear, a pair of jeans and some T-shirts, a wash bag filled with toiletries and a new razor, plus a pair of tan Grenson Oxfords, gambling that it would be a while before he'd be seeing his cottage in rural Wiltshire again. He stuffed the spare clothes into a tobacco-brown leather holdall and set off for an office in Whitehall, from where Don had texted him to arrange a meeting.

Once the security preliminaries were out of the way, and his mugshot had been filed onto yet another government computer, he was ushered to a waiting area furnished with leather sofas. A low table was covered in copies of the Financial Times and official publications of such dryness they could have been used to mop up spills.

He didn't have to wait long. After a couple of minutes, Don strode from the lifts, across the expanse of cream marble flooring, hand extended.

"Hello, Old Sport," he said. "Right, busy day ahead of us. How was your night?"

"Fine, thanks. How was yours?"

"Oh, you know, midnight oil and all that. You OK with the safe house or do you want to find yourself a hotel?"

Gabriel pursed his lips and frowned. Comfort versus anonymity.

"I think I'll find a hotel."

"Perfectly fine with me. Keep all your receipts, and we'll sort out the paperwork later. Now, come with me. There are a couple of people who want to see you."

The journey up to the tenth floor passed in one of those awkward silences that afflict people of every strength of relationship and degree of talkativeness. The two men stared at their hands, the walls, the doors ahead of them as the stainless steel box ground its way up to the meeting rooms on the top floor of the building.

Once the robotic female voice had announced their arrival on the tenth floor, the doors hissed open, and they were out. A few minutes later, after collecting cups of coffee from a kitchen area, they were sitting at an oval table facing the two detectives Gabriel had met the day before. Also seated at the table was the anti-terror officer they'd met the day before with Barbara Sutherland: Gregor Standing.

Don took charge immediately. Clearly, he was the silverback in this particular group of law enforcement officers.

"Morning everyone, thanks for coming. Now, we've all met each other one way or another in the last twenty-four hours, but in a spirit of openness, and just in case yesterday's shocking events have muddled anyone's thinking," he glanced fractionally in Gabriel's direction, "why don't we each give the briefest of introductions?"

"DCI Susannah Chambers," Susannah said, seizing the initiative, no doubt keen to get in before her overboss at the Met. "I'm running the CID investigation of the Oxford Circus bus bombing."

Following her Guvnor's lead, Chelsea introduced herself next.

"DS Chelsea Jones. Coordinating everything on the ground and reporting to DCI Chambers."

"Gabriel Wolfe. Managing Director, Wolfe and Cunningham. I'm working for Don Webster."

"Gregor Standing. I run the Met's Anti-Terrorism Division. Clearly we're digging hard on this one. It's our number-one priority."

"And I," the grey-haired ex-soldier at the head of the table said, "am Don Webster. I run The Department, which is going to eliminate the person or persons unknown who planned and carried out yesterday's atrocity. Well, that's the pleasantries out of the way. I'd like to begin by thanking our colleagues at the Met for accepting our suggestion that Gabriel should be accredited, temporarily, as a consultant on this operation."

"If I may, sir," Susannah said, looking him straight in the eye and brushing her auburn hair back from her face, "it's not like we had a choice."

Don smiled. "No, DCI Chambers, it isn't. However, Gabriel's an easy-going sort of chap, and I don't suppose he sees his role as anything more than that of an observer. At best, a willing helper. But where I want him heading next, it's going to help if he's at your right hand as you get deeper into your investigation."

The rest of the meeting was little more than a recapping of roles and responsibilities, and a securing of assurances that any and all intelligence would be shared with the entire operational team, no matter who originated it. As it drew to a close, Don clamped his hands together on the table in front of him and cleared his throat.

"There is one final bit of business I should like to have out in the open, ladies and gentlemen."

The others straightened up in their chairs and looked across at him, recognising in his tone the impending arrival of something they would all do well to remember.

"You know I report directly to Barbara Sutherland. My team operates with her express approval and at her direct request. I am aware that our methods and code of conduct may not gibe with your conception of British justice." Perhaps the police officers imagined that at this point, he was going to offer a sop to their sense of undermined authority, or their principles. If they were, what he said next dashed their hopes. "Which I understand. But it's something you're going to have to suck up and keep quiet about, I'm afraid. Everyone working on Operation Manticore has signed the Official Secrets Act. One whiff of The Department's existence outside these four walls and the consequences will be bleak. Shall we say, for starters, no career, no pension, and quite possibly a substantial sojourn at Her Majesty's pleasure, a lady, incidentally, who both knows of and underwrites my little group's activities. If there's nothing else?"

There was nothing else, though the thunderous looks on the faces of the two detectives spoke of much they wanted to say, if there'd been even the slimmest of chances it would make a difference.

Gabriel left the building in the company of Susannah and Chelsea, carrying his holdall to their unmarked silver BMW 5 Series saloon. Once it was secure in the boot, and they were on their way to the police station on Savile Row, he judged it safe to speak.

"I won't get in your way, I promise. I had no idea Don was going to deputise me. Just tell me where you want me and what I can do to help."

From the driver's seat, Susannah answered.

"In the background. Help track the fuckers."

16

RESCUING THE FALLEN

A BARROW OF SKINNED COW heads was being pushed across the road opposite Gabriel's hotel. Through the open sash window, he watched the meat porter struggle with the awkward wood and steel contraption, bumping it up a ramp onto the pavement and almost losing part of his cargo. The burly man swore, loudly and inventively, grabbing the head and shoving it back into the pile, then wiping his hands on his bloody white apron.

Gabriel's top-floor hotel room looked out over Smithfield, the Victorian meat-trading market in Farringdon, on the eastern fringes of central London. At this early hour, the place was alive with butchers, meat traders, restaurant and hotel chefs, truck drivers and the odd stockbroker, heading in to work to make a killing on the Asian exchanges before the day proper began. He inhaled deeply, drawing the smell of blood and flesh deep into his lungs.

It starts today.

Dressed in loose pyjama bottoms, he sat in the antique upholstered wing-chair beside the window and let his hands rest lightly in his lap. With his head dropped forward, partially constricting his airway, he closed his eyes and began a sequence of breaths—in for a count of four, hold for one, out for another count of four, hold for one—until he felt a particular sense of calm descend on him. The sounds outside—the diesel engines, the clattering of steel-banded barrow wheels on concrete, the shouts and banter of the meat men—were still present, but they took on the quality of background noise, as if they were coming from an audio feed with the volume lowered.

He visualised a vermilion circle, painting itself anti-clockwise in a swirl of messy orange drips, with a number ten inside it. He began breathing the word "nine" as the invisible artist swirled her brush inside his head. As she changed her hue for a startling acid green and her direction for clockwise, the number inside the circle ticked down to nine and he chanted "eight". Gabriel's brain, partly through long years of practice, and partly because the stimuli he was introducing were already starting to disrupt its logic circuits, adapted itself to the change in oxygen flow and distribution of electrical charge across its surface. Its slow-cycling alpha waves increased in intensity and Gabriel felt the world slipping away from him.

Now. Let's go now.

The bullets were flying.

Crack. Thump.

Crack. Thump.

Crack. Thump.

The air was thick with the smell of cordite and hot brass.

His M16 was vibrating in his hands as it discharged magazine after magazine.

The rebels were screaming. Some because Gabriel and his patrol had sent 5.56mm rounds ripping and tumbling through their unprotected flesh. Some from drug-induced bloodlust.

They'd completed the first half of the mission. Abel N'Tolo, leader of the People's Army for the Liberation of Mozambique, was dead. His plans, in a ridiculous silver attaché case, were in SAS Trooper Smudge Smith's hand.

Then the Kalashnikov round hit Smudge in the back of the head.

Impervious to the bullets that fizzled through his body, ghost Gabriel walked towards his fallen comrade. Smudge was lying dead in the vegetation, the lower half of his face gone, his brown eyes staring up at Gabriel, seeing nothing.

He knelt, slid his hands under Smudge's knees and armpits, and lifted the dead man from the blood-soaked ground.

"Come on, Smudge, let's get you home to see Nathalie one last time."

Smudge focused on Gabriel.

"You left me, boss."

His voice was inside Gabriel's skull, echoing around.

Gabriel's heart-rate shot upwards, his palms were suddenly slick with sweat and his breathing accelerated into rapid shallow panting.

"I tried, Smudge. You know I tried." Gabriel felt the tears coursing down his cheeks, running over the greasy camouflage staining his skin a nightmare mess of black and green.

"It's time to leave me again. For good this time."

Then the body began to shiver and shimmer, losing its solidity as the AK-47s and M16s sang their songs around them and the sun shone down through the trees.

Gabriel opened his eyes. His chest was wet with sweat.

Fuck. I need to get this sorted before it takes me down.

He pulled on shorts and a T-shirt and a pair of running shoes he'd bought the previous day and was out two minutes later, pounding around the huge enclosed market, dodging carts weighed down with sides of beef, striated with white ribs and red flesh.

The PM liked him. Don wanted him. The cops tolerated him. But the person *he* needed was a Muslim by faith and a psychiatrist by profession.

Back in his hotel room, he showered and shaved, and dressed in jeans, T-shirt and a navy windbreaker. One swift breakfast later, he was sitting at the desk calling Fariyah Crace.

"Gabriel. How are you?"

He scratched the back of his neck.

"I'm OK. Yes, not bad. But I think I should come and talk to you. Work's about to kick off again so …"

"So you're wondering whether I can fit you in this week?"

"I know, I know, you just sit around reading celebrity magazines waiting for me to call."

She laughed, a generous, warm sound that made Gabriel feel good in his soul.

"Don't forget the chocolates and champagne."

"What, a good Muslim like you?"

"OK, rose water. That better? As it happens, one of my patients cancelled his five o'clock with me today. So if you'd like it?"

"Yes!" Gabriel almost shouted. "I mean, yes. Please. At the Ravenswood?"

"Yes. At five then?"

"At five."

"I'll let Valerie know. She can put you in my calendar. Though what she'll make of her boss doing her own secretarial work, I don't know."

Half an hour later, Gabriel walked into Savile Row police station. After explaining to the civilian receptionist who he was and the nature of his business, he was directed through a security barrier towards the custody suite and the beginnings of the police machinery.

"Yes, sir," the burly desk sergeant said, narrowing his eyes as he scrutinised the man who'd just walked into his domain.

"My Name's Wolfe. I'm here to see DCI Chambers. I, um, I've been accredited. You should have some paperwork about me."

"Accredited." The sergeant managed to pack enough contempt into those four syllables to make a man turn tail. But Gabriel simply stood there, returning his stare.

"It means …"

"Yes! Sir. I know what it means." Now he bent to his task, riffling through a clipboard full of papers on the desk in front of him. "Wolfe. Wolfe. Wolfe. Yes, here we are, sir. Civilian consultant." More contempt dripping onto the counter between them. "Right, look into this camera, please." He angled a little webcam towards

Gabriel, who composed his face into a bland, slack-muscled expression, eyes neither wide nor squinting, mouth a straight line.

There was a little business involving a transparent plastic badge holder, then whirring as a printer spat out his ID card. With the whole thing attached to a yellow lanyard, the sergeant pushed his clipboard towards Gabriel, tapping with a bitten fingernail against a blank space.

"Sign here, please, sir." Gabriel did as he was told. "Thank you. Now, if you'd take a seat, I'll find DCI Chambers for you."

He pointed at a row of stained, cloth-upholstered seats, some with their cushions split and yellow foam protruding through the rips. Gabriel decided to assert a measure of control over his situation. He moved out of the way but remained standing, leaning against the wall beside the last of the chairs. The sergeant frowned, shook his head, then picked up a greasy plastic desk phone and punched a couple of buttons.

The double doors to the custody suite banged open, slamming back against the walls on either side of the doorway. In burst two uniformed police officers, one male, one female, holding between them a huge man who writhed and twisted in their grasp. The prisoner, his hands pinioned behind him with steel handcuffs, was six foot four or five. His head was shaved and his face was a twisted mask of hatred, thin lips pulled back from his teeth in a snarl. Both arms were sleeved in tattoos, oddly beautiful koi carp and water lilies. *A fan of the Yakuza,* Gabriel thought as he began a quick combat appreciation. *But somehow, I think your tats are all that's Japanese gangster about you. You look pure home-grown thug to me.*

The cops dragged the brute over to the desk sergeant.

"Got a live one here, Sarge," the woman gasped. "Just assaulted a couple of tourists in Leicester Square. Think he's taken something."

"They're fucking parasites," the young thug shouted. "Come here to live on our benefits and steal our jobs. I'm a patriot! Like you lot should be instead of protecting them. Look at me. A white man in a white man's country."

Then, with a convulsive twist of his torso, he wrenched himself free of the grip of the two cops.

Before they had a chance to react, either by drawing their extendible batons or grabbing him again, he reared back and head butted the female cop on the bridge of her nose. She screamed in pain as the bone broke and blood spurted over her face.

The thug turned away from her as she collapsed to her knees, hand clamped over her face, and jerked his knee up between the male cop's legs. The man went down with a cry of agony, clutching his groin.

A screeching alarm went off; the desk sergeant had obviously hit a panic button.

Looking around for a way out, the thug came face to face with Gabriel, who'd moved to block his exit though the double doors.

Gabriel's personal code placed talking above violence.

When possible.

It was not possible.

His right hand shot out, bunched into a fist, and punched hard into the thug's windpipe. He stepped back and hit him twice more with blows to the stomach, driving his wind from him in a gasp. But the thug was tough, and solid, maybe fourteen or fifteen stones of muscle and bone. He staggered back, eyes blazing, but he didn't go down.

With the sound of booted feet running down the corridor getting louder, Gabriel wanted to stop his adversary from doing any more damage. As the thug drew his own right boot back to kick the fallen policewoman, Gabriel used a technique he'd learned from a slightly built Scottish unarmed combat instructor who went by the unlikely moniker of "Ghandi".

He leapt towards his target and, with his right hand bent into a claw, dug his fingers into the guy's eye sockets. Not with the intention of blinding him or, in the charming Scot's words, "enucleating the bastard," but causing him excruciating pain and enough temporary damage to his corneas to stop him from doing any more harm to friendly forces. Two knee-jerks into the thug's groin and the outside edge of his shoe raked down the left shin completed the trifecta of disabling moves.

With a squeal of pain, surprisingly high from such a large chest cavity, the thug crumpled. It was over.

For the second time in the space of a couple of minutes, doors banged back against the walls as a posse of uniforms and detectives tumbled into the increasingly cramped waiting area.

Gabriel was panting. He stood back as four uniformed cops grabbed the man, hauled him to his feet and slammed him face-first into the wall by the booking desk.

"Right!" the desk sergeant bellowed. "Will one of you lot read this fucker his rights so we can stick him downstairs."

"I'll do it." It was Susannah Chambers. She shouldered her way through the throng and planted her not inconsiderable frame in front of the now subdued thug. She grabbed his lower jaw in her right hand, making sure her purple fingernails dug deeply into the skin on his cheeks. "OK, sunshine. Name? And if you say 'Mickey Mouse,' 'you tell me,' or 'fuck off pig,' I'll turn the security cameras off and leave you in here with this lot."

The man grunted something.

"I'm sorry, I didn't hear that, sir. Did you say, 'fuck off pig'? OK, sergeant, turn off the …"

"No! It's Jason Watts."

"Well, Jason Watts, I am arresting you under the Police and Criminal Evidence Act for being a complete cunt. But the record will show you are being charged with causing grievous bodily harm, resisting arrest, assaulting a police officer, and whatever else I can come up with. You have the right to remain silent. But it may harm your defence if you do not mention when questioned something which you later rely on in court. Anything you do say may be given in evidence. Right!" she said, brushing her hands together. "That's the pleasantries out of the way. Here's a little something from me for hurting my officers." She drew back her right hand, balled it into a fist and drove it with some force into the man's stomach.

To laconic cheers and applause, the now drooping thug was dragged away to a cell. Susannah turned to Gabriel.

"Thanks, Gabriel. Sarge just told me what you did. I owe you one. Now, are you ready to stand behind me and do nothing but observe and listen?"

"Yes, Ma'am," he said, tipping her a salute.

"Good. Come on then. Chel's in the forensics lab. We just got some good news."

17

THE WAR OF DRUGS

TORON WATCHED JARDIN PICKING HIS teeth with a long fingernail as he stood thirty yards away from the plane. The Cessna 206 had just taxied to a stop after touching down on Eden's bumpy grass landing strip. Toron observed him from inside the plane, enjoying keeping his business partner waiting. His navy suit was a silk number, reasonably cool, but not a garment to stand around in with the temperature as hot as it was today. He hoped the ridiculous white prophet's robe Jardin affected was keeping him nice and warm. After two minutes had passed according to the stopwatch on his chunky gold Rolex, he opened the door and descended the short flight of steps. Giving an ironic salute, he ambled across the stretch of grass towards Jardin, carrying a tan leather briefcase. He extended his hand as he reached the cult leader whose drug factory he had come to discuss. Closing the gap between them to arm's length, he took Jardin's outstretched hand and pulled him into an embrace, kissing both cheeks.

"Christophe," he said, beaming. "Ready to scope out our facility?"

"Come, Diego, pleasure before business. I have some coffee brewing. From your native Colombia. Walk with me. Oh, and perhaps you would do me the courtesy of calling me Père Christophe while you are my guest."

Toron's eyes narrowed for a split second. In his line of work, it was he who was used to courtesy from others, although he knew it was often born simply out of a fear of drowning. Then he smiled again.

"Why not? It's your place, so I guess I can call you Father. Even though you're not a priest, eh, my friend?" He clapped Jardin on the back as he said this, harder than was strictly necessary, enjoying the brief scowl of irritation that flitted across the older man's face.

They crossed the meeting ground and walked up the path that led to Jardin's house.

Once inside, Toron looked around and whistled. *"Madre de Dios,* you have some fine looking shit in here. They all original, or what?"

"Oh, they're original, my friend," Jardin called from the kitchen. Then he emerged, bearing a silver tray laden with a coffee pot, cups, sugar, spoons, and a plate of cakes, scalloped ovals of pale yellow edged with brown. "Here, I thought you might be hungry after your trip. No room for air hostesses on those Cessnas, eh?"

Toron took a cake and bit it in half, brushing a couple of crumbs off his lapel. "Mmm. These are good," he said. "You make them yourself, or did you have one of your slaves whip up a batch for you?"

Jardin smiled and stroked his beard. "Home-baked, by me. They're called madeleines. My mother's own recipe. One taste of a madeleine inspired Proust to compose *À La Recherche du Temps Perdu.*"

"Sorry, man. English I know for business, but French? Not necessary."

"It means, 'Remembrance of Things Past'," Jardin said, picking up a madeleine for himself. "But what I want to discuss with you, *compadre,* is times future."

"Now who's in a hurry?" Toron said, always happiest when he could force other people to fall in with his pace. "How about some of that coffee?"

"Of course. And help yourself to more cakes."

Coffee poured, and more cakes eaten, Toron finally permitted

Jardin to talk business.

"So, my friend, we go into business together, this is what you want? Maybe we choose a good name for our little joint venture. I know!" he said, clapping his hands together with a loud smack. "*Salvación*. You know, because you are like Jesus to your followers, and people call me The Baptist." Toron laughed loudly, watching Jardin fidgeting with impatience to get started.

"Yes, fine. A name. For the stationery, I suppose. And the corporate jet. Now, how about I show you the site I've picked out? I think it should work rather well."

One of the male Children drove Toron and Jardin out of the village and down a dirt track for a mile until they reached a huge clearing surrounded by a thick screen of trees whose upper branches swayed in the breeze.

"Wait here, Child Raymond," Jardin ordered as he climbed out of the Jeep.

"Yes, Père Christophe," the young man said.

Toron followed Jardin into the centre of the clearing. It was roughly the size of a football pitch. Jardin pivoted on the spot and waved his arm around, taking in the whole circumference of the field.

"I think this would be ideal, don't you? There's a river beyond those trees, a tributary of the Rio Negro. So, one," he held up a finger, "an abundant, reliable water supply." He pointed at the sky. "Two, no commercial air routes cross Eden," another finger flicked up, "so no government snooping." Then he hooked his thumb back over his shoulder towards the village. "And three, a willing and docile workforce. Unpaid, too, so no labour costs. What do you think?"

Toron look around the vast expanse of the clearing. He was already calculating supply routes, tonnages, equipment costs, specialist chemists' salaries, additional freight planes and boats to move product into the US. He was also enjoying keeping Jardin waiting.

18

THE FIRST PIECE OF EVIDENCE

GABRIEL FOLLOWED CLOSELY BEHIND SUSANNAH as she navigated the cramped CID operations room, swerving to avoid detectives shooting back from desks on their wheeled chairs to grab phones, or jumping to their feet to ask her questions on her way past.

She issued rapid-fire orders, responses, and questions of her own without breaking step.

"Follow it up."

"Tell him if he calls again you'll arrest him for wasting police time."

"She sound genuine?"

"Yes, if you're back before the briefing."

"Fuck, no!"

Within thirty seconds, they were through the large square room with its confusion of whiteboards, incident timelines and notices about firearms training and first aiders, and into a narrow corridor. Susannah was marching along, and Gabriel was forced to lengthen his own stride to keep up. She stopped abruptly at a door marked, "Forensics".

She turned to Gabriel.

"They're my little pets in here, and I don't want you to say a word. OK?"

"Sure." He made a lip-zipping gesture and threw away the key for good measure.

Inside, the buzz and banter, ringing phones and hubbub of multiple conversations in CID were silenced. The noise was replaced with a muted murmur. Centrifuges were spinning test tubes full of blood and other liquids. Printers hummed as they churned out documents. Keyboards were being tapped furiously. And below it all was the furious whirring of extremely large brains.

Standing beside a balding, bearded guy, whose brown eyes were magnified by his thick, tortoiseshell glasses, was Chelsea, the Detective Sergeant. They were staring at his monitor.

"Boss," she called, causing all the other people in the lab to look up with varying expressions of annoyance or disgust on their pallid faces. "Steve's got a hit on one of the ball bearings. A print."

Once all three of them were clustered around the forensic analyst's desk, looking over his balding head at the monitor, he pointed at the screen, which was divided into two vertical panes. The left-hand pane was labelled, "BB 79—partial".

He pointed with a bitten fingernail at a pattern of red dots and lines superimposed onto an enlarged fingerprint, which reminded Gabriel of the contour lines on a map.

"We got this off a ball bearing recovered from the bus itself," he said in a nasal voice that suggested he should have had some kind of adenoid surgery as a child. "It's a miracle, really, given the heat the charges must have generated. Maybe someone was smiling on us for once. Anyway, I ran it through …" then he looked up at Gabriel and paused.

"It's all right, Steve," Susannah said. "He's helping us catch the people who did it."

The man sniffed and continued speaking.

"I ran it through the, shall we say, usual databases, and look what popped up ten minutes ago."

He pointed to the right-hand pane, where a complete fingerprint was depicted in pin-sharp resolution, displaying an identical pattern of red lines connecting minuscule red squares. A green banner was flashing across the bottom of the screen. It consisted of a single word.

MATCH.

"So who does it belong to, my darling?" Susannah said, ruffling what was left of the man's hair and causing him to shake his head like a dog objecting to being patted.

He tapped a couple of keys, and a PDF of a police report flashed up onto the screen. He read out the top line, even though his audience were more than capable of doing it for themselves.

"Eloise Alice Virginia Payne. Possession of a Class A controlled substance; specifically, ten grammes of cocaine. Fined one thousand pounds and ordered to do one hundred and twenty hours community service; Woking Magistrates Court, nineteenth of June, two thousand and thirteen."

The colour photograph in the top right-hand corner of the report showed a young girl of maybe seventeen or eighteen. Not particularly pretty. Bad skin, her forehead peppered with spots; long, lank blonde hair; no makeup apart from dark smudges of eyeliner. Sullen expression. Gabriel stared at it. There were similarities with the girl he'd seen leaving the car outside Biaggi's, but he couldn't be sure. Was this her?

"Not much to look at, was she?" Susannah said, stabbing her finger at the picture.

"Why do you say 'was', Guv?" Chelsea asked. "We don't know for sure she was the bomber. Just that she was there when it was made."

"Wishful thinking," Susannah said. She patted Steve on the shoulder. "Good work. Now, print me a copy of that and we'll get out of your hair. No offence."

He smiled. "None taken. You know what they say about bald men, don't you?"

"Yes, I do. And if you want to disappear that lovely wife of yours and run away with me to Zanzibar, we can find out if it's true, can't we?"

"Come on, Gabriel," Chelsea said with a grin. "Let's get out of here before these two start shagging on the carpet."

"Oi! You cheeky little bitch," Susannah said. "Fuck off and get a brew for us. Then see me in my office with wonder boy here."

Chelsea crooked her finger at Gabriel and they left the forensics lab ahead of Susannah, who presumably hadn't finished flirting with her pet.

While they waited for the kettle to boil, Gabriel used the time to find out how the investigation was going.

"So apart from the fingerprint, have you got anything else that might help us?"

She leant back against the fridge in the cramped little kitchen and folded her arms across her chest.

"To be honest? We've got fuck all. All the witnesses who might have identified the bomber are in body bags, or in some cases, freezer bags. Sorry, more cop humour."

He waved the remark away.

"Don't worry about it. Carry on."

"OK, so there's the head. That's our next best hope. It's still with the pathologist, downstairs. He's going to call me as soon as he has something to ID the owner. At least DNA won't be a problem."

"What about CCTV? I'm still sure I saw the bomber. She *could* be the girl in the photo, but if I could see her walking, I'd be more confident."

"Next stop after the Guvnor's told us whatever she wants to tell us. Look, the kettle's boiled. Help me make three mugs, would you?"

The tea made, they carried the steaming mugs through CID and into Susannah's office, partitioned off from the open plan area with stud walls and large plate glass windows. She was already there and on the phone. She waved them to chairs in front of the desk, rolled her eyes and signalled she was trying to wind the call up, rolling her index finger around in a circle. They sat, sipped the scalding tea, and waited. It soon became obvious who was taking up Susannah's time.

"Yes, sir. I know, sir. It's just ... No, I understand the public need to be reassured but we haven't ... Can't we wait for another twenty-four hours before we ... Yes. Yes, sir. Of course, sir. Straight away. I'll get Pam Vickers onto it right away. She's our new Chief Press Liaison Officer. She's ... Yes, I have full confidence in ... yes, thank you, sir. Goodbye, sir."

She held the phone away from her face, which had coloured alarmingly as if she were about to have a heart attack. Her breathing was coming in deep, growling inhalations and exhalations. With a carefully extended middle finger she tapped the red icon to end the call, placed the phone on her desk, then ran both hands through her luxuriant auburn hair.

"That bloody man is going to be the death of me. Chief Superintendent Graham Ford had just ordered me—ordered, mind—to hold a press conference. I mean," she said, her tone protesting, "what the fuck am I supposed to say? A hundred-odd people lost their lives two days ago and so far all we've got to go on is a fingerprint of some bloody teenaged coke-head from a couple of years ago. Oh, yes. Very bloody reassuring. Why don't I go on the morning fucking telly and sit on that luminous bloody sofa and trot out the same platitudes we always have, too? 'Doing everything in our power. No stone unturned. Every officer working round the clock to find the culprits.' Jesus Fucking Aitch Christ, what a fucking mess." She took a slurp of the tea and immediately winced and clamped her hand to her lips. "Shit, Chels. What did you do to it? Taser the fucking thing? I just lost all the skin off my tongue."

"Sorry, Boss. Just the regular boiling water. Oh, wait a moment. Boiling. That might have been it." She risked a wink at Gabriel, who winked back.

"Ooh, not interrupting anything am I?" Susannah said. "You too bonding over the Morphy Richards, were you? Joking about me behind my back when you were dunking your teabags?"

"Sorry, Boss," Gabriel said. "Won't happen again."

Mollified, Susannah put the mug down.

"Here's what I want you to do next. Go and talk to Eloise Payne's parents. Get her last known address, associates, mates, hangouts, the usual drill. And Gabriel, I want you to sit down after you get back from wherever they live and start reviewing all the CCTV footage. I've got one of my lads cueing it all up from the junction of Regent Street and Mortimer Street down to the bus stop at Oxford Circus. I want the car and I want the bomber. If you did see her, we can hopefully get a face and match it to Eloise Payne."

19

I BLAME THE PARENTS

THE PAYNES' HOUSE WAS ENORMOUS, a brick-built, double-fronted Victorian villa set thirty or forty yards back from a leafy avenue on the outskirts of Woking. A varnished wooden plaque screwed to the trunk of a horse chestnut tree announced the house was called "Bellavista".

Chelsea parked the silver BMW on the street, but as they crunched down the pea-shingle drive to the front door, she realised she needn't have bothered. There was space for two or three more cars on the gravel semi-circle outside the front of the house alongside a metallic pink Jaguar XKR convertible and a British Racing Green Aston Martin DB7. Chelsea pointed at the cars as they approached.

"His and hers?"

Gabriel had the same thought flitting through his own head and smiled.

"Obviously. But whose is which, that's the question, Holmes."

Chelsea grinned as she pressed the white china button set into the brickwork to summon, hopefully, the Paynes.

As they waited, Gabriel drew in a deep breath. He'd been in London for three days and was missing the countryside. The suburbs were a poor substitute, but at least out here there were trees. They'd driven past plenty of fields on the journey down to this pleasant commuter town in Surrey, to the south of London. Someone, somewhere, was having a bonfire. The smell of burning leaves filled the air and he picked up the crackle of dry wood burning. A good smell. A bad sound. It reminded him of the distant rattle of automatic gunfire He shook his head. Chelsea was talking.

"What? Sorry, I was miles away."

She tutted.

"I said, I'll do the talking. You're here to listen, OK?"

"Like mother, like daughter, eh?"

"What?" she said, eyes narrowing.

Gabriel pointed at a huge pile of dead flowers and cuttings to the left of the house. "Leaves a trail of destruction in her wake."

Chelsea relaxed a little, still alert to the possibility she was being made fun of. "OK. Well, like I said, you keep shtum."

The sound of footsteps approaching the other side of the door ended the edgy banter between them. A bolt scraped back and a key turned in the mortise lock. The door swung inwards.

The man facing them was about five foot eleven. Slim build with just a hint of a paunch under the heather cardigan he was wearing. Cashmere, Gabriel noted. Nice jumper to be doing the garden in. His face was gaunt and yellowish, cheeks hollow, as if he had weighed a lot more and had shed it all very quickly. His expression was watchful, wary, bright-blue eyes flicking from Chelsea to Gabriel and back again. Before Chelsea could say anything, he spoke.

"It's Eloise, isn't it? What's she done now?"

20

ALL POWER CORRUPTS

WHEN JARDIN HAD SIMMERED long enough, judging by his increasingly twitchy body language, Toron broke his silence.

"What do I think of all this? I think … you forgot something."

"What's that?" Jardin said, frowning.

"Power. You need electricity to make cocaine. I don't see any pylons around here. You got underground cables?"

Jardin smirked, an expression Toron felt he would like to wipe off his face with a slap. "No. Not yet. But among my servants, I have engineers who specialised in hydroelectric and solar power before they joined me. How do you think the air con and the lights work in my house? Yes, I insist my followers live somewhat primitively, but that is part of my brand image. A renunciation of all things corrupting, electrical power among them."

Toron smiled, slowly. "You really are a very evil man; you know that? God must be feeling very forgiving when he looks at what you are doing out here."

"God? Listen, Diego, I know you have your Catholic faith to fall back on like a big spiritual crashmat, but some of us have to make our way in this world alone. And, please, your business operations? Your baptisms? He is OK with all of that?"

"I am a good Catholic. I go to confession. God knows I am weak, but I love my family, I attend mass, and I help the poor. Perhaps," he said, straightening his jacket after a sudden gust of wind blew it back to reveal the butt of a dull black pistol in a shoulder holster, "we should save our theological debates until we have a bottle of something suitable on the table between us. So, we have electricity, or we will have?"

"Enough to light this place up like a Christmas tree any time we want. It will take some time, but I can have a team start work tomorrow."

"Then yes, I think it will work. I will have some plans drawn up for a facility and then we can talk about a schedule, supply routes, and all the other million details our start-up will need attending to."

"No need," Jardin smirked again, stroking his beard and smoothing his fingers along his moustache. "I have architects, too. Let's go back now. We can settle a few terms of business over something cold."

21

WHERE ELOISE WENT

"MR PAYNE? I'M DETECTIVE SERGEANT Chelsea Jones. I'm with the Metropolitan Police. This is Gabriel Wolfe. He is working with us as a consultant. May we come in?"

The man sighed and beckoned them across the threshold.

"I'm Barry Payne. Hold on." He turned away from them. "Lucinda," he called. "It's the police. We're in the lounge."

Then he turned back to Chelsea and Gabriel and indicated that they should go through a white-painted, panelled door to their left.

The room was large, maybe eighteen feet wide by thirty long. At some point in the house's history, the owners—maybe even the current occupants—had knocked down the wall that had originally separated the front room facing the road from the dining room overlooking the garden. Barry Payne sat heavily in a cream leather recliner chair and motioned for them to sit opposite him on a matching sofa. As he opened his mouth to say something, his wife bustled in, wiping her hands on a blue and white tea towel. She was wearing an over-bright smile, as if she'd been told she was going to be on television. Her hair was lacquered into place, shining in the light from a chandelier suspended on a fake antique brass chain, and she was wearing lots of makeup, which reinforced her media-ready appearance. She stood by her husband's side, a hand on his left shoulder. Her face was taut with the effort of maintaining the smile. Gabriel noticed a muscle twitching beneath her right eye, which was highlighted with a broad sweep of shimmering green eyeshadow.

"Mr and Mrs Payne," Chelsea began. "Can you tell us the whereabouts of your daughter, Eloise?"

"Why?" Lucinda Payne said. "Is she in trouble? Oh, Barry, it's those bloody awful people. I told you we should have gone and got her back."

"We just need to know where she's been living and who she's been associating with. Am I right in thinking she doesn't live with you?"

As her husband's scowl deepened, scoring deep lines across his forehead and at the sides of his mouth, Lucinda perched on the arm of his chair. He seemed content to let his wife do the talking.

"She moved out a few years ago. There was a bit of trouble. With drugs. What's this all about please? Why won't you say?"

"We know about Eloise's drugs charge, Mrs Payne. We're not here to talk about that. Can you tell us where she's been living these past few years, please?"

The woman seems on the verge of tears. The smile was slipping, the chin trembling. Barry Payne finally roused himself from his reverie.

"I'll tell you where she's been. With a bloody religious cult, that's where. The Children of Heaven, they call themselves. More like the bloody Morons of Never-never Land, if you ask me."

Gabriel and Chelsea exchanged a quick glance. *Cults do crazy things.*

"No address, I suppose?" Chelsea asked, flipping open her notebook and jotting down 'Children of Heaven'.

"Strangely, no. We don't have their bank details either, before you ask, although they clearly had Eloise's. Emptied her accounts out down to the last bloody penny."

"Barry!" his wife said, her eyes widening. "These officers are only trying to help. There's no need for that tone."

Barry Payne jerked his chin towards Gabriel.

"Officer. Singular. Didn't you hear her. He's a bloody civilian, just like you and me. And I'll use whatever tone I like in my own home, thank you very much."

"Mr Payne," Gabriel said, deciding in a split-second to disobey Chelsea's instruction to keep silent during the interview. She whirled round and glared at him, mouth open. He pressed on. "You're right. I am just a civilian. However, I'm working in an official capacity alongside the Metropolitan Police. My own background is in British Army Special Forces. I've been accredited to work with the police because of my specialist skills and experience. Believe me, all we want to do is find the people who did this. Your daughter may have been duped or brainwashed, but we think she may have been mixed up in the bus bombing in London. So if you can help us in any way, you'd be doing a lot of good."

Payne cleared his throat, then wiped a hand over his face.

"Of course. I'm sorry." Then his eyes narrowed. "'Mixed up' you said."

"Pardon?"

"You said Eloise was 'mixed up' in the bus bombing. What precisely do you mean by that phrase?"

Chelsea was glaring at Gabriel. She looked down at her notepad then up at Payne again. "We found her fingerprint on a component of the bomb."

Barry Payne's face turned white. Beside him, his wife clutched his shoulder so tightly he yelped in pain as her manicured fingernails dug through the fine wool of his cardigan into the flesh beneath.

"Was she there?" she said, in a half-sob.

"We don't know, Mrs Payne. We're still trying to ascertain all the facts. But I'm afraid it does look like she was involved in making the bomb."

At this, Lucinda Payne broke down completely. Her face crumpled, all the features moving independently of each other, the mouth twisting, the eyes squeezing shut, the nose wrinkling. Then she howled. A wide-mouthed moan that started deep in her chest and escaped from her stretched lips in a wail of grief, horror and despair. Payne leapt to his feet and wrapped her in his arms. He looked over his shoulder at Chelsea and Gabriel.

"Her room is upstairs at the end of the hall. Look around all you like, take whatever you like, then leave, please."

Chelsea stood and Gabriel followed her out of the room and up the stairs. Over the sound of Lucinda Payne's pain-wracked crying, Chelsea whispered to Gabriel.

"Think how much worse it's going to be if the head turns out to be hers."

Then she opened the door to Eloise's room. And gasped.

22

A BOMBER'S BEDROOM

THE BLOODSTAINED CUDDLY TOYS DANGLING from nooses were the first things to catch Gabriel's eye as he and Chelsea walked into the last known abode of Eloise Payne. A row of teddy bears hung from the curtain rail on lengths of string as if the sandman had tired of his good guy role and opted for a new career as begetter of nightmares. Posters on the wall featured skeletally thin young girls with ladders of scars climbing their bony little arms and slogans advocating self-harm. IF IT FEELS BAD, CUT IT read one, in scratchy red type echoing the razor marks on the model's skin. He hoped she was a model, anyway.

There was a montage of printed-out photos on the wall above the bed. Teenaged girls in ragged net skirts, torn stockings and smoky black eye makeup draped over each other in poses that appeared to suggest their friendships were based on shared needles rather than music or cat videos.

They stood, silently, for a second or two, taking in this shrine to dysfunctional adolescence. Then Chelsea spoke.

"Seen it all before. Teenage junkie. Hates her parents. Hates the world. Hates herself. Blah blah blah. Right, toss it and collect anything that might give us a lead to where this cult was. Or is."

She started by pulling out the drawers in the girl's bureau and rummaging systematically: to the back, the left, the right then to the bottom. As Gabriel looked around for somewhere to start, and found himself unaccountably nervous, she hissed out a triumphant, "Yes! Diary. Right, we'll have that." She looked round. "Haven't you started yet?" Then she returned to her rummaging.

Gabriel opened the wardrobe. The clothes were all black, red, or white. Lots of vintage lace, silk, and nylon. He squatted and reached to the back, breathing in—but not wanting to—the smell of a troubled girl who was almost certainly dead. Patchouli and sandalwood—joss-stick aromas that made him think of Middle Eastern cafés. He stretched his hand out, craning his neck to keep his face away from the wispy, filmy fabrics, and paddled his fingers blindly over what felt like a shoe box. He grabbed it and pulled it out.

He lifted the lid off, then he turned to Chelsea.

"I've got something."

The box was full of club flyers, gig tickets, postcards, photos, and other artefacts you might associate with a typical teenage life.

She looked over. "Bring it."

After another ten minutes, when they'd failed to turn up anything else, Chelsea felt might lead them closer to the people behind the bombing, she straightened, knees popping. "Come on. I don't think there's anything else here. We can always come back."

They went downstairs together and for one surreal moment, Gabriel felt as though they'd been staying as guests of the Paynes. The faces of the parents dispelled this dreamlike feeling immediately. Both had been crying, and now they were trying to compose themselves for a final conversation about their daughter.

"I know what it looks like. Up there," Barry Payne said. "Some sort of museum of self-harming. But she was a good girl. Used to ask us to give her Christmas presents to charity when she was a little girl, didn't she, Luce?"

"She had her problems. Like we all do, but we thought she was turning the corner. We thought she'd joined a church at first. Like the Alpha Course. You know, happy clappy Christians. Then, one day, she just, just …"

She broke down for a second time, sobbing onto her husband's already damp shoulder.

"She didn't come home," he said. "We got a postcard. It's there on the mantelpiece. Take it. Now please, leave us. And if it turns out she's … gone, please phone ahead. I don't want my wife in any more distress."

Chelsea took the postcard—a red squirrel holding an acorn—and read the message aloud: "Hi Mum and Dad. I am with lovely people. The Children of Heaven. I know it sounds a bit dorky, but they're so cool. I love you. Eloise. Three kisses." She looked up at the Paynes. "Thank you, Mr and Mrs Payne. I'm sorry we had to bring you such distressing news. We'll be in touch."

Then she led Gabriel through to the hall, out of the front door, across the scrunching shingle and into the BMW.

"Fuck!" she said. "I hate those visits. And I'm probably going to have to go back there with even worse news."

"You were brilliant. And I think deep down, they already know. He does, at any rate."

"Yeah. But it doesn't help, does it? Come on, let's get this lot back to Savile Row and show the Boss. At least she'll be pleased."

As Chelsea drove them fast along the A3 back towards London, Gabriel realised he had enough of a grip on the mission parameters to call Britta.

"Hi, you," she said.

"Hi. I know this is short notice but are you free tomorrow? We could do the same place, same time. It's OK if you can't, but I'd really like to …"

"Don't be stupid, Wolfe. Of course I'm free. I'm on holiday by order of the Lord High Mucky Muck of MI5 international cooperation division. Or had you forgotten?"

Gabriel laughed. "No, I hadn't forgotten. I just thought maybe you had other plans."

"Nope. No plans. Though I might go and buy a new dress just for you."

"OK, so see you tomorrow?"

"*Ja, det är perfekt!* Six-thirty. French House. Dry white. I'll be there."

The call ended, Gabriel sighed and put the phone back in his pocket.

"Someone special?" Chelsea asked, keeping her eyes looking straight ahead, hands at the ten-to-two position on the steering wheel.

"No. I mean, yes. A friend. She's Swedish."

"Is she now? Swedish."

"Nothing wrong with that, is there?"

She shook her head, grinning. "Gabriel's got a girlfriend," she chanted.

"She's not my girlfriend."

"No, sweetheart, of course she isn't. She's your friend, isn't she? Your very special Swedish friend. Who's a girl. With long blonde hair and bright blue eyes and big boobs and perfect teeth."

"Not true," he said, smiling now despite the interrogation. "She has red hair and small boobs and gappy teeth."

Ninety minutes later, they pulled into the police station car park and were in Susannah's office five minutes after that. Chelsea placed the shoe box full of souvenirs and the diary dead centre on her boss's desk.

"We got that lot from the girl's bedroom. Looked like a bloody advert for the Samaritans in there. She was into cutting, anorexia, all that shit. No laptop, before you ask. I did look. But," she looked at Gabriel, "we know where she went, after leaving home, I mean."

Susannah looked up and cocked her head on one side. "Well?"

"A cult. The Children of Heaven. It's a lead, boss. A good one, too."

"Good work, Chel. Action Man here behaved himself, did he? No amateur detective shit?" Another look flashed between Gabriel and Chelsea. Which, of course, Susannah picked up. You don't get to be a DCI by missing the bleeding obvious. Especially when it's passing between your DS and a civilian consultant who've just spent the morning together. "OK, spill. Gabriel, you want to fess up or do I have to interrogate you properly?"

"No, Boss. I opened my mouth. Tried to get the dad on-side. But that was it, just a little story about how I was only there because you were throwing all your resources at it."

"It did work, Boss," Chelsea said. "He gave us permission to look in Eloise's room. It was fine, really. Gabriel was good as gold. Well, good as silver, anyway."

Susannah smiled.

"Look, you did a good job. Don't worry Gabriel, I won't bust your balls over it. Just remember who's in charge. Until you and the boys in black balaclavas go in and kill everyone, it's a police case. Now, Chels, you check out these, what did you call them, Children of Heaven? Where they're based. Who's the fuckwit egomaniac in charge. Modus operandi—yes, Action Man, we do still know a little Latin in the Met, thanks for raising your eyebrows —all the usual." She pointed at Gabriel. "You're with me. I've got you a nice little office to watch the CCTV footage in—no windows, no air con, and a subtle bouquet of bad breath, BO, and farts. This way, please."

She manoeuvred herself round her desk and led Gabriel through CID and down a flight of stairs before, as promised, installing him in a windowless cubbyhole furnished solely with a hard plastic chair, a cheap metal and plywood table, and an ageing PC with a flat-screen monitor.

She pointed at the screen, which, when she nudged the grubby black and silver mouse, sparked into life with a grainy but reasonably clear colour still of the north end of Regent Street.

"You use the video controls on screen to play, pause, fast forward, and reverse. You can zoom in by clicking there," she pointed at a button on the screen, "or pressing Control and F1 on the keyboard. Zoom back out by clicking it again or pressing Control and F2. When you're finished with each camera and want to go onto the next one, click that arrow there," another scarlet fingernail tapped against an onscreen button, "and that one there to go back to the previous camera. Any problems, call Roni Shah in IT; she's brilliant. Number's on the side of the PC. Questions?"

"None. Actually, one. What do I do when I find something, or when I'm done?"

Susannah flipped one of her police business cards onto the desk's greasy surface. Call me. I'll come and let you out."

With that, she was gone, her heels ringing on the hard floor tiles outside in the corridor. Gabriel puffed out his cheeks, rocked his head from side to side, making the joints in his neck click, and pressed Play.

For the next ten minutes, he watched intently at double speed, eyes flicking across the screen as the figures scurried this way and that, and vehicles sped into view, paused at traffic lights then jumped forward again and out of sight.

Then he sat straighter. That was the silver Mondeo, he was sure of it. The rear windows were blacked out and the time-stamp on the top right corner of the screen matched the time he was having his coffee. He noted the time and the camera number on his phone then clicked on to the next camera.

This one was placed about halfway between Biaggi's and Oxford Circus. Again, there was a five-minute period when nobody even vaguely resembling the young woman he'd seen passed in front of the camera. But there she was, walking on those stiff, skinny legs towards Oxford Circus, her bulky Puffa jacket a dead giveaway. At one point, she looked straight into the lens of the camera. Her face was a mask of anxiety: skin and muscles around the eyes taut, the eyes themselves wide and staring, the mouth downturned.

"Got you!" Gabriel muttered, noting the time-stamp and camera number again.

Eloise continued down Regent Street until she passed out of the frame. Gabriel clicked onto the third camera. This one was positioned high above Oxford Circus itself. Moments into the footage, Eloise appeared, walking towards a crowded bus stop. She took her place in the loose gathering that constituted a queue and stood, her shoulders hunched, looking left and right at the people around her. They were all intent on their phones and wouldn't have noticed the terrorist in their midst if she'd been wearing a bandolier of dynamite.

A double-decker bus approached the stop. People streamed off from the middle doors and the gaggle of shoppers, tourists and office workers mounted the platform at the front, before being lost from view. Eloise Payne climbed aboard and disappeared inside the bus that was to be her tomb. Gabriel took another note. Now he was sure. This was the same girl. Her fingerprints were on the ball bearing, and she was on the bus.

Suddenly, he realised what was about to happen on the screen in front of him. His finger hovered over the mouse to stop the video. But he couldn't do it. He felt compelled to sit there and wait.

Seconds ticked by and he found he was counting aloud, under his breath, as he pictured her final moments.

"One. Two."

She must have swiped her Oyster Card by now.

"Three. Four. Five. Six."

She's climbing the stairs.

"Seven. Eight."

She's found a seat.

"Nine. Oh, Jesus!"

The bus blew outwards from the top deck then the picture snapped to grey and black speckles as the force of the blast took out the CCTV camera.

Steadying his breathing, he picked up Susannah's card and called her.

"I've got your bomber, Boss."

23

A DEAL TAKES SHAPE

SEATED IN JARDIN'S COMFORTABLE SITTING room, sipping chilled Sancerre from a tulip-shaped glass, Toron once again couldn't help but admire the sheer hypocrisy of his business partner. The man dressed like a hermit, wore his hair like an Old Testament prophet, and subjected his disciples to all manner of privations. Yet he himself lived a life of indulgence, from his paintings to his wine. *What I see when I look at you, compadre, is a smug, egotistical, lecherous con artist. One who I'm sure would double-cross me in a flash if he felt he could get a better deal elsewhere. Better not, though, or you'll find yourself experiencing one final religious conversion in three inches of water.*

Then he noticed Jardin was looking at him with a puzzled expression on his face, brows crinkled, lips pursed.

"What are you thinking about?" Jardin asked, taking a gulp of the wine and wiping the drops from his moustache with his fingers.

"Me? Oh, just how much money we are both going to make from our joint venture out here in your jungle paradise."

"On which subject, perhaps it is time we talked about a split of the profits. I was thinking—"

"Here's what I think," Toron said, leaning forward suddenly and putting his glass down hard enough to make Jardin flinch. "I think I am providing raw materials, management, technical specialists, quality assurance, supply chain, distribution, sales and marketing, plus legal, security, and greasing palms in law enforcement and the DA's office. You are providing facilities, human resources, and power. That being the case, eighty-twenty in favour of Muerte Eterna once all costs have been defrayed."

He sat back, crossed his right ankle over his left knee, and spread his arms along the back of the sofa. Waited.

He got to ten before Jardin spoke. What was interesting, to a student of human weakness, as Toron considered himself to be, was the range of emotions that so clearly flashed across Jardin's face.

Initially, as the ridiculously low percentage proposed to him registered in Jardin's brain, all the colour drained from his face. His skin took on a waxy sheen and his lips tightened into a thin black line as if drawn on with a pen, or cut with a knife. He stroked that damn beard again as he fought to wrest himself back under control. But still he clearly didn't trust himself to speak and played for time by staring up at the ceiling as if looking for divine guidance, which, as an atheist, he was unlikely to receive. Finally, he looked back at Toron, who maintained an indulgent smile as he held his hand, palm out, to one side. *Well, "Père" Christophe, what now?*

Jardin swallowed. "Eighty-twenty?" He laughed, but it was an artificial-sound, mirthless, stagey, too, like he'd learned it from YouTube. "My friend, please do not denigrate our contribution with your management talk of human resources. You know that what we offer here goes way beyond mere 'facilities'." He drew air quotes around this word. "I am offering you a secure manufacturing plant with its own airfield, a guaranteed supply of obedient, free labour, a total lack of scrutiny, and," he smirked again, "I know your loyalty to your wife is total, but for recreation, strictly as a diversion from the pressures of running your considerable business empire, well, let's just say my female children are more than willing to please. Fifty-fifty."

At the mention of his wife, Toron felt a surge of anger race through his body. He clenched his fists and his right hand jerked involuntarily towards his pistol.

"You NEVER mention Dolores, you hear me? *Madre de Dios*, you sanctimonious sonofabitch, if you even breathe her name again I will cut your balls off and make you eat them."

Any other man would have pissed himself with fear at being spoken to like this by Toron. Jardin merely laughed, this time the genuine, twinkly-eyed variety. He patted the air in front of him. "Calm yourself, my friend, calm yourself. I apologise. A poor attempt at humour, that is all."

"Seventy-thirty," Toron said.

"Sixty-forty."

"Sixty-five-thirty-five. And if anything comes out of your mouth except 'deal,' I'm leaving, and your existing contract to fly coke up to Houston is cancelled."

Toron found himself waiting once more.

That infernal smirk appeared on Jardin's face again. God, how he wished he didn't need this man and his posturing.

Jardin took a sip of wine and placed his glass down on the table that stood between them with a soft clink.

"Deal."

24

DOBAG

BACK IN SUSANNAH'S OFFICE, GABRIEL sat facing her across the desk. Her hunched shoulders and crimped mouth told him a lot about what sort of a day she was having.

"So tell me," she said. "How sure are you? That it's her."

Gabriel thought for a second, aware that the woman sitting behind the cluttered desk was going to have to go in front of the media shortly. If he was wrong, she'd probably castrate him publicly in the middle of Piccadilly Circus.

"I'm certain. The car was the same. She was dressed the same. I tracked her from Regent Street all the way down to Oxford Circus. I watched her get on the bus. And I watched the fucking thing explode, forgive my language."

"I don't give a fuck about your language, Gabriel. But I have a full-scale press conference in thirty minutes and if I stand there and say, 'Oh, yes, ladies and gentlemen, the bomber was a nice little middle-class girl from the suburbs called Eloise Payne,' and it wasn't, you will have made me look like a fucking idiot. At which point you are off this case and I don't care what your Mr 'Official Secrets Act' Webster says. Are we clear?"

"As mud."

"Right." She stood up and tugged at the hem of her dark green suit jacket. "How do I look?"

Gabriel looked her up and down.

"Smart, stressed, and sexy. But I'd do up that button or it's going to be your cleavage on the six o'clock news instead of the bomber."

She looked down and fastened her blouse closer to her neck. Then back at Gabriel, a twinkle in her eye.

"Were you looking at my tits instead of listening to me?"

"Me? Of course not! Consummate professional. Plus, you're my temporary Guvnor. It wouldn't be appropriate."

"Oh, no. Of course it wouldn't. And I'm sure you've never done anything you didn't think was *appropriate* in your long and distinguished career, have you? Now, come with me. We've got an appointment in DOBAG."

He stood and followed her out of her office.

"Doe-bag?" he said, once again stumbling to keep up as she swerved effortlessly round swivel chairs, desks and knots of detectives discussing the case.

"Department of Blood and Guts. The Path Lab. You're going to meet our resident slicer-and-dicer, Doctor Henry Haydn, who might give me the final bit of reassurance I need."

The inside of the pathology lab was spotless. Every surface gleamed under the brighter-than-daylight LED lighting, whether it was bone-white porcelain, stainless steel or shining plastic. Gabriel breathed in cautiously through his nose, a frown crinkling his forehead. It smelled of disinfectant, mainly, though he could detect a familiar meaty scent underneath the pine. Classical music was playing from a phone docked into a sleek silver speaker on a bench by the door. Violins and a harpsichord. Maybe a Spanish guitar. The wall on the far side of the room, opposite the door, was divided into twelve rectangular drawer fronts, each about four feet wide by two feet deep.

The central space was filled by three stainless steel tables. Each table had a central depression for a body, sloping from the head-end to the foot, where drain holes led through to deep, oval, stainless steel receptacles beneath. The two outer tables were empty, but the central table was not. Draped in a pale green sheet of thin fabric was an object roughly the size and shape of a deflated football. Standing behind the table, his blue vinyl-gloved hands clasped in front of him, was the pathologist. Dr Haydn was a slightly built man with a shock of white hair standing up all over his tall, domed skull. His spectacles were from another era, black plastic at the top and gold wires around the sides and bottom of the lenses, giving him the appearance of an FBI agent from the 1960s. Unruly white eyebrows leapt and curled from behind the frames. He'd chosen to reinforce the anachronistic image with a tweed jacket, accessorised with a black and white polka-dotted pocket square, and a wine-red, paisley bowtie that appeared, from its lopsided wings, to have been hand-tied.

"DCI Chambers!" he said, then smiled as Susannah and Gabriel walked over to him. "And you have a guest." He turned to Gabriel, snapped off his right glove and shook hands. "Welcome, welcome. No doubt DCI Chambers here has apprised you of her and her colleagues' less-than-respectful name for my laboratory?"

Gabriel glanced across at Susannah, who was grinning at him.

"She may have mentioned it. I thought it sounded cool."

"Cool! You hear that DCI Chambers? I am cool. So, allow me to reveal to you a work I would title 'Head of a Young Woman,' were I curating one of those cabinets of curiosities that pass for art nowadays."

He pinched a corner of the shrouding fabric between thumb and forefinger and whisked it away with a theatrical flourish.

In their own way, all three living people in the room had become used to death, and all the grisly forms in which it might be inflicted on the human frame. There were no indrawn breaths, no mutterings of oaths, no turnings away. The pathologist had spent his career examining dead bodies. The detective had spent hers tracking down those who left them behind. The ex-soldier had spent a fair portion of his creating them.

"Not much of a looker, is she?" Susannah said.

"Ah, the gallows humour once more," Dr Haydn said. "No, she has rather lost her youthful bloom, hasn't she? I dare say we all would, were we to dive fifty feet, face-first, onto a marble floor."

The head that had once belonged to Eloise Payne had been doubly abused, first by the blast and then by the impact with the floor. The skull was crushed and the face was partially folded in on itself. Her blonde hair was cut short and matted with blood.

"I cleaned her up as best I could, but I'm thinking it's nothing the parents should be shown. We received the DNA results an hour ago, ran them through the usual databases and got a match with Miss Payne. So that's fingerprint and DNA evidence for you, DCI Chambers. You have your bus bomber."

"Thanks, Henry. At least that's one incontrovertible fact I can give the jackals for the evening news. And we now know where she disappeared to when she left home."

"Really? And where was that, pray tell?"

"A religious cult. The Children of Heaven. Ever heard of them?"

"No, I haven't. But it does supply an answer to a puzzle that's been niggling at me since I ran a tox screen on the young lady's blood."

"Which is?" Susannah said, checking her watch.

"She had extremely high levels of anti-psychotic drugs in her system, including haloperidol and fluphenazine, which are usually used to treat schizophrenia. Plus, a muscle relaxant called succinylcholine, and a sedative: diazepam. That's Valium. Basically, she was bombed before she bombed, so to speak. These and other drugs have been associated with brainwashing in the past, which would fit with her having been indoctrinated into a cult of some sort."

"What sort of side effects would you expect to see in someone who'd taken that lot, Doctor Haydn?" Gabriel asked.

Haydn smiled, pushing his glasses back up his nose with the tip of an index finger. "A very perceptive question. Your consultant has his wits about him, DCI Chambers. Well, there are many, from impaired liver function to anxiety, although those would be hard to detect externally. But in this dosage, I would be very surprised not to see some evidence of tardive dyskinesia."

Susannah rolled her eyes. "Again, Henry. For the thickos amongst us?"

"My apologies. Tardive, from the Latin *tardus*, meaning slow, or late, onset, and *dyskinesia*, from the Greek, meaning faulty movement. In this case, involuntary, repetitive body movements. Usually of the face, but it can also produce a stiff or uncoordinated gait."

Gabriel looked at Susannah.

"I knew it!" he said. "She was pulling odd, stretched faces and she looked like she'd only learned to walk that morning."

"So the bastards drugged her up, brainwashed her, then wrapped her in explosives and ball bearings and sent her off to commit mass murder," Susannah said, with a scowl.

"So it would seem," Haydn said, pulling the spotted handkerchief from his top pocket and using it to polish his glasses.

"Which is all grist to the mill, Doc, but why did you summon us to your little horror show here? You could have emailed all this."

Haydn replaced his glasses. "Look at the top of her head."

He used a silver ballpoint pen he retrieved from his breast pocket to indicate an irregular black hole in the top of the skull, half-hidden by a hank of blood-matted hair and a mosaic of broken bone. Gabriel and Susannah peered at the cavity.

"What is it?" Susannah asked, wrinkling her nose.

"Patience, my dear DCI Chambers. Watch this."

He crossed the floor to a stainless steel counter and came back with a thin, transparent Perspex rod, about eighteen inches from tip to tip and about the same thickness as a drinking straw. He inserted the tip of the rod into the hole, and pushed it slowly. With a faint squelch, the rod entered the skull. He maintained the pressure, and little by little, with a treacly, sucking sound, the rod disappeared until only half of it was visible.

"Look here," he said, pointing at the ragged flesh fringing the base of the skull. Gabriel and Susannah moved round the table to get a better look. Haydn pushed the rod again and the bloodied tip slid out through a circular hole under the lower jaw. "It is my conclusion that one of the ball bearings surrounding the explosives travelled vertically upwards from this young woman's waist, or wherever the charges were strapped on to her body, penetrated her jaw, travelled on through the brain, and exited through the top of her skull. The hole here," he pointed at the spot where the tip of the rod had emerged, "is approximately twenty-one millimetres across, which matches the dimensions of the ball bearings recovered from the scene. Only someone whose head was directly above the bomb could have sustained this injury."

Susannah pushed her fingers through her hair, scrunching it in her fist. "Right, so we're belt and braces on the perpetrator. Her poor fucking parents are going to need some tranquillisers of their own when this turns up on the telly. We have to go. Thanks, Henry."

Haydn smiled, but his eyes betrayed him. It was a rueful expression that said, another day, another dead human being.

As they walked back to CID, Gabriel touched Susannah lightly on the arm in an attempt to slow her down enough to ask her a question.

"What?"

"I have an appointment at five o'clock. Do you need me any more today?"

She checked her watch again.

"No, you're fine. And, thanks. You're doing well. Chelsea seems to think you have the makings of a halfway decent detective constable. Can you be back here in the morning?"

"Sure. I'll see you then. I've got an idea for what I need to do next. I'll call Don and tell you in the morning. Good luck with your press conference."

She tossed her head back. "The camera loves me, darling! Now fuck off and let me get some lippy on."

Gabriel found a quiet spot behind some filing cabinets. Someone had stacked box files in an untidy pyramid on a tiny steel and plastic table. It made an excellent hide. There was a chair behind it so he picked a paper at random from the topmost box, propped his feet on the edge of the desk, and pretended to read.

He let his eyes drift shut as fatigue stole over him.

Hello, Boss.

Hey, Smudge. Haven't seen you for a while.

Yeah, well, you know, seems you've been kind of busy. How's it going?

I have to get back to Eden.

Wow. That doesn't sound weird at all.

It's under control. Just infiltrate, tab into the centre of the enemy camp, take out the leader, exfil, and extract back to England.

Oh, well as long as that's all…

I know. But it's going to be fine.

You know what, Boss?

What?

It is. Going to be fine, I mean. Fariyah knows what she's doing, and I think you do too, now.

What do you mean, 'now'?

Got to go, Boss. Take care of yourself.

25

SESSION WITH FARIYAH CRACE

"WHERE DO YOU WANT ME?" Gabriel said, looking around Fariyah Crace's office.

The psychiatrist smiled, her olive skin glowing against the shocking pink of her hijab. "Are you looking for a couch, Gabriel? I'm afraid I don't go in for any of that Freudian bullshit. As I think I told you last time. Don't you remember?"

He laughed, briefly. More from nervousness than genuine good humour. "I thought you'd have got one in for me, specially."

"Oh, you're not nearly crazy enough for a couch. You'll just have to make do with an ordinary armchair, I'm afraid. Come on, let's sit down."

She motioned for him to take a low armchair upholstered in a nubbly wool fabric the colour of aubergines. It faced another across a pale, wooden, circular coffee table with a thick sheet of turquoise glass set into the top. He sat, and crossed his right ankle over the opposing knee, then immediately felt this display was overcooked and returned his right leg to the floor. He folded his hands in his lap, then crossed his arms instead.

Fariyah sat in the other armchair, twisting round to turn her phone over on her desk.

"You seem a little tense, Gabriel. Everything OK?"

"I'm fine, really. I'm just having a problem knowing where to put myself."

She smiled that warm, reassuring smile again. "Look. Can you see a clipboard or notebook?" He shook his head. "Or a prescription pad?" Another shake. "We're going to talk. That's all. You have your diagnosis from our first session. It is Post-Traumatic Stress Disorder, as I think you knew all along. So, let your arms and legs find their own place in the world and we'll see what we can do about helping you find yours. Deal?"

He smiled. A genuine, relaxed expression this time. "Deal. Thanks, Fariyah. OK, first question please."

"My first question is, have you been to see Richard Austin yet?"

Gabriel frowned. He'd been intending to call the therapist for a while, but work kept getting in the way.

"Not as such. He's the eye-movement guy?"

"Eye movement desensitisation and reprocessing, yes. It's been shown to have some remarkably quick, and permanent, effects in cases such as yours. Try to get around to it. I think you'll like Richard. And I also think you'd benefit from his approach."

"OK, I will. I promise."

"Good. So tell me, how have you been since we last met?"

Gabriel knew that, unlike the casual enquiry of a friend or colleague, this seemingly innocent question didn't require a generic, "fine". So he drew in a deep breath, let it out in a hiss through his teeth, and began to tell her about the hallucinations. How his former comrade, Mickey "Smudge" Smith, dead from a Kalashnikov round to the back of the head, had become a regular fixture in his day and was now effectively offering him advice on how to do his job; bloody nightmares of lean, dagger-toothed African militiamen walking up the walls of his cottage in Salisbury; sudden urges to sit down in the street and wail with sadness; and others to race his Maserati down to Beachy Head on the Sussex coast and take one final, glorious, plunging dive off the cliff there and into oblivion.

Throughout his tale, the plump psychiatrist sat perfectly still.

Her legs, encased in black, tailored trousers were crossed at the ankle and didn't move an inch as he talked. For most of the time she looked straight at him, though his own eyes flicked away, around the room, before returning to lock onto hers. She smiled encouragement from time to time, but what she was thinking, Gabriel couldn't tell.

He stopped talking. Half an hour had gone by.

Fariyah let a moment or two of silence pass. Then she spoke.

"Your hallucinations where you see Smudge and he gives you advice. In my opinion, that is your subconscious mind donning a disguise. The person giving you advice is you, but your experience in Mozambique has led you to cloak some of your own thoughts in the guise of your lost friend. But that aside, you have amazing strength of character. And a lot of mental resilience. To be carrying that load around with you, well, it's broken plenty of men. Why do you think it hasn't broken you?"

Gabriel scratched his face.

"I don't know. Army training?"

"That seems unlikely. Almost everyone I see for PTSD has had the same training as you. Not the Special Forces element, and it's possible that there are aspects of the psychological techniques for resisting torture that might be helping you, but in all other respects, my other patients have had the same preparation for combat as you. No, I wonder if there's something else. Perhaps earlier in your life? Before the Army?"

"I had an unusual upbringing."

"Yes. You mentioned that at our initial meeting. You didn't settle at school?"

"Ha! You could say that. I got into a lot of fights. And I wasn't that great at taking orders from the teachers either, which is ironic, considering my eventual career choice."

She raised her eyebrows. "Eventual?"

He tipped his head to one side and took a deep breath. He was about to tell her something he'd never told anyone before. "I was considering a career as a gangster."

She sat up straight and uncrossed her legs, leaning forward, eyes wide. "A gangster? Well, you get today's gold star for throwing me. What kind of gangster?"

"In Hong Kong, when I was about seven or eight, there were a couple of gangs who were on the news from time to time. The White Koi and the Coral Snakes. They were trying to control the drugs trade, prostitution, protection, the usual gang stuff, basically. I thought they looked cool, whenever they were arrested. Leather jackets, greased-back hair. I was going to offer myself as a delivery boy for the drugs. You know? A little hoodlum on a BMX bike spinning round the streets with five-dollar baggies of pot down my trousers."

She shook her head. "And did you?"

"No. Turns out I couldn't take orders from them either. I hit one of their boys, got a beating, and was told never to show my face in their territory again. So that was that."

"What changed you? Where did you discover self-discipline?"

Gabriel smiled as he thought back to his Chinese mentor, Zhao Xi, a friend of his parents and the man to whom they'd turned when the only other long-term option for their son looked like juvenile prison.

"Master Zhao, I called him. He tutored me right through from eleven to eighteen. In the beginning, I defied him like everybody else, but he was just … just different. You know that old fable about the reed and the oak?"

"I don't think I do," Fariyah said. "Why don't you tell it to me?"

"Oh, OK." Gabriel cleared his throat, and sat straighter in his chair. "An oak growing close to a river boasted to a reed about how strong he was. And the reed just smiled and said, 'Why don't we ask Wind to set us a test and we can see which of us is the strongest'. And the oak agreed. So they asked Wind to blow with all his strength and whoever was left standing at the end of the test would be the winner. So, Wind blew hard and the oak immediately stiffened himself and braced his trunk and branches against the power of Wind's breath. In contrast, the reed just let Wind's breath move him about, bending him almost to the surface of the river. Wind blew with such force that, in the end, the oak's branches snapped off, one by one, and then, with a terrible cracking and splintering, the mighty trunk shattered and oak was felled. As Wind softened his breath until the air was still, the reed sprang back, undamaged."

Fariyah smiled and mimed applause. "Beautifully told, Gabriel. So you were Wind, your teachers were the oak, but Master Zhao was the reed?"

"Something like that. Except, my teachers didn't break. But their way was a trial of strength. Master Zhao let me blow myself out. When I was finished, he began to teach me. We did the usual school stuff, which kept my parents happy. And we did some really interesting other stuff that kept me motivated."

"Such as?"

"Martial arts. Hypnosis. Meditation. And this discipline developed by the Shaolin monks called *Yinshen fangshi*. It means 'the way of stealth'. It's hard to explain, but you let yourself soften and pull in all your sharpness—that's how Master Zhao explained it to me—until you disappear from people's perceptions."

Fariyah leaned back and folded her hands in her lap, her forehead wrinkled in a frown of curiosity. "Do you know, I have been a practising psychiatrist for thirty years and a professor for five, and I like to think I have read the literature on altered states thoroughly, but I have never heard of *Yinshen fangshi*. Would you give me a demonstration one day?"

Gabriel returned her smile and began speaking.

"Of course I ... could, we'd just need to ... find a time when both you ... and I ... were in the frame ... of mind ... to make it ... happen ... if you'd like to ..."

As he spoke he began altering his breathing and the cadences of his speech, directing his gaze at Fariyah's left and right eyes in a precise coordinated sequence. As her eye movements and breathing began to mirror his, he waited for the telltale sign that it was time to move.

Her eyelids fluttered and her focus slipped.

At that instant, he slid from his chair, retrieved her phone from the desk beside her and tucked it into his pocket. "Check your diary … we could book a time for … me to show you."

Then he stopped speaking and waited, counting in his head.

At five, he leaned forward and tapped her twice on the left knee. With a brief shudder, her eyes refocused on his face.

"Yes," she said. "That would be wonderful. Let me check my calendar." She turned to retrieve her phone from the desk, and frowned.

"Something wrong?" he said, unable to keep the grin from his face.

She looked back at him. "It's my phone. I'm sure I put it here."

Gabriel pulled the phone from his pocket and held it in his outstretched hand."

"Here you are."

Her mouth fell open as she retrieved her phone. Then she laughed.

"You devil! Did you just use the way of stealth on me?"

"You said you wanted a demonstration."

"And I certainly got what I asked for didn't I? That is a very powerful mental technique." She paused and placed the tip of her finger against her lips briefly, then spoke. "Coupled with meditation and the inner strength and discipline you would have gained through your martial arts training, I'm not surprised you've been able to cope with your PTSD for so long. But I'm concerned you may be turning from a reed into an oak yourself. You can only resist trauma for so long without therapy before it fells you just as surely as Wind felled the oak in your tale."

"Which is why I'm here. I need to sort this out. I can't keep carrying this guilt around with me for ever."

"And that brings me to another question. You see, the circumstances in which you lost Smudge, well, they were certainly traumatic, but they lack some of the characteristics that would trigger full-blown PTSD. You were in control, for one thing. You were in battle, albeit under covert operating procedures. The loss of life was not caused by poor leadership or soldiering on your part. That you were unable to recover his body was a great sadness, but in itself not sufficient to account for the severity of your reaction. I don't mean to diminish any aspect of your experience, Gabriel, not the pain, not the grief, not the shock, not the shame, which I know you feel. But in my experience, none of those emotions, or the particular events you've described, are *in themselves* likely to have caused your health problems. I wonder whether there was an earlier event that laid the charge, as it were, that your experience in Mozambique detonated."

Hello, Gable. The nice lady is talking about me.

The voice in his head caused Gabriel to jerk back violently in his chair. His heart began racing and he broke into a sweat.

Fariyah leaned forward, an expression of concern on her face. "Gabriel, what is it? What's the matter?"

He swiped his palm over his face and shook his head. "Nothing. Nothing's the matter. Just a flashback. Talking about Smudge must have triggered it. I'm fine."

Fariyah pulled her chin down to her neck. "Really? Because you reacted only after we'd *stopped* talking about Smudge."

"Honestly, it's nothing."

I'm not nothing, Gable. I'm me.

"Well," Fariyah said, looking at her watch. "Our time's up for today. But I want you to make another appointment as soon as you can. Will you do that?"

"Of course," he said, fighting down an urge to scream. "Yes, I want to. I may have to be away for a while. But yes. Definitely. And thank you."

"It's what I'm here for. And thank you for demonstrating *Yinshen fangshi* to me. I think I could deliver a whole conference paper on that one episode."

Outside Ravenswood, the swanky hospital in the heart of Mayfair where Fariyah ran her private practice, Gabriel leaned against a parked car. He was shaking uncontrollably.

26

ONE HAND WASHES THE OTHER

THE OUTLINE FINANCIAL ARRANGEMENTS AGREED upon, Toron and Jardin were able to relax in each other's company. Another bottle of wine procured and opened, they began discussing operational issues.

"I wonder if, while you're here, you could help me out with a little local difficulty," Jardin said.

"What sort of difficulty?"

"There's a police captain in Nova Cidade, our nearest town. She's been sniffing around my people when they drive over there for supplies. I think she has, what do you say, a bug up her ass about Eden?"

"Does she know anything about your flights?"

Jardin paused before answering. Telling Toron the truth might mean he would be unwilling to do what Jardin required. "I think so. One of the children may have been indiscreet. So, I wondered whether, with your talent for, shall we say, smoothing things over with law enforcement, you might take a trip over there tomorrow."

"You mean kill her. Why don't you ever say what you mean?" Much to Jardin's secret delight, Toron's face betrayed his obvious irritation, lips briefly pulled back from his even, white teeth.

"Oh, if you think killing her would be best, by all means. I was going to suggest possibly a bribe of some kind. Or perhaps simply informing her that we know she has a young family that she no doubt wants to protect from dangerous elements in Brazilian society."

Once again, the deliberate prod at Toron's hardwired belief in the sanctity of family. At least until he felt it necessary to off some judge and leave his wife a widow and his children fatherless.

"She has a name?"

"Rafaela da Silva. Black. Short. Dumpy."

"That's fine. I'll take care of her tomorrow. As it happens," Toron said, straightening his shirt cuffs where they'd snagged in his jacket sleeves, "the Muerte Eterna are also experiencing some unwanted scrutiny. The President of Colombia has appointed a new Minister of Justice. Very young, very ambitious. Boasts of his incorruptibility, which I can personally vouch for. Background in the Colombian military. He's announced a crackdown on the drugs trade, internally and cross-border."

Jardin frowned. "Bad for business."

"Yes, very bad for business. Now, you may not realise this, in your seclusion, but the President of Amazonas State has invited our young firebrand to meet with him to discuss a common approach to tackling 'the continuing scourge of the cartels' as he calls it."

"Yes, yes, I see. But what has all this to do with me?"

Toron leaned forwards to put his wineglass down. "Suppose I tell you that the two men are attending the opening of a new hydroelectric project two months from now. And that the facility is situated just fifty miles from here."

A smile spread across Jardin's lips at this. Killing the state president and the Colombian Minister of Justice would be just the sort of challenge he relished. Although it would need more than just one of his simple-minded followers to achieve a positive outcome. Ah, details, details.

"Wouldn't it be tragic if such a progressive politician, such a clean-hands politician, were to die in a suicide bombing? And the recriminations, of course. 'Surely our friends in Brazil can manage enough security to safeguard the life of one of our most promising rising stars?'"

Toron smiled. "So you'll arrange matters?"

"I will need to find a suitable recruit for the operation, but yes, I'll arrange matters. Leave everything to me."

27

SOMETHING'S UP

A BOTTLE OF WINE STOPPED Gabriel's muscles from trembling. But back in his hotel room after a rushed dinner, he still felt like he was about to crack apart. He opened the door of the minibar fridge concealed behind a fake rosewood door and pulled out a couple of miniature bottles of gin. He cracked the thin metal seals and emptied them into a glass with a tin of tonic. Took a pull on the chilled but not ice-cold drink.

His phone rang, making him jump. It was Don Webster.

"Hello, Old Sport. Forgive the lateness of the hour. I've been with the PM. She wants to know what's happening. So, what *is* happening?"

Don's measured tones made Gabriel realise just how intoxicated he was. He tried to enunciate his words clearly so Don wouldn't think he was drunk on the job.

"OK. What is happening? Eloise Payne, this disturbed teenaged girl, was the bomber. The police have got fingerprint, CCTV, and DNA evidence that confirms it. She'd joined this cult called the Children of Heaven. So my, what I am planning, is this. Join them, the cult, I mean. Get on the inside. Covert op. Find out who's the psycho in charge. Search and destroy. Leave the cult. Job done. Ta dah!"

"Are you all right, Old Sport. The plan's fine but you're not, are you?"

"Oh, just a long day with our friends in the Metropolitan Constabulary. That's all. I'll be OK. Aren't I always?"

"Not counting the PTSD Fariyah's treating you for, you mean? How's that going by the way?"

"Fine, fine. She's good. We're making excellent progress. Look, I have to go. Can I call you tomorrow morning?"

"Better. Come and see me. Usual Whitehall address. Shall we say ten? Sounds like you might need a lie-in before you start getting tooled up."

28

GOING TO SEE A MAN ABOUT A CULT

NURSING A FORMIDABLE HANGOVER, GABRIEL sat in Don's impersonal office on the first floor of an anonymous office building in Whitehall. Unlike his palatial accommodation in the MOD, this room was purely functional: a grey steel filing cabinet, cheap veneered desk, thinly padded chairs. Someone had made a half-hearted attempt to inject a little personality into the room by screwing a print of a vintage hot-air balloon to the wall, but the overall effect was depressing, rather than uplifting. In front of him, a cup of black coffee from a chain of American outlets steamed, the curls of water vapour illuminated by bright autumn sunlight streaming through the uncurtained window. Don's face wore an expression of concern, grey eyes narrowed, chin cradled in the fingers of his right hand.

"So, do you want to tell me what was going on last night, Old Sport?"

Gabriel ran his fingers over his scalp, pushing his short dark hair into spikes.

"It's nothing. Honestly. OK, not nothing, exactly. I saw Fariyah yesterday for a session and something came up. You know, very cathartic—isn't that was the shrinks call it?"

"It is. And there's a word for what you're doing right now. Bullshitting. But you're a grown-up. So deal with whatever you have to deal with, but promise me you're fit for the mission or I'll pull you out and find someone else to do it."

Gabriel took a sip of the coffee and let a few molecules of caffeine percolate into his brain before he spoke.

"I'm fine. I can do it. Plus, for what I'm thinking, a bit of a ragged-edged psyche could work in my favour."

"And what's that exactly?"

"I'm going to join the Children of Heaven."

Don leaned forward, steepling his fingers under his chin. "Continue."

"I'm going to be an exemplary recruit, or acolyte, or whatever they call them. I'm going to get close to the leader and I'm going to take him out. Then I'll give you a call and you can come in and round up the rest of them and deprogramme them or whatever the process is called."

"Sounds perfect. Just remember, we don't want any more innocent deaths. And no martyrs, either."

"Oh, don't worry about that. I'll find a way. Maybe he's into kiddie-porn, or satanic abuse—that would work."

"Fine. Agreed. Just let me know if you need anything once you're inside. Our cyber guys are always hot to trot. And we can supply anything you might need in the way of weapons or equipment."

"I will. But I'm thinking of keeping it low key as it's on British soil. After all, most accidents happen in the home."

Gabriel tried for a smile, but he felt his lip quiver and wiped the half-formed expression away with the palm of his hand.

His next stop was 27 Savile Row. The redheaded Police Community Support Officer on duty at reception smiled when she saw him and waved him through the security door into the main part of the station. He passed quickly through CID, unchallenged—amazing what a piece of plastic on a lanyard can do for you—looking around for Chelsea, but not seeing her at her desk or in the kitchen area. He knocked at the closed door to Susannah's office.

"Come!" a voice barked from within.

He pushed through the door and found Chelsea with her Guvnor.

"Morning all," he said, with a natural smile this time. He'd grown to like these two officers with their swagger and their "lippy" in the sweaty, testosterone-soaked environment of the CID.

"Ah! If it isn't our favourite trainee detective," Susannah said, putting her hands on her hips.

"Hi, Gabriel," Chelsea said, from her chair across the desk from Susannah. "So what's the news from the men in black?"

"I'm going undercover. Joining the cult. Getting the membership badge and the stickers."

"And then conducting an extra-judicial execution on the British mainland," Susannah said, her initial mocking tone replaced by something altogether darker. "Great. Makes you proud to be a police officer, doesn't it, Chels?"

Chelsea gave Gabriel a small smile. "The boss is pissed off because we're off the case. Because we identified Eloise Payne as the bomber, they're saying it's closed. Murders were committed, a murderer was found. The evidence confirms her guilt. End of story."

"Except it isn't end of story, is it?" Susannah snapped. "There's a terror cell operating in London or somewhere close, taking out our people, and we are this close," she pinched the air, "to finding the real evil bastards who ordered the attack, and suddenly, it's, 'Oh, no, this is *much* too important for you simple plods to handle, leave it to the grown-ups'. So forgive me if I'm not jumping for joy at your new life as a fucking Jesus-freak-assassin."

Gabriel watched as the colour returned to Susannah's cheeks, and her chest stopped heaving. Judged when it would be safe to speak.

"Look, I understand how this looks to you, but," he continued quickly, as Susannah's mouth opened again, "I'm just doing my job. I have my orders, same as you. I just came in to say goodbye. And that, well, it's been an honour to work for you, even for just a couple of days. And also," he turned to Chelsea, "thanks. For the other day, I mean. In Regent Street. Stopping to see if I was OK. That was kind. Really kind."

His speech was genuine. Maybe the two detectives saw that, or felt it, because the atmosphere in the office changed in that instant.

"Oh, fuck, come here, you overgrown toy soldier," Susannah said, rising from her chair. She stepped round the desk and crushed Gabriel in a hug, then stood back and planted a hard kiss on his cheek. "Just get the fucker for us."

Chelsea stood too. She stuck her hand out, but as Gabriel took it, the gesture turned into an awkward hug. No kisses this time. "It was OK, working with you. And you were great with the Paynes. Good luck."

Then the farewells were over. He had a new job to do.

Search.

And destroy.

29

BLASPHEMY

JARDIN WAVED AS THE CESSNA TOOK off from Eden's airfield. His smiled stay glued in place until the little white plane had banked left over the trees fringing the field and was lost from sight. Toron had left him with a promise that he would return in two weeks with a team of engineers and builders to begin construction on the factory. As the drone of its engines faded, replaced by the rustle of the wind in the palm leaves and the resumption of birdsong and insect noise, his shoulders dropped and he let the grimace slide off his face. He stood, facing the sun, enjoying the sensation of its light and heat on his skin. Then he spread his arms wide.

"Can you hear me, God?" he shouted to the sky. "Are you enjoying the actions I carry out in your name? The blood? The mutilations? The deaths? Do you enjoy eavesdropping while I fuck those young girls in your name?" He cupped a hand to his ear and leaned forward, eyes scrunched tight, as if straining to catch a faint sound. "Nothing to say? Of course not. Because you don't fucking *exist*, do you? Fools like Toron with his confession and his stupid churchgoing believe in you, but I don't." In a sudden spasm of activity, he stripped off his robe and sank to his knees, arms wide. "I tell you what. Kill me. Kill me right now. Send a lightning bolt. Give me a heart attack, a brain haemorrhage, a stroke. I *dare* you."

Jardin maintained the pose for a few seconds more, then scraped up two handfuls of grass and the rich loamy soil it grew in. He stood, and flung the clods of earth skywards in curving sprays, laughing hysterically as the fractured clumps pattered down onto his upturned face. "I am the power here!" he screamed. "I control life and death. And you, you are like a bribe of candy to get a toddler to behave. I created you to serve ME! Let me give you an example of my contempt for you."

He leaned forward and hacked at the earth with the heel of his right shoe, pulling it back until he had gouged a two-foot long scar. Moving to one side he repeated the action to create a rough cross in the sod. Then he unzipped his trousers and urinated into the earthy crucifix, all the while giggling and muttering obscenities. Suddenly exhausted by his blasphemies, he bent to retrieve his robe, rearranged his clothing into Père Christophe's customary humble garb and walked back to the village. Hunger was cramping his stomach and making him irritable.

30

HELLO, AND GOODBYE

GABRIEL GRIPPED THE COLD BRASS handle of the door to the French House and went in. Even though it was only early evening, the small pub was already full. The majority of the drinkers looked like his former advertising agency colleagues. Mostly young, mostly funky, all talking loudly while knocking back pints of beer or glasses of wine. You could spot the account managers because they were smarter than the creative types, who in their desire for nonconformity had dressed identically in jeans, T-shirts, and scarves for the men or cute dresses, leather jackets and Doc Martens for the women.

He looked around, standing just out of the crowd around the bar. Then he saw her. Alone at a small round table in a corner sat Britta Falskog, a former Swedish Special Forces soldier who now worked semi-permanently for MI5. Her red hair flamed in the light coming in through a stained glass window behind her. It looked like a bundle of fine copper wire twisted into a plait that fell forward over her collarbone. She held her hand up in a wave and called to him.

"Gabriel! Hi. I got you a glass of Chablis."

A few of the men near him looked around at the husky sound of her voice with its lilting Swedish accent, and then at him.

"Ooh, Chablis!" one of the more fiercely funky creative types cooed at him, winking. Gabriel momentarily considered decking the boy then smiled and manoeuvred past him on his way to meet Britta. She stood up as he arrived at the table. The dress she'd bought was simple. A scoop-necked, emerald-green, silk sheath that fitted closely all the way from her chest to her hips then flared a little before ending just above the knee. She had matching green stones in her ears, and at her throat on a fine silver chain.

They kissed, almost formally, on the cheek, then Britta grabbed his head on each side and planted a real kiss straight on his lips. There was a small cheer and some clapping from the group of men he'd just passed.

"Hi," Gabriel said. "You look amazing."

"I thought you'd been killed," Britta said, by way of reply, whispering, though with all the background noise from the other patrons, there was no need. "I heard the explosion on your phone then it went dead."

Gabriel shook his head, noticing, again, how pale her skin was beneath the spattering of freckles across the bridge of her nose. Her blue eyes bored into his with an urgent look.

"And yet, here I am," he said. "Just wasn't my time. But those poor souls who were on the bus. Jesus, Britta, it was bad."

"As bad as that day in Bosnia?"

"Yes. And that place in Rwanda. As bad as any bad place you or I have ever been."

She took a sip of her own drink, a dry Martini with two olives.

"So tell me, what's Don got you up to this time?"

"It's not Don. It's me. I called him. I'm going after the person or persons who planned it. And I'm going to deliver the Queen's Message."

"Ha! I never understood your SAS lingo. You're going to give them a bullet in a perfumed envelope?"

Gabriel smiled and took another sip. It was so good to be in her company again, making gentle fun of each other as they had so many times in the past, often when enemy combatants were shooting Kalashnikovs at them in a firefight or sniping down on them from ruined sandstone buildings.

"You know perfectly well what the Queen's Message is. It's our way of saying 'you just crossed a line' so she doesn't have to."

"Yes, and your writing implements are so elegant. Very sharp nibs."

"And don't even get me started on our pencil sharpeners."

She laughed, throwing her head back. Gabriel looked for, and found, a little triangle of freckles just under her jawline. He reached out and touched it gently with the tip of his finger. Britta dropped her head forward and fixed him with a hard stare.

"Go and deliver the Queen's Message. And stay safe."

"You know I will. Now, how about dinner? I could eat a cow."

"Don't you mean a horse?"

Gabriel waited a beat. Raised his eyebrows a fraction.

Then Britta realised what he was doing.

"Are you taking the piss out of my English, Mr Wolfe?" She leaned across the table and poked him in the chest. "There are punishments for that, you know."

"Show me later."

Later turned out to be eleven o'clock. They'd had dinner at a tiny restaurant on Lexington Street. The bottle of wine they shared disappeared without their noticing, so intent were they on catching up with each other's exploits. A black cab had taken them along Piccadilly, round Hyde Park Corner, past Harrods and onwards to Chiswick. Britta had snagged a one-bedroom, top-floor flat in this leafy, middle-class part of West London that was worth as much as Gabriel's three-bedroomed rural cottage.

Letting herself in with a giggle as she fumbled the key into the lock, Britta turned and shushed Gabriel theatrically.

"Quiet! I do have downstairs neighbours, you know."

Inside, the flat was decorated in high Scandinavian style. The walls were all white, the floors were sanded oak boards, the pictures on the wall were abstracts: blocks of sand, cream and saffron punctuated with slashes of blood-red and buttercup-yellow.

He held her lightly by the shoulders and turned her to face him. She stepped into his embrace and tilted her face slightly to meet his lips with her own. They stood like this for a minute or two, hardly daring to move, reacquainting themselves. Gabriel tasted wine on her and breathed in her perfume: a light floral smell that reminded him of tropical beaches.

In her bedroom, they undressed and then faced each other before sinking onto her bed entwined in each other's arms. They fell into an easy rhythm, Gabriel above Britta, looking down into those wide blue eyes. She reared up as she came, clenching her hands round his arms. Gabriel reached his own climax moments later, moving urgently inside her as she moaned softly into his ear.

Gabriel woke in the night and checked the digital clock at the side of the bed. It was 3.00 a.m. Of course it was. Had he ever woken up with fear ricocheting around in his stomach like a pinball at any other time? He rolled away from Britta, onto his back, and folded his arms behind his head. Outside he could hear traffic on the A4, clattering taxis, and a few lorries moving up through the gears after being stopped at the lights. No planes yet; they wouldn't start their nose-to-tail procession towards Heathrow for another hour or so. Britta stirred beside him.

"What's the matter?" she asked, in a sleep-muffled voice.

"Nothing. Just thinking about what I have to do next."

She propped herself up on her left elbow and looked at him. Moonlight glinted on her eyes through a gap in the curtains.

"I wish I was coming with you. Maybe they'd let me. My masters at MI5, I mean. Especially if Don asked them for me specially."

"I do too, but this is strictly off-the-books stuff. You know how Don works."

"Well, I don't, as a matter of fact. Just he's some kind of super-spook with people like you running around with better toys than the rest of us."

"It'll be fine. Go to sleep."

"Only if you do, too."

"Deal."

Gabriel held his arm out for her to slip inside. Pressed against him along the whole length of her body, Britta placed her palm flat over his heart.

"Stay safe, Gabriel Wolfe," she whispered.

Gabriel left her later that morning with a promise to call her once the mission was over. He headed for the tube and was sitting in a half-empty carriage heading into London at 11.30.

31

WEALTH DOESN'T BRING YOU HAPPINESS

SUSANNAH'S PARTING GIFT TO GABRIEL had been a small-but-useful piece of intelligence. The Children of Heaven had some sort of recruiting centre just behind Sloane Square, at the top of the King's Road. "In Chelsea, ironically," she'd said as she told him. "They wander about offering tickets to a talk or a presentation or some fucking nonsense. Just stand around looking lost, and they'll find you."

He emerged from the exit to the tube station at just after midday. He stood with his back to the wall of the station and took in the crowd, trying to split it down into manageable categories. The bustling pedestrians began to slow down in his mind as he let his gaze roam over them, separating out the different tribes. Office workers, dressed more funkily than the ones he'd seen in the City of London's financial district, in sharp-tailored outfits of teal, tobacco brown, and sky blue. Tourists ambling along the pavements, eyes upturned, selfie-sticks held aloft like divining rods, searching out the perfect shot. The odd wino pushing a wire trolley laden with bulging, wind-tattered plastic bags still displaying upmarket supermarket logos. And everywhere, the carefree, elegantly dressed offspring of the capital's rich.

For his infiltration, Gabriel had decided simply to backtrack a couple of years and clothe himself in his advertising agency persona. A former soldier who'd served his country and then become disillusioned with the place and the job he'd come back to. A confident salesman who'd suddenly become sick of the shallow lies he was peddling. Don had suggested keeping his identity standard, since there was no way of telling what sort of background checks the cult would run on him. All his work for The Department was so far off the books that invisible ink would have looked like permanent marker in comparison.

The day was warm. Gabriel paused in his stroll through Sloane Square, turned his face towards the sun and let its warmth caress his cheeks. Standing around with your eyes closed and pointed heavenwards in central London is an activity that might charitably be described as unusual. And less charitably as, "acting like a bloody fool," which was how a middle-aged man wearing a regimental blazer, rose-pink twill trousers and a bristling grey moustache referred to Gabriel after bumping into him while texting. Having extricated himself from the retired colonel's personal space and made his apologies, Gabriel wandered on, attempting to cultivate an air of dissatisfaction with life in general. He pulled his brows together and turned his mouth down and sighed theatrically every ten steps or so.

He had just entered the King's Road proper when a young couple approached him. They were both in their early twenties, dressed all in white and extraordinarily good-looking. Like models, was Gabriel's first thought. They both had short hair; hers was a rich coppery colour cut into a fringe, his sandy and combed neatly into a side parting.

"Are you OK?" the young man asked. "From your little tangle back there, I mean?"

"Oh, yeah, sure. Of course. It was nothing. I was just daydreaming. Should have been looking where I was going, I suppose." He sighed again and tried for a sad expression, corners of the mouth pulled down, eyebrows pulled together. It seemed to do the trick.

"It wasn't your fault," the young woman said touching him lightly on the arm and giving him a quick sympathetic smile. "Everyone's in such a hurry these days. Nobody has time for anyone else any more, do they?"

And here you are, to show me the way.

"You're right. I sometimes feel like, you know, what's the point? I mean, is this all there is?" he swung his arm round in a vague half-circle, taking in the department store on the corner and the expensive designer shops to each side.

"We know how you feel," the young man said, adding a pat on the shoulder to the subtle grooming process. "I'm Zack. This is Sophie. Listen, have you got anywhere you need to be right now?"

"Huh! That's the point, isn't it? No job, no prospect of getting one. So, in answer to your question, no, I'm as free as a bird."

"Cool. I mean, not about the job, that's terrible. But it's cool that you have some free time. Listen, we've got a really great place to hang out, grab a free coffee if you like, or a water. And we've got a really inspirational talk starting in twenty minutes. It's all about finding meaning in our lives. Maybe you'd like to come along? Sophie can take you, if you like."

Sophie smiled at Gabriel. "Of course! You can tell me about yourself. Shall we?"

"Why not?" Gabriel said, "It's not like I have anything else to do, is it?"

"Lush!" she said, slipping her arm through his. "Come on then. What's your name, by the way?"

"Gabriel."

"Oh wow, that is so awesome. Like the archangel."

The building she led him to, a couple of streets back from Sloane Square, was a four-storey Georgian house, painted white, with gold-tipped black iron railings along the front. Etched onto a thick, translucent sheet of blue-green glass above the door were the words,

. . .

ARE YOU CONNECTED?

Gabriel pointed. "What does that mean?"

"Like, an electrical circuit, you know? Connected. To yourself. To other people. To the Universe. To a higher power."

"Oh. OK. Cool."

"I know, right?" she said, her eyes flashing wide and her smile even wider. "It's like, there's this big spiritual battery and you need to be connected to it and then you can share the power with others."

So who's sharing their power with you, Sophie? That's what I need to find out.

To each side of the front door stood an olive tree, pruned into a loose ball on its gnarled trunk and planted in a galvanised iron cube at least a yard on each side.

"They symbolise ancient wisdom because they can live to be a thousand years old. They're mentioned a lot in ancient texts, too," Sophie said, with a disarming smile that exposed perfect white teeth. "Come on, let's get a coffee and something to eat. I'm famished!"

Inside, the character of the house changed completely. An extremely clever architect had remodelled the interior, giving it the feel of a modern university campus or marketing agency. Everywhere he looked, Gabriel saw pale wooden tables, moulded plastic chairs in shades ranging from a dazzling peacock blue through burnt orange to a mint green, and beanbags. Lots of bean bags. There were plenty of tablets and slim silver laptops plugged in to floor-mounted power outlets, some being used, many waiting to be tapped into life. The floor was sanded and polished floorboards, scattered with rugs and mats in more bright, rainbow hues and abstract geometric patterns. If he was looking for signs of God, he was disappointed. It felt more like some communal creative living space for artists or graphic designers, or maybe app designers. Although the uniformly attractive men and women thronging the massive space shared very little with that tribe beyond their youth.

If it was a cult, its public relations people had succeeded

brilliantly in disguising the fact. The white clothes were odd, but they reinforced the impression of health and well-being that seemed to emanate from the inhabitants' pores.

"Come on, Gabriel. What do you fancy? Latte? Cappuccino? Fruit juice? It's over there."

Sophie pointed to the far side of the room where a counter beneath one of the abstract paintings groaned with bowls of fresh fruit, bagels, pastries, jugs of fruit juice, bottles of mineral water, and a couple of pop-in-a-pod coffee machines.

"A latte would be good. And I might have one of the Danish pastries. I haven't eaten for a while."

"Oh, poor you!" Sophie said, pouting and putting her head on one side. "You have to eat."

They stood together at the counter, making drinks and picking a couple of pastries each. Then Sophie led him to a spare table. He took a sip of the coffee. It was good, and he hadn't been lying about not eating for a while; he'd skipped breakfast, not wanting to risk throwing up in Don's office. While Gabriel munched the pastries, which were also delicious, made with fresh raspberries and thick, creamy confectioner's custard, Sophie talked non-stop. Not a word about religion, or God. Just about how she and her 'mates' wanted to make a difference in the world, to be 'connected'.

Then, "Oh, look," she said, pointing at a huge railway station clock bolted to the opposite wall. "The talk's almost starting. Come on, let's go in and get a good seat."

She stood up and brushed a few buttery flakes of pastry from her thighs. Then she held out her hand. Taking it in his own, Gabriel stood. Once again, she led him through the tables. He noticed that couples all around were standing and making their way in the same direction as he and Sophie were, towards a door at the back of the room.

The door led directly into a darkened room that looked as though it would hold about fifty people. It reminded Gabriel of one of the smaller screens in his local cinema. The seats were similar, too—high-backed and comfortably upholstered. The first couple of rows were already filled, so Sophie ushered him towards two adjacent seats on the next row back.

Amid the hubbub as people continued filing in to the room, Gabriel looked around. Half the people wore white; half were dressed in street clothes. All were more than averagely attractive, he judged, resisting the urge to denigrate his own looks in their company. He'd been told often enough that his intense, dark brown eyes, black hair, and scar on his right cheek were catnip to women, most recently by his friend Julia, back in Salisbury, when they'd been walking her dog together.

"Don't be so bloody modest," she'd told him. "If I wasn't married, I'd give you one. And you know how high my standards are."

When he returned his gaze to the front, he saw that the previously dark lectern was now illuminated by a single LED lamp on a bendy, black swan-neck fixture clamped to the side of the pale wooden platen. To its rear stood a tall, slim man in his mid-forties, dressed in white like Sophie and her fellow devotees. In his case, this meant tailored chinos and a loose, collarless shirt. His silver-grey hair was cropped short to his skull and he looked out at his audience with piercing, ice-blue eyes that glittered behind shallow, rimless glasses.

Robert Slater stood, perfectly still, observing his audience, smiling as a patient father might smile as he watched his children play together. Then he leaned forward and gripped the lectern with both hands. The murmur of subdued chatter died away in seconds. Once silence had fallen, Gabriel started to count. The man was using an old trick Gabriel had been taught at Sandhurst. The instructor called it "the headmaster's pause"—that moment of suspense when you hold the audience in the palm of your hand and make them wait.

32

LET GO OF YOUR TROUBLES

THE SMILING MAN BROKE THE silence. His voice was warm, and he spoke slowly and steadily, his voice rising and falling like a preacher's.

"Violence. Greed. Consumerism. Crime. Family breakdown. Racism. Corruption. Does it ever seem to you that this world of ours, this *beautiful* world of ours, has something rotten at its core? Do you ever stop for a second and ask yourself, 'Was I really put here just to take photographs of myself and put them on Facebook?'"

There was a titter at this, and a few people nodded.

"Well, my friends, let me give you a straight answer. No. You were not. You were not put here to yearn for empty material success. You were not put here to engage in mindless, transitory sexual relationships with strangers. You were not put here to squander your short, beautiful lives in pursuit of empty goals that bring not satisfaction, but more emptiness. Will the perfect phone bring you spiritual fulfilment? Will more likes or retweets bring you contentment? Will a promotion to a new job where you work even longer hours make you a better person? No. No. NO!"

He shouted this last word, and a few of the people in the front rows reared back at the sudden violence of his delivery. In his persona of world-weary fugitive from all that the smiling man was railing against, Gabriel felt he could nod along vigorously like the other outsiders sitting beside their white-garbed minders. Other than that, he simply saw a smooth, polished huckster who was part of a terrorist organisation and whom he would cheerfully strangle with his bare hands if they were in a place where the rule of law was more readily flouted. The smiling man, who wasn't smiling any more, continued his speech, only now he stopped attacking his audience and began a subtle bonding process.

"It is not your fault. You did not ask for this world. You have the potential for purity of thought, word and deed. Of a spiritual life free from the curses of this sullied, commercialised world they have built around you. But beware. There are those who would sell you cures," he made air quotes around this last word, "that are nothing but stickier strands of the same spider's web of deceit. Believe me, my children, eating like a caveman, stealing grains from Bolivian peasants to sprinkle on your breakfast cereal, hanging crystals in your bedroom, twisting your body into knots, repeating nursery babble in your head—these will not bring succour. They are mere spiritual baubles, as fragile as those you hang on a Christmas tree, and capable only of delivering the same fleeting pleasure."

As the sermon, or motivational speech, or whatever it was, continued, Gabriel noticed one or two people getting up and leaving. They stooped as they left, as dissatisfied theatregoers will if they find they cannot tolerate a moment more of the drama, anxious not to draw attention to themselves. The man did not acknowledge them. He spoke on, and Gabriel noticed that references to God had, finally, surfaced, like trout rising for flies on the surface of a chalk stream.

"Let me ask you a question. Do you believe in anything at all beyond what you can discern through your five senses? Beyond money, jobs, material goods, and worldly success? Let me see your hand if you have ever wondered about that."

About half the visitors in the room put their hands up, a hesitant, bent-elbow gesture, no doubt encouraged by their minders, all of whose hands shot up like eager children in a classroom.

"That's good. Now, I don't know what you call that, that *thing* you believe in. Some call it mindfulness. Some call it Gaia. Some call it energy. Some call it bliss. Let me tell you what I call it. I call it connection. We are connected. We are connected to each other. We are connected to every other human being on this planet. We are connected to nature. And we are connected to God. Now," he patted the air in front of him with both hands, "I'm not talking about some old bearded guy in a long, white robe flinging thunderbolts around," there were more titters, "but about the fundamental, basic, connecting force of love in the Universe. Did you see the question above the door as you came into this house? Are you connected? We talk about connections here. Because we are *all* connected. But it has a truer, deeper meaning. We are connected to God."

At this, there was a scraping of chairs and another handful of people got up and left, keeping their eyes down as they did so. That left about eleven or twelve visitors, along with their wide-eyed and smiling chaperones. Sophie reached out and squeezed Gabriel's hand.

"I'm so glad you're still here Gabriel," she whispered, bestowing on him another radiant smile. "Robert is so inspirational, don't you think?"

Actually, I think he's full of weapons-grade horseshit, but OK.

"Totally," he said. "I can feel God's love pouring out of him."

She turned to him, eyes glistening. "I know! It's like he's speaking God's truth to us right in this room, isn't it? I love him."

"He's really something," Gabriel whispered back.

The speech was drawing to a close. Exhortations to live a purer life. To release oneself from the shackles of doubt and greed and a whole lot of other unsavoury personality characteristics. And, most importantly, to join the organisation of which Robert was the local shop steward: The Children of Heaven. Gabriel tuned back in for Slater's concluding remarks.

"If you are ready, come to God now. Do it now. Now is the time to begin to live as God intended you to. We have everything you need here. Clothing. Home-cooked food. Warm, comfortable, safe accommodation. Meaningful work. Friends." He paused. "We even have Wi-Fi!"

There was a big laugh at this, though Gabriel saw it for what it was, a disorientating juxtaposition of a cutting-edge contemporary reference with some fairly old-school talk of redemption and purity. He looked around the room. Apart from himself and Sophie, there were five other lost souls still with their smiling handlers. The rest of the audience consisted of initiates or whatever they called themselves. He turned to Sophie.

"What about my stuff? My rent? My whole life is still out there. I can't just put it on hold."

"Oh, you don't put it on hold, Gabriel. You press 'delete'. Join us and you won't ever have to worry about anything ever again. It's a life of blissful connection."

Until you make the ultimate electrical connection, you mean.

Gabriel frowned, ran his hand through his hair, looked around, rubbed his chin. Performed a little act for Sophie: 'the waverer'.

"You know," she said in a low voice, closing the distance between them and placing her right hand on his knee. "When Robert talked about transitory sexual relationships with strangers, he meant out there. Not in here. I mean, I'm not a nun." She widened her green eyes a fraction as she stared into Gabriel's dark brown ones.

Gabriel decided it was time to stop wavering. He inhaled deeply and let it out with a smile, then spoke.

"And I'm not a monk. Where do I sign?"

She clapped her hands and her face lit up with what appeared to be a genuine smile of happiness. Her eyes crinkled at the corners and she showed those immaculate teeth again.

"Oh, Gabriel. I'm so thankful. Come on. Let's go and meet Robert."

33

HOW TO KILL A POLITICIAN

OVER THE YEARS, JARDIN'S TASTE for killing had mutated. In the early days of Eden's existence, he'd amused himself by driving out into the rainforest in a 4x4 pickup with a high-powered Mossberg hunting rifle equipped with a telescopic sight. The rifle had been his first purchase in Brazil, and he had become an expert shot. The local Indian tribes were peaceful, unused to seeing white people. When he first glimpsed one of them, pin-sharp through the precision-ground optics of the sight, he'd been entranced by the man's utter focus as he puffed out his shiny, ochre-daubed cheeks to expel the poison-tipped dart from the end of his blowpipe. A black and white monkey crashed through the lower canopy and bounced off the thick leaf mould beneath, the scarlet feathers of the dart like a splash of blood at its scrawny neck.

As the man straightened after picking up the monkey by a hind leg, Jardin fired. It was a perfect kill, straight through the heart. The man dropped in a heap, crushing the monkey's carcass underneath his own. Jardin didn't bother to bury the man's corpse, reasoning, correctly, that scavengers would do a far more effective clean-up job than he could.

Exhilarated, he'd returned to Eden and summoned two of the

most beautiful female Children to his house. The following morning, as the girls had lain sleeping in each other's arms, he'd driven into Nova Cidade and purchased five more boxes of shells for the Mossberg.

Even though he was careful, and restricted himself to very occasional trips into the forest, he knew the local Indians would eventually become suspicious of the tribe of white people living next door to their lands.

He'd planned the first attack on the outside world a year to the day after shooting the hunter. It was a gun attack on a nightclub in Berlin. He'd had one of his Children there secure a job in the kitchen, then simply begin her shift armed with a mini-Uzi submachine gun and two spare thirty-two-round magazines under her chef's whites. Fifteen clubbers had been seriously injured or killed, and the Child herself had been shot dead by police as she left the club by the front door, still carrying the smoking Uzi. Media reports described her as smiling, "beatifically".

From that moment on, he'd abandoned retail killing for wholesale slaughter. Initially, he'd found the sheer pleasure of wielding such power and control over people utterly fulfilling. But purely by chance, he'd discovered that he could also turn his amusements to financial advantage. After he'd arranged the murder of half the board of directors of a French bank at a charity football match, the bank had become the subject of a fierce takeover battle among two of its closest rivals. The shares, of which Jardin held 200,000, doubled in value inside a week. His profit was almost five million euros. It was, as he confided to one of the Aunts at Eden, "my conversion on the road to Damascus".

From then on, he had contrived to find ways to benefit financially as well as emotionally from the attacks. By spreading his operations across the world, he'd managed to go undetected by the various law enforcement agencies who would always spring into impotent action every time one of his disciples detonated a suicide bomb, shot up a government building, or unscrewed the valve on a canister of poison gas on a crowded underground train. Oh, they might claim to have leads, but that was just posturing for the media.

The Children never survived; he'd programmed them not to, and there was never enough of a pattern for police or counterintelligence agencies to join the dots. When it amused him, he would even arrange for the local Aunts and Uncles to make anonymous calls to the principal news media outlets, claiming responsibility on behalf of this Muslim group, or that Trotskyite gang. Neo-Nazis worked brilliantly if he wanted to blow up a centre for refugees from the Middle East. And when was there ever a shortage of those to target?

And now, his business partner, a man who definitely favoured the one-victim-at-a-time approach to the business of killing, had asked him for help taking out a couple of interfering politicians. What a challenge!

Spread out before him on his dining table, a deep-red slab of mahogany cut from one of his own trees, was an aerial photograph of the Santa Augusta Hydroelectric Generating Station. Blown up and printed out on a sheet of paper the size of a bus-stop poster, the photo showed every detail of the plant's layout, from the dam itself, to the pumping station, control room, substation, and management offices. The network of pylons and high-tension cables snaked away from the plant like strands of pale grey barbed wire laid across the deep, rich green of the forest.

According to Toron, the opening ceremony was to be held in a small courtyard in front of the pumping station. A large, fake 'start' button would be mounted on a wooden box attached to the dais, and when the two men jointly pressed it, a worker inside the control room, watching on CCTV, would press the real button and start the generator turbines.

Clearly, the best approach would be to have one of the Children insinuate themselves into the crowd marshalled by the state president's media minders to applaud dutifully at his clichés. Someone with the strength to muscle his way to the front, but also the ability to blend in and not draw attention to himself. Yes, it would have to be a man. Someone preferably with a background in the military, as Jardin could imagine there might be a need to deal with security personnel on his way to the event's climax. Which was a problem. Having consulted his database, he knew that he had any number of junior bureaucrats among the Children, whether from the world of business or that of officialdom. There was also no shortage of over-privileged brats from families so wealthy they'd had no need to learn a trade or get their hands dirty. But the one category of disciple he lacked was ex-soldiers.

He lacked them at the moment, at any rate. He opened the lid of his laptop and composed an email to all the members of the Elect around the world.

34

HOW TIME FLIES

THE FREEING, THEY CALLED IT. Along with the five other recruits he'd seen in the house behind Sloane Square, Gabriel had taken part in a ritual of destruction that reduced two of the three women in the group to tears. Whether of joy or sadness, it was impossible to tell. They had stood in a circle and placed their phones in front of them, plus any MP3 players, tablets, and laptops they'd brought in with them. Then, to the background of a softly sung piece of baroque choral music—Gabriel hazarded a guess at Bach—they had stamped and ground their heels into the slivers of technology. The screens cracked, the cases splintered and, for one or two devices, bright white sparks leapt and fizzled from their ruined interiors, releasing an acrid smell of ozone and burnt plastic. Next were their purses, wallets, and handbags. Banknotes, plastic cards, all forms of ID, credit card receipts, and even dry cleaning tickets were cut in half, dropped into a steel bowl half-full of a transparent gel, and finally set alight, whereupon they released greenish-blue flames and the unmistakable aroma of burning petrol.

They followed Robert Slater through a corridor into a room blazing with blue-white halogen light where two older women, both with grey hair cropped short, handed out loose white trousers with drawstring waists and matching smock-like shirts. They looked around for changing cubicles, but there were none.

"Do not feel shame, Children," one of the women said. "You were made in God's image, and you are beautiful in his eyes."

And so, shyly, without making further eye contact, they changed out of their own clothes and assumed the uniform of the Children of Heaven. They were a mixed bunch: an overweight young man with black plastic discs in both earlobes and a wispy beard, whose pallid, doughy flesh looked as though he had spent his entire life indoors, possibly behind closed curtains; two young girls of maybe seventeen or eighteen, gym-trim and toned; and a woman, maybe mid- or late-twenties, whose voluptuous frame reminded Gabriel of an Old Master painting of Venus.

Out of the corner of his eye, Gabriel noticed racks of thin scars on the insides of both the skinny women's arms—just like those on the poster model in Eloise Payne's bedroom. The plump woman lacked the scars, but her back was decorated with a tattoo of a Geisha that stretched from one shoulder blade to the other. The older grey-haired woman who hadn't spoken yet gathered up their clothes into a multi-coloured bundle and left through a side door.

That was when the cult revealed its true nature. Separated from their friends and families, colleagues and contacts, with no way of reaching the outside world, no money, and no way to get any, Gabriel and his fellow inductees were powerless within the grip of the Children of Heaven. He supposed he could have fought his way out if he'd wanted to. But he doubted that was an option for the others. Even the two younger women, who looked fit enough, were unlikely to be much good at punching anything harder than a personal trainer's sparring glove.

They were ushered into a small room with twelve red plastic chairs arranged in a circle. Six stern-looking cult members, all between eighteen and twenty-five, he judged, were sitting in alternate chairs. Once they were all sitting, Slater walked in. He sat in the twelfth chair and looked round at the new recruits. A stern, unsmiling gaze. Then he spoke.

"You have all done terrible things in your lives. Things of which you are ashamed. Things that make you wish you could go back and undo the damage you did. Now is the time to confess those deeds. Cleanse yourself of this guilt. Let it out and let it go."

His tone was not kind, but earnest. He stared at each of them in turn until one of the women broke down in tears. She related a story of how she'd bullied another girl at her private boarding school until her victim had first begun self-harming, then taken a craft knife and slit the arteries in her wrists and feet and bled to death in a bath full of warm water. Her story opened the floodgates and soon each of them, including Gabriel, had unburdened themselves with stories of romantic betrayal, criminality, cheating in university exams, even, in one young woman's case, animal cruelty. Gabriel had enough demons of his own to trump all their stories put together, but he contented himself with a fabricated narrative of spying on a work colleague and revealing his affair to his wife.

This 'cleansing circle,' as Slater put it, was merely the first in a series of demeaning and shaming exercises that went on for three days, from five a.m. until one or two in the morning, the cult members taking turns to sit in on and run the meetings. Such food as they were allowed may have been home-cooked, but it was served in tiny portions and consisted of steamed vegetables and plain rice. The starvation diet, the endless cleansing circles, the sleep deprivation, and the lack of any contact with the outside world, or even the other 'Children,' depleted their energy and psychological resilience to the point that the new recruits were listless, fretful, and often in tears. For Gabriel, it was a delicate balancing act. He had to maintain a facade of helplessness while drawing on deep physical and mental reserves instilled by Master Zhao and by his SAS instructors to stay outside the closed world the cult was building around its latest members.

Now, though, that period of indoctrination had ended. They had been driven in a minibus out of London, along the M4 motorway to a manor house set deep in a wooded estate in the Berkshire countryside. Gabriel had developed an aversion to such residences during an earlier mission and experienced a flutter of anxiety as the rambling Elizabethan building came into view.

Elysium, they called it, and it housed almost a hundred cult members. Most were the so-called Children—young people, very few of whom looked older than twenty-five and many younger than twenty, from privileged backgrounds. Their names were a giveaway: Tabithas and Jemimas, Emilys and Sophies; Rafes and Jeremys, Jontys and Florians. Not a Dean, Crystal, or Tiffany in sight. Their voices were another. Cultured, cultivated drawls, now inflected with a bright, breezy tone that Gabriel quickly found wearying, even as he affected the same shining-eyed wonderment at their apparent good fortune.

Aside from the Children, there were the Uncles and Aunts. These were the officer class. Sentinels, whose job it was to maintain discipline, assign tasks each day, and, most importantly, conduct the regular sessions of breast-beating, confession, and question and answer meetings on matters of cult doctrine.

On his first day at Elysium, Gabriel was interviewed by a woman who called herself Aunt Christine. She wore the prescribed white outfit, in her case a snug trouser suit that outlined her muscular frame. Her sandy hair was cut in a short bob that she pinned back with two white plastic clips, and she smelled strongly of honeysuckle. In a sterile, white office equipped with a computer, fax machine and a row of white filing cabinets, she had him run through his background, from childhood to the day he had walked into the house behind Sloane Square. At his mention of the Army, she looked up.

"Which regiment?" she asked, pursing her lips, her fingers hovering over the keyboard.

"Paras to begin with, then SAS."

Her fingers danced over the keyboard, and she smiled as she typed.

"Excellent. I think Père Christophe will be delighted to hear you have joined us, Child Gabriel."

"Who is Père Christophe, Aunt?" he said.

"He is our leader. Did Sophie not mention him to you at your

Freeing? How forgetful of her. I must speak to her later. He is a wonderful man, a deeply spiritual shepherd of his little flock. He has studied the Bible in the original Hebrew. He has also studied the other great religious works—the Torah and the Koran, the Bhagavad Gita, and all the rest—and has divined the flaws in each. The places where their authors misread the simple truths God offered us in return for our salvation."

"Can I meet him?" You see, I have this contract on his life from the prime minister, and I would very much like to fulfil it.

"That is not for me to say. And anyway, he does not live here."

"Where does he live?"

"In Eden." She smiled at him, waiting for a response that, he guessed, she'd heard many times before.

He let his mouth drop open and widened his eyes.

"Eden? You mean…"

"It is our true home. Père Christophe founded Eden some years ago. A paradise, yes, but alas, for the moment merely an earthly one. In Brazil. Many of our Children—your cousins—live there with him, far from the corrupting influences of the world outside."

"But do you not wish you were there with him? In Eden?"

She looked out of the window, her eyes shining in the weak Autumn sunlight.

"Of course I do. But my place, for now, is England. We search out lost souls. There are so many in London. We have another house in Manhattan and one in Paris. One day, yes, I will join Père Christophe in Eden. But it is not my position to question his will. I serve him, that is all."

And that was indeed all. Having completed his file, she dismissed him. He returned to his allotted chore for the day, which was feeding the pigs that lived in a field on the estate. As he slopped the swill from the bucket into the silvery-grey, galvanised trough, he breathed in the aroma of vegetable peelings and yesterday's leftover apple crumble and custard. At least the Children were fed better now. They'd had roast pork, too.

The pigs jostled and shoved him out of the way to get to the food, and he moved off to one side, trying to figure out a plan. He'd assumed the cult leader would be based in the UK. That plan was simple: get in, kill him, forge or fabricate some damning evidence that would place him beyond the moral pale, and get out again, turning the remnants over to Don and his shrinks and deprogrammers at The Department. In a sudden flash of insight, he wondered whether that was how Don knew Fariyah. Perhaps she used to be a military psychiatrist. Lord knew there was enough material to work with, let alone all the PSYOPS shit the spooks were always talking about.

The grunting of the porkers was oddly soothing, and he stood there, watching his breath condense in the air around him, feeling his way towards Plan B.

35

ASK AND YE SHALL BE REWARDED

AS HE READ THE EMAIL from Aunt Christine in London, Jardin's pulse increased markedly. He could feel it behind his eyes and in the mysterious tubes in his ears, a rushing sound like when you put a seashell there, until your father swipes it from your grasp and tells you, "we've been at the beach all day, Christophe, it's time to go home and when are you ever going to grow up and stop daydreaming?"

From: AuntChristine@coh-anon-remailer.com
    Subject: A very special Child

Dear Père Christophe,

God be with you.

. . .

We have a new Child amongst us. His name is Gabriel Wolfe. You asked me to contact you if any new Children possessed certain skills. Gabriel does.

He is obedient and good. The Freeing and our initial prayer and devotional sessions with him have proved very effective. He sees himself as a servant of God through your will.

Awaiting your instructions, as always, with prayers in my heart for your continued good health,

Aunt Christine

He paused for a moment, the tips of his spidery fingers twitching. Then they scuttled over the keyboard, tapping out a short reply.

From: PereChristophe@coh-anon-remailer.com
    Subject: Re: A very special Child

Chère Aunt Christine,

You have done well.

Send him to me.

God be with you, always.

                          . . .

Père Christophe

36

SUMMONED TO EDEN

IN THE END, PLAN B came to Gabriel. After a meeting where the Children meditated and listened to a webcast from Père Christophe, the woman known as Aunt Christine crooked her finger at Gabriel as he was heading out of the ballroom. He walked over to join her, where she stood underneath a seven-by-four-foot portrait of one of the house's former owners, a Victorian industrialist, judging by his immense mutton chop whiskers, corpulent belly, and self-satisfied expression.

She was smiling as he approached.

"Child Gabriel, I have such exciting news for you."

"What is it Aunt Christine? A new job? I've grown to like the pigs."

"Oh, no, silly," she said, wagging her index finger. "After my last report to Père Christophe, he got back in touch with me. As I thought he would do," she added, with a wink. "It is such an honour. He has summoned you to join him in Eden."

"When? How? I don't have my passport with me or anything. After the Freeing, well, you know, I came here with nothing."

"You have leave to fetch it. We will provide your tickets and money and some essentials for your journey. Go to your room, change into your old clothes—they are there waiting for you. I have booked a taxi to take you to your home."

"But Aunt, I live, I mean lived, in Salisbury. That would be so expensive."

She smiled again. God, these people did a lot of smiling. "Don't worry about the cost. As Père Christophe teaches us, it is a grave mistake to imagine God and Mammon can't be reconciled. We are living proof. For did He not endow us with money as well as faith? Now, go. Be outside on the drive in ten minutes."

As he changed out of his cult-approved white garb, Gabriel wondered whether he'd be able to get a message to Don. Tell him the quarry was in Brazil and not in the UK at all. He'd no mobile any more, but the cottage still had its landline. Shit! Don's numbers —for his mobile and his offices in Whitehall and MOD Rothford— were all on his phone. And who bothered to remember people's numbers anymore? He had a couple of hours to think of something. Time to move.

He was downstairs and outside on the gravel drive five minutes later, just as a gleaming silver Jaguar XF saloon pulled up outside. "Apollo Executive Cars" read the green capitals along its doors. Below the name was a slogan, "Your comfort is our mission," and a Reading telephone number. He climbed in to the back and fastened the seat belt.

"Where to?" the young black driver asked, turning round in his seat to smile at Gabriel. "I'm Joseph, by the way."

"Salisbury, please, Joseph. Well, a village just outside. I'll give you directions when we get closer."

"No worries. You just relax. Like it says on the door. There's an iPad in the seat pocket in front of you if you want some entertainment. It's got a ton of games, and we've got Wi-Fi if you want the Internet. Do a little surfing, email, whatever."

"Thanks. Maybe I will." *Yes, thanks. Truly.*

As the Jaguar powered southwest, Gabriel retrieved the iPad and launched a browser. Then he realised he hadn't a clue what to type into the search engine. Somehow, he didn't think "The Department + contact us" would get him very far. Or, for that matter, "secret British government black ops". Then he had a brainwave.

He typed in the name of Don's club and up popped a basic name, address, and telephone listing. He leaned forward.

"Excuse me, I need to make a phone call. It's very important. Please, can I use your phone? It's just to a London number."

"Sure. Go ahead."

The driver held his phone out over his shoulder so Gabriel could take it. He dialled the number for the club and waited. When he'd almost given up hope, the call was answered. Gabriel spoke, aiming for a tone of voice that conveyed urgency without lunacy.

"Hello. I am a friend of Colonel Donald Webster. It is extremely important that I speak to him. I don't suppose he's at the club, is he?"

"I'm afraid, sir, we make a point of never revealing the whereabouts of our members. It's club policy."

Gabriel pictured some uniformed flunky enjoying keeping the riff raff away from the sanctum.

"And I totally understand that. I don't want to sound melodramatic, but it's a matter of national security."

"I see. May I ask, sir, what is your name?"

"It's Wolfe. Why? Did Don say I might call?"

"And, if I may, sir, what might one be referring to, if one talked of 'Don's Bombs'?"

"They were his jokes!" Gabriel said, sensing that his old boss was one step ahead of him, as usual. "In the mess. He used to crack us up. Even got the Queen once."

"Hold the line, please, sir."

Gabriel waited, heart pounding, listening to Vivaldi's *Four Seasons*, while the man on the other end presumably went off to make enquiries. Then there was a click and a buzz.

"Hello, Old Sport. Thought you'd gone off and left us."

"Oh, Jesus, Don. It's good to hear your voice. It was just a wild guess you'd be at your club."

"I'm not. George just patched you through. I'm with the PM, actually."

"Wow! I imagined those St James's clubs were still holding out against the march of technology."

"Oh, things have moved on a bit. And as you may have deduced already, I left instructions for what to do were you to make contact. So, how's the mission going? Have you identified the target yet? Or better still, have you taken him down?"

"Yes and no. Listen, I'm in a cab so I can't say much. They call him Père Christophe, so I'm guessing he's a French national. And get this: he's in Brazil. I've been summoned to meet him. In Eden."

"Ha! Might be a long flight."

"It's what he calls his base, or compound, or whatever. And the place I've been staying in is in Berkshire. It's called Elysium. A massive old Tudor pile with huge grounds. It'll probably be in some parish record under a different name. It's about twenty minutes due north of Reading."

"OK, that's fantastic intel. Proceed according to plan. If you can report in again, great. If not, don't worry. When you've completed the task, find a way out of there and get a message to me via George. Exfiltrate from Eden and set up an extract point, and we'll come and pull you out. I have to go. The PM's tapping her watch. She says hello, by the way. Good luck, Gabriel."

"Thanks, Don. Speak soon."

Gabriel returned the phone to the driver then leaned back in the seat and closed his eyes.

"Journalist, is it, boss?"

He opened his eyes again. "I'm sorry?"

"Journalist. You investigating those weirdos up at Elysium, are you?"

"Oh, yes. Yes, we're, er, doing an exposé on cults in the UK. You can keep a secret, can't you?"

"Me? Absolutely. 'Discretion comes as standard.' That's another one of our Guvnor's slogans. She's got loads. Like, 'Speed, safety, security.'"

"Security?"

"Yeah. We do some high-level stuff. You know, celebrities,

footballers, that kind of thing? She only hires ex-forces or ex-police for drivers on account of we've got what it takes."

"Which are you?"

"Forces. Five years in the Rifles. Took a bullet in the shoulder, got my honourable discharge."

"Well, like I said, if you could keep it on the QT, I'd appreciate it."

"No problem."

An hour and a half later, they pulled up in Gabriel's drive. He hadn't seen his cottage for ten days, but it felt like he'd been away longer. The bombing, the police investigation, tracking down Eloise Payne's family, joining the Children of Heaven … had that all really happened in under a fortnight?

He entered the four-digit code in the key safe screwed to the wall beside the kitchen door, extracted the key and let himself in, reflecting on the fact that so many of the cult's other recruits must never see their homes again. Did they just leave them unoccupied until either their landlord took them back, or the bank or building society repossessed them for non-payment of the mortgage?

He fetched his passport from his office filing cabinet and came back through to the kitchen. He was just about to leave when a niggling worry about the taxi driver prodded his anxiety circuit into life. Supposing discretion didn't come as standard? Supposing the driver served two masters? Not God and Mammon, but his boss at Apollo and one of the Aunts or Uncles at Elysium? Snatching the landline receiver from its cradle, he redialled the number for Don's club. The same man answered.

"Is that George? It's Gabriel Wolfe again."

Yes, sir. How can I help you?"

"I need to get this message to Colonel Webster. Are you ready?"

"Absolutely, sir. Fire away."

"There's an executive cab company in Reading. They're called Apollo. They have a black driver called Joseph. He may need to be removed from circulation for a while."

Gabriel concluded his message with the registration number of the Jaguar and then ended the call. He was back in the car a minute or two after that and drifting off to sleep, earbuds in, Ella Fitzgerald singing to him of backyard blues as the car merged with traffic on the A303 dual carriageway heading back to Elysium.

"Sir? Boss? We're here."

Gabriel woke with a start. Someone had been calling to him while he sank to the bottom of a lake, green water all around him, and the word "Gable" echoing in his ears.

The Jaguar sat, idling, outside the front door of Elysium. He thanked the driver, got out and made his way inside to find Aunt Christine.

37

WHERE THE NUTS COME FROM

GABRIEL'S PREVIOUS TRANSATLANTIC FLIGHT HAD been in the company of an extremely rich and unpleasant man he was pretending to work for called Sir Toby Maitland. They had at least travelled First Class. On this flight, Gabriel was in the rear of the plane. The Children of Heaven could afford to live in Eden, but apparently, a certain amount of self-mortification was required before you got there.

The fat businessman next to him spent the first ten minutes of the flight getting himself comfortable, which seemed to involve jabbing Gabriel in the ribs and arm every fifteen seconds or so. As the man huffed and puffed, Gabriel began to fantasise about the best way to kill him and dispose of the body without being discovered.

"Bloody seats," the man said, shuffling his immense bottom from side to side and pressing his warm flesh up against Gabriel's right hip. "I swear they're getting smaller."

Because that's more likely than you getting fatter, you big oaf. Why don't you try going easier on the expense-account lunches instead?

"And for a man in your shape, that's got to make a deep vein thrombosis a racing certainty, hasn't it?" Gabriel said.

The man stared at him open-mouthed, then opened a copy of Forbes magazine with a snap and buried himself in its pages.

Twenty-six hours and fifty minutes later, Gabriel was standing outside the arrivals lounge at Brigadeiro Eduardo Gomes—Manaus International Airport, having transferred onto an internal flight at Rio de Janeiro International Airport. It had been sunny, warm, and humid as he emerged from the air-conditioned vault inside the airport terminal. But then a squally wind had arrived from the direction of distant, tree-covered hills, and with it bruised-looking clouds of charcoal and purple. The wind whipped his thin jacket against his chest and stinging drops of freezing rain beat against his face. Now what? He realised he had no firm idea of how he was to reach Eden, beyond an assurance from Aunt Christine that he would be taken care of by Père Christophe.

Amid the endless procession of yellow and green taxis—old American models mostly, Ford Crown Victorias dominant among them—a white Range Rover hove into view. It towered above the cabs as it bore down on Gabriel. The huge car pulled up next to him. The front passenger window slid down and a young woman in a white T-shirt leaned over and smiled at him through the opening.

"Gabriel?" she asked, though it was clear she already knew.

"That's me," he said, bending to pick up his bag.

"Jump in!"

He did as he was told and found himself in close proximity to surely one of the most beautiful women he had ever seen. Her russet hair was cut short, like all the other Children of Heaven women he'd met in England, both in Sloane Square and Elysium. On her, it framed her face, which was almond-shaped, and concentrated his gaze onto her mouth, which was wide and full-lipped. She had light caramel-coloured skin that offered a soft contrast to her bright green eyes. A tiny bump on the bridge of her nose only accentuated her good looks.

"I'm Eve," she said, flashing a brilliant smile at him and offering her hand.

"Eve," he said. "And you live in Eden."

"I know, right?" she said with a grin. "My job's tending the apple tree. Ha! Just kidding."

She spoke with an American accent, somewhere on the West Coast to judge from the lazy vowel sounds. The silent interior of the Range Rover smelled of her: a musky perfume of fresh sweat and clean hair. He inhaled deeply and let the molecules of scent activate pleasure circuits deep inside his brain. He smiled, the first time he'd felt like it since speaking to Don.

"Where are we going?" he asked her.

"Hold on," she said, swinging the car around a taxi that had just pulled up sharply in front of her and giving him a good blast on the horn, "OK. Yeah, so we need to get to another airport. Well, airfield, really. It's a little commercial place out in the boonies, and we fly from there to Eden. We have our own landing strip."

"OK, cool. I hope you have decent showers, too, because I'm starting to feel a little too human for my own good."

She looked over at him. "God, you English and your accents. I swear I could listen to you read the phone book. Anyway, yes, we have showers. All mod cons."

"So what about your accent? You're American?"

"San Diego, born and bred."

"And how come you joined the Children of Heaven?"

She glanced over at him, then back to eyes front.

"How does anyone? My life sucked. My stepdad, like, totally abused me from pretty much day one after he moved in with my mom. I was ten when it began. Hadn't even started my periods. She wouldn't do anything. Told me I was a liar and a slut. I got into a bad scene, staying out at night, running with the wrong kids, you know? Starting doing this …" she held her right forearm out to show him a now-familiar ladder of thin white scars, "… then doing drugs. On the day before my sixteenth birthday, my stepdad is like, 'I got you something real special, for once you're a woman,' and he's leering at me. I know he's gonna rape me, 'cause up until then, he's just been touching me, you know, with his fingers. Or getting me to touch him. Next thing I know, I'm standing on the edge of the

Coronado Bridge thinking about just letting go when this woman calls out to me. She says, and I will always remember this, 'God loves you, child. God loves you, even if nobody else does.' So I climb down and I take her hand." She looked across at Gabriel, her face serene where he thought she'd be angry or in tears. "At that moment, I left my old life behind."

"Wow! I'm sorry I put you through that. I was just making conversation." Gabriel ran a hand over his head and scratched the back of his neck.

"Hey, no problem," she said, smiling brightly again. "We leave our negative energy at the door when we enter Eden, right? That's what Père Christophe teaches us. And here's a funny thing. When I was shopping in Nova Cidade—that's our nearest town—I saw a newspaper. We don't have them at Eden, but it's sort of allowed if you peek at one in a bookstore or a gas station. My stepdad? He was killed by a minivan a month after I arrived here. A hit and run, right outside their house. Who knew? It was, like, divine retribution. So, how about you? What's your story?"

"Me? Oh, you know, I lost my way, I guess, after the Army. Started wondering what I'd been fighting for. Then I went to a meeting at the place in Sloane Square. Do you know it?"

She shook her head. "Not really. I mean, I know we've got other places outside of Brazil, but I've been here for the last five years straight. Never want to leave. Père Christophe's, like, so cool. As long as you follow the First Order, you know?"

"Serve God through Père Christophe's will?"

"That's the one! And, I mean, we all do, right? From morning prayers right through to bedtime. I just hope one day he gives me the Second Order."

"What's that?" Gabriel said.

"Didn't they teach you that in England, yet? Maybe you got invited out here before they had the chance. OK, so the Second Order is the ultimate test of your devotion. There are so many evil forces in the world, Gabriel. That's what Père Christophe teaches us every day. Governments, big corporations, trade unions, organised crime, law enforcement agencies, universities, the UN, NATO:

they're all a massive international conspiracy. Even the so-called world religions are in on it."

OK, here it comes, the nut at the centre of the cake. "In on what?"

"Trying to prevent ordinary people from touching God, of course! I mean, look at us, right? No possessions, no property, no stabbing each other in the back to climb some corporate greasy pole. Just love for God. That's a subversive message, Gabriel, it really is. Père Christophe teaches that if everyone was just allowed to love God, they'd stop buying all that worthless stuff and cluttering up their lives with fear and hatred. All the drug companies peddling their tranquillisers and antidepressants? They'd go out of business overnight."

"Oh, yeah. I mean, of course. That's what's really wrong with the world. The conspiracy."

"Exactly! So, like, the Second Order is when Père Christophe asks you to give your life for God. 'Give your life to cleanse the world of sin,' is, like, the official version. He doesn't want to do it, on account of, obviously, you're leaving him, and he loves you so much, but he knows even he has to submit to God's will. It's such an honour, when you go to your glorification. And then you're there, actually there, in heaven, with God. One of the chosen. Père Christophe says in the end we'll all have to follow the Second Order, and we'll be reunited in God's love. Till then, we just obey Père Christophe in all things."

She smiled at him again and patted him twice, lightly, on the thigh.

"So, have many of us received the Second Order? I mean, here, in Eden?" he asked.

"Wow, you ask a ton of questions. But, yeah, six this year. It's not, like, an everyday thing, you know? But there is a lot of sin that needs burning out of this world."

Gabriel had a sudden flashback: a burning tangle of twisted, blackened metal, draped with body parts, and ball bearings rolling to a stop in pools of blood. He clamped his lips together to stop himself saying anything.

They turned off the main road into a little industrial estate—just a handful of workshops with smashed up cars outside and a few warehouses—and drove along an access road that snaked through the buildings. As the Range Rover emerged from between the last two warehouses, Gabriel gasped. Ahead of them was nothing but hundreds of miles of forest, stretching into the distance in bands of green that lightened progressively with each range of hills. Directly in front of them was a hangar, its massive doors open to reveal a handful of small, white planes including a couple of twin-prop models with space for maybe six passengers apiece. The airfield was just that: a close-cropped landing strip of grass, maybe a third of mile long and a couple of hundred feet across.

Eve killed the engine and unbuckled her seat belt. "I'm going to find José; he's our pilot. Have a look around if you like, but stay where we can find you, OK?"

"Sure, you're the boss."

She flashed him another dazzling smile and walked back towards the hangar. Her white shorts and T-shirt did amazing things for her, not least revealing most of her smooth, brown skin. As he watched her disappear into the hangar, he noticed a small group of people checking parachutes. Members of a club, presumably. Nice place for that kind of hobby. Gabriel thought back to his early days in the Parachute Regiment. All those hundreds of jumps. Everybody had their favourite, but his was the LALO—Low Altitude Low Opening. A burst of wind in his face as he left the plane at around six hundred feet, then he yanked the ripcord and was down before he'd had time to take in the scenery. No time to deploy his reserve chute if the main chute failed. A real death or glory jump.

The weather had settled after the earlier squall. It was hot again, but the humidity had gone. There was a light breeze blowing towards him and he stood facing into it, feeling the sweat evaporate off his face and arms. The place smelled of aviation fuel and the heady perfume of a huge flowering vine smothered in dark purple blossoms that sprawled over the corner of the hangar and along a low breeze-block wall that ran away from it at right angles. Gabriel went to sit on the wall. He closed his eyes and took a deep breath in, then let it out through his open mouth. Rotating his head on his neck he took the moment of quiet to prepare for his inevitable meeting with the man who had summoned him here, to a cult compound in the depths of the rainforest in Amazonas State. Questions. And answers.

Who are you? I am Child Gabriel.

Why did you join the Children of Heaven? Nothing in my life made sense any more.

What is the First Order? Do God's bidding through you, Père Christophe.

Are you a spy? Or a journalist? No. I am, I was, lost. Now I am found.

Would you give your life for me? For God? I would do anything for you, Père Christophe. Especially help you on your way to meet Him.

38

TARGET ACQUIRED

A CALL FROM EVE ROUSED Gabriel from his meditation. She'd shouted his name and when he opened his eyes, he saw her walking back towards him and waving. He levered himself off the wall, its surface rough under his fingertips, suddenly aware of a great fatigue dragging at his muscles, and went to join her in front of the hangar.

"José's basically ready to leave. He says the weather's OK. It's the Cessna with GZ108 on the side, the one nearest the door." She pointed to the plane. "Come on. I bet you can't wait to meet Père Christophe."

"You're right, I can't. It feels like I'm meeting someone I was always meant to connect with."

"That is so weird. That is *exactly* how I felt."

Ten minutes later, they were flying fifteen hundred feet over the rainforest. Below them, the Rio Negro twined through the millions of trees, a silver ribbon woven into a tapestry of emerald, sage, lime, light, dark, pea, mint—more shades of green than Gabriel had thought possible. Beside him, Eve sat silently, her eyes closed, her lips moving. Praying, he guessed. For guidance, maybe. Or else she was just a nervous flyer. But the little plane was stable, not even a bump from clear-air turbulence or a slewing dip from a crosswind. He enjoyed flying in light planes and he craned his neck to see the river beneath them. At one point, it widened out into a lake, maybe a few hundred yards long, and he could see alligators, or crocodiles, massed in the shallows, their long, dark bodies recognisable from a thousand nature documentaries. There wouldn't be much left of you if you ended up dumped in their dining room. Nothing at all, in fact.

Thirty minutes' more flying brought them directly over Eden. Gabriel realised he'd been expecting something akin to a large farmhouse and maybe a couple of acres of land around it. As José banked the plane round to give him the tour it became clear just how vast this jungle paradise really was. How did you get to own that much land out here? Who did you have to bribe? And with what?

Eden's airfield was another strip of mown grass with a corrugated iron hangar abutting it and a prefabricated office building off to one side. José brought the Cessna in for a perfect three-point landing, and a few minutes after that, Eve and Gabriel were inside the office waiting for their lift to the village in the centre of the cult's land, named The Heart of Eden.

The ride into The Heart of Eden wasn't quite as pleasant as their air-conditioned trip in the Range Rover. This was a beaten-up, old, American Jeep that looked as if it had first seen active service in Korea, if not World War II. Its olive-green paintwork was giving way to rust, and there were numerous bullet holes in the bodywork. The driver was a young man Eve introduced as Child Soren. He was Danish, with blonde hair and bright, pale-blue eyes. He drove skilfully, but the Jeep's failing suspension was no match for the ruts in the track that led from the airfield to the village. Eve had her left hand clamped to the open side of the car; her right was squeezing Gabriel's left forearm.

Five minutes of bouncing into and out of potholes and juddering across the corrugated red earth brought them to the centre of the village. A cluster of adobe huts with colourful fabrics in the windows faced a central square that also housed a larger building with a huge wooden cross outside—some sort of meeting hall or church, Gabriel assumed. Behind the square, down a beaten-flat, earth path, stood an imposing, single-storey, timber-framed building. Dismounting from the Jeep and shouldering his bag, Gabriel wondered whether this was the dwelling of Père Christophe.

His suspicions were confirmed when a man with long, greyish-blond hair and matching beard and moustache came out of the house's front door and waved to him.

"Look," Eve said, nudging Gabriel in the ribs. "It's Père Christophe. He's come to greet you personally.

The man Gabriel had been sent to kill ambled down the path towards him. He held Gabriel's gaze the whole way, like a snake approaching its prey, and walked so slowly it took him a full minute to close the thirty yards between them. As he got closer, Gabriel used the time to study his target. Jardin wasn't tall, an inch or so shorter than Gabriel. His build was slight, though as a breeze blew his loose white robe against his torso, neatly defined abdominal muscles became briefly visible. *You work out, then.*

Arriving, finally, in front of Gabriel, he held his arms wide. Gabriel stepped into the embrace, letting himself slump against the older man, and relaxing his own muscles. Jardin kissed him on both cheeks, then held him by the biceps, at arm's length. He had thin, delicate, pianist's fingers tipped with long nails that gave his hands the appearance of claws. His face was disfigured with deep, pitted acne scars on his cheeks. His eyes, still burning into Gabriel's, were an unsettling deep purplish-blue, and his nose was straight and classically fine.

"Child Gabriel," he said, speaking English in a breathy voice still coloured by his upbringing in Paris. "Welcome to Eden. Aunt Christine told me of your background. You were sent by God to me, and I am grateful."

Feeling that some sort of obeisance was required, Gabriel sank to his knees and kissed the other man's sandaled foot, whispering, "Père Christophe, you are my saviour". He stayed down, counting the hairs on the big toe and wondering whether he had overdone it, until Jardin more or less hauled him to his feet again, a flicker of a grin chasing itself off his thin lips.

"Come now, my child. I am nobody's saviour. I am just a lowly messenger, a servant of God." He turned to Eve, who was standing, entranced, her green eyes glistening. "And you, Child Eve. Thank you for bringing Child Gabriel to us. Your flight, it was not too frightening?"

She looked down, but he lifted her chin with a delicate grip of thumb and forefinger.

"It was fine, Père Christophe. I was much less frightened than last time."

"Good, good. We will cure you of your phobia yet. Now, I wish to spend some time with Child Gabriel, alone, so forgive us. I am sure you have chores to attend to."

She smiled at him. "Of course, Père Christophe. And yes, I mean, I have chores. It is my turn to help prepare the evening meal."

"Very good. God be with you." He waved her way with a languid flap of his hand, his attention focused entirely on Gabriel. "Come, then, Child Gabriel. I have many questions I want to ask of you."

They walked back up the path together, Jardin placing his arm across Gabriel's shoulder. All around was the sound of birdsong. Not the garden birds familiar to Gabriel from his life in rural Wiltshire. These were louder, brasher, more strident calls, and exotic songs full of trills and fluting sounds. He looked up just as a flight of half a dozen blue and yellow macaws clattered out of a palm tree and swooped into the branches of another on the other side of the village.

Inside the timber house, the air was at least thirty degrees cooler than the temperature outside. Gabriel shivered as gooseflesh prickled along his arms and over his chest. The entrance hall was dark after the bright sunlight outside, and Gabriel's eyes took a few moments to adjust to the gloom. Jardin steered him by the elbow into a room at the far end of the corridor. Another adjustment was needed, psychological this time, rather than visual. It was a huge room, lined with books, CDs and, in the spaces between the rows of floor-to-ceiling shelves, some extremely valuable works of art. Gabriel would make no claims to scholarship in matters cultural, but he recognised a couple of the works as being by Andy Warhol and another as one of Picasso's paintings of his muse, Dora Maar.

Jardin watched as Gabriel turned a full circle, taking in the magnificence of his surroundings compared to the rudimentary architecture and fittings of the adobe huts outside. He was smiling and stroking his beard as Gabriel returned his gaze to his own.

"What are you thinking, Child Gabriel?" he asked.

"That God truly has smiled on you, his servant, Père Christophe. The paintings are exquisite." He pointed to the Picasso. "Is that a Renoir?"

Jardin snorted. "A Renoir? Do they teach you nothing in that country of yours? Such philistines. No, that is by the master himself, Pablo Picasso. Now, sit there and relax and let me bring you some tea."

He pointed to a vast sofa piled with silk-covered cushions in shades of rust and gold. Gabriel sat, grateful both for the rest and the chance to conduct a fast situational analysis while Jardin was out of the room. Standing beside the sofa was a three-foot-high sculpture of a naked woman, cast in bronze from what appeared to be an assemblage of thumb-sized lumps of clay. She was as slender as a baseball bat. He caressed the top of her head and took an experimental grip around her elongated neck. Could he beat the man to death and begin the clean-up operation before he'd even had a meal in Eden? He stood and picked up the sculpture, hefting it in his hands. No. No martyrs; that was Don's order. A straightforward bludgeoning would definitely create one. He replaced the sculpture on the floor and resumed his seat.

Jardin reappeared at this moment with two yellow gourds, each the size of a grapefruit, with wisps of water vapour curling off the liquid within. Silver straws rested against matching silver rims. He gave one to Gabriel, who looked down at a floating mat of beige leaves, and took his own to sit at the other end of the sofa, where he twisted round to face Gabriel.

"This is *chimarrão*," he said. "Elsewhere in Latin America, they use the Spanish name *yerba mate*. It will perk you up a little. I know you have had a long day."

Gabriel bent his head and sucked on the silver straw. The hot liquid that spurted into his mouth made him first wince, then gasp. The flavour was an unpleasant combination of wood smoke, dried grass, and very weak coffee. Almost instantly, he felt his pulse pick up and settle at an elevated rate of maybe eighty or eighty-five. He broke out in a sweat and put the gourd down on a side table to wipe his forehead.

"It's very strong," he said, as the blood rushed in his ears and his heart jumped and stuttered in his chest.

"Caffeine. Lots of it. Some say it has a bigger hit than amphetamines … for the uninitiated. Now," Jardin said, putting his own gourd down, untouched, "tell me, Child Gabriel, why did you really join the Children of Heaven?"

Gabriel tried to formulate an answer, but something was wrong with his tongue. It seemed to have swollen inside his mouth and he couldn't get it to move. Jardin's face was blurring then swinging back into focus. He tried again and heard a stranger's voice as if through a thin hotel bedroom wall, "I was in crisis. I was lost. I felt life had no purpose." He'd rehearsed the mantra thousands of times on the flight from Heathrow to the airport in Rio.

"Really," Jardin said, not even trying to conceal the contempt in his voice. "How unfortunate for you. Was the security business not fulfilling your spiritual needs?"

39

EXPOSED ...

"WHA-WHAT YOU MEAN, SECURITY BUSINESS?" Gabriel said, trying to steady himself by gripping the armrest of the sofa and aware, as he stared at Jardin, that red light didn't normally emanate from people's eyes.

"Wolfe and Cunningham. Your business card. Very nice website by the way. Very ... professional."

"But we, in the fire. Everything. We freed ourselves from, you know. Everything."

"Yes, you did. And when you left the ceremony, we extinguished the flames to check your identities. Running a cult leaves one open to prying from all kinds of undesirable people."

Gabriel could feel his heart hammering in his chest. It took on a samba rhythm as Jardin's face wavered in front of him.

"I don't feel well, Père Christophe."

"That would be your *chimarrão*. I prepared it slightly differently from mine. *Yerba mate*, yes, and just a dash of sodium thiopental supplied by a friend of mine. It's what they call a truth drug. Now, once again. Why did you join the Children of Heaven?"

"To kill you. Because of the bus bomb." Gabriel giggled as he said this, but Jardin wasn't smiling.

"Who do you work for?" Jardin said, standing up and leaning towards Gabriel to stare into his eyes from a hand's breadth away.

"Don Webster. Who do you work for?" Gabriel laughed again.

"Who is Don Webster?"

"He runs The Department. You know," Gabriel put his finger to his lips and *shushed* loudly, "getting rid of bad people. Like you."

Jardin stood back. "Thank you, Child Gabriel. You have been of great service. But that is nothing compared to the duties I have planned for you."

Then he picked up the same statuette Gabriel had been hefting just a few minutes earlier, swung it back, and brought it round in an arc that ended at a point on the side of Gabriel's head.

40

... AND ALONE

THE ROOM WAS A CUBE. Its walls were painted white. There were no windows, although there was a six-inch diameter circle of tiny holes drilled into a corner of the ceiling. No furniture, either. It smelled of disinfectant.

Gabriel fell asleep again on the hard mud floor.

He dreamt of Britta Falskog. Her red hair streamed behind her as she swam, naked, in the Amazon, among grinning crocodiles.

Wake up, Gabriel, she said.

He tried to sit up, but the explosion of agony in his left temple put him down onto the floor again, groaning and suppressing a wave of intense nausea. He fought to stay awake, but the heavy, sweaty blanket of confusion that surrounded him muffled his consciousness once again. He slept.

At some point he wet himself. The next time he surfaced, the stink, and the cold, clammy feeling of his thin cotton trousers, finally broke whatever spell he'd been under.

His throat was dry, and he was overtaken by a fit of hacking, dry coughs that made him retch as his empty stomach churned.

He sat up. Then he stood up. Taking slow, even paces, he measured the floor. Eight feet by eight.

There was a door, but it had no handle on the inside. He backed up and charged at the rectangular outline in the white wall. Apart from bruising his shoulder, he achieved nothing. Or not nothing, precisely. His awareness flickered back into life, fully active, and fully aware of the utter shit he'd got himself into.

A single, bright bulb burned in the centre of the ceiling, suspended from a short length of white, plastic-sheathed flex.

Gabriel ran his fingers along the edges of the floor, around the outline of the door and as high on the corners between the walls as he could manage. Nothing. A master carpenter couldn't have made cleaner or smoother joints.

He slumped to the floor, his back wedged into a corner.

Fuck! I need a plan.

"Maybe I can help," Smudge said, from the opposite corner. His customary, jawless smile was absent for once, though his face still looked unstable, as if a sudden movement might dislodge the flesh from the skull beneath.

"Any and all suggestions gratefully received," Gabriel said, aware, as he spoke, that his former comrade was nothing more than a PTSD-induced phantasm.

"You're not going to fight your way out of here, Boss. But you're not dead, either. He could have killed you with another whack from that sculpture. So he wants you alive. That's your Get Out of Jail Free card. Everything else, you have to play by ear."

"Good enough, Trooper," Gabriel said. "Now fuck off and leave me in peace, will you?"

He blinked, and the ghost of Smudge Smith was gone.

That was when the music started.

Gabriel's tastes in music were wide-ranging. Jazz and old-time blues were his natural home, but he enjoyed classical music, rock, so-called 'world music,' anything that happened to move him. This did not extend to German 'oom-pah' music. As the tubas, trumpets, and bass drums began their assault, he hunkered down into a corner and shoved his fingers in his ears.

. . .

Three hours later, as the boisterous musicians began again on their waltz-time serenade, he curled into a foetal position and began to cry.

Three hours after that, he began to scream.

Two hours after that, he passed out, whether from hunger, dehydration, or fatigue no doctor would have been able to pronounce.

Britta stood before him, water running over her freckled breasts. She swept her long coppery hair behind her ears and squeezed the water out. Three parallel slits on each side of her neck gaped obscenely, their fringed red interiors pulsing as she drew oxygen into her lungs.

"Listen to me, Gabriel Wolfe," she said. "I didn't come all this way to watch you give up. So get off your arse and give me ten, soldier!"

He opened his eyes. The music had stopped. He flattened himself against the whitewashed floor and executed ten very poor press-ups. His arms almost buckled after five and he had to use his knees to finish the pathetic set. With his biceps and triceps quivering, and his breath heaving in his chest, he flopped to the floor and lay there, knowing that whatever was going to happen next, he was going to fight with every sinew and breath to regain control.

The door opened, banging back against the wall. A man stood there. He was tall, dressed all in white. He was heavily built, muscular arms hanging loosely by his sides. Maybe twenty, twenty-one. He looked like a college football player. He bent and grabbed Gabriel by the arms and hauled him to his feet.

"Come with me," he said, in a flat, emotionless voice.

He dragged Gabriel out of the room, down a white-painted hallway, and pushed him through a door into another white room. This one was larger. A single, empty wooden chair faced a row of seven others, each occupied by a white-garbed acolyte of Père Christophe. Their faces were, variously, stern, bland or amused, smiles here and there, but no intensity of emotion that might yield a clue as to what was about to happen.

The young man forced Gabriel down onto the empty chair, then left, closing the door behind him with a soft click from the latch.

"Are you thirsty, Child Gabriel?" the young woman in the centre of the row of chairs facing him asked. She was tall, with an athletic build, her ropy arm muscles corded with thick veins under the skin. He noticed rows of punctures in both ears, all the way around the edge from the lobes upwards. There were matching dots in both nostrils and under her lower lip.

"Yes," he croaked, breaking at once into a dry, heaving cough that lasted for almost a minute.

"Here," she said, proffering a bottle of water that had been standing on the floor by one of the rear legs of her chair.

He leaned forward and grabbed it, breaking the seal on the lid and swigging half of the precious fluid in one go before pausing to gasp for air, then returning the neck of the bottle to his cracked lips and finishing it.

"Thank you," he said.

"You're welcome. Now, let's begin. Repeat after me, 'I am a liar'."

Gabriel looked into her eyes, a beautiful shade of brown, or maybe that green-brown they call hazel. Her eyelashes were thick and dark. He said nothing.

She glanced to her left, at a heavyset young man with black hair cut close to his scalp. He looked like the US Marines Gabriel had occasionally fought alongside, impassive but utterly confident of his abilities.

The man stood and closed the distance between his chair and Gabriel's in two long strides. He whipped out his right hand and delivered a ringing slap to Gabriel's left cheek that knocked him to the floor. A thick band of silver on his middle finger raised a white welt on Gabriel's cheekbone.

"Child Thaddeus is an instrument of God," the woman said. "Each blow he strikes causes him intense suffering. I will have to counsel him later. You would not want his suffering on your conscience, would you? Repeat after me, 'I am a liar'."

After the tenth, or the twentieth, time she instructed him to repeat her words, Gabriel's face was running freely with blood. Thaddeus's ring had opened several deep cuts on his cheek and the pain was the only thing keeping Gabriel from passing out with exhaustion.

Britta tapped him on the shoulder. *"Yield, soldier,"* she said. *"This isn't the battle to win."* Then she bent to kiss his mangled face, and disappeared.

"I am a liar," he said.

They let him sleep after this, his first confession. Two whole hours. Then they brought him back to the room with the chairs. The Children facing him were different. The routine was the same. This time his reward for compliance was a meal. A bowl of rice and some small fatty pieces of meat.

Over the next month, Gabriel Wolfe was subjected to a regime of shouting, finger-pointing, chanting, a continuing restricted diet, long periods of solitary confinement in the white cube room, and sleep deprivation. In the early days, his SAS training and long years of instruction by Master Zhao helped him withstand the cult's brainwashing. During the time they left him alone in the windowless cell, he practised his own meditation, repeating the mantra, "Alone on the landscape, always strong". Smudge and Britta added their own messages of support from time to time, and he began to have long conversations with each of them during the rare moments when his tormentors let him be.

"You are losing weight, Child Gabriel," one of the young

women said to him, as he sat facing her one, what? Morning? Evening? "Here." She held out a bar of chocolate.

He grabbed it from her and crammed half of it into his mouth at once. At the intense hit of sweet, creamy flavour, tears formed in the corners of his eyes and rolled down his cheeks to mingle with the smears of melted chocolate around his mouth.

"Thank you, Child Britta," he mumbled.

She frowned. "I am Child Yasmin. But it is Père Christophe you must thank. Look." She pointed to the door.

It was him. Père Christophe was standing there, smiling down at Gabriel. He walked over and laid a soft hand on Gabriel's shoulder as he finished the rest of the chocolate.

"I love you, Child Gabriel," he said, looking down into Gabriel's upturned face.

"I love you, too, Père Christophe."

The Children applauded at these words.

The next session began with a bottle of water, without Gabriel's having to earn it. As the water entered his stomach, the purified extract of what the Brazilian Indians called *caapi*, and their cousins across the Peruvian border called *ayahuasca*, delivered its harmala alkaloid molecules into his bloodstream. Propelled like bullets by Gabriel's elevated pulse, they crossed his blood-brain barrier about forty-five seconds later. He retched and fell to his knees, vomiting up a thin stream of water and half-digested rice. The Children sat, unmoving, watching his spasms. When he finally stopped and slumped unconscious to the floor, they left.

Père Christophe was talking. A beautiful, deep voice that seemed to come from inside Gabriel's mind.

"See how the condor flies, Child Gabriel. See how she soars."

"I see her, Père Christophe."

"She is coming for you."

The huge bird landed between them, spread its wings and enveloped Gabriel in the soft black silk of its feathers.

"She will protect you, Child Gabriel, when you carry out my Second Order. When you give your life for me."

"She will protect me, Père Christophe."

The bird smiled down at Gabriel. She had soft, slanted eyes. Like his mother's. Dark brown.

Then she spoke.

"Père Christophe is good. Père Christophe is love. He loves you more than I ever could, Gabriel. Do you love Père Christophe?"

"Yes, Mum. I do. I love Père Christophe."

"Good boy. Now, come, I want to show you something."

She held him tightly as she spread her great wings and took to the blazing blue vault of the heavens, sweeping her wings in huge, whispering beats that seemed to echo the sound of Père Christophe's voice.

He smiled, eyes closed, as he rested against her, taking in the vast tract of rainforest below, with its golden threads of rivers.

"You love Père Christophe," she said.

"I love Père Christophe."

"You love Père Christophe."

"I love Père Christophe."

A hundred times the condor said it.

A hundred times he repeated it.

A thousand.

A million.

Until the end of time and the edge of space, the beautiful bird flew with him safe in her embrace.

"I love Père Christophe," he said.

It was true.

Then the condor began speaking her name to him. Over and over again. And with it a command.

41

A TEST OF FAITH

HIS BRAINWASHING COMPLETE, GABRIEL was led to a small hut in the centre of the village by one of the female Children. She tucked him up in a narrow single bed, beneath a blanket woven from coarse, thick wool in a pattern of red, brown, and cream stripes.

Every four hours, one of the Children would look in on him and report back to their Aunt or Uncle.

On the eighth visit, Gabriel stirred as the young woman was about to leave. She turned and went to sit beside him on the edge of the bed. Wincing with pain, he levered himself up onto his elbows.

"Child Gabriel," she said, softly. "How are you feeling?"

He looked up into her pale blue eyes.

"Who are you? Am I dead?"

She smiled. "No, you are alive. You are in Eden. I am Child Rebecca. We are all Père Christophe's Children."

At the mention of Père Christophe, Gabriel relaxed and slumped back onto his pillow. "I love Père Christophe. He sent me with the condor."

"I love him, too," she said. "Come, he wants to see you."

"I will serve God through Père Christophe's will. It's the First Order."

"Yes, it is," she said, then laughed, a light sound that made Gabriel think of someone he once knew. He couldn't remember her name. It didn't matter. Only Père Christophe mattered.

Ten minutes later, he was sitting in Père Christophe's living room, sipping tea from a white china mug and eating a bowl of fruit salad. His saviour spoke.

"Gabriel, I am so glad you joined our family. I have such plans for you. The angels will smile when they meet you, for you have a divine purpose here at Eden."

Gabriel finished the mouthful of sweetly scented papaya and guava, spiked with fresh lime juice, and put his spoon down.

"How can I serve God? Please tell me."

Père Christophe smiled and stroked his beard, then stood. "All in good time, my Child. But first, God wants to be sure of your faith. Have you finished your breakfast?"

Gabriel slurped up the last of the juice in the bowl, gulped down his tea, and got to his feet. "Where are we going?"

"To meet someone. Someone who will test your faith. Come, walk with me."

Together, they left the house and crossed the village square, leaving between a pair of adobe huts painted in bright shades of turquoise and rose pink.

"It's a beautiful day, is it not?" Père Christophe said. "You can smell a change in the air." He sniffed loudly. "A change in the seasons and in man's fortunes."

Gabriel followed his example and inhaled deeply. "I can smell wood smoke, Père Christophe. What are we burning?"

"Oh, I have some friends visiting. They are building a workshop for us. Where we can pursue God's work."

"That is good. You have many friends, Père Christophe."

They walked on, along a grassy path cut through the forest, until they emerged into a small clearing. In its centre were two older men and a young woman. They all smiled as Père Christophe and Gabriel approached. The young woman's eyes were heavy-lidded, and her smile was a little lopsided. The men were holding her by her arms. She swayed between them.

"Child Gabriel, these are your Uncles Joseph and Samuel. And this is Child Elinor. She is your test of faith."

"What should I do? Are we going to pray together?"

"No. Not pray. I have given Child Elinor the Second Order, and I wish you to carry it out for me. You know how to take a life, I think?"

"I do."

"Then place your hands around her throat and take hers. For me."

The young woman looked at Gabriel and spoke.

"I have been chosen for my glorification. I am grateful to Père Christophe. Thank you, Child Gabriel."

Then she shook herself free of the two older men and closed the gap between them in two unsteady paces.

Gabriel smiled back at her and encircled her slender neck with his hands.

Above them, a howler monkey boomed out a call and was answered by shrieks and hoots from its rivals.

Gabriel began to squeeze, digging his thumbs into the soft flesh just above the notch in Child Elinor's throat.

He looked down into her eyes, which were beginning to bulge from their sockets. Tiny carmine flares erupted in the whites as their oxygen supply was choked off.

Her mouth opened and her tongue, a darkish purple, poked out. She was on her knees now. And he leaned over her, maintaining the pressure around her neck, observing the whiteness around his knuckles.

Death was close now, but he knew better than to let go.

A minute more.

Just to be safe.

42

BLESSED ARE THE BOMB MAKERS

CHILD ELINOR WAS ALMOST DEAD. Faint gurglings were the only sounds to escape her stretched lips. Gabriel stood over her, staring down into her bloodshot eyes as he choked the life out of her to please Père Christophe.

"Enough!" It was Père Christophe who shouted this command. "Release her, Child Gabriel."

Gabriel relaxed his grip around the young woman's throat, and she collapsed onto her side, gasping and weeping as she filled her lungs. Her throat was marred by an ugly circlet of dark purple bruises, and the imprints of Gabriel's thumbs stood out in stark relief on the pale skin at the base of her throat. He stood back from her and turned to Père Christophe.

"Is my test over? Have I passed?"

"Yes," Père Christophe said. "You have passed. Now, help us with Child Elinor. She will need some time and healing in our infirmary."

Gabriel squatted beside the still-weeping girl and hoisted her up and into his arms, one hand under her armpit, the other supporting her under her knees. He carried her back to the village where he left her with the two Uncles.

"Come with me, Child Gabriel," Père Christophe said. "We have much to discuss.

Inside Père Christophe's house again, Gabriel found himself looking at the aerial photograph of the hydroelectric complex.

"Do you know what this is?" Père Christophe said.

"It's a factory of some kind. No, wait. Is that a dam across the river? Yes, it is. I know what this is. It's a power station, isn't it? Hydroelectric."

"Very good. Yes, it is the Santa Augusta Hydroelectric Generating Station. And next Friday, there will be a grand ceremony to open it. But there is a grave problem."

"What is that?"

"The men who are presiding over the ceremony are evil men, Child Gabriel. They have poisoned the well whereof they drink and whereof their cattle drink. They have sought mastery of the waters of the Earth and the rains of Heaven. And now they seek to destroy us. They would disperse the Children of Heaven to the four winds like chaff after the threshing. I will not allow them to do that. They must be brought low by the righteous. By you!" He whispered this last, short, phrase.

Gabriel nodded. "What do you want me to do?"

"Revelation, sixteen-four: 'The third angel poured out his bowl into the rivers and the springs of water, and they became blood.' You are my third angel. Even your name is a sign. You are our avenging angel. You will make the waters blood."

"But how, Père Christophe? I was a fighting man. I know how to shoot and how to kill. But I can't see how I can destroy a whole power plant."

"That is not your concern. Those friends I mentioned? Whose fires you could smell. They are helping us. Now, go find Aunt Maria. She has some work for you in the garden. I will summon you soon. There is someone I want you to meet."

With Gabriel gone, Jardin called Toron, who was supervising the work on the cocaine processing facility.

"Diego. I have our man. He is perfect. Ex-British Army. Special Forces. One hundred percent docile and controllable. I just had him choke a pretty young girl almost to death. He would have finished her off if I'd let him."

"Good. Because those damned politicians are going to be congratulating each other on their war against the cartels unless we stop them."

"When can you get hold of the parts we need?"

"Give me two days. I'll be back here then with everything."

As good as his word, Toron arrived back at Eden two days after the call. As he descended from the Cessna, he was carrying a brushed aluminium flight case big enough for most tourists to live out of for a week. On this occasion, there was nobody to meet him, so he wandered to the village and up the path to Jardin's house. The door was open, so he strolled in, dumped the case on the table in the dining room and called out.

Nobody answered. Shrugging, he went into the kitchen and helped himself to a beer from the fridge, marvelling once again at the way Jardin managed to keep his followers living in a state of near-poverty while enjoying for himself all the luxuries modern living could offer. As he swigged the cold beer, he caught a movement from the corner of his eye. He whirled, FN Five-seveN pistol yanked from its worn leather holster inside his jacket, tracking left and right. The pistol was a gift from the boss of a Mexican cartel. Its 5.7mm rounds were capable of piercing body armour, giving it the informal name amongst its illegal users, *mata-policia*, or cop-killer.

Jardin stood in the doorway, hand aloft, a mocking, wide-eyed smile signalling that he wasn't in the least bit afraid.

"No need for that, my friend," he said. "There are no threats inside Eden. Just outside. Which is why you're here, I hope."

Toron grunted his displeasure as he reholstered the Five-seveN. "Creep up on me like that again, my friend, and you'll never have to worry about enemies ever again." He drained his beer in one long swallow and belched loudly. "It's in your dining room. On the table."

The two men went back to the dining table. Jardin stood back and watched Toron flip open the catches holding the flight case closed. The last catch unfastened, Toron lifted the lid and settled it back on the table. The case was lined with grey foam. Set into individually cut recesses were a professional video camera; six one-and-a-quarter pound M112 demolition blocks of C-4 plastic explosive, two by one-and-a-half inches thick and eleven inches long; four clear plastic zip-lock bags full of ball bearings; a button-operated, electrical remote detonator; batteries, detonator cord, and blasting caps. Lying across the top was a laminated ID badge marked MEDIA in bold blue capitals and declaring that the bearer, Gabriel Da Costa, was a cameraman for TeleGlobo. The mugshot, taken by Jardin when Gabriel was being indoctrinated, was pixelated and deliberately poor quality, but he was recognisable, and that was all that counted.

"Excellent. That should be enough to exterminate those two pests," Jardin said. "Wait here. I want you to meet Gabriel. Help yourself to another beer, if you like."

Ten minutes later, Jardin returned with Gabriel at his side. They entered the dining room to find Toron asleep in an armchair. Jardin turned to Gabriel, winked and held a finger up to his lips. Then he kicked Toron's left foot.

Toron woke with a start and was reaching for his pistol as Jardin let out a high-pitched giggle. Scowling, Toron continued the movement, withdrawing the gun and pointing it at Jardin's face.

"You know, Père Christophe," he said, laying extra stress on the word 'Père,' "one of these days, I swear to God by the Holy Virgin, I will put a bullet in you just to stop you jerking my chain." But he put the gun away nonetheless and looked up at Gabriel. "This is your boy, yes?"

Jardin nodded. "Gabriel, I want you to meet one of my ... spiritual advisers. This is Diego Toron. He is the man supervising the construction of our new building."

Gabriel stepped forward and shook hands with Toron, who had got to his feet.

"How do you do?"

"How do I do? *Madre de Dios*, you're English?"

"Is that a problem?"

"No, no, my friend, no problem at all." Toron laughed. "And Père Christophe here tells me you have a background in the military. That right? You were a soldier for Her Majesty Queen Elizabeth?"

"That's right. Parachute Regiment then the Special Air Service. That's a bit like Delta Force in the US."

Toron scowled again. "Yeah? Well you better be glad you're on my side. I really don't like Delta. Those sons of bitches are always on my back trying to fuck up our operations back in Colombia."

Jardin touched Gabriel lightly on the shoulder. "Which is why I asked you here, Child Gabriel. Do you have experience with explosives? Can you make an IED?"

Gabriel looked down at the contents of the flight case. "With that? Easily."

"Good. Because that's what I want you to do. There are two corrupt government officials who are planning to destroy our community. A Colombian government minister and the President of Amazonas State. They hate everything we stand for: prayer, obedience to God's law, public service, selflessness. We must be strong and fight them. They have sown the wind. Now they must reap the whirlwind."

Gabriel nodded, held rapt by his master's carefully measured cadences. "With this, we can burn them from the face of the Earth, Père Christophe."

"Exactly, my Child. Now, let me bring you some tools and you can begin. Diego and I have some other matters to discuss, so we'll leave you to God's work."

Jardin returned within a minute carrying a black plastic tool chest with a yellow lid. He dumped it on the table next to the flight case. Gabriel pulled out a chair and sat, already focusing on the task ahead as Toron and Jardin left the house. He lifted the camera out

241

of the flight case and weighed it in his hands before placing it on the shiny, polished wood of the table top.

The camera's casing was held together with eighteen tiny, cross-head screws, which he removed and lined up in two rows of nine, like soldiers on parade. With the camera laid on its side, he eased the casing apart. Concentrating, he removed all the internal components and mechanisms of the camera until nothing remained but a hollow shell. Swift slices with a box cutter opened the M112s' black film wrappings, which he swept onto the floor. With the oily, burnt plastic smell of the C-4 making his nostrils sting, he squashed the separate blocks together into a rough cube. He carved and shaped using the box cutter until the block of plastic explosive fitted inside the camera body with a quarter-inch gap all the way around. The ball bearings were next. He slid the fastenings on the zip-lock bags open and began inserting the silver spheres into the C-4, pushing each one down until only half protruded from the surface. When he was finished, each shiny ball bearing reflected Gabriel's serene face back at him. He pushed in a blasting cap and attached a yard of detonator cord.

With the charge seated inside the camera, he reassembled the casing and tightened the screws in place. An experimental shake revealed that he'd judged the fit perfectly. There was no noise from the ball bearings against the inner surface. He'd threaded the detonator cord through a hole in the casing designed to take an external mic. Now he wired it into the detonator. He didn't insert the batteries. Better safe than sorry. He stood, and hefted the camera onto his right shoulder. It felt about the same weight as it had before he'd modified it. He inhaled, then began to speak, in a quiet monotone.

"If I sharpen My flashing sword, And My hand takes hold on justice, I will render vengeance on My adversaries, And I will repay those who hate Me."

Then he pressed the detonator's red 'fire' button.

And smiled.

43

SEMPER FIDELIS

AS THEY WALKED BACK FROM the clearing where their cocaine factory was rising out of the grass like an ark, planks being hammered and nailed into place, even some drywall panels being nail-gunned with rapid-fire pops onto the wooden studs, Toron and Jardin were arguing.

"You're telling me you'd run away if the government sent police over here? Leave all this," Toron waved his arm around him. "And that?" He stopped abruptly, grabbed Jardin by the bicep and swung him round so he could point at the factory.

"I'm telling you," Jardin said, shaking himself free of the other man's grip, "that I'm not interested in getting into a shooting match with the Brazilian police. If the plan fails—and it won't, by the way —but if it does, well, all I'm saying is I have an escape route planned. We can restart somewhere else."

"And what I'm telling *you*," Toron jabbed a finger into the other man's chest, hard enough to make him wince, "is that the Muerte Eterna do not run. I have men—*many* men—with all sorts of skills. If the police come, we do what we've always done. We fight them off, kill as many as possible, capture a couple, and use them to send a message back to the media, the president and their families.

Believe me, this is a tried and tested method of keeping them out of our hair. We do it in Colombia, and we can sure as hell do it here."

Ever the manipulator, Jardin decided on a different tactic. His voice softened, and he stopped to face Toron, drawing him into the role of follower. "Diego, you are a powerful man. Yes, you have men at your command. You are a soldier. But I am a man of God." Toron snorted at this but stayed silent. "A firefight? No, that is not the right way to go. You are on my land now, and we do things my way. I said there's an alternative to a gunfight at the OK Corral and there is. A much better alternative."

Toron frowned. Looked back at the factory, then at Jardin. Then he burst out laughing. "I tell you what, you have *cojones*, my friend. Big fucking *cojones*! OK. Fine, whatever. Let's just hope your boy Gabriel does his thing next week."

"Oh, have no doubts. He will do his thing exactly as I have programmed him to. Now," he checked his watch, "let's go and find a news channel. My message to Hollywood is about to be delivered."

Child Zack was twenty-four. He'd been captain of his university's water polo team, a member of a fraternity and a star scholar in his chosen field: business management. But when his girlfriend died after taking a single white tablet supplied by a Puerto Rican drug dealer outside a club in Boston, Zack had found it impossible to hold himself together. A DUI charge was narrowly averted only because his father, a hedge fund manager, bailed out his drunken son with a promise to the police lieutenant to have him attend therapy and buy the other motorist a brand new car. After that, Zack dropped out of college and began drinking seriously. He found the Children of Heaven, or they found him, in the open air market at Faneuil Hall down by Boston's waterfront.

Now he sat behind the wheel of a late-model, white Ford Transit Connect minivan heading for a film company lot at the end of a long street running north off Melrose Avenue in West Hollywood.

His left leg was jittering, and he felt as though there were a frightened version of himself blanketed in a calmer outer layer. The effects of the special sacrament he had received that morning, he supposed.

Behind the partition, separating him from the load space, were six, fifty-gallon plastic drums filled with petrol. A detonator sat on top of the centre-left drum, connected by a length of household bell wire to a trigger device in Zack's lap—a simple electrical switch activated by a red button. He was to drive through the gates, bursting them open if they were closed, head at full speed into the busiest part of the lot he could see, then press the button.

He made a right turn onto North Detroit Street. At the end of the road, he could just make out the ornate gates of the film studio, surmounted with its name in curling steel capitals: Monstrous Regiment Pictures.

Thirty minutes earlier, Jardin had placed calls to half a dozen media outlets advising them that, should they want a hot story concerning a particularly attractive Latina actress, they should have their helicopters airborne and ready to film above the studio lot.

As Zack locked his elbows on the steering wheel and jammed his foot down hard on the accelerator pedal, he was dimly aware of the chatter of rotor blades above him. He smiled, despite the distant nerves jangling deep inside him. He was ready.

The guard on duty that day at the studio's front gate was Frank Hemmings. Unlike his counterparts in the studio security department, Frank wasn't an overweight ex-cop, or even a moonlighting real cop. Frank, at fifty-four, was a trim, one-fifty-four-pound former US marine. He still wore his grey hair in a military buzz cut and carried himself upright, gut—what there was of it—sucked in, shoulders thrown back, chest out. 'Ramrod,' his colleagues called him behind his back. He knew, and didn't care. Liked it, in fact.

He looked up at the choppers hovering a couple of hundred feet above the lot and wondered what the jackals were after. There was a rumour that Cora Mendes and Lane Bradley were doing a nude scene on a closed set today, so maybe that was it. Idiots! There'd be nothing to see from the air or the ground. The studio had the whole place on lockdown until the scene was in the can. That meant there were a hell of a lot of extras and non-essential crew milling about outside the soundstage. But that was hardly worth scrambling six choppers for.

Back at ground level, the distant roar of a vehicle engine grabbed hold of Frank's attention. Shading his eyes against the sun, he squinted along the street. He didn't like what he saw. A van accelerating hard towards the lot. Frank had served two tours in Afghanistan and done guard duty outside the US Embassy in Kabul. He'd seen what truck bombs could do, and he'd developed a finely tuned sense for when a vehicle's driver wasn't planning on delivering bread. It was broadcasting on full alert right now. He pressed a button marked 'CLOSE' and stepped out from his kiosk by the right-hand pillar as the electrically powered hydraulic rams began pushing the heavy steel gates together.

The van roared onwards.

Standing in front of the gates, Frank unsnapped the press stud on the highly polished brown leather holster on his right hip. He drew his weapon, a Beretta M9 semi-automatic pistol he'd used in his Marine Corps service. As the van roared towards him, closing now to three hundred yards, Frank racked the slide to feed one of the fifteen 9mm Parabellum rounds from the magazine into the chamber. He brought the pistol up in front of his eyes in a two-handed grip and looked along the barrel, lining up the iron sights on the windscreen.

Now the van was close enough for Frank to make out the driver. It was a male, face a blurred blob at this distance, blonde hair. Tall on the driver's seat. Both hands on the wheel.

He knew the driver wasn't going to stop. It wasn't a feeling or an intuition. It was hard-edged knowledge, gained and proven in combat. The engine note of the van, whose white and blue oval grille emblem told him it was a Ford, rose steadily, then dropped a couple of semitones as the auto box changed up. Frank waited. His weapon was reasonably accurate at ranges of up to fifty-odd yards. He wanted a good clean kill shot, but he also wanted to take it before the van got so close it detonated its payload at or near the studio.

When the van had closed to a distance of fifty yards, Frank opened fire. He put the first five rounds through the driver's side of the van's windscreen, the M9 jerking in his hands, deafening him with the explosions from the muzzle and filling his nose with the sharp stink of burnt propellant from the cartridges being ejected from the chamber. He must have hit the driver because the van slewed left, then right, as Frank emptied the rest of his magazine into the side of the cab. The van smashed into a couple of parked cars, setting off their alarms. As it bounced back into the centre of the road and overturned on the hot tarmac, the driver, dressed all in white, was flung through the shattered windscreen to land in a bloodied heap on the far side of the road. The horns of the damaged cars blared in asynchronous frenzy. Then, with a roaring explosion, the van exploded outwards in a boiling cloud of tangerine flames.

Figuring somebody else would already have hit nine-one-one, Frank raced to the inert form of the driver, slamming a new magazine into the Beretta. The heat from the flames was intense and the pool of flaming petrol was spreading across the road. He'd hit the boy high in the chest on the right-hand side and again in the left shoulder. Terrible grouping, his firearms instructor would have said, but good enough to put his man down. He checked for a pulse, pushing two fingers none too gently against the carotid artery on the left side. It was faint, but it was there. He took out his handkerchief and wadded it against the chest wound and pushed down hard with the heel of his left hand, keeping the muzzle of the Beretta against the boy's head.

The wail of approaching sirens told him help was on its way, and two minutes later, a posse of black-and-whites, ambulances, and a fire truck screeched round the corner of Melrose Avenue and North Detroit Street. Frank stood aside as paramedics raced from their ambulance and began stabilising the boy. Frank knew he'd be wanted for questioning by the cops later, but right now he needed to call the head of studio security and brief him on what had almost happened.

* * *

Three thousand nine hundred and seventy-eight miles away, Jardin watched with growing satisfaction as the aerial footage from the US TV stations' choppers relayed the unfolding drama. While everybody else would be focusing on the huge square roof of the sound stage, he was looking at the street on the edge of the picture. There it was! A van emerged from the edge of the frame, paused, then raced down the long street towards the studio entrance.

Then, "No!" he shouted, his face contorting into a mask of rage, as a security guard left his little building and took up a shooter's stance in front of the closing gates.

He jumped to his feet and knelt right in front of the TV screen as the guard began firing. The excited chatter from the commentator drowned out any noise of the gunshots, but Jardin could see plainly the moment Child Zack was hit. As the van swerved and smashed into the parked cars, he jabbed an impotent finger at the screen.

Toron didn't leave the sofa behind him. But his sardonic voice made Jardin whirl round.

"Not quite the result you were hoping for, Christophe? I don't suppose your Chinese friends will find that worth a trip to Los Angeles."

Jardin bit back his words. He didn't want to fall out with Toron, and the choice phrases trying to batter their way past his teeth would almost certainly put an end to their relationship.

"There will be other opportunities. I am a patient man."

44

AN UNWELCOME INVITATION

GABRIEL WAS WEARING AN OUTFIT chosen for him specially by Père Christophe. Khaki chinos, running shoes, a white T-shirt, and a cream cotton waistcoat festooned with pockets, press-studded compartments and woven straps closed with D-rings. A black baseball cap with a TeleGlobo logo stitched in white completed the picture.

"There," he'd said, as he lassoed the ID card on its lanyard over Gabriel's head. "Every inch the media professional."

That had been ninety minutes earlier. Together with a second man, Uncle Peter, they'd flown out of Eden to Nova Cidade. For the duration of the flight, Père Christophe had stared into Gabriel's eyes, held his hands and asked him the same two questions, over and over again:

"What is your name?"

"Gabriel Da Costa."

"Why are you here?"

"To film the speeches."

After landing, they'd picked up the Range Rover in which Child Eve had driven Gabriel into Eden that first time. Père Christophe had prayed briefly with Gabriel before leaving him in the care of Uncle Peter.

* * *

Now, the white Range Rover rumbled over a red earth road heading for the Santa Augusta project, maintaining a steady fifty. The big car's suspension soaked up the worst of the ruts and the rain washouts, but the odd pothole caused it to lurch left or right. Uncle Peter was holding the steering wheel too tightly, Gabriel could see that. The man was about forty-five and paunchy. He had wispy, sand-coloured hair that framed a boyish face, disfigured by a port-wine birthmark that covered his right eye like a bandit's mask.

"Uncle Peter, let the wheel play a little through your hands. Guide the car, don't force it."

The man's frown deepened into a scowl. "Thank you, Child Gabriel, but I think I'll drive the way *I* want to, if it's all the same to you."

"Of course," Gabriel said, returning his gaze to his own window and the rainforest that began at the edge of the road and extended for thousands of miles away from them. He leaned against the glass and let its delicious coolness spread across his forehead.

"How are you feeling?" the man asked.

"Feeling? About what?"

"About carrying out the Second Order."

"I am blessed, of course. After my glorification I will be with the Almighty Father. I will have served Père Christophe faithfully to the end of my days, and I will sit at God's right hand to wait until he calls Père Christophe to him. 'Be strong and of a good courage, fear not, nor be afraid of them: for the LORD thy God, he it is that doth go with thee; he will not fail thee, nor forsake thee'. Deuteronomy, thirty-one six."

The man nodded and relaxed his grip on the wheel. He drew in a deep breath and let it out in a sigh. Gabriel spoke again.

"Are you all right, Uncle Peter?"

"Yes, yes, I'm fine. Are you hungry? Thirsty? We could stop if you like. There's a diner coming up."

"If you want."

The man nodded once, then braked for the diner and swung the Range Rover into the dusty parking lot behind the building, which was little more than a corrugated iron shack painted yellow, green, and blue.

Inside, the place smelled of *churros* and coffee. They sat at the counter on chrome and red vinyl stools, which were bolted to the floor. The young girl behind the bar, made up like a Hollywood starlet, put her phone down and sauntered over.

"What can I get you?" she asked.

Uncle Peter ordered two coffees and a plate of *churros*, tempted perhaps by the smell wafting from the steaming pyramid of sugary doughnut sticks the girl had just lifted from the frying basket with a wide slotted spoon.

With their food and coffees in front of them, Uncle Peter turned to Gabriel. "Good?"

Unable to speak through his hot mouthful of coffee and deep-fried dough, Gabriel nodded and smiled, his cheeks bulging like a hamster's.

Uncle Peter leaned closer. "Listen. Gabriel. You're not going through with the bombing, OK?"

Swallowing, Gabriel looked round sharply. "What do you mean? Père Christophe gave me the Second Order. It's my glorification. It's my duty."

"No, it isn't. You don't have to do this. He's tricked you. Like he's tricked everyone. I'm leaving, and I want you to come with me. There are people who can help you. They'll talk to you, get you to understand how Père Christophe has messed around in your head. Not just you, everyone."

"I don't understand. Why are you saying this?"

"I met some people, about a year ago, in Nova Cidade. From the Brazilian police. I go in every two weeks to run errands for Père Christophe and buy supplies. They spoke to me and gave me something to take. A drug, you know? To counteract the effects of that shit he pumps into us all. I started meeting them regularly, for deprogramming, they call it. But when I asked to leave with them, they said, no. I had to stay to gather evidence for them. You are that evidence, Gabriel. You!"

Gabriel shook his head. "No. This isn't right. You're lying. Père Christophe is a good man. A holy man. 'A good man out of the good treasure of the heart bringeth forth good things: and an evil man out of the evil treasure bringeth forth evil things.' Matthew, twelve thirty-five." Frowning, he slid off the stool, and walked to the door. "Come on. We have to get there with the rest of the media."

Outside, squinting against the sun, Gabriel made his way round the side of the diner to the Range Rover. It was still locked, but that didn't matter. He stood waiting for Uncle Peter by the driver's door.

As the man approached, thumbing the unlock button on the key fob, Gabriel stood back to let him grab the door handle. He looked around. The car park was empty. There were no cars in sight on the highway, either.

Gabriel curled his right hand into a fist, pulled it back and delivered a massive blow to the back of Uncle Peter's head, driving it forwards into the steel pillar between the front and rear doors with a bang. Catching him as he fell, he wrapped his arms around the man's head and neck and wrenched them violently in opposite directions. The snap was audible as the cervical vertebrae parted company, severing the man's spinal cord.

Gabriel opened the door, pressed the button that lifted the tailgate, then hauled the corpse round to the back and up into the load space beside the camera.

"The Devil seduced you, Uncle Peter. You were Satan's instrument. And I am God's."

"He was an evil man, but I won't fail you, Père Christophe. I will prove myself worthy of your faith," Gabriel said as he drove south towards Santa Augusta. His eyes flicked left and right, looking for a spot to dump the body. Then he slammed the brakes on, dragging the car to a juddering halt. He reversed for a few yards then turned the wheel onto full lock, pushed the gear selector back into drive and wove down a narrow track.

After five minutes, the track turned through a right-angle and ran parallel to a wide, fast-flowing river. Gabriel pulled up and a few minutes later was standing with the limp body of his former Uncle on the riverbank. The water was a muddy green, cloudy with silt and algae. Gabriel let the body fall to the grass and shaded his eyes with his hand to look downstream, into the sun. He smiled at what he saw: a dozen or so long, dark, brownish-green, knobbly shapes, near the far bank, half in, half out of the water.

Getting to his knees, he pushed and rolled the body until it slid off the bank into the water with a small splash. He stood again and watched as it sank from view. He knew what would be happening beneath the surface. The body would start to roll and twist in the current, bouncing off rocks and tree branches. Perhaps it would snag and stay submerged, to decompose until the crocodiles could smell it. Perhaps it would bloat and rise to the surface, where they could see it. Or maybe it would simply roll and tumble all the way to the sea. It really didn't matter.

He was back in the Range Rover and heading south again ten minutes later.

45

GABRIEL WOLFE, SUICIDE BOMBER

THE BRAND NEW TARMAC ROAD was glassy smooth, the white line down the centre flecked with reflecting chips of mica and still unmarked by rubber from truck tyres. Gabriel had turned off the highway two minutes earlier and was now driving towards the hydroelectric plant. Ahead, its white-painted turbine hall and control building stood out like a modernist cathedral plonked down in the middle of the rainforest. They were still a mile away, but the road was arrow-straight, drawing the eye towards this example of man's mastery of the environment to deliver that precious, invisible commodity: power. At this distance, Gabriel couldn't pick out any details. The haze wavering off the hot road surface rendered the buildings as simple three-dimensional shapes: a cube, a rectangular block, a sphere.

The Range Rover was silent as he cruised towards his glorification. No tyre roar or wind noise penetrated the cabin. His mind was quiet, too, his thoughts sluggish, as the double dose of his morning Valium purred through his veins, finally taking effect.

Then he saw a group of shimmering black shapes on the road. He craned his neck towards the windscreen and squinted. Finally, he smiled and a lazy laugh escaped his lips. He took his foot off the throttle and coasted for another two hundred yards before braking smoothly and bringing the car to a stop. In front of him, ambling across the road, was an adult tapir, a mother presumably, and three miniature versions of herself, striped and spotted where she was a deep, chocolatey brown. Their questing noses, really more like short little trunks—*Ha! truncated trunks*—twitched as the petrol-scented air from the Range Rover's bow wave floated across them. They were taking too long.

"Come on," he said. "Shift yourselves. We've still got a day's march ahead of us."

Then he frowned and shook his head.

He slipped his right foot off the brake pedal and onto the throttle.

Feeding a sip of petrol into the engine, Gabriel eased the car forward until its front bumper was touching the mother's right flank.

That was enough. She hurried her brood off the road and into the trees.

After that, he put his foot down and was at the main gate ninety seconds later.

Pulse? Sixty-two. Breathe. Focus. Still your mind. Pulse? Fifty-nine ... eight ... seven ... Cameramen do not look nervous.

Inside Gabriel's brain, two sets of psychoactive chemicals were skirmishing for advantage. The benzodiazepines administered by the Uncle at the end of his row at morning prayers were exerting a calming effect. The adrenaline and cortisol that his adrenal glands were secreting were doing the opposite. The benzodiazepines won. Coupled with his meditation and breath-control, they lowered his pulse and refreshed the blood supply to his skin and facial muscles. All was calm once more. Gabriel Wolfe was ready to die.

Three paramilitary cops stood in front of the gate, two men and a woman, feet apart, khaki caps pulled down low over their eyes, grey shirts marked with sweat stains visible where their black body armour ended under their armpits. One of the men had his sleeves rolled up, secured with straps attached to press-studs, revealing muscles like road cobbles, laid in close formation under his brown, tattooed skin. The woman wore hers rolled down, but her stance said, "I may have tits under the Kevlar, but I'll put you down without thinking about your wife and kids for a second". All three had black assault rifles carried diagonally across their torsos.

Somewhere in the locker room of Gabriel's swoony brain, an old bit of his training surfaced, complete with an extract from his photographic memory for international firearms makes and models. Combat appreciation, yes, sir! Three enemy combatants. Fit, hard, trained. Weapons, Imbel IA2 assault rifles, curved magazines chambered for 5.56mm NATO rounds. Taurus PT 24/7 9mm semi-auto pistols. Tear-gas grenades. Tasers. Compliance best option, sir!

The woman broke away from her two colleagues and strode over to the Range Rover. Gabriel buzzed the window down as she drew near.

"TeleGlobo," he said, smiling, knowing his hastily assembled Portuguese mini-vocabulary would get him through this encounter.

"ID?"

Gabriel flashed his laminated media accreditation.

She scrutinised it for ten seconds or so, flicking her gaze back and forth between the grainy digitised photo on the ID and Gabriel's own impassive face. *Pulse? Fifty-five.*

"Gabriel Da Costa?"

He nodded. "Cameraman." He jerked his thumb over his shoulder at the boot.

She strolled round to the back of the Range Rover, her finger crooked over her rifle's trigger guard.

"Open it," she called.

Gabriel pressed the tailgate release switch.

She waited while the heavy door swung open, then leaned into the load space. The camera was secured with a length of black webbing to a couple of chromed D-rings screwed to the insides of the wheel arches.

Gabriel unclipped his seatbelt and twisted round in his seat to watch.

If she asked him to switch it on, the glorification would be at an end. The detonator was stored in the glovebox and the black detonator cable had been coiled and clipped to the camera body, but in the absence of electronics, the heavy camera's masquerade would be discovered.

She poked at the camera, then scanned the rest of the load space, but there was nothing else there.

"OK, close it," she said.

Gabriel thumbed the switch again and listened to the hum of the powerful electric motors as they pulled the tailgate closed, then latched it.

The cop came round to the driver's window again. She pointed beyond the gate.

"Down there to the end. Turn left. Park with the others. Follow the signs and do what you're told."

Then she called over to her colleagues.

"Open it!"

One of the men strolled over to the galvanised iron pillar supporting the gate and pressed a button. The gate jerked to the left with a clang then slid back behind the razor-wire-topped fence.

All three cops stood aside as Gabriel drove through the gate and inside the plant.

46

HOW TO DEAL WITH CHILD ABUSE

A SCREAM PIERCED THE CLATTER and thud of the building work. Not of pain, but of fear. Stark terror. It stopped abruptly just as it was rising in pitch, so the screamer clearly had breath left in her lungs. Toron and Jardin were standing at one edge of the clearing watching the factory's roof being laid onto the wooden rafters. The Children working on the factory all stopped, as did Toron's men, who were nominally supervising the work, but mainly standing around smoking.

Jardin pointed to a stand of açaí palms maybe seventy-five feet away from where they were standing.

"Over there!"

He set off at a run, surprising Toron with his speed. Toron followed, pulling his Five-seveN, and swearing under his breath. He'd noticed that one of his men was missing from the building site. Ramón, always leering at women in the street, wolf-whistling at secretaries on their way to work.

He was panting heavily as he caught up with Jardin, who was standing on the other side of the trees, yelling at a man with his back to him. Shit! It was definitely Ramón. Then he noticed the girl between Ramón's legs. Her thin white cotton dress was rucked up around her waist revealing white panties that she was struggling to pull back up, but not before he caught a glimpse of her dark pubic triangle. The girl was young, no more than seventeen, and her face was blotchy and red, wet with tears.

"Leave her alone, you animal!" Jardin shouted, marching up and delivering a ringing slap to the side of Ramón's head.

Men had died, quickly and bloodily, for lesser insults than that, but Ramón saw that his attacker was accompanied by Toron, so he contented himself with a snarl at Jardin and finished zipping his trousers.

Jardin whirled round at Toron and marched up to him.

"The Children are under my protection, Diego!" he shouted, flecks of spittle clinging to his beard and moustache. "They are mine! My property!"

His face was dark with rage, and his eyes were staring, the whites showing above and below the purple-blue irises. Toron decided appeasement was in order. There would be plenty of time to discipline Ramón later.

"I'll talk to Ramón. To all my men. It won't happen again."

Jardin unclenched his fists and smiled, then took a step closer to Toron.

"Thank you my friend. After all, transgressors must be punished, yes?"

He seemed to fall against Toron. As the younger man bent his knees and reached out to support his business partner, Jardin lunged to his left and grabbed Toron's pistol.

He spun back to face the foiled rapist.

He racked the slide.

He took aim, holding the gun with both hands cupped around the grip.

And he fired.

Ramón died with an expression of equal parts shock and pain on his face, a fist-sized hole punched through his chest and a torrent of blood staining his yellow silk shirt all the way down to his belt.

The girl scrambled to her feet, looked once at Jardin, mouthed "thank you," then ran off towards the village.

Toron's fury, though slow to arrive, burned with an intensity that had earned him a fearsome reputation in Bogotá. When baptism wasn't an option, he was known to be equally comfortable leaving those who had crossed him with a 'Colombian necktie,' a savage mutilation where the victim's throat was cut and their tongue dragged out through the gaping wound and left flopping and bloody on their chest. If the offence was severe, the necktie would be inflicted while the victim was still alive.

The fire was banking up now.

"Ramón was my cousin. You should not have killed him."

"Your *cousin* was about to rape a teenaged girl under my protection. On my land."

"What, and you haven't been fucking those little *chicas* all this time?"

"They're here to serve me. I don't force them to do anything."

"You fucking brainwash them! You feed them fucking Valium like it's their breakfast. Of course you don't force them. You just fucking zombify them instead."

Jardin opened his mouth to speak, then closed it again. He smiled and cocked his head to one side. He looked down at the gun in his hand. Toron followed his gaze. Looked back at Jardin. Those eyes were unreadable. Shit! Jardin was unreadable. Was he insane? Toron doubted it. He was always rational and clearly enjoyed normal pleasures like most other men. Was he normal? One hundred percent, no. There was something seriously off about this hippie Frenchman. A personality disorder, or maybe he was a psychopath. The fact he never seemed even remotely afraid of Toron made the cartel boss wonder.

The gun floated between them, gripped in Jardin's right hand. The barrel ascended slowly and Toron tensed himself. But then it pointed left and Jardin transferred his grip to hold the muzzle and offered the pistol to Toron.

"Trust is important, don't you agree, Diego?"

Taking the pistol and holstering it, Toron nodded. "So is respect, Christophe."

"Respect goes two ways."

"So does trust."

"Do you respect me?"

"Do you trust me?"

In the pause that followed, Jardin stroked his moustache, smoothing it over his top lip, giving Toron that damned superior smile.

"*Naturellement.*"

"*Sí.*"

Jardin laughed. "Then we are good. I am sorry for your loss. We can give Ramón a decent burial out here, if you like. He can spend eternity looking up at the rainforest canopy."

"Do not push my patience. We'll fly him back to Bogotá. He was married you know. Two children."

"Your decision. Now," Jardin checked his watch, "why don't we go up to the house and turn on the TV? They're live casting the ceremony, and we wouldn't want to miss the climax, would we?"

Keeping his simmering temper under control, Toron took one last look at his cousin's corpse, then turned away and followed Jardin. He stopped on the way to give instruction to two of his men.

"Get Ramón to the plane. Fly him home. Give Elena fifty thousand US and tell her I'll see that she and the boys are OK when I get back to Bogotá."

The two men nodded, then trotted over to retrieve their friend's body.

For one brief moment, Toron considered catching up to Jardin and putting a bullet in the back of his head but then dismissed the idea. Patience, Diego. Build the factory, set up the supply chain, start shipping product. Then maybe we'll take that blasphemous freak for a trip to the baptistry.

* * *

Jardin had already turned on the TV by the time Toron entered the house. He could hear the jabbering of the news presenter in that bastard language of theirs. It always sounded to him like they had badly fitting false teeth. Why they couldn't speak Spanish like the rest of the damn continent escaped him.

"Come in," Jardin called. "They're about to go over to Santa Augusta. We might even catch a glimpse of Child Gabriel."

Grabbing a beer from the fridge, Toron turned his head to watch the TV, then walked into the living room and sprawled out on the sofa, arms spread along the back, claiming the whole piece of furniture for himself.

"Look," he said in a quiet voice. "There they are, those sons of bitches who want to shut me down."

47

TWO RED BUTTONS

IN THE CAR PARK, GABRIEL sat in the back of the Range
Rover to perform the last few tasks required for his glorification.
The detonator was a short, stubby cylinder of black plastic pushed
inside a bicycle handgrip of black, ribbed rubber. He unscrewed one
end with a coin, inserted the two batteries and twisted the cap back
on. Next, he unclipped the coil of detonator cord and connected it
to the detonator using a 3.5mm jack plug. At the other end from the
jack was a small, cylindrical, red plastic button with a flat top.
Toron's electrician had built it with a two-in-one action. Press to
arm the bomb, release to detonate. That way, Gabriel could
complete his mission even if the police killed him.

He hoisted the camera by the carrying handle and tucked the
detonator into a waistcoat pocket. The walk to the control building
took less than a minute, where a small crowd had gathered to hear
the speeches and gawp at the spectacle.

In the end, no muscling to the front was required. The media
managers had set up a dedicated filming area directly in front of the
platform where the two politicians were to give their address. The
platform was about two feet high, ten wide, and five from front to
back. It was draped in a huge Amazonas State flag: two horizontal

white stripes enclosing a red stripe—like a jam sandwich, Gabriel mused. In a corner, a blue rectangle enclosed white stars.

In the centre of the platform was a four-foot tall varnished mahogany box, eight or ten inches to a side. Let into the top was a domed red button five inches across and about two inches high. Beside the box were two mic stands with wires trailing off to the PA system at the side of the platform.

Gabriel secured a spot dead-centre in the front row of the media enclosure between a huge guy who smelled of last night's beer, and a skinny little runt with bad body odour. He breathed through his mouth as the two aromas contested the space under his nostrils.

According to the slim young woman in black who'd addressed them from the platform ten minutes earlier, the president and the justice minister would arrive to begin their speeches at noon. He checked the black digital watch Jardin had fastened onto his right wrist before they left Eden. Allowing for the Brazilian concept of punctuality, Gabriel estimated that they might be kept waiting for at least thirty minutes more.

Around and behind him, the cameramen and photographers were checking lenses, batteries, mics, and cable connections. Gabriel fiddled with his own camera, aiming for a look of professional diligence combined with world-weariness, sighing occasionally and looking up at the sun, which was throwing warming rays onto their heads. He was grateful to Père Christophe for the baseball cap. The camera's rubber grip felt slippery. He transferred it to his other hand and wiped his palm on the side of his leg.

Sweat was dribbling from his hairline into his eyes, the salt stinging and making him blink. Somewhere deep in the pit of his stomach, a faint fluttering started up.

A miniskirted woman of maybe thirty or thirty-five stepped out from the control building and mounted the platform. Her high-heeled black shoes meant this last manoeuvre had to be executed with extra care were she not to show her underwear or topple backwards into the dirt.

The crowd quieted and the media people stopped adjusting

lenses and tweaking controls. She waited for a few more seconds until she had everyone's attention before speaking.

"Ladies and Gentlemen. Enrique Salazar, President of Amazonas State, and Bernardo Menel, the Colombian Minister of Justice."

There was a brief burst of applause, and a whirring and chattering from the two dozen or so video cameras and digital SLRs in the media pen. She smiled and stood to one side of the two mics.

Onto the platform bounded two men. Both young-looking, with full heads of dark brown hair, combed in side partings. The state president was the older of the two, forty-four according to the official biography in the press pack. Deeply etched lines fanned out from the corners of his eyes, which were set wide apart behind his round, tortoiseshell glasses. His guest was thirtyish, the youngest-ever Minister of Justice in Colombia's brief but violent post-Indian history. He had been elected—"catapulted" would be a better word —into Colombia's parliament on a "no corruption" platform and had been appointed to his ministerial role a few months later. He smiled, revealing horsey teeth, and brushed his hair back from his forehead. The sharply tailored suit gave him the appearance of a junior executive anxious to please his boss.

Watching the men with his left eye, Gabriel pressed his right to the rubber eye-cup of the camera and pointed the blind lens at the mahogany tower that housed the dummy switchgear. With his free hand, he reached into his waistcoat pocket for the detonator, pulled it out and transferred it to his trouser pocket.

He closed his hand around the rubber grip.

Placed his thumb over the button.

And pressed down.

He felt the click. The bomb was armed.

Now all he had to do was let go and the president, the Minister of Justice, the pretty press aide, the media people around and behind him, and a goodly proportion of the crowd behind them, would be killed. Those not killed outright by the blast would be mutilated by the Tears of God, with a high chance of dying from blood loss. *And me, Gabriel Wolfe? What will become of me? I will die. I will sit at God's right hand.*

The state president stepped forward and grasped the mic. Gabriel noticed he had black hairs on the backs of his fingers.

"Today, we take another important step in the fight to make Amazonas State self-sufficient in energy. The Santa Augusta Hydroelectric Generating Station will produce enough power to reduce our dependence on the national grid supply by seventeen percent in its first year of operation. But there is another fight in which we are engaged. A fight against corruption. And against the befouled well from which that corruption creeps like a plague. You know, ladies and gentlemen, that I am speaking of the drugs trade and of the cartels who control it. With intimidation, bribery, and violence."

Nice link. Smooth. As it's your last speech, it's good you've made the effort.

Gabriel could feel the tension in his left hand. How easy it would be to release it and himself. Then someone nudged him in the back. He turned, but the men directly behind him were focused intently on the president.

As he turned back, he saw a familiar figure had replaced the skinny man with the personal hygiene problem.

"Hello, Boss."

"Hello, Smudge. You're looking good."

Smudge touched his chin. "This, you mean? I know. Seems to have healed up nicely, doesn't it? You going to kill everyone, then?"

"Looks like it."

"You want to do that, do you? Really?"

"I do. It's my duty to Père Christophe. He gave me the Second Order."

"What's that then?"

"Give your life to cleanse the world of sin."

"Fucking strange order, Boss. Who authorised it?"

"Père Christophe."

'What? So you're saying this Christophe geezer sent you out here to murder a load of innocent people and yourself, and he authorised his own kill order?"

Gabriel frowned. "Yes, he did. But they're not innocent. Those men are evil"

"How d'you figure that out, then?"

"I didn't. Père Christophe did. He told me."

"Oh, well as long as he told you, that's all right then, isn't it? Come on, Boss, this isn't you. You're better than this. What would Master Zhao say?"

"How do you know about Master Zhao?"

"Or your Dad? Or the one who called you 'Gable'?"

"What?"

"You heard. The one from before you joined up. The one from way back."

Gabriel blinked. His thumb was quivering, and he began to unwind the muscles that kept it clamped down on the button.

48

RELEASE

GABRIEL MADE A SMALL ADJUSTMENT to the bomb. Then, with a tiny smile, he released the button.

"Well done, Boss. I knew you could do it. We'll speak again."
"Thanks, Smudge. Bye for now."
"Bye, Boss."

49

MISSION RESUMED

GABRIEL LET THE DISCONNECTED JACK plug drop. Then he put the disarmed detonator back in his pocket. Excusing himself to his skinny neighbour, he shuffled out of the media pen, drawing a fleeting frown from the Colombian justice minister. He walked away from the crowd towards the downstream side of the dam. Nobody was watching him. The security detail were focused on their bosses, the media people on the journalists, the crowd on the bigwigs who were now berating previous governments for cowardice in the face of the threat from the cartels. *If only they knew.*

Rounding a corner, he found what he was looking for. He ran down a narrow pathway between two windowless concrete buildings towards a retaining wall set on the cliff that separated the plant from the two-hundred-foot drop to the river below. He leant over the parapet. Far below, the green water looked as though it was barely moving. Five streams of water from the sluices at the foot of the dam kept the current flowing, leaving white feathers of bubbles trailing out into the river.

He took a final look behind him then turned, swung his arm back, and hurled the bomb towards the middle of the river.

It tumbled end-over-end through the air, diminishing in size until it disappeared before hitting the surface with a foamy, green-white splash. No sound reached him. He wound the cable around the detonator, tucked the end with the jack plug under the final coil and flung it far out into the air. It vanished after a couple of seconds, and if it made a splash, Gabriel didn't see it.

His head still felt fuzzy from the increased dose of Valium, but the mental conversation with Smudge had reset his brain's rational circuitry. Best of all, he felt himself again, as if he'd been mired in a fever-dream for months. But now he had a job to do. A job he was going to enjoy. Kill Père Christophe. End his terror campaign. And get back to England, and his sanity.

As he drove up to the gate, one of the pumped-up paramilitary police turned at the noise of the Range Rover's engine and frowned. Then he unshouldered his rifle, pointed at Gabriel and made a 'turn off the ignition' gesture, twisting an imaginary car key in the air in front of his shoulder. Gabriel coasted to a stop. He got out and came round the door to face the cop through the bars of the gate, feeling as though he were in prison, talking to someone on the outside.

"Why are you leaving?" the cop said.

"My boss called. Hospital fire. I have to go film it." Gabriel shrugged and pulled the corners of his mouth down as if to say, orders are orders.

"Bloody vultures. OK, hold on."

Gabriel got back in and started the car again. Then a jolt of adrenaline shot through him. *What if he asks to look in the back again? There's no camera.*

He started calculating. Three against one. Full-auto assault rifles against a thin-skinned Range Rover. Accuracy versus speed. The advantage of surprise. Or claim I lent the camera to a colleague. But then what are you going to use to film this alleged inferno, compadre?

The gate juddered and began its journey along the well-greased rail let into the tarmac.

It clanged to a stop.

The cop stood to one side and beckoned him forward.

The female and the other male cop started to walk into the centre of the road. They wanted to talk.

Gabriel looked down.

He twisted the gear selector to Sport mode.

Then he jammed his foot down hard on the accelerator pedal, mashing it into the thick black carpet, and slid down in the seat. No sense in giving them an easy head shot.

Even with a kerb weight of over two tonnes, the Range Rover was a hugely powerful beast of a car. The five-litre, supercharged V8 engine instantly remapped for high performance over comfort and launched the car forwards.

The cops leapt back as the Range Rover surged through the gate. It took them a good two or three seconds to realise that he wasn't going to stop.

With the exhaust howling behind him, and the engine raging up front, Gabriel was not, at first, aware of the clattering of the cops' rifles as they opened fire. Then a round hit the rear window, shattering the glass before exiting through the passenger window, having been deflected by the front seat. That was their only hit on target. They'd had their weapons set to full auto, so they had very little control over their accuracy. And they were cops, not soldiers, so they probably hadn't spent as much time on the range, or with their instructors, as they should have done. By the third second, Gabriel was out of effective range, and he could see in the mirror that they'd turned and were running back into the plant, presumably to warn everyone that someone had planted a bomb.

He drove for two hours without stopping then pulled in to the side of the road. He slammed his palms against the steering wheel.

"Fuck!" he shouted.

How am I supposed to get from here to Eden? There's no road: we flew out. Only now, I need money to hire a plane. And you don't give a suicide bomber spending money, do you?

50

THE WAR ON DRUGS

TORON LEANED FORWARD AND JABBED his finger at the screen. His face had darkened into a scowl. He spoke.

"When's your boy going to detonate the bomb? Those sons of bitches are still up there, all in one piece."

For once, Jardin's face betrayed his emotions. No smirk this time, no look of otherworldly calm. He was chewing his lower lip and had drawn his brows down, furrowing his forehead with five or six parallel lines of wrinkled skin.

"I don't know. I really don't. He was properly conditioned. He was drugged up to his eyeballs on Valium. He should be a red splatter at the bottom of a crater by now."

On the screen, the Colombian justice minister had started wagging his finger at the cameras. Jardin felt the gesture was aimed directly at him. Bernardo Menel reached the climax of his speech.

"Here, ladies and gentlemen, is where the new war on drugs begins. You are witnesses to the first shot in that war that we, together with our partners in Amazonas State," he looked to his right and bared his horsey teeth at the state president, "have begun against the lawless, evil men who run Colombia's cartels, specifically, the Muerte Eterna, under the leadership of Diego Toron. And now, we have intelligence that the Muerte Eterna are in business with a pseudo-religious cult called the Children of Heaven right here in Amazonas State. President Salazar will tell you more."

The older man stepped forward to his mic.

"Thank you, Bernardo." He cleared his throat and smoothed his hair back. "Working undercover, at great personal risk, agents of the state government's anti-cartel squad have learned of plans by Muerte Eterna and the Children of Heaven to start manufacturing cocaine right here in Amazonas State." He looked directly into the cameras, so that he appeared to be looking straight at Jardin himself. "I have news for you, Senhor Toron. And your business partner. We are coming for you."

As the speech drew to a conclusion, Jardin leapt from his seat and kicked the huge flat-screen TV over, smashing the screen with a shower of sparks and a curl of white smoke that stank of burnt plastic.

"No!" he shouted. "This is not right. They should be dead. I ordered it. I gave the Second Order."

Toron stood, too. He looked at Jardin, who was running his fingers through his hair as he paced around the sitting room.

"Maybe someone gave him new orders. To save his skin and blow the whistle on us."

"Don't be a fool," Jardin said, turning on his partner. "He's been brainwashed. The best techniques the Chinese and the Russians could come up with, modified with some nice little tweaks courtesy of the CIA. And he's been under direct supervision since he arrived."

"You call me a fool?" Toron's mouth hardened into a slit and his eyes narrowed. "You? The man who dresses like Moses then watches TV and uses the Internet? Let me ask you something. Who plans a drugs operation then lets one of his people rat us out to the authorities? Who sends a suicide bomber who doesn't fucking commit suicide? No, my friend. It is you who is the fool. And my only foolishness was to believe you could be trusted to keep your side of the deal." Toron pulled his pistol and pointed it at Jardin's face. "I could kill you now and nobody would ever know. Give me one reason why I shouldn't use my *mata-policia* on you. Just one, hey?"

Realising he had overplayed his hand, Jardin lowered his voice and tried for a smile. He stroked his moustache as he calculated the best way to save his financial relationship with one of Colombia's most powerful crime bosses. And his own life.

"Diego, forgive me. I was upset. Justifiably, I think you'll agree."

"Fine," Toron said, breathing more calmly now and lowering the barrel of the pistol. "But we still have a major fucking problem. It won't take them long to find this place and then we're fucked. All that work. Wasted."

Jardin paused before speaking. He was weighing the pros and cons of a fairly drastic course of action. Yes, it was time.

"Listen. I had a backup plan all along. I'm sure I told you. We're going to scrap the factory here. In fact, we're going to scrap Eden altogether. It served its purpose, but now we need to leave and set up somewhere more … conducive."

"I'm not flying you and your fucking followers anywhere. There's hundreds of them."

Now Jardin did smirk. "I'm not asking you to. Just me. I'll give them all the Second Order. Tomorrow. Listen, you know the Diazepam you supply."

"Of course. You've got your own little zombie army haven't you?"

"Exactly. And every morning they queue up for their medicine. My orders."

"So?"

"So, I have an alternative formulation stockpiled. I'll line them up to take my sacrament and within ten minutes they'll all be dead. Who's to say I'm not among them? Nobody knows me. My identity disappeared in France years ago. When the cops and the soldiers arrive, this place will be a mass graveyard. Nobody knows what I look like. They'll assume one of the Uncles was the leader. I'll be long gone. Then we'll find a new site, maybe in your country, closer to home for you, eh? I'll find some new recruits and we can start anew. Believe me, there's no shortage of young kids willing to believe there's a better life for them just around the corner. Maybe I'll play up the environment next time. Gaia's Children, what do you think? Plenty of empty-headed, eco-handwringers would buy that message."

Toron's eyes widened. "Really? You'd kill them all?"

"Why not? They all want to go to a better place. I'll just send them all at once."

"You know, you are a very cynical man."

Jardin grinned. "Come on, you can help me mix a very special batch of our sacrament: one part Diazepam, one part phenobarbital, and just a splash of cyanide, courtesy of a former professor of botany at the University of Texas. You'd be surprised how many plants out here are full of the stuff. We might need to add a bit more cordial this time."

51

DAYLIGHT ROBBERY

APPROACHING A BAR, GABRIEL SLOWED. It appeared to be hosting some sort of family celebration, a wedding maybe, or a christening party. The car park was full of 4x4s, cars, and motorbikes. About thirty people were sitting round a long outdoor table covered in a white cloth, scattered with bottles, glasses, dishes of food, and plates. Gabriel kept driving.

After another thirty minutes, he saw a sign shimmering in the heat haze ahead. Decelerating, he gave himself time to scope it out. *No cars or bikes parked outside. Good.* He pulled in to the gravelled parking area and killed the engine.

Inside, the bar smelled of last night's beer and cigarette smoke. An ancient air conditioning unit was fixed into one of the windows facing the road. It was doing a reasonable job, although the cost was a noisy rattle from the motor, and a flapping from half a dozen strips of coloured plastic that fluttered in the artificial breeze. Behind the counter, a man was drying beer glasses with a dishcloth so thin from washing it was almost transparent. He was thickset, with cropped grey hair. His forearms were massive, decorated with tattoos of lizards, skulls and flowers. Gold hoops dangled from both his ears. He looked up, took in Gabriel with a glance and said, in English, "Help you?"

"A beer, please."

Gabriel settled himself on a stool that wobbled as it took his weight and placed his elbows on the thickly varnished bar. The wood looked like toffee.

The man pushed a stemmed glass of Brahma beer in front of Gabriel, which he drank off in a single, long draught.

"Thirsty, huh? Again?"

"Please. How did you know to speak English?"

The bartender put another beer in front of Gabriel. "You're not Brazilian. Figured you were US media, whatever the cap says. But you're British, right?"

"Yeah. Freelancing for TeleGlobo. You speak English very well."

"Thank my wife. She's from California. Pasadena. You're a long way from home. How does an Englishman wind up working for a TV company in Brazil?"

"I burned out in the UK. Took off on a trip. Ran out of cash in Rio. Friend of a friend put me in touch with the head of production at TeleGlobo. Bingo! Here I am."

"OK. Well, shout if you need another beer."

With that, the man turned and started wiping down the rear shelf where bottles of tequila were ranged in order of price, Gabriel assumed, from the stuff you'd chuck down between licks of salt and bites of lemon to the classier brands you'd probably savour like a fine cognac.

He took a deep breath and let it out slowly. Silently, he slid off the bar stool, placed the flat of his right hand on the wooden surface and vaulted over the counter, kicking the man in the back with his booted feet.

The man let out a yell as his face hit the edge of the shelf and he fell to his knees. Gabriel was crouched ready, his weight on the balls of his feet, and with a hard chop to the side of the man's neck he put him down on the ground. He drove the ball of his right thumb into a small pit on the back of the man's neck, just under the bony ridge at the back of his skull. The man's struggles subsided almost as soon as they began and he slumped, unconscious, to the floor.

Gabriel ran to the end of the bar, hit the button on the till to open the cash drawer and scooped out the paper money held under three spring clips. He returned to the prostrate form of his latest victim and rifled through his pockets. He was in luck. A creased and worn brown leather wallet shoved into the right hip pocket yielded more notes. Gabriel made sure the guy was face down with his head to one side, so he wouldn't choke if he vomited. Then he ripped a couple of bar towels into strips and bound his wrists behind him and tied his ankles to one of the steel legs supporting the bar.

He was back in the Range Rover and pulling out of the car parking area twenty seconds later. He wasn't precisely sure of the exchange rate for the Brazilian Real, but he didn't think he had enough to hire a plane back to Eden. It was a start, though.

The Range Rover would be a liability now. With more time, he could try to sell it to a garage owner in a small town, but time was against him. The cops back at Santa Augusta would have radioed the State Police and the Federal Highway Police and now he had a seriously pissed-off bar owner on his case, too. Time to ditch the wheels and find an alternative source of transport.

Ten miles down the road he saw a sign: '*Ponto de vista 1 km*'. A viewpoint. Perfect.

After a few minutes he came to the turn and swung off the highway down a bumpy dirt road. Another five minutes brought him to an empty scrape of earth bordered by a low, steel-rail fence. Beyond the rail was the rainforest. Millions of square miles of trees that started a deep intense green and faded towards the horizon, ending in a pale, misty grey. Gabriel wasn't interested in the view. He was more concerned with what lay below the rail. Which was a good two thousand feet of air. He stood on the edge of the cliff and leaned over. He'd never suffered from vertigo or any kind of fear of heights. His training for the SAS had included a jump from the UK mainland to a three-hundred-foot column of basalt, nicknamed by the locals, Old Tom. The gap had been negligible, five feet at most. He'd done it with ease. Unlike Smudge, who he'd saved from plummeting to his death with a hand like a crane grab that closed round the falling man's wrist, pulling up him to safety and a job in the Regiment.

There was more forest at the foot of the cliff. At this distance, it resembled a mottled green carpet, wreathed in silver wisps of mist. He walked back to the Range Rover, which he'd left with the engine running, and reversed up the road for sixty yards. Under the floor of the load space, where, until recently, there'd been a homemade bomb, he found a white polypropylene tow-rope and a small toolkit. He took out both and slammed the tailgate shut again. To hold the steering at the straight-ahead, he tied one end of the tow-rope to the passenger door grab-handle with a bow-line knot. He ran it through the steering wheel, then looped it around the driver's seat before securing it to the steering wheel again with a reef knot. He wasn't sure his father, a keen amateur sailor, would have approved, but it would do the job for the ten seconds or so it would need.

Gabriel tugged the bonnet release lever and went round to the front of the car. Using the pliers and a screwdriver, he wedged the throttle open and closed the bonnet. The engine screamed in Neutral as the revs rose to the redline. One last task remained. Gabriel popped open the fuel filler cover and unscrewed the cap. The sharp tang of petrol wafted up into his nostrils. Crouching just inside the driver's-side door, he shoved the brake pedal down with his right hand, the brushed aluminium cool against his palm. With his left, he twisted the rotary gear selector knob one damped click clockwise into Drive. Instantly, the transmission strained against the brakes, pulling forward, and he simply let go with both hands and rolled away into the dirt.

The Range Rover picked up speed rapidly over the short run down to the fence. By the time it hit the steel rails, it was doing over forty miles per hour. There was a brief screech as the metal rails ripped free of the stanchions and a bang as the heavy car tore through them and leapt out into the abyss.

Gabriel sprinted back to observe the descent. He arrived at the gaping gash of metal just as the car, which now resembled a tumbling sugar cube, disappeared into the trees. One heartbeat later there was a brief flash, visible through the hole the Range Rover had torn in the canopy, followed half a second later by a boom, as the petrol tank exploded. A ring of whitish-grey smoke rolled out of the trees as if blown by a skilled cigar-smoker, then dissipated in the air currents that raced up the sun-drenched cliff-face.

Now all Gabriel had to do was find more cash and an airfield. Hitching seemed the best move.

52

BLOOD AND WINE

JARDIN LED TORON FROM GRACIOUS living room to fully-equipped chemistry lab. At the back of the house, behind the kitchen, was a door. He pulled on a dirty length of string that hung round his neck, and from inside his robe a brass key appeared. The lock turned easily with a series of soft clicks. Beyond the door, all trace of the tropical luxury hotel disappeared. Jardin turned on the lights. As the fluorescent tubes over their heads clinked and flickered into life, Jardin spread his arms.

"Welcome to my vestry."

The room beyond the door was spartan and windowless, twenty feet long by fourteen across. Set into a stainless steel counter that ran the length of one of the long walls was a huge stainless steel sink, wide and deep enough to hold a full-grown man. Beneath the counter were racks of drawers and doors with slots for handles, and there were eye-level cupboards running right round the room's circumference. The centre of the room was dominated by a table of the sort referred to as a butcher's block. Four sturdy legs on castors supported a foot-thick solid slab of pale wood, five feet on one side and three on the other. Against the wall opposite the sink were three tall refrigerators. They were huge, professional models with brushed steel doors and hard, right-angled corners, humming in an unsettling, disharmonious chord as their pumps moved the coolant around the pipework, struggling to keep their contents chilled.

Jardin walked over to the nearest fridge and pulled the door open. The seal gave with a dry, sucking sound. Inside, stacked floor to ceiling on heavy-duty steel racks, were ten tall aluminium canisters, eighteen inches high and eight inches in diameter. They resembled miniature milk churns, with tops closed against their rubber seals by lever-catches.

"Help me with these, would you?" Jardin said. He lifted a canister from the shelf and carried it round the butcher's block before dumping it on the stainless steel counter.

Toron grunted but took off his navy suit jacket, folded it, and placed it on the counter then grabbed a second canister.

"Which is this?" he asked, placing his canister next to Jardin's.

"The Diazepam. The regular sacrament."

Jardin returned for a second canister and Toron followed. They repeated the process three more times until the ten canisters of Diazepam were arranged in two ranks of five, to the left of the sink.

After pushing the plug down into the sink, Jardin turned to Toron.

"We'll start with this," he said, then popped the catch on the nearest canister and tilted it until the clear, syrupy liquid glugged from the lip of the canister into the sink. Toron grabbed another canister and followed Jardin, emptying the contents into the shallow pool that spread out over the sink's shining floor. He leaned over the growing pool of liquid and sniffed, then wrinkled his nose and drew his head back.

"Smells like guava going bad," he said.

"You wait till we get to the third fridge. You'll like that even less, my friend. We'll have to do it in batches. Put another load in."

The two men heaved two more canisters onto the lip of the sink and simultaneously popped the catches. This time, Toron kept his nose out of the way as he poured out the liquid tranquilliser.

"Right!" Jardin said, rubbing his hands together and smiling. "Now for the second ingredient in our little *soupe du jour*. Come with me." He crossed the room and pulled on the middle refrigerator's door. Inside it resembled the first, just a tightly-packed array of dull, silver-grey canisters. "This is the phenobarbital. Sleeping pill juice. Hendrix, Monroe, Garland: it did for all of them, you know."

Four canisters crossed the room and were emptied into the Diazepam. The sink was half full, and the liquid, smelling of sweetly rotting fruit, swirled and eddied as Toron and Jardin added each fresh canister to the mixture.

"And for the icing on the cake, perhaps you'd fetch the canister with the blue band round it from the third fridge," Jardin said.

Toron came back with a single cylinder that he set down by the sink with a slosh and a clank. "You know," he said, "a lot of people would say you're a crazy man, killing all those people like that."

"And you? What would you say?"

"I say, it's your party, do whatever you want. If you can live with it, so can I."

"Well, as it happens, I *can* live with it. Now, pour that stuff in, and we'll refill the empties with my signature blend." Jardin giggled. "Those poor fools. They followed me out here in search of paradise, and now I'm sending them all to hell."

Toron frowned, but he opened the catch and added the cyanide to the sink. The smell of bitter almonds that wafted up from the sink's contents made both men jerk their heads back and turn away.

Pulling the front of his robe up over his mouth and nose, Jardin lifted a long metal spoon from a rack over the sink and stirred the liquid for a few seconds. "Come on. We'll refill the empties and make another batch. That will be enough to put my flock to sleep for good."

Half an hour later, the work was done. Twenty-one canisters stood on the floor in three rows of seven, each filled with a lethal cocktail of muscle relaxant, sedative, and good, old-fashioned poison.

· · ·

"I've enjoyed my time here, you know," Jardin said, once they were outside. "Look around you. Life is simple. I do what I want, when I want, with whom I want. And nobody tells me what to think or believe or do."

"Yeah. Until your disciple slipped the leash."

"I know. And if we ever come across him, I will gladly help you deal with him in any manner that you think fits his transgression. But for now, we need to pull out. Your pilot can fly us all out tomorrow as soon as our special sacrament has done its job. It'll take a couple of trips, but I guess your men won't mind waiting."

"They'll do what I tell them to."

Toron placed extra emphasis on this statement, which Jardin noticed. Its implied criticism, "unlike your people," wasn't lost on him. Oh well, maybe one day he'd dose Toron up with a little *soupe du jour* of his own. But for now, he was useful. And setting up a new compound in Colombia would be easier with his connections.

"Indeed they will," Jardin said with a big smile. "Now, how about a drink? And I have an idea for how we can deal with Child Gabriel."

Inside Jardin's house, the two men sprawled on the comfortable sofas, sipping cool sauvignon blanc from Chile. Jardin was speaking on the phone.

"Vasco, it's Christophe. Listen, that favour you owe me? I'm calling it in. One of my flock has absented himself from Eden. He failed to do what was expected of him today, and I want him dead … Today … Yes, he's short, maybe five eight or nine. Medium build. Very dark hair, almost black. Looks like he could have had someone oriental in his bloodline. Be careful, he's tough. Just go in hard and don't ask questions." Jardin listened for a minute or so. "Yes, that's a good plan … fine, fine, we can set up another deal next time you're passing through."

He ended the call. Toron spoke.

"Who was that?"

"Vasco Cabral. Runs a biker gang. He's going to put his men out looking for Child Gabriel. They've got hundreds of members. If he's coming back here to find me, they'll intercept him."

53

POKER FACES

FOR FIFTEEN MINUTES, NOT A single vehicle passed. Then an oil tanker bore down on him, sun glinting off the massive silver cylinder behind the red-painted cab. He stuck his thumb out, but the driver just sounded the air horn, which Doppler-shifted down from one angry note to another as the truck blew past him, pulling a vortex of road-dust in its wake, making Gabriel screw his eyes shut and turn away from the stinging grit.

Rubbing his eyes, he swore after the departing truck. Maybe the company had a policy against picking up hitchhikers. He neither knew nor cared. There was another long wait, during which time the only vehicles he saw were a couple of mid-sized saloons heading back towards Santa Augusta. They appeared to be driven by travelling salesmen to judge from the jackets hanging from hooks in the side windows.

Finally, a possible ride approached. Another mid-sized saloon, heading away from Santa Augusta. Gabriel stuck out his thumb, and this time, the car slowed to a stop beside him.

"*Onde?*" the driver said though the lowered window. Where are you going?

"*Perseverança*," Gabriel said. It was the next big town along; he'd driven through it with Uncle Peter on the way in. "*Obrigado.*"

"*Nada,*" the driver said. He didn't seem to want conversation, which would have been difficult anyway. The company was clearly enough.

Forty-five minutes later, they arrived in the centre of Perseverança. After thanking the man, Gabriel found himself in a central square, a church at its centre and fringed with brightly lit bars that were just starting to warm up for the evening. One in particular caught his eye. It appeared to be some sort of student hangout, to judge from the young men and women standing and sitting around outside, smoking and holding drinks, checking their phones and draping toned, brown arms around each other.

Among the scooters and beaten up, old cars parked nearby, one vehicle stood out: a vintage camper van, orange with a white roof and a big chromed VW logo on the front. Gabriel wandered over and idly conducted an appraisal. It looked to be in mint condition, a far cry from the shabby examples he'd seen all over the world. He settled down to wait, back against a cool wall in a corner of the square.

After an hour, a small group of young men emerged from the bar. They were heading for the camper van. Gabriel jumped to his feet, brushed himself down and jogged over to intercept them.

At ten feet, he called out.

"Excuse me!" At the sound of his voice—and that unmistakable accent—the five young men stopped and looked at him. Gabriel closed the distance between them to a few feet and stopped, wide smile on his face. "I'm terribly sorry to bother you," he said, playing up the 'Englishman abroad' act. "I don't suppose you chaps could give me a lift, could you?"

The man who speaks first is usually the leader. Gabriel paid close attention. This group's alpha male was a young guy with floppy blonde hair swept back from his eyes and held in place with a red and white spotted bandanna. He looked obscenely healthy— tanned, fit, clear skin, laughing blue eyes, and good teeth, revealed as he smiled. The other four looked like they'd been cut from the same cloth. *College kids?*

"English, right?" he said. Gabriel nodded, still smiling. "Kind of in the middle of nowhere, aren't you?" The young man's accent was American, maybe somewhere on the East Coast. Cultured, anyway, with a tone that spoke of easy living. *Maybe rich college kids, then?*

"My last ride dropped me here. He was delivering beer to a bar." Gabriel nodded back past the rear of the camper van.

"So where are you headed?"

"Nova Cidade. But," Gabriel added, holding his hands wide, "I mean, wherever you chaps are headed would be fine by me. My money's pretty much all gone, so you know …" He let his voice tail off as if embarrassed.

"We're not exactly 'headed' anywhere. It's more of a road trip. So why don't you ride with us for now, and we'll see whether we can get you closer to your destination."

"Thank you so much. My name's Gabriel, by the way."

The man did the introductions. "Cool. I'm Marcus. These guys are Evan and Josh …" The two men each side of him held out their hands to shake. "… and they're David and Nico." More handshakes.

Marcus climbed in, taking the driver's seat, with David beside him. Sitting in the back of the van with Josh, Evan, and Nico, Gabriel looked around as they pulled away from the kerb. "Nice," he said, and meant it. The VW's interior was decked out with pale orange LEDs in the ceiling, like a constellation. The bench seats were upholstered in white leather with orange piping.

"Yeah," Josh said. "Marcus's dad gave it to him for getting into Yale."

"Shouldn't you guys actually be there, then? In college, I mean."

"Nah. We're taking a break before Thanksgiving. My dad owns a freight company. He flew the van down here for us, and we picked it up last week."

Gabriel looked around at the young, gilded men with whom he was sharing the camper van. He took in their sprawling, relaxed poses and expensive, casual clothes; their understated watches and knotted leather bracelets fastened with silver clasps; their athletic physiques and good looks that generations of careful mate-selection in their bloodlines had produced. *I'm in a WASPs' nest!*

"So how 'bout you, bro?" This was Evan who spoke. Preppy horn-rimmed spectacles made him look like a writer in a 1950s film about Hollywood. "What's your deal?"

"Well, this is going to sound a bit freaky to you, but I belong to the Children of Heaven. We're a religious group based just beyond Nova Cidade. I got separated from my friends, so I'm trying to get back by riding my thumb." He smiled in what he hoped was a disarming fashion, spreading his hands wide and sticking his thumb out for good measure.

"The what of what?" The one called Josh brayed a laugh that sounded cruel rather than humorous. "What are you, one of those cults that hang around in malls giving out flowers?"

"Not exactly. We believe that the world is full of sin and we have to serve God though our leader."

"Your leader? Oh, this is too much. We've just picked up an honest-to-God, bible-thumping, religious fanatic."

They all joined in the laughter. Gabriel guessed their own brand of religion would be something quiet and respectably middle-class. Episcopalians, maybe, or Presbyterians. Certainly nothing that involved living in a communal village in the middle of the Brazilian rainforest. Although, he reflected, plenty of the Children came from exactly the same comfortable, Ivy-league backgrounds as these five.

They were back on the highway now.

"Hey, Marcus," Evan called. "Why don't you show Gabriel what this baby can do?"

"Hold on tight," Marcus shouted, then dropped down a gear and floored the throttle.

The camper van took off like a sports car, exhaust emitting a flat bark Gabriel recognised. But he decided to play dumb.

"Wow! Is that a standard engine you've got in this thing?"

"You wish," David called over the noise of the engine. "It's a three-point-six Porsche engine from a 911. Totally remapped and custom-fitted. She's good for one-eighty-five, but the van'd probably part company with the engine."

"So, your leader. He's super-holy? Vegetarian, hair shirt, all that?" David said, craning his neck to look round at Gabriel from the passenger seat up front.

"Not exactly. We eat meat. But he preaches that the things that will truly make us happy aren't to be found in shops, or on the Internet or TV. We're just trying to fill a spiritual void."

"Dude, that's what church is for," Evan said.

"He teaches us that mainstream religions have lost their way. That they cater to the needs of their priesthoods. That they seek power, that they cause wars."

"That's ridiculous," Josh said. "My dad is a deacon in the Episcopalian Church. He does a ton of charity work. He's not seeking power or causing wars. Now Islam, on the other hand. There's a dangerous religion. I mean …"

"OK, Josh," Marcus said, before his friend could expound on his theory. "We've heard it all before. Peace-loving Muslims are just terrorists who haven't thrown a bomb yet. But what about that shit storm up in Maine last year? That wasn't Muslims. That was some fucking nut-job white guy with an assault rifle and a God complex."

This seemed to be an old conversation rehearsed many times before, and, as the camper van sped northwest, Gabriel decided to change tack.

"I don't suppose you've got a pack of cards have you?" he said. "We could play to pass the time."

"Your guru OK with that, is he?" Josh said, his lip curling with evident disdain.

"What the eye doesn't see, the heart doesn't grieve over."

"You're off the leash for a few hours, that what you're saying?"

Gabriel smiled. "Sure, why not? So, cards?"

Evan rummaged through a drawer set into the bench-seat. "OK, here you go. Do you play bridge, Gabriel?" He exchanged a look with his friends that was no doubt meant to be invisible to Gabriel. It wasn't. It was a sly look, under lowered eyelids, accompanied by a tiny grin. It said, shall we have some sport with this simple fellow and relieve him of his money?

"I'm afraid not. But I can play a little poker. Five-card stud any good for you guys?"

"Oh, I think we could manage that," Josh said. "What kind of stakes were you thinking? I mean, assuming you managed to beg enough alms on your road trip."

Gabriel emptied out his pocket onto the black-carpeted floor between them. That's all I have. It's enough for a grub stake, wouldn't you say?"

Josh poked a finger through the untidy pile of banknotes.

"Fine. So, let's make it a twenty-forty, fixed-limit game. That OK with you, Gabriel?"

"Fine by me."

The terms and betting limits settled, Josh shuffled, invited Gabriel to cut, then dealt the cards.

Gabriel contrived to lose the first three hands, folding his last—three kings and a pair of tens—without revealing his cards to the others. Then he began to play in earnest. Greed had kicked in hard with his opponents, as he saw them, and they were betting rashly. *Time for a little* Yinshen fangshi, *my over-privileged friends. You can afford to lose, and I really, really need your money.*

54

CHEATS NEVER PROSPER

GABRIEL'S CASH PILE GREW STEADILY LARGER as he began winning hand after hand. He was fairly certain Master Zhao had never intended him to use the Way of Stealth to cheat at cards, but equally, his old teacher had reminded him that we make our own luck in this world.

The Ivy League boys weren't so happy now they were losing, and had begun exchanging furtive glances. Their flicking eyes didn't go unnoticed and Gabriel decided he needed to finish them off before they decided enough was enough and put their depleted stakes back in their wallets.

"So did you ever play anyone with a real tell," he asked Josh, pulling the young man's gaze to his eyes and subtly altering his speech pattern and breathing. "You … know, you … blink when you've got a weak hand … or you … rub your nose if you have a strong one?"

"What? Why? Shut up and let me concentrate."

"Yeah, bro," Evan said, looking up from his own hand. "Shut up and play."

"Sorry, Evan," Gabriel said, altering his tone of voice and eye movements to bring the other man into his slightly altered reality. "I

… I guess I should be concentrating on my cards … I don't want to … lose your money … for you."

Little by little, Gabriel wove an ancient Chinese spell over his three opponents. Not magic, but a combination of techniques practised by monks since before the time of Christ to disorientate others they wished to influence. His current hand was a strong one: a royal flush. He took the betting way up, all the time encouraging the others to keep pace. Finally, they cracked, one by one.

"I fold," Evan said, throwing his cards down in disgust.

"Fold."

"Fold."

Gabriel smiled innocently, eyebrows raised, as he scooped the pile of bills over his own. "Lady Luck is favouring me with her attention," he said.

"Yeah, well, either that or you're cheating," Josh said, almost pouting. Of the three Americans, he'd lost the most.

"Josh!" Evan said.

"I just can't believe he's doing this well. I mean, I founded the fucking poker club in Phi Sigma Kappa, for Christ's sake."

Time to end this, Gabriel thought, noticing that they'd just blown through a one-horse town with a petrol station, a couple of cantinas and a minimarket. It was his deal. This time, Lady Luck was definitely looking the other way. Once all the cards were dealt, he was looking at what his father would have called, "a bit of a ragbag". A pair of fours and three more cards of singularly unimpressive value: seven of clubs, nine of diamonds and Jack of hearts. He watched the others from beneath lowered lids.

Evan blinked.

Nico blinked.

Josh rubbed his nose, and smiled too, for good measure. Obviously the founder of the frat house poker club was feeling confident.

Five minutes later, the smile was gone, replaced by a glowering expression that knitted his bushy ginger eyebrows together and pulled the corners of his mouth down into a scowl.

"Fuck. I fold," he said, slamming the cards down.

"Yeah, me too. Again," Nico said.

Evan wasn't giving up though.

"See your twenty and raise you forty," he said.

"See your forty, raise you another forty," Gabriel said.

The betting between the two remaining players continued until the pile of Reals between them was almost six inches high.

"Come on, Evan," Josh said, "take him to the cleaners".

"You tell him, Josh," Gabriel said, with a smile, pushing the word 'tell' just a little.

He waited.

Began counting.

Looked Evan in the eye.

Evan blinked.

And folded.

As Gabriel was gathering up the cash and stuffing the bills into his pockets, Josh spoke. This time there was a nasty edge in his voice. A cruel tone. A tone that said, "I come from money, I'll have more money, and you're not supposed to have *my* money".

"Nobody plays that well. What are you up to?"

"Me? Nothing. Why, are you not used to losing? You know what Rudyard Kipling wrote. 'If you can meet with Triumph and Disaster and treat those two impostors just the same …'"

"Fuck Rudyard Kipling! And fuck *you*! Marcus, stop the van. He's getting out."

"Yeah, yeah, Josh, fine. I'm getting tired of all of you in the back, bitching like a bar full of queens."

Marcus pulled over onto the gritty hard shoulder and killed the engine.

Josh stood and squeezed past Gabriel to open the door then jerked his thumb at the gap.

"OK, you, out."

Gabriel stood and stepped towards the door, but as he reached the opening, Josh stuck his foot out to trip him and shoved him hard in the back. It was a clumsy move, and one Gabriel was expecting. He rolled as he hit the ground and was back on the balls of his feet a second later, just as Josh jumped down, fists up, teeth bared.

Gabriel didn't feel good about putting the college kid down, but there was more at stake than the kid would ever know.

As Josh hit the ground, bleeding from a split lip, there was a shout from inside the van.

"He decked Josh!"

Nico bailed out next, followed by Evan. In seconds, they'd joined Josh, moaning for breath and winded after hard punches to the solar plexus. That just left the two men from the front seats. David was out next, and Marcus rounded the front of the van almost at the same time. They both charged him, apparently aiming to grapple him to the ground rather than engage in any Queensbury rules-style boxing. It did them no good. Gabriel simply seized them by the necks and slammed their heads together with a noise like two blocks of wood meeting at speed. "Stay down!" Gabriel shouted, pointing at Josh, who was struggling to his knees, "Or I'll put you down."

Josh subsided, but to judge from his high colour, his fury at being bested in a fight as well as a card game was about to detonate something deep inside his brain.

"What are you going to do?" he asked.

"I'm going to take the van. You guys look fit enough to walk back to the last town we passed. I'll leave it somewhere conspicuous with a note saying it belongs to five entitled American frat boys. I'm sure it'll find its way back to you."

As he climbed into the driver's seat, it was to a background chorus of most un-Yale-like oaths. He twisted the key, blipped the throttle then took off, pushing the engine right up to the red line in every gear. When the camper van was almost flying, he eased off a little and held it at a steady one-twenty as he powered down the highway towards his flight to Eden.

55

FILHOS DE SATAN

AFTER BLOWING THROUGH A COUPLE of towns, each consisting of little more than a bar, a few shacks, and a petrol station, Gabriel felt his own fuel levels dipping dangerously low. He pushed on for another ten miles until he came to another of the ribbon-like settlements strung out like beads on the straight concrete thread of the highway. This one was called Castelo do Norte.

He pulled in to a petrol station, fuelled up, then went inside to pay. While he was waiting for his burrito to heat up in the microwave thoughtfully provided by the owner, he heard the roar of motorcycle engines from the road. He looked over to the window, which was partly obscured by posters advertising a nearby festival. Five or six bikers had pulled in at the pumps.

The microwave pinged. He grabbed his burrito and a can of Coke from the next-door cooler. He paid at the till with one of the crumpled bills he'd taken from the frat boys. The woman behind the till looked the motherly type. She was plump, with dyed black hair, big gold hoop earrings, and a smudge of rouge on each cheek. She nodded at Gabriel then inclined her head towards the window and frowned. She spoke one word as she handed him his change.

"Problema."

"Obrigado," he said with a smile.

"De nada, senhor."

He took a bite of the hot burrito, savouring the flavours of chicken and chilli sauce, as he stepped out onto the gravel surrounding the pumps. Clustered around their machines were half a dozen leather-jacketed bikers, skin tones ranging from pale caramel to a brown so dark as to be almost black, with tattoos, gold earrings like the petrol station woman, and deep brown, hooded eyes, which he could still read. Their leathers were adorned with patches advertising oil companies and bike parts makers. Two of the men had their backs to him. Their jackets bore shoulder-to-shoulder patches with a winged skull and the legend, *Filhos de Satan.*

The camper van was on the other side of the pumps. Gabriel strolled over and reached into his pocket for the key. Getting in meant squeezing between the side of the van and the pump. It also brought him within an arm's length of the nearest biker. As he climbed in, the man turned and looked him straight in the eye. He was an ugly brute. Short, thickset, and with piggy eyes set close together in a face pockmarked with acne scars. Gabriel stared back.

"Bom dia," he said. *Might as well be polite.*

The biker said nothing. He did grin though, exposing snaggled dentition with at least as many gaps as teeth. *Time to be on my way.* The others were also watching, and their conversation proceeded in Portuguese too rapid for Gabriel to understand fully. He did catch one phrase, and it didn't fill him with optimism: *"mata lo e despejaremos."* It was close enough to the Spanish for him to translate it perfectly. "Kill and dump him". *Sorry boys, not going to happen. And what is it with bikers? Why are you always so fucking hostile?* Gabriel had had dealings with Hells Angels, these bikers' cousins in upstate Michigan on a previous excursion to the Americas. It hadn't ended well. For the bikers.

He started the engine and peeled out of the forecourt, changing up through the gears and flooring the throttle each time. The Porsche engine did what it had been designed to do, and soon the town was a blur in the heat haze coming off the tarmac.

Unlike the Harley Davidsons favoured by their North American counterparts, the Sons of Satan were mounted on faster, nimbler machinery. As he'd left the shop, Gabriel had checked them out: British-made Triumphs and Japanese Suzukis and Kawasakis. Each with an engine displacement of at least nine hundred cubic centimetres and a kerb weight well under a quarter of a tonne, their power-to-weight ratio dwarfed the camper van's.

That disparity explained why, five minutes later, he clocked a tight group of six mainly vertical silhouettes growing steadily larger in his wing mirror. He drove the throttle down, but the van maxed out at a hundred and thirty. It felt like it was about to shake itself to pieces anyway. Maybe the boy's old man had the mechanics install a limiter.

Inside the cabin, the noise made thinking difficult. Tyre roar and wind noise added to the blare from the exhausts and the engine's thrashy bark. Gabriel made a decision.

A minute or two later, the leading bike pulled away from his lieutenants and accelerated up alongside the camper van until he was level with the driver's window. Gabriel glanced left. The big man was smiling, revealing a mouthful of gold teeth. Then he pulled a sawn-off shotgun from a scabbard strapped to the bike's frame and swung it around until the black figure eight of its side-by-side barrels was pointing directly at Gabriel's face.

Gabriel smiled back and touched the brakes. Then, as the man matched him to keep level with the front of the van, he jabbed the throttle at the same time as he swung the steering wheel hard over to the left. With a bang, the front wing smashed against the bike's rear wheel.

It doesn't take much to upset the equilibrium on a fast-moving motorcycle. A tap will do it. This was more like a roundhouse from a super-heavyweight. The front forks turned through ninety-degrees and the tyre dug in, catapulting the bike and its rider ten feet into the air. By the time they crash-landed on the tarmac, Gabriel was accelerating down the road. The distance gave him a great view of the bike in his rear-view mirror as its tank exploded, covering its former rider in burning petrol.

Now he had the remaining five to deal with. Would they stop to try and extinguish their leader or come after him? No honour amongst thieves, apparently. They spread out and accelerated hard, three to the left, two in single file to the right, trying to come between Gabriel and the hard shoulder. *Fine, we'll do it your way, boys.*

He waited until they'd drawn level, like a vicious-minded escort, semi-auto pistols drawn and held in their left hands aiming in at the windows. Then he stamped on the brakes, almost standing the camper van on its nose. Relative to his position on the road, the five bikers hurtled ahead. Two of the three to his right were trigger happy. They were still shooting as he disappeared from their field of fire. The shooters' gang-mates on Gabriel's left took rounds to the body that punched them off their bikes and out of the game. *Careless. Now it's three to one. But I'm in an armoured truck compared to your rides.*

Dropping down a couple of gears, Gabriel floored the throttle once more and barged straight into the back of two of the bikers. He was close enough to read the script on their leathers before their bikes shook violently like bucking broncos and threw their riders off to skid and tumble down the road at close to ninety miles per hour.

The final rider had finally wised up to the fact that he was in trouble. But he still had his pistol. He braked suddenly and pulled in behind Gabriel then loosed off three shots that shattered the back windows. Gabriel suspected that the man would have been able to shoot him clean through the back of the head under ideal conditions. But these weren't ideal conditions. Not even close. Pulling behind had probably seemed a clever move. And it was, until Gabriel repeated the trick with his own brakes, which clearly had been upgraded at the same time as the engine.

With a satisfyingly loud, crunching bang, the last remaining bike smashed itself against the rear of the van, spun off sideways, and deposited its rider into the scrub at the side of the road.

In all, the chase had lasted no more than three minutes. For Gabriel, time had slowed down until it felt like hours were ticking by, each collision a slow-motion scene in a movie. His heart was pumping, but not particularly quickly. He inhaled deeply then let it out in a great sigh.

"I really *hate* biker gangs."

56

RUMBLED. AGAIN

GABRIEL DROVE ONTO THE AIRFIELD at Nova Cidade. His arms were sore from holding the vibrating steering wheel for hundreds of miles. Without sunglasses, his eyes felt rough inside their sockets from squinting into the sun for so long. He rolled up to the hangar, switched off the engine and climbed out of the van. Stretching and leaning over, first to the left then the right, feeling rather than hearing the muted pops as his spine unkinked itself, he could see the office was shut for the night. That was OK. He could wait until morning.

Well, you don't have much choice do you, Old Sport?

Funny how Don's voice would pop into his head at moments like these, reminding him that sometimes, what felt like a decision was just force of circumstance.

With nothing to do until morning, he turned around, climbed into the camper van, and drove back into the nearby town, aiming for food and drink. Then he'd simply drive back to the airfield, pull the curtains and sleep in the van.

Compared to the tiny settlements he'd driven through since meeting up with Marcus and his friends, Nova Cidade was a hive of activity. The bees were certainly buzzing when he got out of the van after parking on the street outside a bar called Cantina Moravia. Smartly dressed office workers were milling about outside drinking tall glasses of foamy amber beer, dewed glasses of white wine, and the odd Mojito, mint leaves crushed amongst the ice cubes.

He pushed through the swing doors into a blessedly air-conditioned interior where a band were warming up in a corner. As they vamped a few jazzy chords, Gabriel walked to the bar, which was free apart from a couple of young women drinking caipirinhas.

The barman wandered over, clearly more interested in the girls than in serving a gringo. He lifted his chin. Gabriel pointed at the girls' drinks and held up a finger. They turned as he ordered and bestowed smiles on him: white teeth, beautiful dark skin, deep brown eyes fringed with heavy lashes. Any other day, any other time, he would have enjoyed making conversation, or trying to, but he was shattered from the day's events. He nodded at them and stared at the bottles behind the bar while the barman made his drink. It arrived a minute or two later. Gabriel put a ten-Real note on the bar and downed the drink in one.

The cold hit of sugar and lime mixed with the fiery sugarcane spirit revived him almost at once and he let the last few drips fall from the rim of the glass into his open mouth, holding the ice cubes and lime wedges in place with the edge of his thumb. He signalled the barman for another and watched as the man, buff-bodied and clearly proud of it in a skin-tight white vest and white jeans, repeated the process, smashing sugar and limes together in the bottom of the heavy glass tumbler before adding the clear *cachaça*.

The girls beside him were giggling and stealing glances in his direction, whispering behind their hands. He added another ten-Real note to its sister and took a sip of the new drink. He hooked a tall barstool over with his foot and took a seat, resting his elbows on the zinc surface.

One of the girls touched his left arm and spoke in halting but good English.

"Hello. You're American?"

"Hi. No, sorry. English."

"Oh. That's OK, we like Englishmen."

"Your English is very good."

"We're students. International business."

"Well, you have no idea how nice it is to hear a friendly voice. It's been a very long and trying day."

The girls swivelled and slid their stools to face his, and the three of them exchanged names and clinked glasses to their newfound friendship.

They were called Mariana and Beatriz and were eager to try out their English on Gabriel. That suited him just fine; he didn't have a lot of energy left for foreign language conversation. After ten minutes or so, Mariana, the girl who'd touched his arm in the first place, checked her phone. She looked up at Gabriel and pouted her disappointment.

"It's my boyfriend. I have to leave. We're going to the movies. It's been lovely to meet you, Gabriel."

She leaned towards him and they kissed on each cheek. Gabriel was almost overwhelmed by the fresh floral scent of her perfume. Suddenly he wanted to be out of Brazil and back home. Back home with Britta Falskog, curled up in front of an open fire, preferably not wearing very many clothes. Then she—and the vision of his Swedish on-off-but-mostly-off girlfriend—was gone.

"That outfit," Beatriz said, plucking at his shirt. "I see Enrique isn't the only one around here who goes for all white. But yours looks like it could do with a wash."

He looked down. The shirt and trousers were smeared and grimy with road dust and sweat.

"God, I look a mess, don't I?"

"I'm sure God doesn't mind. And Père Christophe probably doesn't either."

Gabriel had often read in books about people's hearts skipping beats. He'd always assumed it was a writerly cliché. That was, until his own pump did a kind of jerk in his chest, sending a spike of adrenaline coursing through his bloodstream.

"Père who?"

She winked at him. "Very good. So you're not a member of the Children of Heaven? You don't know about a place in the rainforest called Eden? And you don't have a leader who calls himself Père Christophe?"

57

PASSPORT, TICKET, MONEY

CHRISTOPHE JARDIN, BORDERLINE PSYCHOPATH, CULT leader, serial rapist, murderer, terrorist, and narcissist prepared to leave his jungle paradise. He stood in the middle of his living room and turned through a full circle, taking in the gracious proportions of the house he'd had his slaves build for him all those years ago. It was a monument to his ego, as was the entire Eden complex, from the generator room to the vegetable gardens, the laundry to the temple. There was cash enough in the numbered accounts held in his name in a trio of Swiss banks, but when was it ever about money? Look at his mother and father—avowed Marxists for their entire adult lives, yet living off interest from inherited wealth and spending freely on that most bourgeois of all commodities, fine art.

He stalked over to a bookshelf and swept his right arm along the top, scattering tribal artefacts he'd bought in the early days, crude clay figurines of pregnant women with grossly exaggerated breasts and buttocks, priapic males with erections that threatened to poke them in the eye. Worthless now. Utterly without value. He'd been betrayed by one he'd assumed would be his to command. He could feel it. And that smug, self-satisfied politician he'd watched on the

TV, pointing at him and threatening him with shutdown. Cunts! All of them. They neither saw his genius nor cared for it. Yet here he was, forced to run like a rat down a sewer while these, these pygmies crowed about their prowess and their rectitude. Who the fuck do you think's paving our way north, you idiots? A bundle of cash here, a tumble with a fresh-faced female follower there. It's all corruption, however you look at it. At least he, Christophe Jardin, was honest about the process. You take what you want, and one way or another you pay for it. Just don't preach about "the war on drugs" before you return to your campaign headquarters to open a bottle of wine or chop a few lines of coke for your hardworking "team". Jesus! It was enough to turn a man to God.

Jardin barked out a hoarse laugh at this thought. "God?" he shouted. "There's a joke. Do you kill those millions of children with malaria out of compassion? Are paedophile rings your way of saying, 'Behave yourself or else?' I send teenagers wrapped in explosives and ball bearings to slaughter innocent people BECAUSE I FEEL LIKE IT, and what do you do about it? Sorry?" He cupped his right palm around his ear. "I missed that. WHAT? Oh, nothing. You're OK with the slaughter of innocents. Good! Because listen up, old man. I have plans that will curdle your fucking ambrosia. I'm going to test you to the very fucking limits of belief. By the time I've finished, they'll be turning to Satan for a sympathetic hearing. I. Will. BEAT YOU!" Jardin screamed these last words, breaking into a squawking cough as his screeching caught in his throat.

58

COMPETITION

BEATRIZ SIPPED HER CAIPIRINHA, WATCHING Gabriel silently over the rim of the glass. She seemed in no hurry to fill the silence. Which was a shame, as it would have given Gabriel more time to think. In the end, he settled on the truth. Or most of it.

"OK, yes. I belong to the Children of Heaven. But you're a very pretty girl, and I thought you'd mark me down as a weirdo and leave if I admitted it."

"Thank you. For the compliment as well as the truth." She put her tumbler down on the bar. "Here's the thing. I'm not a student. I'm not even Brazilian. I'm with the DEA. You know what that is?"

"Yes. The Drug Enforcement Agency. Père Christophe says they're part of the problem."

"Which is?" Beatriz had stopped smiling now.

"Governments. Their agents of repression. Organized religion. Multinational corporations. The UN. NATO. Banks. The mass media. The Internet companies that control our lives."

"OK, OK," she interrupted, holding up both hands in an 'I surrender' pose. "I get the picture. Everyone's in on some evil global conspiracy except your Dear Leader. That about it?"

He nodded, hoping his loyal follower act would be sufficient to keep Beatriz from asking more searching questions.

"Can I ask *you* a question?" he said.

"You just did. But, sure, why not? Ask away."

"Is Beatriz your real name? Was Mariana DEA too?"

"That was two questions. Naughty boy." She wagged a finger at him. "No. It's not my real name. Which is Alana by the way. Alana Losanto. And yes, Mariana is DEA." She crinkled her nose. "On which subject, that's an unusual phrasing, don't you think?"

"What is?"

"You said, 'Is Mariana DEA too?', not, 'Is Mariana *in the* DEA?'. Or 'Does Mariana *work for the* DEA?'"

"So what?"

"So what? So, civilians don't say it like that."

Gabriel took a sip of his drink, realising that this, too, was a giveaway. A bit of business to buy time, which his counterpart would surely notice. Then he had a brainwave. One that would account for his language and his guilty behaviour. "Look," he said, looking directly at Alana, "I'm not supposed to, but when I come in to get provisions, sometimes I sneak into a movie. I love those action films. Always have. We don't get much entertainment at Eden. I must have picked it up from one of the films."

Alana pressed her lips together. Clearly not convinced.

"Suppose I believe you. Suppose I think you really are some brainwashed zombie who thinks the sun shines out of Père Christophe's ass," she put air-quotes around the cult leader's name, "and not some deep-cover British spy." She paused for a beat, but Gabriel was ready and kept his facial muscles relaxed and still. "Last week he sent one of his followers, an ex-Ivy League dropout called Zack Framingham, to firebomb a film studio in LA. Only the kid failed and got himself taken into custody. He eventually gave us the last piece of intel we needed to nail your leader, Christophe Jardin. So now we're going to flush that little creep out into the open and deal with him with appropriate severity. We could do with someone we can trust on the inside of his little rainforest paradise." She took another sip of her drink. "I just thought that might be you."

Oh, Alana, it would be so helpful to have backup. Added firepower, boots on the ground. But my orders are clear. He's mine and I won't let him disappear. Either deep into the forest or deeper into the America legal system.

"I'm sorry. Père Christophe rescued me. He loves me, and I love him. Now, if you'll excuse me, I have to go."

Alana shrugged. "Your funeral. But you might want to take a long walk in the rainforest, day after tomorrow. I saw a weather forecast and it's going to get very hot out there."

Gabriel nodded. He left without saying another word, or looking back.

He bought some fried chicken and rice from a street vendor and ate it with the wooden spoon the man gave him as he walked back to the van. He passed a bar and slipped inside to buy a half-bottle of vodka.

He was back at the airfield thirty minutes later, setting up a bed inside the camper. He closed all but one of the blinds, hoping sunrise would wake him.

With his head on the pillow, he closed his eyes and let his mind quiet, helping it along with a breathing exercise taught him by Master Zhao. In for four, hold for one, out for four, hold for one. 'The ten-second breath,' he'd called it. As the breath pattern became automatic, his lungs inflating and deflating like a machine-controlled bellows, Gabriel focused his attention on another organ: his heart. It was beating at around sixty-five to the minute. An excellent rate for most people, but Gabriel's resting pulse was closer to sixty, the high fifties on a good day. He pictured the throbbing, four-chamber pump and willed its movement to slow.

Sixty ... fifty-nine ... fifty-eight ... fifty-seven ...

... from its appearance, it's clear that Oxford Street has hit hard times, maybe from another recession, because how else to account for the vines and lianas hanging from the lampposts and the upper-storey balconies, and the lush vegetation thrusting its way up through cracks in the road and out from the smashed windows of the shops, and those trees, leaning towards each other from either side of the street, their higher branches almost touching overhead like the canted roofs of Elizabethan buildings, and there's no merchandise left, of course, the looters have seen to that, and up in the tree canopy, monkeys leap from branch

to branch in search of fruit, while scarlet-beaked birds of prey hunt them down, pulling their heads off with loud popping sounds as Gabriel walks down the centre of the road, M16 held loosely in the crook of his right arm, keeping well away from the crocs with their burnt-black scales that lurk in the shadows, whispering to each other in Portuguese, while his stomach churns with fear, and the heat makes him sweat even more than the anxiety; he looks around, but the other members of his patrol have disappeared. Troopers "Daisy" Cheaney and "Smudge" Smith and Corporal "Dusty" Rhodes are nowhere to be seen and then a scream pierces the noise of the jungle, and it's a pleading note riding high on top of the visceral sound of a man in agony as he calls out …

"Boss! Help me!" and Gabriel knows that the voice belongs to Smudge, so he breaks into a run, cocking his M16, head turning left and right, looking for him, but when he next looks ahead, he sees something that brings him to a stop. It's one of the lampposts that's out of position, in the centre of the road instead of at the edge. Two dull grey horizontal branches fork away from the main upright about ten feet off the ground, where he sees a lean, brown-skinned figure dressed in tracksuit trousers and an Adidas T-shirt climbing head-down from the crosspiece on long spidery legs, an AK 47 slung over its back, and it's getting closer. Gabriel sees what the figure has left behind, sees Smudge, crucified on the lamppost, machetes driven through both palms and into the steel crosspiece, so Gabriel tries to run faster, but his knees seem locked and he can only stumble on stiff legs, trying to shout out to Smudge, but his mouth won't emit any sound at all. He can feel it twisting into a rictus grin, tongue poking out between his teeth, then the spidery creature is standing in front of him, legs apart, arms hanging down by its sides, and its body has the lean, brown, corded look of a People's Army for the Liberation of Mozambique fighter, but the head is that of a girl, a girl with short blonde hair with closed eyes and a smiling mouth, a mouth filled with row upon row of sharp-pointed, yellow-white teeth and it says,

"Come closer, Captain Wolfe."

Gabriel takes a few more paces, terror welling in his throat and making him gasp in short, shallow breaths and he knows he doesn't want to see the fighter up close but he can't stop moving until, eventually, they are standing face to face, whereupon the fighter's terrible grin widens until the corners of its mouth tear open with a ripping sound and its lower jaw falls to the jungle floor and then it slowly opens its eyes, which are not brown, nor blue, nor green, nor grey, but silvery and shiny and smeared across their steely corneas with congealed blood, making Gabriel open his mouth to scream but he can't. It's jammed full of more of the obscene spheres, splintering his teeth as he tries to spit them out, then the grinning figure draws a machete from its belt and rests the blade against Gabriel's left cheek before snapping its hand back and bringing it forward again with a swish

59

NOW ALL I NEED IS A RED BERET

GABRIEL JERKED AWAKE AS THE sun crept above the roof of the hangar and sent a beam of yellow-white light in through the open blind above his head. Like a caul round a newborn baby, the nightmare still clung about him, making him shudder.

Ten minutes later, he was outside the airfield office. He could see what he wanted hanging from a hook on the wall, beneath a promotional calendar displaying Señorita November, who had forgotten to put her top on before working on her plane. Using a couple of bits of steel wire he'd pulled from the engine bay of the camper van, he picked the lock. It was so simple, a child could have done it. He snagged the bunch of heavy keys then wedged the door ajar with a folded piece of card from the wastepaper basket.

It was far too early for anyone to be around, but Gabriel moved quickly, nonetheless. No sense in being caught by Brazil's only early-rising aircraft technician. He jogged over to the huge sliding door of the hangar and started trying keys in the lock of the door set into the massive sheet of steel. Master Zhao spoke to him.

Slow down, Wolfe cub. Think first; act second.

He took a deep breath, and examined the lock, looking for a maker's name. Yes! There it was. A laser-cut logo: La Fonte. He found the matching key and pushed it home. The door opened silently.

Once inside with the door closed and latched behind him, Gabriel felt along the wall for a light switch. His fingertips grazed a block of switches with a cold metal conduit leading from the top. He flicked down the six toggles, one after the other, and the gigantic space was lit by twenty-four industrial pendant lamps suspended way above him from the pitched, corrugated iron roof. The small white planes occupying the centre of the space like a sleeping flock of geese were packed in prop-to-tail, their wheels chocked.

He jogged round the periphery of the hangar, looking for the gear locker. On the third side of the square, he found it. He repeated the process with the keys, taking only a few seconds to find a Yale that fitted the lock. He pulled the door wide and breathed a small sigh of relief. Stacked inside, in their thick black nylon covers, were a dozen parachutes. He pulled one out and rearranged the others to mask the gap. The condition of the cover was immaculate: no rips, scuffs, or tears. It looked brand new. The surface was smooth and even, with no suspicious lumps or bulges to indicate a badly packed chute. The ripcord was shiny and coated in a thin film of light oil. Another tick in the checklist that was headed, "Careful, safety-conscious owner". Next, he checked the straps and buckles. Again, they were in excellent condition. No fraying on the webbing, no nicks or tears, no scratches on any of the buckle components.

After locking the hangar door and replacing the keys in the office, Gabriel didn't have too long to wait. He heard the distant clatter of a well-used diesel engine coming from the road. Five minutes later, a battered, red Toyota Hilux pickup rounded the corner of the hangar, crossed the tarmac apron in front and pulled up a few yards away from the camper van.

The man who emerged squinted into the sun as he took in Gabriel's white-clad form. Then he rubbed his hand over his stubbled chin and scratched his neck. His eyes were reddened, and he had the enlarged, purple nose of the serious drinker. He wore a much-scuffed brown leather flying jacket with a shearling collar over a grubby white T-shirt, and he carried a scruffy canvas bag slung over one shoulder.

Was he a pilot or just the handyman? In some ways, Gabriel hoped he was the latter.

The man lifted his chin by way of greeting. Gabriel pointed at the chute at his feet. Then at the sky.

"How much for a private flight?" he asked. Then, in Portuguese, "*Quanto?*"

The man looked at the chute then at Gabriel, who was aiming for the image of a jump-gypsy, working his way round the country in return for flights.

He sniffed, then spoke in English. "Three hundred. Dollars."

It was a wildly optimistic price, and Gabriel felt sure the man knew it. Slowly, he pulled the roll of banknotes from his pocket and counted off six hundred Reals. He pushed the handful of crumpled bills towards the man. It was worth a hundred and fifty dollars, a decent enough price for a single flight.

The man, perhaps sensing he had a captive buyer, shook his head.

"Two-fifty."

Gabriel counted off another four hundred Reals and offered them to the man. He held his gaze and matched his breathing pattern for a few seconds then leaned forward and moved his hand fractionally closer to the man's right hand.

The man nodded. "OK," he said, and stuffed the wad of bills into the pocket of his flying jacket.

Gabriel picked up his chute and together they walked over to the landing strip. The pilot led the way to a Cessna 208, its cabin hooded with a fitted blue tarpaulin like a horse wearing a fly mask. He whisked it away and rolled it casually into a sausage shape that he slung over his shoulder while he unlocked the cabin door. In it went, chucked behind the seats to join a wreckage of soft drinks cans and old flying magazines. Gabriel was wondering whether he'd picked the right pilot after all, but he didn't have the luxury of a buyer's market. He pushed his parachute over the back of the seat to join the tarp, then climbed up and into the co-pilot's seat and buckled the harness over his shoulders and lap. He watched as the pilot pulled the chocks out from under the wheels then rounded the front of the plane and climbed in.

This close, Gabriel could smell the booze coming off the man in sickly-sweet waves. *A heavy night, then. Just hope you're OK to fly this thing close enough to Eden for me to jump without killing us both*. The pilot ran through a worryingly brief set of pre-flight checks, which mostly consisted of rapping the back of his knuckle against the fuel gauge and altimeter. Then he flicked on the master switch, fuel supply switch, and fuel cutoff valve. With a toothy grin, he stuck his thumb into the aluminium collar of the ignition switch and fired up the engine. It coughed a couple of times and emitted a cloud of dark grey smoke from the exhaust, then with a whine from the starter motor, the prop started turning. It juddered round for a few revolutions, then the engine fired and the whine changed to a buzz-saw rasp as the revolutions built.

The pilot turned to Gabriel and spoke in English.

"Where you going, man?"

"Eden? You know it?"

"The white people?"

For a moment Gabriel tried to remember whether all the Children of Heaven were Caucasian. Then he saw that the pilot was pointing at his clothes.

"Oh! Yes. *Sim*. The white people."

"No problem!"

The pilot sniffed, wiped his nose on the sleeve of his flying jacket and eased the throttle lever forward. The Cessna rolled and bumped over the grass towards the end of the runway.

Gabriel had flown in many planes on many missions, from Lockheed C-130J Super Hercules transports so huge you wondered how they ever got airborne, to helicopters, light planes, even gliders on one memorable occasion when a silent approach over the capital of a central African country was ordered. But there was something about this flight—this pilot, especially—that set a kaleidoscope of butterflies loose to flitter and swirl in his stomach. If the man wasn't still drunk from the night before, he surely had enough blood-alcohol to seriously impair his judgement.

The plane accelerated towards the end of the runway, and still the pilot kept the flaps neutral. Gabriel stared at the trees that demarcated the end of the airfield. They were now approaching at around fifty miles an hour. He felt his arms and legs bracing involuntarily and realised he'd clenched his jaw. He'd pushed the back of his head hard against the seat back and was breathing shallowly. Now the pilot was singing. A samba tune, something about a girl with brown eyes. Surprisingly melodic, he thought. As the trees rushed closer, he clenched his fists against his thighs and squeezed his eyes shut.

"*Vamos!*" the pilot shouted and hauled back on the control column.

With a sickening lurch that left Gabriel's stomach thirty feet below his boots, the Cessna pulled up into a steep climb. Gabriel opened his eyes just in time to see the tops of the trees rush by beneath the plane.

"Good pilot, yes?" the man said, with a laugh, elbowing Gabriel in his bicep.

Not up to a reciprocal laugh, Gabriel contented himself with a tight-lipped smile. "Yes. Very good."

"You with them?" the pilot asked, pointing again at Gabriel's shirt.

"Visiting."

"By parachute?"

"It's a surprise."

"Fucking big surprise. You gonna land on the big man's head?"

"Something like that. You know him?"

"A little. I flew stuff out there for him when he came to Brazil." He turned to look at Gabriel and tapped the side of his head. "You want to watch yourself with him."

Gabriel nodded. "I intend to."

After this brief flurry of conversation, the man lapsed into silence, and they flew on, towards Eden.

60

ONE LAST DAY IN PARADISE

CHRISTOPHE JARDIN WOKE EARLY. THE girl next to him was eighteen. She lay with her slender limbs spraddled across the sheets like a dropped marionette. She'd told him her name was Rebecca. Appropriately Biblical. And in a couple of hours, she'd be dead. He grinned, stroking his moustache and staring up at the bullet hole in the ceiling. Why wait? He slid from under the sheet and wandered, naked, into the kitchen.

Having selected a deep-bellied cook's knife from a magnetic bar attached to the wall, he went back into the bedroom. The girl was still sleeping. She looked very peaceful, her unlined skin so pale as to be translucent. Not having been at Eden very long, she had yet to acquire the golden tan that made all the other Children, Uncles, and Aunts look like residents at some sort of exclusive health club deep in the rainforest.

She stirred in her sleep, mumbling some nonsense in a whisper of outflowing breath. Then she rolled over, arms flung wide as if greeting the sun, which was creeping across her torso through the uncurtained window.

Jardin crossed the room and eased himself onto the bed beside her. She had a mole on her left breast, just above the nipple. Pale brown, like a drop of spilled *café au lait*. It made a good target.

"*Bonjour, Rebecca,*" he whispered. And then, "*Adieu.*"

He raised the knife to the limit of his reach, gripping it in his right hand, paused for a second, then brought it down, fast, plunging the long blade through the mole and into the girl's heart. Her eyes opened wide as she died, and she gasped out a mist of red droplets. Jardin left the knife sticking out of her chest and went to shower off the blood.

Half an hour later, he was sitting at his dining table, eating breakfast with Toron.

"How are your quarters," he asked the cartel boss.

"They're fine. Everything ready for your little group of followers?"

"More or less. I thought I'd give them a little sermon before we administer the final sacrament. Something to put them in the right frame of mind to meet their Maker."

"I thought you didn't believe in God. I heard you screaming at him yesterday."

Jardin smiled. "I don't. But they do. And they believe I am his conduit. The Messiah. It's the least I can do, leaving them to die with a smile on their faces."

"Good. Because this has been a massive waste of time and money, my friend. There's a half-built coke plant out there and we're just going to leave it all behind."

"Would you rather wait for the Brazilian anti-cartel squad to arrive with guns and tear gas?"

"Why not? We've done it before. In Colombia we don't just run at the first scent of danger."

"I know you don't. But without a workforce, you'd be left with a shed and some machinery."

"Round up some Indians. Give them Levi's or TVs or whatever the fuck they want. Drug them, why don't you?"

"I've made my mind up. I have a feeling things are going to get a little too hot around here for comfort. No. We stick to the plan. Your plane will be here at ten, you said?"

"Should be. A Beechcraft King Air. Plenty of room for us and my men and anything you want to bring out."

"Good. Well, I'll leave you to finish your coffee. Help yourself to whatever you want from the fridge. After all, we won't be coming back."

"Don't take too long. We need to go back to Bogotá and make some serious plans for our future operations." Toron paused and looked Jardin in the eye, then leaned across the table and poked him over his heart, "… if we *have* a future together."

Jardin smiled. "No need for the melodrama, Diego," he said. Then he poked Toron back, hard, enjoying the look of fury that flitted across the younger man's face. "Where there are human beings, there is weakness. And where there is weakness, there is also money to be made. Now, get everything ready. And relax." He smiled again, calculating just how wide he could make it without irritating Toron to the point he pulled a gun. Or a knife. "I'll be back soon enough."

With that, Jardin left, strolling down the path from his house towards the main kitchen. Inside, the Elect were preparing the sacrament, lining up the silvery canisters and decanting bottles of fruit cordial. They turned as he entered, bowing to him and then standing, waiting for him to speak.

"Good morning," he said, injecting a cheery note into his voice. It was what the poor fools expected, after all.

"Good morning, Père Christophe," they chorused, smiling at him as he walked among them.

He stopped beside one of the women, a former bookkeeper from Cincinnati.

"Aunt Nina, God be with you," he said, his hand alighting on the small of her back.

She looked down, blushing. "And with you, Père Christophe."

"I think it will be a good day, today, don't you?"

She looked up and smiled. "It's always a good day here."

He smiled back, letting his hand slide down over her ample buttocks, noting her look of surprise and, was that pleasure? Then he walked on, absorbing the smiles and looks of gratitude and of love from his chosen lieutenants in the biggest mass slaughter in Brazil's history. Of course, they would also be dying today, so their culpability would be a matter of purely academic debate. One for the murder ghouls only.

"We will meet in the square at nine-thirty this morning. I have a few words I wish to say to the Children."

"Very good, Père Christophe."

He left the way he had come, continuing his leave-taking. All around him, the Children of Heaven were walking to their allotted chores: gardening, feeding livestock, mending clothes, repairing machinery. There was singing coming from a clearing behind a row of the simple adobe huts.

Jardin watched from behind a palm tree. He saw a group of about twenty young men, with guitars and tambourines, singing some dirge one of them had composed about loving God and doing good. Or maybe it was loving good and doing God. He suppressed a snigger. *Who fucking cares, you idiots! Enjoy your little sing-song while you can.*

As he turned to go, a young woman stepped out in front of him. Her face was a mask of worry.

"Yes, my child," he said. "And what can I do for you?"

"I am troubled, Père Christophe. Can you help me?"

He pursed his lips and stroked his moustache, then spoke.

"Why not? What's wrong, my child?"

61

LALO

GABRIEL LOOKED OUT OF HIS side window, then down. Below them, the rainforest, a vast tract of green interrupted only by the sinuous golden ribbons of rivers and the lakes they fed. From the south, a flock of flamingos rippled above the canopy, thousands of flickering pink wings setting up a rhythmic pattern that shifted and pulsed as the flock maintained the gaps between its individual members. He pondered the best way to proceed once he was on the ground. Without a weapon, he would either have to improvise or use his hands. Both suited him fine. There'd be plenty of timber, so a clubbing weapon would be an easy option. Maybe there'd be a rock in a stream bed. Or, higher risk, he could break into the tool shed by the vegetable gardens and snag a machete or a pruning knife. Or he could just snap the bastard's neck.

"Hey," the pilot said, breaking his train of thought. "You hungry? Thirsty?"

Gabriel realised he was. Both. "Yes, very."

The pilot reach down and pulled out the canvas shoulder bag, then handed it across to Gabriel.

"Coffee and sandwiches. Help yourself."

"Do you want some?"

"When I get back. Knock yourself out."

Gabriel poured a cup of coffee from a dented aluminium flask and took a gulp. It was very strong and very hot. He gasped.

"Wow! Is this how you deal with hangovers around here?"

The pilot laughed. "Good, huh? My wife makes it for me every morning. Woman's a saint."

Gabriel unwrapped one of the foil packages shoved down inside the bag. It contained a sandwich of rough, homemade bread filled with thick slices of cold pork, and slathered with a sweet-sharp apple sauce. He took a bite and sighed as the food hit his stomach.

"You should take care of your wife. She's a very good cook."

The man nodded. "She's a fucking good mechanic, too. Keeps this baby flying, anyway."

Gabriel smiled, acknowledging the pilot's good fortune. For the next five or ten minutes he munched contentedly on the sandwich, taking restorative draughts of the coffee.

"We're getting close," the pilot said. "You got a drop zone you want me to hit? Wind can be unpredictable out here, so much above ten thousand feet you may have problems sticking your landing."

Gabriel thought back to his training in the Paras. And his favourite jump.

"Somewhere a few miles from the village. Any clear spot. But we don't want to go high."

"No?" the pilot frowned.

"No. A thousand feet will do it, even a little less. No lower than six hundred, though."

"A thousand?" The pilot whirled in his seat to look at Gabriel. "You crazy? You'll get about ten seconds tops, and you're gonna kill yourself anyway. What the fuck do you want to go in so low for?"

"I'm in a hurry to see my old friend."

The man looked at Gabriel steadily for a few seconds, pursing his lips. "I only know one kind of person goes in on a chute below five thousand feet. Couple of the boys I used to hang with back in the day did it."

"Oh, yes? Who were they, then? Extreme sports enthusiasts?"

"You could call it that. Used to have special equipment for the kind of sports they did, though."

"Really?"

"Yes, really. Government equipment, know what I'm saying?"

"As you can see, I don't have any special equipment."

"But you want to do a LALO."

"A what?"

"Please, my friend. Don't insult me. You turn up out of the blue dressed like a member of our local religious cult, only you sound like that ain't your bag. You pay way, way over the odds in cash for a jump—and by the way, I recognise that chute, and it ain't yours—and you want to go in like a paratrooper. To my way of thinking, that's a pretty strange kind of a deal. What are you up to?"

"Like I said. I'm dropping in on an old friend."

"Oh yeah?" A note of irritation, mixed with suspicion, had crept into the man's voice. "Well the boys I was telling you about? Before? They were *Comando de Operações Especiais*. You know what that means?"

An easy translation job for an ex-SAS linguist. "Special Operations Command."

"Exactly. So when they dropped in on people, those people kind of stayed dropped in on, if you know what I'm saying."

Gabriel stared straight ahead. More complications. He had cash left in his pockets. So he could buy the man's silence, at least for a while, hopefully till he was out of the country. Or maybe he could tell him the truth. Or some of it. He sounded like he might be ex-military. And he clearly thought Jardin was crazy. Gabriel made his decision.

"Their leader is called Christophe Jardin. He's been organising bomb attacks. In Europe and here in Brazil. I work for some people who want him stopped."

He waited. The pilot took his time answering.

"He slapped a girl," the man said.

"Pardon?"

"He slapped her. One of his, you know, followers. I was flying them back there after they'd been on some sort of shopping trip in Nova Cidade. Pretty little thing, too. With that short hair he makes them all have. She dropped one of the packages and something inside it smashed, and he just yelled at her, then he slapped her. Hard, I mean, knocked her off her feet."

"He's not a very nice man. Slapping girls is probably the least bad thing about him."

"Whatever. So you're going to go in there and read him his rights?"

"Something like that, yes."

"Fine. And if he can't hear you no more, well, you can still read them can't you?"

"I guess I can."

"OK, then. Eden, clearing, three miles out, Low Altitude Low Opening jump. Coming up, chief. Hey, you need anything else?"

Gabriel shook his head, then clambered into the back of the plane and buckled himself into his chute. He checked and double-checked every strap, latch, and buckle. And was grateful again for the care its owner had devoted to its maintenance. In another three minutes, the pilot called over his shoulder.

"You see down there? There's a clearing. Looks like someone's been building something."

Gabriel looked down as the pilot banked into a turn. Through the Plexiglas window, he could see a huge clearing with what looked like a half-built wooden building of some kind, little more than the exterior walls, half the roof and piles of discarded timber and other hard-to-identify materials.

"That looks perfect," he shouted back.

"OK. I'm going to go out a ways then lose some altitude and come into the wind at a thousand feet. You go when you're ready, and send that fucker my best wishes."

The pilot banked again and took the Cessna maybe a mile away from the drop zone. Then he turned and eased the throttle back and the nose down. As the thrum of the propellers decreased in pitch and volume, Gabriel felt the plane losing altitude. He hoped he could remember all his training. If he hit the ground wrong and smashed his ankle, it was game over.

He pulled the door to one side and latched it. The inrush of air roared about his ears as he readied himself for the jump. Holding on tight to the vibrating door frame, he leaned out just enough to check the approach to the clearing. The pale green expanse was coming up fast. He looked down. The trees were clearly distinguishable as separate specimens now.

Then the knobbled green canopy flicked out of his field of view and they were over the clearing.

He took a breath.

And jumped.

Yelled, "one-one-thousand".

And pulled the ripcord.

With a fluttering snap, the chute deployed above his head.

The ground was rushing up to greet him.

The rigging opened the edge of the chute, and it gulped in air before bellying outwards like a huge, white jellyfish.

His descent speed was slashed by ninety percent as the chute grabbed at the air above him, jerking him out of his freefall, and Gabriel let out the breath he'd been holding since leaving the Cessna.

After what seemed like just a few seconds, he hit the ground, yanking upwards on the rigging lines at the last second and rolling to his left in a perfect landing.

"Ah, Scotty, you'd have been proud of me," he said, as he freed himself from the harness and began cramming his chute into a messy ball of nylon. Ralph MacArthur Scott had been Gabriel's jump instructor in his training for the Parachute Regiment. Scotty was a man of boundless patience and few words, most of which had four letters apiece.

He stowed the billowing mess of nylon under a thorn bush, whose inch-long spines hooked into the chute and prevented the wind snatching it away to possibly inflate like a hot air balloon and give away his presence. Before, he'd not paid much attention to the landscape, being physically and mentally drained for most of the time, and under Jardin's psychological and chemical influence. Now he needed to find the village. He needed to find Jardin. Gabriel aimed his watch's hour hand, which was currently just past ten, at the sun, then split the angle between it and twelve. That marked south.

"OK, Wolfe, so you've got directions. But where's the village from here?" He looked around, staring at each corner of the clearing. "If they're building here, they must be bringing the materials in from somewhere else."

There! In the northeast corner was a dark space in the trees. A gap, in fact. A gap where a road entered? He began making his way round the clearing, keeping ten or twelve feet inside the treeline to avoid detection if any of the Children should be out for a morning constitutional. The temperature was climbing and his grubby white clothes were soaked in sweat by the time he reached the gap in the trees. It was a track, rutted and scored by off-road tyres. He leaned against a tree fern, its thick, ridged trunk almost as tall as he was and at least twice as thick around its middle. The rosette of deeply cut leaves above his head cast striped shadows across his arm.

Something tickled the back of his neck.

62

A FATHER'S DISCIPLINE

"IT'S CHILD RYAN. HE HAS made, you know, advances to me. Physical ones. He knows we are dedicated to your service, but he said 'what the eye doesn't see the heart doesn't grieve over'."

"Did he now?" Jardin said, frowning. "Remind me, my child, which one is Child Ryan?"

She turned and pointed at a tall youth strumming a guitar. "That one, Père Christophe, with the tiger tattoo on his neck."

Jardin turned to face her and cupped her cheeks in his palms, bestowing on her a smile of what he hoped was bottomless compassion. "Leave Child Ryan to me. Now, be on your way." He pulled her head towards him and kissed the top of it, breathing in the smell of her hair as he did so.

The girl gone, Jardin ground his teeth together so hard they hurt. Fixing a smile on his face, he stalked into the middle of the group of singers. The music died, mid-bar as they realised who had come among them. Jardin walked up to the man known as Child Ryan.

"You play the guitar very well, Child Ryan," he said. "Perhaps you would come with me and show me how you form those wonderful chords."

At these words, the young man's chest puffed out.

"Of course, Père Christophe. Gladly. Did you know I played in a band before I saw my future lay here with you? You should have heard me playing my old axe."

"Axe! What a strange word to use for a musical instrument."

Jardin held the young man by the left elbow and guided him away from the clearing towards a stand of bamboo. Their stems were as thick as a man's arm at their bases and broke up the sunlight into hundreds of stripes of light and shade. He pushed his way into the centre of the bamboo, making the hard stalks rattle against each other. Standing facing Ryan, in a space no more than a yard or two across, he held out his hand.

"May I try?" he asked.

Ryan handed over the guitar. "Do you know how to hold it, Père Christophe?" he said.

Jardin grasped the guitar with both hands around the neck, enjoying the sensation of the steel strings digging into his palms.

"You hold an axe like this, no?"

63

BEASTS OF THE FOREST

GABRIEL BRUSHED AT THE IRRITATION with his hand and felt something move off his neck and down his shoulder. He glimpsed something dark brown and furry out of the corner of his eye. His first thought was that a mouse or a rat had run onto his arm. But mice generally manage quite well with four legs. Short little legs that are hard to spot under their slim bodies. This creature seemed to have won the legs lottery and doubled its money. *Fuck! Don't even shudder. Keep absolutely still.*

Gabriel had known some of the toughest men in the Regiment who'd suffered from phobias. No, not suffered from them. *Had* them. They'd learnt to suppress their reactions to snakes or creepy-crawlies or heights or enclosed spaces, so desperate were they to enter the British Army's elite. In his own case, things with eight legs —eight scuttling, hairy legs—aroused his particular hatred.

Now one of these creatures was picking its way across the rough cotton fabric of his right shirt sleeve. It was so big he could see the individual black beads of its multiple eyes and the huge palps housing its venomous fangs, each as long as the top joint of his fingers. When its trailing legs were still disengaging from his bicep, the leading limbs were feeling their way across the middle of his forearm. Drops of sweat were running freely into his eyes as he tracked the outrageous spider's path. The spider made its way onto his wrist. Gabriel tensed every muscle in his arm and then, with a convulsive spasm, jerked it straight and shook the revolting beast onto the ground. He raised his foot and stamped down hard onto its fat, hairy body. It burst with a cracking sound, squirting yellow and brown viscera out to the sides of Gabriel's shoe.

"Jesus Christ! Like I need any more fucking enemies around here," he muttered.

A shout echoed through the trees. A man's voice. He dropped into a crouch and backed into the undergrowth. Another, answering, shout. Spanish, not Portuguese. Easier to understand, at any rate. He drew some fallen palm leaves towards him and draped them over his shoulders as best as he could to camouflage his white clothes, which were still high-contrast and out of place in this world of green, despite the sweat stains.

"Hey, Jacobo!" the first voice shouted again. "Hurry up. The boss says we're leaving soon."

"OK, fine. But the bitch just bit me."

"Well, give her a slap."

There was a percussive crack and a muffled scream. Gabriel crouched lower.

Two minutes later, two men dressed in jeans and brightly coloured cotton shirts printed in tropical patterns of yellow, red and orange came into view on the track. Between them they were dragging a girl dressed in a white dress. The front was ripped, exposing one breast. She was sobbing but her head was down and she wasn't attempting to break free or even scream.

Combat appreciation, Wolfe. Now.

Yes, sir. Two enemy combatants, armed with semi-auto pistols. One civilian prisoner. Female. Combatants no threat once disarmed. Intention rape. Objective, free prisoner, kill combatants. Use weapons to prosecute rest of mission.

Very good, Wolfe. Mission ratified. In you go.

Gabriel waited until the ungainly trio had passed his position. Then he crept clear of the undergrowth and stood. He moved quickly and silently, using *Yinshen fangshi*. Three long strides took him directly behind the right-hand man. In a single, fluid move, he pulled the pistol, a Glock 19, from the man's belt-mounted holster. With a shout, the man dropped the girl's arm and whirled to face Gabriel, just in time to catch a double-tap between his eyes that blew his brains out through the back of his head in a pink mist.

Now the girl did scream as she twisted free of the other man's grip. He was still trying to process what was happening as Gabriel's gun arm swung through ninety degrees and shot him three times in the chest, directly over the heart. He crumpled without making a sound, his arteries fire-hosing blood through the massive exit wound.

Gabriel bent to retrieve the second man's Glock, checked the magazine—full, nothing in the chamber—and stuck it into the back of his waistband. The girl stood, pulling the tear in her dress closed across her chest.

"Child Gabriel, is it you?" she asked, eyes wide with shock.

"In one," he said. "But it's plain Gabriel now. I'm sorry, I don't remember your name."

She smiled. "That's OK. It's easier to remember the new faces than the crowd. I'm Child Sarah. Well, one of them, anyway. There are seven of us."

"Are you OK?" he asked.

"Yes, yes I am. Thanks to you. Those men were …" Tears rolled down her cheeks.

"I know. But you're safe now." He checked the watch Jardin had given him. Half past ten. "How come you're out here? Isn't it time for Père Christophe's sermon?"

"It is. But they grabbed me as I was leaving my house."

"Who are they? Were they, I mean?"

She looked down at the bodies, then turned back to look at Gabriel.

"They came with that man Père Christophe's always with. I heard them talking. His name is Diego Toron."

"And he's here now? This Toron character?"

"I'm not sure. He's been around for a few days, in and out by plane."

"OK, look. I don't think you should go back to the village. Not for a while. I've got something I need to do there, and it's better you stay clear."

Her eyes flicked down to the corpses. Blood was pooling in the grass between them, already attracting flies and beetles. "Don't make me stay here. Not with … not with them."

He looked around. "You see the building over there?" He pointed to the half-finished factory in the middle of the clearing. She nodded. "Go and wait there for me. I'll come back for you. I promise. But go now, I have to move."

Perhaps sensing the purpose in his voice, the girl ran off to the centre of the clearing, looking over her shoulder once or twice. Then she darted inside and was lost to view.

Gabriel ran along the access road. Then he heard men's voices. He veered off into the trees at the side of the track, pulling the second Glock out of his waistband, and crouched behind a tree whose massive trunk provided perfect cover. These two had no captive. One was tall, and musclebound, like a nightclub bouncer. Dressed like the other two in denim and a bright shirt, white with red flowers this time. The second man was shorter, and dressed in a navy linen suit with a white shirt. Was this Toron? Bosses usually dressed better than their hirelings, in Gabriel's experience.

While he watched the men approach, hoping they'd pass him and allow him to continue towards the village, a narrow column of ants emerged from a pile of dead leaves by his right foot. One, straying from its fellows, started climbing the toe of Gabriel's shoe. It crossed the short expanse of protective leather and walked onto the bare skin of his ankle. Absentmindedly, as he continued to watch the two men, Gabriel brushed at the ant. The ant did what ants do. It attacked, sinking its jaws into the skin of its enemy. Gabriel stifled a yell as the hugely powerful jaws closed, drawing a bead of blood. But this was just the warm-up act. The main attraction happened next. Curving its abdomen down, it thrust its stinger into Gabriel's ankle. The pain was agonising and he shouted out as the toxins flushed into his bloodstream.

The two men yanked out their pistols and dropped to their knees, facing Gabriel. They fired a handful of rounds each, which tore through the foliage around Gabriel, ripping chunks of bark from the tree that had become his torture chamber as well as his shelter. With tears of pain coursing over his cheeks and what felt like a white-hot knife driven through the flesh of his leg, he stumbled away from the men, and the column of ants, deeper into the forest. The men gave chase, crashing into the trees behind him, still firing. He should have been counting their shots, but the agony from his leg was making thought impossible. Ten yards ahead, he saw a fallen tree. He sprinted for it, managing to ignore the pain for a moment, and hit it at waist height. He rolled over and collapsed on the far side. His pursuers would be on him on seconds and he needed to drive them back and take the initiative.

Keeping his head down, he popped the two Glocks up over the top edge of the trunk and fired three rounds from each pistol. That stopped the men and he heard them swearing in Spanish and scurrying for cover. Another two shots held them down while he gathered his thoughts.

They'll be expecting you to run. So don't. Go wide. Get behind them. Attack.

He belly-crawled behind the dead tree for the entire thirty yards of its length. The men were on their feet again, but they were heading for his firing position. And he was no longer there. Standing, he began working around in a circle, taking his time now and silently swearing in a stream of inventive Anglo-Saxon that Scotty would have enjoyed, had he been there to listen.

Behind them now, Gabriel could see the taller man about forty feet away. Too far for a head shot and risky even to try to take him centre-mass. Crouching, he started to work his way closer, ready to shoot if the giant or his boss should turn and come towards him. The forest floor was carpeted with soft leaves, but he was on the lookout for anything dry that could give him away with a rustle or a snap. His quarry was still pushing deeper into the trees. But the thick vegetation was slowing them down. The big man was now just twenty feet away. Gabriel adopted the shooter's stance—gun held up and level with the head, not dropped with the head lowered—that he'd learned working ops in Northern Ireland with a unit called 14 Company. He hated to say it, but they made the SAS look like amateurs when it came to undercover work.

"You SAS boys are all the same," a 14 Company operator called Lewis had told him on patrol. "Zapata moustache, bomber jacket, tight stonewashed jeans and trainers. Why don't you just hang a sign round your necks saying, 'SAS' and have done with it?" At the time, Lewis was dressed in the skankiest grey acrylic trousers Gabriel had ever seen, paired with a nylon zip-fastening cardigan and pair of scuffed and worn-heeled tan slip-on shoes.

Now, Gabriel faced his target, left palm cradling right, which was wrapped around the Glock's butt, pushing forward to steady the gun.

64

RELICS ...

RYAN SMILED AND REACHED FORWARD. But before he could correct his master's grip, Jardin brought the guitar back behind his shoulder and swung it forwards with all his strength. The edge of the body connected with Ryan's left temple, shattering the thin bone beneath the skin and driving sharp-pointed fragments into Ryan's brain. The young man collapsed to his knees, swaying, his eyes unfocused and rolling in their sockets. The spruce and rosewood guitar cracked and splintered from the impact.

Jardin took a step back, raised the smashed guitar behind his head, and brought it down and across in a driving blow into Ryan's face. The force broke his nose, which spurted blood over his mouth and chin and down the front of his white shirt. One of his eyes was pushed from its socket and lay on his cheek suspended from shreds of optic nerve and muscles.

"Do not take what doesn't belong to you!" Jardin shouted, battering the now lifeless head with all his might until the fragile wooden construction of the guitar's body imploded with a bang under the tension of the strings. He flung the remains of the guitar onto the ruined face of his former disciple, then looked down at the blood spatters across the front of his robe and tutted.

"Doesn't matter. I'll be changing for the flight anyway." He laughed as his pulse returned to normal and his breathing settled.

He returned to his house by a circular route, pausing to watch a blue and yellow macaw flying amongst the topmost branches of a date palm.

"I'll be joining you soon," he told the bird.

Toron had gone by the time he arrived back at the house. Gone to ready his men, presumably. Jardin pulled a leather holdall from a cupboard. He'd bought some street clothes on his last trip into Nova Cidade. Jeans, T-shirts, a cotton zip-fronted jacket, underwear. He changed into one set, then stuffed the rest into the holdall. Then he crossed the bedroom and knelt in front of a wooden cabinet, its front, top and sides carved with feathered serpents, winged lizards, men with grotesque bulging eyes, women with multiple sets of breasts. He turned the key in the lock faced with a brass plate and opened the door.

Inside the cabinet was a black steel safe locked with a combination dial. Jardin twisted and spun the dial clockwise and anticlockwise. He was humming as the internal ratchets and cogs ticked and clicked. When the final spin had dropped the last tumbler into place, he cranked the steel handle down and opened the door. He began pulling out the contents of the safe and placing them beside him on the floor.

What emerged in his hands were thirty, inch-thick blocks of tightly-banded hundred-dollar bills. In total, six hundred and ninety-nine thousand dollars. This constituted the dollar cash balance of his inheritance, after he had sold the art and founded Eden all those years ago. He wasn't sure whether or how he would access the money tied up in Switzerland. Those suave, oily bankers were more than happy to hold onto Jewish gold and art treasures looted by the Nazis, but just recently he'd noticed on the news a troubling willingness to cooperate with international law enforcement in terrorism cases. His passport, meticulously renewed through the years, followed.

Finally, he pulled out a small, zipped case, about three inches wide by seven long, and perhaps an inch and a half thick. The covering was made from snakeskin in irregular bands of red, white, and black. He pulled the tab on the zip and opened it out onto the floor between his knees. Inside were a three-inch long pencil-shaped piece of blackened wood, several inch-long, roughly cylindrical bones and a stoppered vial of oily and clotted plum-coloured liquid that glowed a deep red as he held it up to the light.

These were his 'relics'—the final proof, if his disciples had ever needed any, that their leader was truly a divine. "A piece of the true cross," he'd explained in the early days. "The bones of Christ's right hand. Blood from his side where the Roman centurion's spearpoint penetrated his body." There was a mahogany tree in the compound with a short gouge in its trunk, a dead howler monkey missing a hand buried in the earth under one of the adobe huts, and empty bottles from an art supplies store jettisoned along with the trash years back. He re-zipped the case with a smirk and stuffed it down to the bottom of the holdall.

"Now," he said, brightly, "just a few things for the flight, and we're done here."

He stood, not bothering to close the door to the safe and went to a drawer in the kitchen. Inside were dozens of slim, white cardboard packets. These were the knockoff pharmaceuticals manufactured by Toron at one of his facilities in Colombia. Low-level stuff for the most part: painkillers, sedatives, amphetamines. No labels—printing was an unnecessary expense for the segment of the market Toron served. The poor living in the barrios of Bogotá and the up-country peasants couldn't afford real doctors, or real drugs, but they could scrape together enough cash to buy some of his pills when a child was bitten by a dog or a wife became catatonic with post-natal depression.

Jardin used both hands to scoop out the packets and returned to dump them on top of his things.

"There! All done."

He closed the holdall.

At the back of the house was a small wooden shed. Jardin opened the padlock that fastened the hasp and stepped inside. He retrieved a jerry can of petrol and stepped back into the sunlight. The can was heavy—full almost to the neck—and barely sloshed as he carried it to his living room. He checked his watch. Then he turned and left, back to the Children of Heaven for one last morning ritual.

65

... AND REGRETS

THE YOUNG PEOPLE WHO'D FOLLOWED Jardin out to the Brazilian rainforest, or, in some cases, been summoned or escorted, were gathering in the village square. Jardin watched, silently, through the knotted fringe edging a hammock, sunk so deeply into the brightly coloured woven sling that nothing but the very top of his head was visible. He rolled a little, this way and that, to set the hammock in motion. The movement soothed his fevered thoughts as he looked at the women in particular. So much beauty, so much youth, so much potential. He sighed. *If there were another way, my Daughters, believe me, I'd take it.*

The Children were forming rows like a school assembly. No chairs, of course, but they were used to standing. Used to waiting for Père Christophe to make his appearance. Among them, the Aunts and Uncles walked, patting a head here, stroking a shoulder there, whispering reassurance into those trusting ears.

Jardin amused himself as he waited by trying to spot all the girls he'd had brought to him. He leaned forwards a little, craning his neck to get a better view. He could only see the first couple of rows, but that was enough. There was Rowena, a middle-class black girl who couldn't deal with her bourgeois parents' aspirations for her.

Two along from Rowena was Elinor. Sweet Elinor who'd run away from an abusive father at age thirteen and been picked up living rough on the streets in Los Angeles by one of his scouts. Behind her, he could just make out the fiery red hair of Madison, as stupid as fuck but with a body Jardin had once ravished for two days without letting her leave his house. *Ah, Daughters, such times we've had here. But there will be others. The world is full of people who need to believe someone else is responsible for what happens to them. I just take that need and … tweak it a little. God has served me well as a pimp here, and I'm sure he or some other spiritual figurehead will be happy to continue serving that purpose somewhere new.*

Now the Elect were setting up the folding tables alongside the rows of the Children. Out came the tall, curved stacks of white paper cups, ribbed like spinal columns. Out came the heavy canisters, their usual contents laced with cyanide this bright November morning. Out came the jugs of fruit cordial, gleaming in the sunlight like potions from a fairy tale.

Jardin rolled carefully out of the hammock. Years earlier, one of the Children, startled by his silent approach, had made a too-hasty exit from his hammock to greet him, landed awkwardly and broken his neck. No room in Eden for quadriplegics, so Jardin had smothered him in his sleep after administering a triple dose of that morning's sacrament.

He composed his features into a thoughtful half-frown, turned up the corners of his mouth, just a little, and marched down to address his flock for the last time.

There was a hum of anticipation, murmuring voices, shuffling feet, as the Children of Heaven saw their leader approaching. Their gazes were all identical—wide-eyed, open, smiles, no worry lines on their perfect skin. A couple of mouths actually hung open. *Dolts! Why are you boys always the ones to do it?* He mounted the podium in front of them and waited for silence. He smiled at Rowena. Then he found Madison's adoring gaze, held it for a moment, then winked. She blushed and looked down.

Silence fell. Jardin waited. He loved this moment. Several hundred people kept in suspense until he chose the moment to break the tension. He counted. He liked to count at times like these. Once, he'd reached two hundred and still those idiots stood there in the boiling sun. *Had one fainted? Can't remember. Doesn't matter. Look at you all. Trusting a perfect stranger to tell you the route to salvation. Fucking idiots. Oh, how my parents would have loved you. Proof positive of the failure of Western capitalism and its bourgeois adherents.*

He looked up, caught a quiver of mass movement at the edge of his vision as hundreds of them followed his gaze, perhaps hoping a giant hand with a pointing finger would emerge through the clouds and a booming *basso profundo* voice would intone, "It is time. Père Christophe was right. You are the saved. Now, form an orderly queue and no pushing at the back". It was almost too much. He coughed to mask a laugh and covered his smiling mouth with a hand. Then he began.

"My Children, God be with you." *Wait for it.*

"And with you, Père Christophe." *Idiots.*

"You have chosen a life of purity, of reverence, of simplicity. A life devoted to God. A life guided by the First Order." *Again, please.*

"We serve God through Père Christophe's will." *Fools.*

"Some of you have displayed the utmost devotion and have followed the Second Order." *And…*

"Give your life to cleanse the world of sin." *Morons.*

"My Children, you have no need of mass media. You have renounced all that is worldly, all that is corrupting. But on your behalf, I do follow world events. I must know how the ungodly think and act. And they are planning to act against us."

There was a low murmuring at this, at its core a note of anxiety.

"The Brazilian and Colombian governments are planning to come here with guns and take you away from Eden, away from me."

The murmuring gave way to a rumble of dissenting voices and even a cry from one of the female Children. Jardin patted the air in front of him in exaggeratedly large movements that even those at the back could discern.

"Do. Not. Worry. God will throw his arms around you and keep you safe in the bosom of his love. And I, your Père Christophe, I will go to meet them and to turn them back. This is Eden, my Children. This is our paradise. And nobody is going to take it away from us!" Aware that he was shouting, and that the faces of the Children were clouded with frowns and tight, worried-looking eyes, Jardin waited for a count of three before he continued, in a lower tone.

"Today will be a day of prayer. All chores are suspended. Pray for me as I venture to meet Satan in human form, for the international conspiracy of sin will not defeat us today. God bless you, my Children."

"God bless you, Père Christophe," they murmured, though the unity of the chant was ragged compared to their opening responses.

Good. If you're scared maybe you won't notice the taste of the poison.

"One final instruction today, my Children. Receive your sacrament, but do not drink. Not straight away. Return to your place and wait for my assent. Today, we will make this a very special act of devotion."

He'd instructed the Elect to make up the sacrament extra strong this morning, "to fortify them with a little extra sweetness for the trials ahead," was how he'd phrased it. Now he watched them lining up to receive their medicine. The Elect would serve themselves last, as they always did.

When every single human being gathered in the square was standing, facing him, their hands clasped around their paper cups, Jardin spoke.

"In a sense, you obey the Second Order every day at Eden. You give your life to cleanse the world of sin simply by being here and serving God's will through me." There were smiles at this, nods here and there. *You love it when I flatter your piety, don't you?* "So, let this day be a very special one in your lives. Let this be another day when you obey the Second Order. Now, drink."

Time to go. Night, night, sleep tight.

He stepped down from the podium and returned to his house.

66

A QUIET COUNTRY VILLAGE

THE BIG MAN STOPPED. HIS boss, who had been leading the way, turned and walked back to him, coming into Gabriel's sightline. His eyes flicked right, over the muscleman's shoulder and looked straight into Gabriel's.

"There!" he shouted in Spanish. He was still raising his Glock when Gabriel fired. He fell backwards, blood spattering the trees behind him.

The big man was too slow. Gabriel shot him three times between the shoulder blades, the Glock jerking in his double-handed grip. The man fell forwards, half-covering the body of his boss.

In the silence that followed, Gabriel closed his eyes, straining to catch the sound of onrushing boots, shouts in Spanish, more gunfire. But other than the ringing in his ears from the reports of the Glock, there was nothing. Soon enough, the jungle returned to its multi-layered soundscape of birdcalls, monkey hoots and the relentless buzz and chitter of millions of insects.

His ankle was still hurting badly. He bent and pulled up his trouser leg to get a better look. A shiny red welt the size of a two-pound coin had blossomed over his ankle bone. It had a white centre and the tiny black puncture wound stood out like a bullseye on a target. But the pain was bearable. A long time ago, he'd been trained to take it until he passed out. He wasn't going to pass out now.

He dropped the magazine out of one of the Glocks and pushed the remaining rounds into the palm of his left hand. Six. He repeated the process with the second Glock. Nine. He reloaded the second pistol with all fifteen rounds, then stuck the first into his waistband.

Jogging along the track, it took him fifteen minutes to reach the outskirts of the village. He paused only once, when he heard what sounded like a woman's scream. But it was probably a monkey or a bird of some kind and he ran on. The white adobe huts looked abandoned. Nobody was moving among them, carrying laundry or talking in pairs or small groups. There was no sound of singing or musical instruments, no guitars being strummed or drums beaten. Apart from the natural sounds of the rainforest and the wind sighing through the trees, Eden was utterly silent.

67

DEATH IN PARADISE

THE SCREAMS BEGAN JUST AS Jardin reached his front porch. He smiled and went inside, not bothering to close the door behind him. After a while, the noise began to irritate him, so he put a CD on the hi-fi—Mozart's *Magic Flute*—and ramped up the volume until the house vibrated to the music. He lay back on the sofa and massaged his temples. *Why does everyone conspire to ruin my plans? Why can't they see that what I'm doing harms nobody—well, nobody who doesn't deserve to be harmed anyway.*

No! The Mozart is definitely not helping.

He jumped to his feet and kicked out at the small silver cube into which he'd inserted the CD a few minutes before. The opera arrested in mid-aria as the player shot back off the low table and parted company from the speakers with a crash.

Jardin dumped his holdall on the front porch then went back inside. He grabbed a box of matches from the kitchen counter and the jerrycan from under the dining table, and unscrewed the lid. He splashed the petrol over the soft furnishings first: the sofa, the cushions, the rugs on the floor, the curtains. Then he swung the can round to spray more over the floor and walls. He trailed it behind him, leaving a lake of fuel all the way down the hall to the front door. Once it was empty, he threw it back inside.

When he stepped out of the house, his holdall bumping against his thigh, it was for the last time. He turned, struck a match, used it to light its sleeping fellows still in the box, then tossed it, flaring, into the hall. The petrol ignited with a soft pop, and Jardin watched for a second as the blue flames danced along the floor towards the sitting room where the soaking furniture ignited with a louder roar.

He walked away without looking back, whistling Papageno's tune from the opera. He continued on towards the village square with its mounds of dead followers, many of whom appeared to have clutched each other in their final moments. Then he turned left and began picking his way through a few of the Children who had staggered away from the others, perhaps hoping to reach water. The plane was a good half-hour walk away if he set a good pace, but he was in no hurry. Toron could wait, and it was a nice day. The sun was out, a cool breeze was whispering to him through the trees, and some late-blooming jacaranda were drenching the air in their sweet, almost cloying scent.

68

CONDOR

GABRIEL CARRIED ON WALKING BETWEEN the huts, head scanning left, right, ahead and behind, looking for the Children of Heaven and for his target, the man he would never again refer to as "Père Christophe".

Then, directly ahead of him, in the direction of the village square, there was a *whoomp* and a roar. Seconds later, a plume of greyish-white smoke boiled up into the air above the roofs of the nearest huts.

He ran towards the smoke, Glock held in a firing-ready position in front of him. He rounded one of the squat white huts the Children lived in and stumbled to a halt.

What he was seeing made no sense. Why were all the Children of Heaven asleep on the ground in the village square? His mouth dropped open and he covered it instinctively with his free hand. His rational brain had switched off for a second at the sight, but now its circuits rebooted, carrying with them the knowledge that the bodies he was looking at were not sleepers but corpses. Hundreds of them. All those beautiful boys and girls. And the older ones too. The Aunts and the Uncles. All dead. They looked as though they had died of sunburn, with faces a bright cherry-red.

357

Gabriel had seen death many times before. Had caused it when circumstances dictated. Had suffered, grievously, from one death in particular, that of Smudge Smith, whose brown-skinned ghost continued to haunt his nights and, occasionally, his days. He had witnessed scenes of mass slaughter, in places where normal people never travelled or would want to. Where children were kidnapped then brainwashed and abused into committing atrocities on their former communities with Kalashnikovs, clubs, and machetes. But this. This, somehow, was worse. This was the will of a single, crazy man. He could not advance war or tribal tensions or ideology as a reason for his actions. He'd just done it because he could.

Gabriel knew it in his heart. And now he was going to make Jardin pay for his crimes. All of them.

The village square was a carpet of white-garbed corpses, all with the same bright red faces, some with lips drawn back in their death agonies, some clutching each other in some final gasping desire for human contact. And all around them, as if a huge children's birthday party had been abandoned in the rush to play sleeping lions, lay paper cups, each lined with a thin slick of green, purple, or orange. The bodies were too freshly dead to be smelling of anything, yet the air reeked of bitter almonds. Gabriel knew the smell from a course he'd undertaken in Quantico, under the auspices of the FBI. It was cyanide.

"Shuts down the body's ability to take oxygen out of the air," their instructor had intoned, while she waved a test tube of potassium cyanide under the crinkling noses of her trainees from a dozen different NATO Special Forces commands. "Symptoms pretty much the same as for strangulation, only no petechial haemorrhaging in the corneas and no ligature or finger marks round the neck. Only giveaway is your victim's going to look like they had a pretty bad case of sunburn."

So you poisoned them all, you bastard. Hundreds and hundreds of them, just to feed your monstrous ego.

Gabriel's jaw was clenched tight. Gripping the Glock tighter, he picked his way among the dead, avoiding looking at their faces, searching for movement. Searching for Jardin.

There he was. Wearing jeans and a T-shirt under a zip-fronted windcheater and carrying a bulging brown leather holdall. And smiling. The bastard was actually smiling as he skirted the square. Gabriel broke into a run, leaping and swerving to avoid the corpses as he closed with the man Don Webster had sent him here to kill.

Fifty yards.

Forty.

Thirty.

Twenty.

Jardin caught his movement and looked left. Saw him. And smirked.

Gabriel brought the Glock up and slowed his run, getting ready to kill the man and complete his mission. But Jardin did something that surprised him.

As Gabriel came to a halt, the pistol held in both palms, the iron foresight glued to Jardin's heart, the man simply dropped his holdall and held his arms wide. No flinching, no frantic dash for cover. No dropping to the knees and pleading for his life. In short, none of the reactions the seasoned fighter in Gabriel Wolfe was ready for. Instead he smiled, then uttered a single word.

"Condor."

As the final, soft 'r' left Jardin's lips, Gabriel's arms fell to his sides, the Glock still gripped in his right hand.

Jardin was smiling wider than ever as he held Gabriel's gaze with his own. He closed the gap between them to just a few feet, not bothering to watch where his feet went now, treading on arms, torsos, and chests, rising and falling as he traversed the corpse-strewn ground.

"Child Gabriel," he said. "Back to kill me, I see. After all I did for you. I gave you the chance to sacrifice your life for me, and you threw it back in my face. And brought the wrath of two governments down on my head. Or three, I suppose, if we count the British."

Gabriel watched Jardin approach as if through gauze. His voice sounded both very, very close and as distant as the far mountains. He could feel the brush of feathers on his skin.

"What? What are you doing to me?" he muttered through slack lips.

"Why, aren't you feeling yourself?" Jardin laughed, then took a step closer and prodded Gabriel between the eyes before stepping back. "I gave you the second order, Child Gabriel, but guess what? I buried a third order inside it. You hear it? Condor. A magic word, yes? I knew you were a high-risk recruit. All that training. All that psychological conditioning. So I planted a little post-hypnotic suggestion in that stupid soldier's brain of yours. I give the third order and you return to being my slave."

Gabriel tried to lift his right arm but it hung, useless, at his side.

"I … will … kill …"

"Yes, yes, yes. Of course, you will kill. Of that I have no doubt. I engineered it so that you would. But it is not I that you will kill, Child Gabriel. No." Jardin stroked his beard between his thumb and fingers. "You will shoot," he paused, "yourself. Do it now."

Gabriel stared into Jardin's narrowed, purplish-blue eyes, trying to break away. Then he saw his right forearm levitate to the horizontal out of the corner of his eye. It rotated from the shoulder and locked into a right angle. Then his wrist flexed, bringing the muzzle against his right temple.

Sweat broke out on his forehead and trickled into his eyes, stinging as the salt hit the soft inner skin of his lower lids.

His index finger tightened on the trigger, taking up first pressure.

Jardin stood opposite him, smirking. Waiting. He checked his watch. Then returned to staring into Gabriel's eyes.

Gabriel could feel the muscles in his right hand quivering. No, please. Stop. This wasn't supposed to happen. Help me, Master Zhao.

69

SMUDGE REDUX

THE HANDS THAT CLOSED AROUND Gabriel's own weren't those of Master Zhao.

They were brown-skinned. They seemed not to be connected to any arms that Gabriel could see. Then a familiar voice spoke, deep inside Gabriel's mind.

"That ain't a good idea, Boss. Bloke could do himself a mischief firing a Glock into his head. Fariyah'd agree. Here, let me help."

The strong brown hands gripped tighter and began to guide Gabriel's own hand. Gabriel strained every muscle and sinew in his right arm and felt it begin to straighten, inch by painful inch, pulling the muzzle of the pistol down and away from his temple.

In front of him, Jardin's smirk slid away to be replaced by a look of puzzlement, eyes narrowed, brow creased in a frown of incomprehension. Then, in its place, came a look of purest hatred. The top lip was pulled back, the front teeth were bared and the skin looked greasy and taut.

"I said, shoot yourself!" he screamed. "I said, *Condor!*"

"And I say we off him now, Boss. This guy's a pain in the fucking arse."

The gauze burned away, and the sounds of the forest sharpened in Gabriel's ears.

Jardin turned and ran, straight towards the centre of the village square.

As Jardin hopped and leapt to avoid tripping on the scarlet-faced corpses of his former followers, Gabriel found he had regained control of his own limbs. He shook his head, then set off after Jardin, weaving amongst the dead and trying to keep his target in range.

Jardin looked over his shoulder. It was a mistake. His holdall swung in front of him and altered his centre of gravity so that he stumbled left and caught his leading foot under the thigh of a redheaded female corpse. He fell heavily onto the holdall, winding himself as the bag punched the air out of his lungs.

As Jardin staggered back to his feet, Gabriel dropped to one knee, held the pistol out in front of him cradled in both palms, and squeezed off a shot. It took Jardin on the outside of his right thigh, a through-and-through that drew a high-pitched scream from him. He hobbled off, blood running freely down the side of his leg from the entry and exit wounds. Perhaps realising flight was no longer an option, he stopped and turned to face Gabriel, who was now walking towards him. Jardin's former disciple held the Glock in both hands, aimed directly at Jardin's head.

Jardin spread his arms wide, wincing from the pain in his thigh, placing his weight on his left leg.

When Gabriel caught up with him, he began speaking.

"Child Gabriel, don't kill me. Help me. Come with me. Toron and I are planning to restart our operation in Colombia. You could join us. Be my second-in-command. You could become a very rich man."

Gabriel drew his lips back from his teeth.

"Toron's dead. I killed him. And his men. Nobody's getting rich. Especially you. Not after what you did in London. Not after, after this." He let go of the gun with his left hand to wave it around them at the sea of dead bodies. "How could you do it?"

Jardin smiled, grunting with the effort. "Them? They were my followers. You know. Like Twitter." Gabriel jerked his head back in shock. "Oh, yes, Child Gabriel. I know I look like a ragged old prophet, but it pays to keep up. So, like I said, they were my followers. Mine to do with as I wished. And I wished them dead. Now they *are* dead."

"And London? The bus bomb? Eloise Payne?"

"I saw how many died. Less than a hundred, wasn't it? Do you know how many people get killed in traffic accidents in the UK every year? Do you? Let me enlighten you. Seventeen hundred. A year! And how about the Americans? Twelve thousand gun deaths a year. Their military forces killed thousands of civilians in their foreign adventures in the Middle East. So forgive me for not sharing your horror, but death is everywhere."

Gabriel straightened his arm again. He aimed the Glock at Jardin's forehead. At this range he didn't need to go centre-mass for the kill shot. He was gratified to see Jardin flinch. He tightened his finger on the trigger, remembering the carnage at Oxford Street.

"Wait!" Jardin shouted, eyes wide with terror. He put his hands out in front of him, palms towards Gabriel. "God doesn't want you to kill me, Child Gabriel."

"Nice try, Jardin. Maybe He doesn't. But Barbara Sutherland does."

Gabriel fired twice in quick succession, a double-tap to the head that threw Jardin backwards, blood and brain tissue spraying from the exit wound as the bullet tore away the back of his head.

Gabriel thought he heard a voice saying, *"Nice one, Boss."* He shook his head and looked around. But Smudge was gone. Or not completely. There *was* a voice inside his head, faint but audible.

"Nathalie, Boss. Go and see her. For me. Tell her what happened,"

Then it was gone and the sounds of the rainforest returned. And with them, the realisation that the mission was over. He turned to look at the dead. All those believers. In what? The promises and bluster of a self-made messiah. Why did they trust him? Why come all this way to live with nothing but the promise of being allowed to kill yourself and many others? He realised he would never know. He was a fighting man, not a philosopher. And right now, the thorniest question facing him was how he was going to get out of Eden.

But first he needed to set the stage for the Brazilian police. Give them a clear-cut narrative that would make sense in terms of their mission.

Jardin lay face upwards, eyes wide but already dulled as if coated with matte varnish, staring sightlessly at the Brazilian sky. His arms were flung wide and his legs were twisted around each other. Gabriel got to his knees, then lay on his back on top of Jardin. He grabbed the outstretched arms and pulled them down over his shoulders and across his chest like the straps of a Bergen. Then he rolled onto his stomach, dragging Jardin with him so the dead man rested on Gabriel's back. He pushed up onto his knees and then, holding the corpse's arms, got to his feet.

Carrying the deadweight of Jardin's body was a struggle, but Gabriel was still fit enough to manage. He carried the corpse at a fast walk back the way he'd come until he reached the bodies of Toron and his henchman. Turning to face Toron, he released Jardin's arms and let the body fall behind him.

Next, the pistols. He ejected both magazines and emptied the remaining rounds from the one he'd used to shoot Jardin onto the ground. Using his shirt, he meticulously cleaned both pistols, the magazines and the rounds, before reloading, this time sharing the remaining rounds equally between the two Glocks.

He pressed one of the Glocks into Jardin's unresisting right hand and curled the dead man's index finger round the trigger. He fired a couple of shots into Toron's body.

Then he went over to Toron with the second pistol. Gabriel lifted the corpse's right arm and let it fall. He smiled grimly. The body was still flexible. He wrapped the dead man's fingers around the Glock's grip and pushed his index finger through the trigger guard. Holding the hand out in front of him, he aimed into the trees and fired twice to ensure some gunshot residue ended up on Toron's fingers. Then he let the hand holding the gun fall, and stood. He bent to recover the brass, then stopped. The police would find it odd that Toron and Jardin had killed each other in a dispute over a drugs deal gone bad then somehow contrived to vanish their spent cartridge cases.

He walked away from the scene, figuring he'd head back to the clearing where the planes flew in and out from. Which is when he remembered.

Child Sarah.

Apart from himself, she was the only survivor of Christophe Jardin's murderous reign.

He ran back through the huts and onto the track. Fifteen minutes of jogging brought him back to the clearing.

He cupped his hands round his mouth and shouted out to her.

"Sarah! Child Sarah! It's safe."

She didn't emerge from the abandoned factory, so he walked towards it, calling out every few paces. At the halfway point between the edge of the clearing and the building, he tried again.

"Sarah! It's me. Gabriel. It's over. You can come out."

He stood, hands on hips, panting, waiting for her to emerge.

Just when he had resigned himself to having to cross the remaining expanse of grass to fetch her, a flash of white in the doorway caught his eye.

70

LEAVING THE GARDEN

GABRIEL STOOD PERFECTLY STILL, ALLOWING her to see that he was alone. That there were no gangsters or gunmen waiting to grab her. He held his arms out wide.

Hesitantly at first, then with a sudden burst of speed, she came towards him, closing the gap between them in thirty seconds before flinging her arms around his neck and burying her face in the crook of his neck.

"It's OK," he murmured into her hair. "It's OK. He's gone."

She jerked her head up. "Who? Who's gone?"

"Jardin. Père Christophe, I mean. He's dead."

Her eyes widened and her chin trembled. "What do you mean, dead? How? Who's going to look after us now?"

"Sarah, listen to me. I killed him. He was evil. I'm afraid there is no 'us' now. Everybody else is dead. He poisoned them. He would have poisoned you too."

"No!" she hissed. She writhed in his arms and tore herself free. "You didn't. You can't. He was good. He was going to save me." She stood in front of him, eyes red, hands covering her mouth.

"He wasn't good. He brainwashed you. He brainwashed

everyone. Me as well. You need to come with me. I'll show you. Come."

He held out his right hand to guide her towards the track. She surprised him by taking it and letting him lead her back to the village.

As they stood on the edge of the square, Sarah began to sob. Wet spots from fallen tears blossomed on the top half of her dress, turning the white cotton grey. More flies and beetles had found the bodies, alerted by the scent of decomposition, even if the humans' noses weren't alive to the subtle changes in the air around them.

"They're all dead," she wailed. "All my brothers and sisters."

When Gabriel tried to pull her away she stood her ground at first, then, as if someone had thrown a switch inside her, all the resistance disappeared. He placed a protective arm around her waist and led her back to the clearing.

As they neared the end of the track, Gabriel cocked his head.

"Do you hear that?" he said.

Sarah closed her eyes and mirrored his pose.

"Yes," she said. "It sounds like a plane."

"Come on, quick."

Holding hands, they ran towards the end of the track where it opened out into the clearing. Way above the trees on the far side, a white shape was growing larger. It was the plane Toron had ordered to take him and Jardin back to Bogotá.

They watched as the pilot brought the small craft down for a perfect three-point landing. The prop roared then died to a soft buzzing as the pilot cut the throttle and taxied towards them, past the factory.

A figure descended from the cabin and stood by the side of the plane, arms folded, legs apart. A figure wearing a leather, shearling-lined flying jacket. It was the same man who'd dropped Gabriel from a thousand feet just a few hours earlier.

"Come on," Gabriel said. "Someone's smiling on us today."

They ran across the open ground to where the pilot waited for them.

"Greetings, my friend," the man said as they arrived, red-faced and out of breath. "We meet again. And you found us an extra passenger."

"You worked for Toron all along?" Gabriel said.

The man smiled. "No. But I had a funny feeling you might be needing a ride out of here. I know all the pilots, including the guy who usually flies Toron. I bought the job off him."

"I'll pay you back. I mean, I don't have enough cash left, but I'll get the money to you."

"No problem. It felt like I was doing the right thing, you know? Now, we could stand around talking or we could get out of here. Which is it to be?"

Once airborne, Sarah became talkative. It was as if leaving Eden had unlocked a part of her that Jardin had suppressed all the time she'd been there.

"I have no money. And nowhere to live. And no clothes. Apart from these," she plucked at her torn dress. "How am I going to live? *Where* am I going to live?"

"Do you have any family?" Gabriel said, twisting around in his seat to talk to her.

"My mom and dad, but they're the reason I joined the Children of Heaven in the first place. They just don't understand me. I can't go back to them. They'd never forgive me for leaving."

"You might be surprised how much forgiveness there is in the world. The real world. Look, let's get to Nova Cidade and talk about it all then. I still have some money. Enough for two hotel rooms and something to eat."

Sarah seemed pacified by this and lapsed into silence, her face turned away and pressed against the window. Gabriel faced forward again.

"So, I'm guessing I won't be making any more flights to Eden then?" the pilot said.

"Not unless it's to bring police out here. And would you mind just calling me by name? Please. It's Gabriel. It would mean a lot to me right now."

The pilot turned and offered his right hand with a smile. "Sure, Gabriel. I'm Tiago. Short for Santiago, you know? But only my momma calls me that, eh?" He laughed then, a friendly sound in the cramped cabin that made Gabriel smile in response. Mothers. They wrapped you up and protected you for as long as they could, but then … *No! Not now. Save it for another session with the good Doctor Crace.* He turned to check on Sarah. She was fast asleep, her head slumped forward on her chest, and snoring. While they flew on, he closed his eyes and began a sequence of meditation exercises, going deep into his memory to find Don's mobile number. He'd called it many times, and though he'd forgotten it during his time with the children of Heaven, he knew it was there somewhere.

Tiago landed at the airfield in Nova Cidade thirty minutes later. He stared at Gabriel and Sarah as they faced him outside the plane.

"You know," he said, "you two don't exactly look like the ideal hotel guests. Are you hungry? You want a shower?" Gabriel and Sarah nodded in unison. "OK. I got a suggestion, and don't go all polite on me. My momma lives about ten miles from here. Nice big house, plenty of space, hot and cold running water, all that. Let me make a call."

He turned his back on them as he fished his phone out of his flying jacket. Either Tiago was very persuasive or his momma was very hospitable because after a few minutes he turned back to them, pocketing the phone.

"We're good?" Gabriel said.

"All set. Come on. My truck's out back."

Forty-five minutes later, Gabriel and Sarah were sitting at a scrubbed pine table in Mrs Rosario Pereira's spotless kitchen, eating a spicy rabbit stew that apparently she'd been cooking anyway.

She'd fussed over them from the moment they crossed the threshold of her home, Gabriel in particular. She applied an herbal salve to the ant bite on his ankle, which, miraculously, stopped the pain almost immediately. She'd found clothes for both of them, "my late husband's," she'd said to Gabriel as she handed him a stack of neatly folded trousers and work shirts; "my daughter's, from when she used to live with me," to Sarah, as she offered a dress.

"Mrs Pereira," Gabriel said, "May I …"

She placed her flat palm against her chest and rolled her eyes. "What's that? I feed you my best *ensopado de coelho* and you call me, 'Mrs'? No, no, no, Gabriel. Anyone who eats in my house calls me Momma. Now, you were saying?"

He smiled, happy to be bossed around by someone with no motive beyond feeding and clothing a house guest. "Momma. I have to make a phone call. An international phone call. It might be expensive. I have money."

As the words left his lips, he knew what her response would be. It was almost comical in its intensity.

She opened her mouth into an "O" and dropped her head back, replacing the fan of fingers across her bosom.

"You have money? Good for you! So do I! Gabriel, I am not some peasant from the forest. I own a business. I am an *empresária*! Please do not come to my house and insult me with offers of money. Now, go, you silly boy. The phone is through there."

She pointed to the hall, letting him see just the hint of a smile as he excused himself and left the table.

He punched in the number he'd brought to the surface during his in-flight meditation session. While the local, national and international exchanges talked to each other, routing the fourteen pulses of the number along copper wires and fibre-optic undersea cables, he tried to condense his narrative into some sort of situation report.

The phone at the other end of the line rang. Twice.

"Don Webster."

"Don, it's me."

There was warmth in the voice. Real, fatherly warmth.

"Hello, Old Sport. Been wondering when I'd hear from you. How are you?"

"I'm fine. Jardin's no longer a problem. There were some complications. I dealt with them too. But listen. He gave them all poison. His followers, I mean. There must be five or six hundred bodies out there. Someone needs to deal with them."

There was the briefest of pauses.

"Right. I'll put wheels in motion. We'll have to leave this to the Brazilians, but we'll work on a story they can give their media that leaves you out of it. Now, we need to extract you. Where are you?"

Gabriel smiled. "Well, right now I'm in the home of a businesswoman who insists I call her Momma. But the city is Nova Cidade. I'm not alone, though. I pulled one of Jardin's followers out with me."

"Do you want to bring her along?"

"No. She's American. But can you fix her up with some kind of consular assistance to get her home?"

"Consider it done. OK, look. Can you stay where you are?"

Gabriel laughed. "I have a feeling your main problem will be extracting me from Momma's clutches."

"Sounds like a hospitable lady, so mind your manners. I'll call you back when we're ready with a flight plan. Give me your number there."

Gabriel read out the number on the little slip of paper beneath its Perspex cover on the phone.

"OK, Old Sport, stand by to stand by."

71

A BLAST FROM THE PAST

BACK IN LONDON, GABRIEL STOOD, glass in hand, staring out of the window of his fourteenth-floor hotel room. Don hadn't scrimped on his accommodation budget, and the view was spectacular. He could see St Paul's cathedral from his balcony, its golden dome luminous against the night sky. Or he could turn to the river, and the light sculptures of the South Bank arts complex. Further away, the London Eye, that high-tech Ferris wheel, was lit with red spotlights around its circumference.

But he wasn't seeing the view. Wasn't seeing anything. His senses weren't dead, though. He could hear perfectly well. Acutely, in fact. And what he could hear was a child's voice. A young boy's voice. And it kept saying the same, single word.

"Gable."

His heart was racing and nothing he could do would make it stop. He felt like he had before his first parachute jump without a static line to open the chute for him. He turned and walked to the armchair. Sat down heavily. Put the tumbler of gin down on the table with a clunk, slopping some onto the polished cherrywood.

I need to talk to someone. But who can I talk to? Mum and Dad are dead. No relatives they ever spoke of. No friends from that time. Unless …

Master Zhao, I need you like I never needed anybody before.

Since he'd joined the Army, Gabriel hadn't spoken to Zhao Xi. He revered the man but associated him with the past. And Gabriel wanted to move forward. Had to move forward. Like a shark. Stop moving and you die. He went online using his new phone and found Zhao Xi's number in seconds. He taught martial arts classes and even had a website.

From almost six thousand miles away he heard the muted purr as Zhao Xi's phone rang. He pictured the house, high in the hills above Victoria Harbour. What time it was in Hong Kong, he hadn't bothered to figure out. The last words Zhao Xi had said to him were as fresh in his mind as if he'd heard them yesterday. "Make your way in the world, Gabriel Wolfe, as the cub leaves the litter. But remember where you first found safety."

The ringing stopped, mid-purr. Gabriel's pulse jumped upwards.

"Master Zhao, it's me."

"Me who? I know many 'me's.'"

"Gabriel! Gabriel Wolfe."

"It has been many years. Are you still a warrior?"

"I am. But not a soldier. Now I fight the enemy on a freelance basis."

"And you are very good at it, of that I have no doubt. It is good to hear your voice, young Wolfe cub. Even at a quarter to three in the morning."

"I'm sorry, Master Zhao. But something happened and I really need your help.

"Then speak. Speak. I will help if I can."

"Master, did I have, I mean, does the name Michael mean anything to you?"

There was a short silence.

"It means many things to me. Pop stars. Basketball players. Sculptors."

Say it. Just say it!

"No. Not them. I'm talking about Michael …" Gabriel heaved a deep sigh, "… Wolfe."

There was a longer silence, during which Gabriel could hear his old teacher's breathing on the line.

"I always wondered whether you would ever ask me that question. And now you have, I am so far away. But your parents' instructions were quite clear on the matter. Tell you everything as soon as you asked. Hide nothing."

"So?"

"Michael was your younger brother. Though I suspect you have already worked that out if you're calling me."

"Jesus! Hold on." Gabriel drained the gin and tonic, which tasted bitter in his mouth, wiped his lips with the back of his hand, and resumed speaking. "I *can* remember him. I mean, I can remember his name. But nothing else. Until a few hours ago, I would have sworn blind I was an only child. Why? Master Zhao, what happened to Michael? And why can't I remember?"

"Ah, Gabriel," Zhao Xi said, with a note of infinite sadness in his voice. "How I wish we were sitting together for me to tell you this." There was a deep sigh. "Michael drowned in the Harbour. He was five, you were nine."

"Drowned? How? And why don't I remember any of this? Why can't I even remember what he looked like?"

Another silence followed this question.

"Your mother had taken the two of you to the park at the Harbour near your parents' house. You took a rugby ball with you. You used to be so keen on the game, do you remember that?"

"Yes. I used to play sevens. It was the only sport I enjoyed at school."

"Just so. You were very fast. A great winger. Your mother told me you kicked the ball and Michael couldn't catch it. It went into the water and you told Michael to fetch it out. Your mother called him back, but he idolised you, so he jumped straight in. He was a good swimmer for his age, but he banged his head and went under. You went in after Michael. By the time you found him, it was too late. After the funeral, you went into a blank state for a fortnight. You drank only water and ate almost nothing. You didn't speak or even move unless your parents or I moved you."

Gabriel felt empty inside. As the story unfolded, he still couldn't picture the drowned boy, much less find the place a brother should have occupied in his heart.

"So what happened after two weeks?" he asked, finally.

"You woke up one morning and asked for a boiled egg. But your mind had let Michael go. You couldn't remember him. Your parents tried to remind you, but in the end, the stress was too great, for them and for you, and they quietly removed all the photographs of Michael from the house. After you left to join the Army, we did talk about what had happened to you. That is when your parents gave me their instruction. And now I have fulfilled it. I am so sorry you had to hear it like this."

"It's OK, Master Zhao." Gabriel swallowed, trying to push the lump in his throat down. "I believe you, and I know you're telling the truth. It's just, I still don't really remember. Except, one more thing. What did he call me?"

"He called you Gable. He always found it hard to say your name correctly, and in the end, it just became a family nickname."

"I remembered that, at least. But how can I get to all the rest? I can't even picture his face."

"Maybe in time, now you have opened the sluice gate, enough memories will flow through. Be patient, Gabriel, but be ready in case the dam bursts. You can always call me, you know that."

"Thank you. I will. But this is just, I'm not, you know, I've repressed this memory so completely and for so long. I'm sorry I haven't called you before. I have to go. Goodbye, Master Zhao."

"Goodbye, Wolfe cub."

Gabriel remained sitting in the armchair in the hotel room. He refilled the glass at his elbow from time to time, but otherwise remained unmoving. He closed his eyes, but sleep did not come. Nor did hallucinations. No dead soldiers. No drowned boy, as he had half-expected, half-dreaded. Just a dead, cold, black silence stretching back through history to the late 1980s when, apparently, he had ordered his younger brother to his death in the murky green waters of Victoria Harbour.

"Oh, Michael," he said, finally, as the sun came up. "I'm sorry. I wish you were here to forgive me. I wish Smudge was, too."

72

CLEANUP

WHEN STILL ALIVE, CHRISTOPHE JARDIN had known a lot about exploiting people's weaknesses. But he did not have a monopoly on those insights. The commander of the operation to round up the Children of Heaven was similarly knowledgeable about human psychology, which is why she ordered her armed officers into the grounds of Elysium House several hours before dawn. Her counterparts in the German *Bundespolizei*, American FBI, the French *Gendarmerie* and the Metropolitan Police's Special Branch were issuing identical orders.

All the residents of Elysium House were taken into custody. "Protective custody" was how it was framed for the media. Clinical psychologists, hypnotherapists, and specialist social workers went to work on the members of the cult, 'deprogramming' them before handing them back to the police to be interviewed in connection with a series of global terrorist attacks. The older members were subjected to considerably more forceful interviewing techniques than the younger.

* * *

Later that day, a team of forensic analysts and Brazilian Special Forces soldiers flew into Eden. They were accompanied by detectives from Rio de Janeiro, Bogotá, and Miami, and a neatly turned-out phalanx of FBI agents from their Quantico headquarters and the field office in Houston. More than one hardened veteran of wars in Vietnam, Bosnia, Afghanistan, and Iraq wept as they witnessed the corpses of so many young people.

* * *

Five days later, at 11.00 a.m., Gabriel sat on a squashy, yellow, chintz-covered sofa facing Don Webster and Barbara Sutherland in the sitting room at 10 Downing Street. They were drinking tea from bone china cups decorated with a pattern of pink roses, which clinked politely every time they were settled back into their delicate saucers.

"Well, Gabriel Wolfe, you did us proud," Barbara said with a smile. "You got that bastard before he could cause any more suffering."

"Not really. They're probably still toe-tagging six hundred corpses in the middle of the rainforest." Her eyes flashed. *Oops. Still the PM, Gabriel. Probably best not to be too familiar.* "Sorry. I just meant …"

"It's all right, my love. I know what you meant. And I should have chosen my words more carefully, shouldn't I? Before he could order any more attacks. Is that better?"

Gabriel nodded, feeling a blush creeping onto his cheeks.

"He almost got you too, didn't he, Old Sport?" Don said, before taking another sip of his tea.

"Yes. I was all ready to press the red button myself and take out two politicians and a few dozen civilians."

"Now look, Gabriel," Barbara interrupted. "You and Don don't need me for all the detailed debriefing. And I know all about his rules of engagement and standard operating procedures and all that quasi-military bollocks. So I won't be offering you a medal or anything like that. Although, God knows, you bloody deserve one.

But is there anything else I can do for you? It's a cliché, but you do, actually, have the gratitude of a nation."

Gabriel thought for a moment.

Saw a pair of strong, brown-skinned hands guiding his own to pull the muzzle of a pistol away from his head.

Heard a soft South London voice talking about his daughter.

Then the same voice screaming for her.

"We left one of ours behind on my last mission in the Regiment. Mozambique."

"Yes?"

"I'd like to bring him home."

She paused for a moment and looked at Don. Then she looked back at Gabriel.

"We'll have to see what we can do then, won't we?"

The End

ACKNOWLEDGMENTS

Thank you to my first readers: Katherine Wildman, Vanessa Knowles, Merryn Henderson, and Giles Elliott. You helped ensure I had the makings of a good story in its early days. I am also indebted to the members of my Readers' Group Inner Circle.

Thank you to my friends in the Salisbury Writing Circle: having people to talk writing with has enriched my life.

As always, I want to thank my friends and military advisers for keeping my vocabulary and tactical descriptions vaguely within the realms of acceptability: Colonel Mike Dempsey and Giles Bassett. Also Chief Superintendent Sean Memory for helping me understand some of the intricacies of police operations.

In this book I borrowed a couple of episodes from other people's lives and embroidered or tailored them to fit the story. To one modest man in particular, I want to say thanks: Mark Budden, for a story of everyday heroism that I borrowed and allowed Gabriel to inhabit briefly at Oxford Circus.

My editorial and publishing team continue to amaze me with their talent and skill. Thank you to my editor, Michelle Lowery; my designer, Darren Bennett; my proofreader Jessica Holland; and the production team at Polgarus Studio, Jason and Marina Anderson.

And to you, my reader, for buying this book, I thank you from the bottom of my heart.

Andy Maslen
Salisbury, July 2016

ALSO BY ANDY MASLEN

THE GABRIEL WOLFE SERIES

Trigger Point

Reversal of Fortune (short story)

Blind Impact

Condor

First Casualty

Fury

Rattlesnake

Minefield (novella)

No Further

The DI Stella Cole series

Hit and Run

Hit Back Harder

Hit and Done

Let the Bones be Charred (coming soon)

Other fiction

Blood Loss - a Vampire Story

Non-fiction

Write to Sell

100 Great Copywriting Ideas

The Copywriting Sourcebook

Write Copy, Make Money

Persuasive Copywriting

AFTERWORD

To get a free copy of Andy's first novel, *Trigger Point*, and exclusive news and offers, join his Readers' Group at www.andymaslen.com.

Email Andy at andy@andymaslen.com.

Follow and tweet him at @Andy_Maslen.

Join Andy's Facebook group, The Wolfe Pack.

ABOUT THE AUTHOR

Andy Maslen was born in Nottingham, in the UK, home of legendary bowman Robin Hood. Andy once won a medal for archery, although he has never been locked up by the sheriff.

He has worked in a record shop, as a barman, as a door-to-door DIY products salesman and a cook in an Italian restaurant.

As well as the Stella Cole and Gabriel Wolfe thrillers, Andy has published five works of non-fiction, on copywriting and freelancing, with Marshall Cavendish and Kogan Page. They are all available online and in bookshops.

He lives in Wiltshire with his wife, two sons and a whippet named Merlin.

* * *

News of the fourth Gabriel Wolfe thriller on the next page...

FIRST CASUALTY

FIRST CASUALTY

FIRST CASUALTY

73

FIREFIGHT

A FOREST. NORTHWESTERN MOZAMBIQUE—27 DECEMBER

GABRIEL Wolfe looked down at the bloody bullet wound in his right thigh.

"Britta! I'm hit!" he shouted.

Britta Falskog whirled round, still firing her SA80 assault rifle in five-round bursts over the top of the fallen tree she was using for cover.

"I'm coming. Can you move?"

"Not sure. Hurts like fuck."

"OK. Hold on."

She ducked down, rested the SA80 against the rough bark of the tree, then unclipped her two remaining grenades from her belt: a white phosphor and a high explosive. Holding one olive-green steel sphere in each hand, she pulled the pins out with her teeth, let the springs fly, then counted to two and lobbed them into the path of the incoming fighters.

Three seconds elapsed, during which she retrieved her rifle and crawled over to Gabriel, who had cut away his trouser leg and was staunching the bleeding with a QuikClot sponge he'd pulled from his medical kit.

With loud bangs a half-second apart, the two grenades exploded. There were screams from the enemy fighters as the shrapnel fragments hit them, tearing open gaping wounds. The white phosphor was worse, exploding outward in a cloud of burning chemicals that stuck to the skin and kept burning all the way down to the bone.

Britta pulled her pistol, grabbed the SA80 with her left hand, and popped up again, spraying rounds into the small clearing where the enemy fighters had fallen. None returned fire. Their AK-47s lay on the ground near their owners, who were maimed, burning, bleeding, or all three. She vaulted the log and rushed towards them, killing each man in turn with a double-tap to the head.

Now she rushed back to Gabriel. His face was white and his lips were drawn back from his teeth.

"Help me with the field dressing," he said, grunting rather than speaking.

She unravelled the bandage and wound it tight round his thigh, holding the QuikClot sponge in place against the wound. He drew in a sharp breath through his clenched teeth. She checked on the other side of his leg.

"No exit wound. Round's still in there. Fuck!"

"We need to go," he said. "Get me up."

She shouldered her SA80 and bent to grab his arms and pull him to his feet. He pulled upwards and transferred his weight to his good leg. Gingerly, he put some weight on the right and almost collapsed, biting back a scream as the pain intensified. Blood squelched out round the edges of the anti-clotting sponge and through the dressing, and ran over the pale skin of his leg and into his boot.

In the distance, they could hear shouts and gunfire. More fighters. More Kalashnikovs. More machetes. More trouble.

With Britta supporting him, Gabriel was able to limp along.

What worried him was the amount of blood flowing down his thigh. Their progress was agonisingly slow. The undergrowth was thick and Britta had to slash at it with her parang every few steps to clear a path he could negotiate. Even with the razor-sharp blade, it was slow going, and the enemy fighters were getting closer.

"Wait," Gabriel said, pulling Britta to a stop. "We won't outrun them. Not with me like this. I'll hold them down and you go. Get back to base. Try and get some support out here for me. Whatever happens, Don can pull you out."

Her blue eyes flashed. "Fuck you, Wolfe! I'm not leaving you. We'll fight these fuckers off, then I'm getting you out of here or we'll go down together. OK?"

Gabriel nodded, his mouth set in a grim line of determination and pain. "Over there," he said, and pointed to a clump of tree ferns with fat brown trunks covered in a scales of tough, hairy bark.

Britta half-dragged, half-carried him to the ferns and they flopped behind them, backs to the trunks.

With a grunt of effort, he unshouldered his own SA80 and pulled back the cocking lever.

"How are you for ammunition?"

She patted the bandolier that ran diagonally across her chest. "Got three clips. Thirty rounds. How about you?"

"Not as wasteful as you. Five. Plus whatever's in the mag."

"OK, so we've got maybe ninety rounds between us. SIG?"

"Two full mags and a handful loaded."

"I've got one spare, one just loaded. MP5?"

"Out. Dumped it."

"Me too."

"It's going to be tight."

She swiped the back of her hand across her high forehead then pulled the plait of copper-red hair straight out from the back of her head. "When was it ever not?"

Then a burst of automatic fire shredded the foliage of the ferns as somebody opened up with an AK-47.

They rolled away from each other onto their bellies and

shimmied sideways along the ground like crabs, taking up firing positions on each side of the clump of ferns.

"Come out, British cowards. Die like men," a voice called from about thirty yards away. Its owner sounded like he was laughing. "Or we can come and get you. You can eat your own balls while we watch, if you like."

There was another burst of fire. The Kalashnikov's 7.62mm rounds slammed into the trunks, spattering Britta and Gabriel with sharp chips of bark.

She looked across at him.

"British?" she mouthed.

"Balls?" he mouthed back, grinning despite his wound, as adrenaline neutralised the worst of the pain.

They looked into each other's eyes and nodded. An old, familiar signal.

The man who'd issued the threat went down with half his head missing as a three-round burst from Gabriel's SA80 hit him in the face. Three more lean, brown men replaced him, rushing forward, AKs held at their hips, set to full auto and spraying bullets at Gabriel and Britta.

Britta hit the leftmost man in the groin, doubling him over and leaving him screaming in the mud. The centre and right-hand men swerved to their left, only to be caught by a long burst from Gabriel that took them both in the torso, tearing great holes through their bodies, smashing and liquefying internal organs before exiting from their backs in showers of blood, bone, and tissue.

Gabriel was starting to believe they might, just, get out of the unholy shit storm they'd got themselves into when a sound he hated almost more than any other shattered the calm that had descended after they'd put down the four militiamen.

A booming, thudding, and very, very loud, automatic weapon had opened up from way back beyond their last position. A "Dushka." Officially, a Soviet-manufactured DShK heavy machine gun that wouldn't kill you so much as obliterate you. It could destroy light vehicles, helicopters, buildings, or firing positions thanks to its 12.7mm calibre rounds, each possessing enough kinetic energy to put a football-sized hole through anything softer than armour plating.

Whoever was behind the Dushka had them pinned down and was methodically chopping away at the tree ferns. Huge umbrellas of leaves tumbled from the tops of the ferns and fell to cover Britta and Gabriel. As the Dushka's rounds crashed into the trunks, they tore out lumps of wood that fragmented into lethal shards with points and edges sharper than the best tactical knives.

"Switch to single-shot," Gabriel shouted over the roar of the Dushka rounds.

Britta nodded again, discerning his meaning. If they were to stand any chance against the remaining fighters advancing on them, they had to take out the Dushka.

She was the better shot of the two of them and had completed a sniper training course in her Swedish Special Forces training. Now she began listening hard, trying to pin down the position of the heavy machine gun. Gabriel peered through the broken fern fronds, trying to identify the firing path of the rounds still smashing into the trees in front of him.

They both reached the same conclusion. The shooter was off to their right, two o'clock. Probably standing in the bed of a pickup, a Toyota Hilux probably, or a Land Cruiser if they had a bit more cash. That would put his head about ten feet off the ground and his torso and the Dushka maybe two feet below that.

Gabriel closed one eye and sighted down the SA80's barrel, aligning the iron sights on an imaginary machine gunner. He tightened his finger on the trigger and squeezed, slowly and steadily as his gunnery instructors in the SAS had taught him, until the rifle almost seemed to fire itself. The 5.56mm round tore into the trees. The Dushka kept firing, pouring red-hot, copper-jacketed lead into the rapidly diminishing cover hiding Gabriel and Britta.

Now Britta began firing, too. She was systematic. One round high, one low, one to the left, one to the right. The Dushka kept firing.

Then it stopped. Gabriel's heart leapt. She'd done it! The super-

Swede had actually taken out a Dushka that was completely invisible.

The roar of the heavy machine gun was replaced with taunts.

"Come out, pussies!" one voice called, a high-pitched giggle following the words.

"We're going to fuck you up bad, man. Yes we are," called another, deeper voice.

"Take your heads into Maputo and go bowling," yelled a third.

Then the Dushka started up again, only now its deep, bass roar was joined by the excitable chatter of three AK-47s being fired in unison and clearly in full expectation of a quick victory. The shooters burned through their magazines in a matter of seconds and had to stop to reload.

In the gap, Britta squeezed off another six rounds in quick succession. There was a scream. One more down.

But the enemy were still firing, even if they'd lost a man.

There was a slashing rustle ahead of the tree ferns. Someone had cut their way through the undergrowth into the small clearing. Gabriel risked a look. A tall, grinning man stood there, machete in his left hand, Kalashnikov held by the pistol grip in his right. Gold teeth glinted across the front of his mouth. A single round from Gabriel's Glock put him out of action, his heart smashed by the 9mm Parabellum round that left a gaping exit wound big enough to put a fist into.

"How're you doing," he whispered to Britta. She didn't reply.

He looked over.

Britta Falskog was lying on her back. Her eyes were closed. Blood was running down her forehead, obscuring the freckles that spattered her face like caramel-coloured snowflakes.

He crawled over to her and pulled up her right eyelid. The eye was rolled back in its socket. He bent to her chest and listened for a heartbeat. Couldn't hear one. Put his ear to her nose. No breath either. "Britta!" he whispered hoarsely. "Come on!"

He knelt astride her and began thumping her chest. Not the interlaced fingers of TV medical dramas. These were full-power punches that would crack ribs. He leaned forward, pinched her nose and covered her mouth with his own before blowing fiercely into her, trying to put breath back into her lungs.

"Too late, my friend," a voice said from above him.

He looked up into a brown face, incised with dozens of V-shaped scars on both cheeks. The man grinned, revealing a double row of gold teeth. Then he drew a pistol.

Printed in Great Britain
by Amazon

77992449R00231